T E C H
TRANSFER

SCIENCE, MONEY, LOVE, AND THE IVORY TOWER

D A N I E L   S.   G R E E N B E R G

Kanawha Press
Daniel S. Greenberg
3736 Kanawha St. Nw
Washington, DC 20015-1874
Tel. 202/244-4135
E-mail: danielg523@aol.com

AUTHOR'S NOTE:

Daniel S. Greenberg is a science journalist based in Washington. He is the author of three prior books: "The Politics of Pure Science," "Science, Money, and Politics: Political Triumph and Ethical Erosion," and "Science for Sale: The Perils, Rewards, and Delusions of Campus Capitalism," all published by the University of Chicago Press. He formerly was a reporter for the *Washington Post*, news editor of *Science*, and founding editor and publisher of *Science & Government Report*. He has contributed to many professional and popular publications and lectured widely at universities.

To the next generation of scientists. Good luck. (You'll need it.)

A P R O L O G U E

Within the walls of the university, the professors come and go as they choose, occasionally teaching, but most often indifferent to the students. Professors with abilities of value to commerce, such as those versed in law, or in navigation arts, or in compounding medicinals, seat themselves in the comforts of the university, but devote their time and skill to personal gain. Their rapacity is exceeded only by their hatred for each other and disdain for the citizenry. Upon being called to attend to their established duties, they bitterly complain of intrusions on their freedom. In the universities, it is a woeful situation.

Gianfredo Capitoliano, Rector, Bensilatano University, in "Lament of the Learned," 1435. In 1437, in his third decade as Rector, Capitoliano was assassinated by a deranged doctoral candidate.

∾

The university strikes many critics as a kind of anarchy, ill-suited for any purpose other than securing the comfort and convenience of the tenured professors. Officials of the university have very little authority over their senior faculty. The latter have virtually complete license to do as they choose, thanks to the security of tenure buttressed by the safeguards of academic freedom. Since it is difficult to monitor closely the work of highly educated professionals, faculty members can travel more than the university rules allow or remain at home tending their garden or enjoying their hobbies without much fear of detection. So long as they meet their scheduled classes and refrain from criminal acts, they can stay happily in their jobs until they retire.

Derek Bok, President, Harvard University, 1971-1991, in "Universities in the Marketplace: The Commercialization of Higher Education" (Princeton, 2003).

∽

We find everywhere a type of organization (administrative, commercial, or academic) in which the higher officials are plodding and dull, those less senior are active only in intrigue against each other, and the junior men are frustrated or frivolous. Little is being attempted. Nothing is being achieved.

C. Northcote Parkinson, in "Parkinson's Law Or The Pursuit of Progress" (John Murray, London, 1958).

CHAPTER 1

"These rats never sleep and they don't crap or piss."

"Sort of like a jet-lagged tourist?" Lou Crowley asked, wide-eyed with mock wonder.

"Cut it out," Collin Marson pleaded. Nearly 30, about half Lou's age, he reacted like a kid teased too hard by an elder. Lowering his voice in the crowded restaurant, Collie explained, "I didn't want to say anything on the phone. But like I said, they don't do any of them, and that's the important thing scientifically. I think we've got a big one."

After only two years, Collie Marson was a fast-rising member of Lou's venture-capital company. Lou had long prospered in real estate and other conventional investments. But now with Collie, who described himself as a "lapsed scientist," Lou's firm was making progress in a little-known, unfamiliar investment niche: mining gold from research in universities. A high-school dropout who started in a Wall Street mail room 35 years ago, Lou never made the proverbial ascent to titan of finance. Brash, socially unburnished, he wasn't material for the elite, white-shoe firms that dominate high finance and are synonymous with Wall Street. But he was savvy about raising and profitably investing money, and was upbeat about his young science guru pointing the way to bigger profits.

Collie still resembled the youthful, trim, distracted graduate science student that he once was, until the profession coldly signaled—not unfairly, he accepted—

that Collie Marson was not destined for success at the lab bench. An outcast from science, and still learning his way in the investment business, Collie was cautious in dress and manners: Dark, well-fitted suits, undemonstrative neckties and plain white shirts, and a friendly, unthreatening persona as he made his way in a new profession—one so very different from his life-long ambition.

Realizing now that Collie was serious, Lou retreated. "So, what the hell is this about?"

Collie delicately speared a shrimp from his salad, held it aloft for a moment, and did a quick scan of nearby tables. A couple of people he recognized were lunching nearby, and one casually nodded when Collie glanced at him. An unsurprising coincidence at a popular restaurant near the Kershaw University campus, in Manhattan. Collie ingested the shrimp and resumed the conversation.

"Remember that odd-ball professor, the guy with the pigtail when we were at that dog-and-pony at Aspen last year?"

"Brusolowitz. Brucie, they called him," Lou said, recalling a private get-together at the ski resort where researchers from a dozen major research universities discussed the commercial potential of their work with scouts from venture-capital firms. It was a typical get together in the new world of academic science, commercial opportunity, and restless finance. "Brucie," Lou repeated. "Sure. When everyone else is complaining about not getting money, he's the guy who keeps getting more. The feds love him. Except we never heard about it from him. He just listened and didn't say anything. Very cool."

"Right," Collie said. " Brucie. The guy's quaint, let's say, but he's a producer. Turns out research papers easy as pancakes. He's got a pile of patents, and all the best grad students and postdocs want to slave for him."

Lou nodded understanding. From Collie, he was getting the hang of the university science culture. A winner's lab drew top young talent because it could provide a boost up the career ladder. "But wait a minute," Lou said. "He doesn't have the Nobel Prize, does he? How come?"

"No, not yet. They don't award it posthumously—that's the rule. So, there are a lot of old guys in line for it before they die. Brucie is young. He'll get it someday."

Collie continued. "He runs a big lab—it's more like an institute—with lots of projects and money from all over, NIH, Department of Energy, foundations. And some of it is from the Army, actually lots of it. About five years ago he worked out some kind of new field ration for them that weighs a couple of ounces but makes you feel like you've eaten a 16-inch pizza with all the toppings. Everything. It's a beautiful piece of research. Brilliant. Actually nothing to do with food. It's a drug that controls hunger, really controls it in a smart new way while you get real nutrition from concentrated stuff. The U.N. buys it by the shipload for humanitarian relief after hurricanes and earthquakes and for refugees in Africa. I won't try to explain it to you. Let's say Brucie is a hormone genius. The Army took it away from Brucie before he thought it was ready. Now, the FDA thinks it could have some serious health problems, and won't let it on the U.S. market. But who needs it here? And the Army doesn't care about what the FDA thinks."

"This is all amazing," Lou said. "What about the U.N.?"

"I don't know. That's their problem. But that's not what we're interested in. Brucie is a frigging genius. That's why they keep giving him money."

"Good for him," Lou said. "So this sleep stuff. Anyone who takes it can't shit and can't sleep? And can't piss. Is that it? They'd better check into the Mayo Clinic and see a specialist. No, they'll need three." Lou hah-hahed several times, appreciative of his own humor.

"Cool it, please," Collie said. "It might take a while to sink in, because this is unusual, but, believe me, it's big, bigger than anything we've ever heard of. I don't know all we'll need to know, but this is not about one of those miracle pills that don't work, or maybe kills you, but makes a billion or two."

"Don't knock 'em," Lou advised his excited young colleague. "We've bought into a few of those ourselves, and we're working on others. At this very moment, as we speak, the pharmaceutical guys are ghosting papers for a couple of big shot professors to put their names on and publish in a big medical journal."

"Yeah, I know," Collie said cheerlessly. The union of science and capitalism sometimes made him wince. "But this is something else. This gets into the whole economy. The whole goddamned economy. Trouble is, we got to figure out how to get a piece of it, a big piece."

Now more than ever, Lou felt he had chosen wisely in recruiting Collie. His instinct for the deal, coupled with Collie's knowledge and enthusiasm, told him that his youthful partner was onto something good, great, maybe extraordinary. Though Dr. Collin Marson, Ph.D., would never be in the running for the Nobel Prize, he knew a lot about science, and Lou didn't—except how to make money from it.

"Okay," Lou said. "Inform me. What's the deal?"

"It's like this," Collie said. "Brusolowitz gets this new contract from the Army. They want something so soldiers can stay up for a week, maybe a month, and march and fight or do whatever they have to do without any fatigue. No sleep. Wide awake. We're not talking about coffee or caffeine or amphetamines. They've taken them as far as they can go. They want something new. It's been done to some extent with fruit flies, but you can do almost anything with fruit flies. The Army promises him a shitload of money—as much as he needs—and tells him to go for it. But they said he's got to keep it quiet, because they don't want any stuff in the news about turning soldiers into sleepless zombies. So all this is secret, classified, with security checks and all that hocus-pocus. Brucie sets up the research in a separate, closed-off wing of the lab. Screw academic freedom. All the secrecy stuff that isn't supposed to happen in universities, but they get away with it. It's the Army. They do whatever they like. No one notices, because Brucie is running lots of other projects at the same time right out in the open. The Army is in awe of the great scientist, and the university gets its cut in overhead money. Everyone is happy. If by some chance someone asks questions about the secret lab, they say it's basic medical research and the security is because of bio-terrorism regulations. But no one really asks any questions. So Brucie in his usual manner messes around in the lab with lots of different possibilities. He parcels out pieces of the research to grad students and postdocs, because there's a lot to do. But he holds all the strings and doesn't cut anyone in on the whole picture."

"Okay. So what's he got?" Lou asked in an impatient whisper.

"I'll tell you," Collie said, lowering his voice as he came to the point. "He's got a big goddamn colony of rats that haven't slept, shit or pissed for three months, maybe four, and are doing just great. A cage cleaner found out and came to Brucie to ask what was going on—nothing to clean. He thought someone was trying to horn in on his job. Brucie told him to shut up or he'd have him deported. The whole thing was unbelievable. Brucie at first worried that it might be a joke, some kind of prank by the idiot graduate students who maybe had gotten wind of what he was doing. So he put a video camera on it. There they were, the goddamned rats, night and day, running in the exercise wheels, digging into their chow, mating, reproducing. Big and healthy, wide awake around the clock. Brucie even gives them the rat IQ test and they pass just fine. Three months for a rat is like a lifetime for us. Everything normal, except—."

"The things they don't do!" Lou gasped, with the voice of discovery.

"Right. The three things they don't do. It's absolutely fantastic," Collie said. "And think what this means. Forget about the Army, because this is going to get out sooner or later. Impossible not to. Soldiers who are on the stuff will talk about it. The whole goddamned civilization. I mean, where do you begin? Hotels, the mattress business, toilet paper, sewage systems. Who needs them? Everything goes 24/7. Workaholics will pay anything to get this stuff. Parents will want to keep their kids up for studying so they can get ahead in school. Cross-country truck drivers. Athletes training. Dictators could put it in the water so people can work around the clock. Stalin would have killed for this stuff. Very rarely in history do you get a discovery that changes everything, I mean everything. Think of electricity, the birth-control pill, the computer chip. This is just like them."

Collie's normally relaxed speech became excited. "Figure that sleep takes up a third of our lives, even more for some people. One-third of the world is always asleep. Figure this: For every three soldiers in the Army, if they don't sleep, it's like getting a fourth for free. What happens if no one sleeps anymore and just keeps going? You can't even begin to think about it without—."

Lou motioned for calm. "You'll still need beds and hotels and mattresses for screwing. Especially some people," he said with a winking salute to his young colleague's crowded social life. "And changing clothes when you're traveling. But I see what you mean."

"Okay, okay," Collie said. "You get what I mean. The whole world can operate around the clock. There could be a vaccine. One shot and you've got it for life. Or maybe pills. It will be like sleep never existed."

With a troubled expression, Lou pondered the prospect of a world without sleep. "So how does this work? What's in the pill or the vaccine?

"I don't know," Collie said, "but figure that Brucie started out in endocrinology—that's hormones. And then he did some famous work on synthesizing enzymes. And he also got in early on gene splicing, taking genes out of strands of DNA, juggling their sequence, modifying them. These days that's easy. Kids in high school labs are doing it. And Brucie is a whiz at chemistry. That could be something else in the picture. Like I said, I don't know how he does it, but if it can be done, he's the guy to do it. What you got to understand about research is that when you find the answer to a problem, you realize it was there staring you in the face all the time. The great people like Brucie find it fast. The rest of us can keep on looking and never see it."

Lou nodded. Collie continued. "There are sleep labs all around the country, but no one really understands anything about sleep. Why do we sleep, why do we collapse if we don't sleep, what it is that sleep does for us? One big mystery. Brucie's the guy to figure it out, or at least to make it go away."

"Okay," Lou said, strained by another of Collie's dumbed-down science lectures. "I think I get it so far, maybe. But what about the crap and piss? How do they disappear?"

"Again, we don't know," Collie said. "But just figure. Maybe he's found a way for the body to make more efficient use of nutrients and liquids. Enzymes can serve as a catalyst."

Lou appeared increasingly puzzled. "Just forget about that," Collie said. "Just figure there's less waste to dispose of—maybe very little, or none at all. Then, consider that all matter is solid, liquid, or gas. So, if there's a way to convert it all to gas, maybe it could be exhaled—no solids or liquid. Might even be pure and odorless. Sounds crazy, I know," Collie said, "but, who knows?"

"Pure and odorless," Lou said. "I hope so."

Always interested in how his young colleague operated in the inscrutable halls of science, Lou asked, "How did you hear about this?"

"That's a story too," Collie said. "There's this guy, Charles Hollis, who was in grad school with me. He got his degree, but even after a couple of postdocs he couldn't get a decent university job. So he took the best he could find at the time, a civilian job with the Army. He's a project manager in the Army Research Office. Charles is a big church-goer, a Quaker or something, and a do-gooder type. In his spare time he builds houses for poor people. But no decent job offer in research. So, he signed up with the Army because they do a lot of humanitarian work—hurricane relief and earthquakes. They told him he could do research on water purification and emergency food supplies, but that never really worked out. He's got a wife and kids, house payments, student loans, a sick mother. Usual story, and now he's got some seniority with the government, and it's hard to move. He's stuck. I just now ran into him at the bio-chem meeting in New Orleans. We had a drink and he got all soppy about being a failure and never making anything of himself. Then he starts telling me about how the humanitarian work has been side tracked by the Army and about this big project he's been assigned to as project officer. He's in charge of doling out the money to Brucie and taking progress reports about the project and pushing him to go faster. He originally looked up Brucie because of his work on emergency food rations. And so they got to know each other, and when he mentioned that the Army was looking for a contractor for this new project, Brucie got all excited and said he wanted a piece of it, a big piece. Actually, to make it easier to keep it quiet, he got all of it. One hundred percent. The Army's given it a project name, Zap-Hypnos because Hypnos is the Greek god of sleep. Cute. You get it?"

"I suppose that's a big joke," Lou said. "But, seriously, if we can't deal with Brucie, will your friend Charlie tell us more about this, keep us informed as it moves along? I'm beginning to think that some of the Big Pharma guys might really go for this, and we can cut ourselves a pretty good deal."

"That's a problem," Collie said. "I'll get to it. But one thing first, in case you ever meet Hollis. Don't call him Charlie or Chuck. He goes bananas if anyone does that. It's Charles. No other way. He's a very formal, very sensitive guy."

"Okay, he's just plain Charles," Lou agreed. "So what's bugging him?"

"I'll tell you," Collie said. "He was practically crying. He tells me he has no say about going ahead with this, and actually thinks it's a bad idea, dangerous, but the Army brass is pushing hard to speed it up, and he's helpless to do anything about it. Says he's agonizing. Says he's worried about testing it in humans—that still hasn't been done. He's worried that it violates some rules of nature. There's the question of whether it's reversible. Maybe it's even hereditary. Can you put things back like they were before? And what happens long term? So far, there's no way of knowing, he told me. You can't judge from rats. And then he shut up. The poor guy's a wreck. Said he had told me too much. And that was that. He clammed up, and I don't think I should try, at least for now, to get anything more out of him. It's weird, isn't?"

"Yeah," Lou agreed, as a flood of questions filled his mind. "Let's say your friend Charles and Brucie come up with exactly what the Army wants. The project is a success. Before they can use it, it still has to pass one of those review boards and be tested on humans, won't it, and be approved by the FDA or somebody? They can't just—."

"Yes and no," Collie said. "First comes the Institutional Review Board, the IRB. Every university is supposed to have one. Federal rules. They have to make sure that volunteers for the clinical trials know what they're getting into—informed consent—and that the risks aren't too great. That's federal law. But that's no big deal. The boards are made up of people from Brucie's own university, his own buddies, plus an outsider or two for window dressing. That's the way they're all set up. You advertise for volunteers for experimental trials, and if you pay them enough, you can get all you need. And if they sign the consent forms and the IRB okays them, you're covered if anything goes wrong. The IRBs can make a stink about paperwork and dotting the i's, but they don't want to be the skunk at the picnic. It's you okay my project and I'll okay yours. Everything will pass ethical review. And the FDA won't tangle with the Army. Brucie will get by when he's ready. No problem."

"What's this ethical review?"

"I don't know. It seems to be catching on everyplace. You got a bunch of doctors, lawyers, and religious experts called bio-ethicists. I don't know who the hell they are. Probably a lot of losers. They sit around and piss and moan and write reports. But nobody pays any attention to them."

"Good," Lou said. "We don't have to worry about the ethics bullshit. That's none of our business."

"I guess so," Collie mumbled unconvincingly, recalling his friend's anguish.

Recognizing his doubt, Lou said, "Look, this guy's a big boy. What the hell did he think he'd be doing when he joined the Army? Handing out coffee and muffins after a hurricane? C'mon, he's not working on poison gas.

It's a drug, and like ninety-nine out of a hundred, probably nothing will come of it."

"You're right," Collie said, aiming for harmony with Lou. Having failed at his initial choice of a career in scientific research, Collie sorely wanted to succeed in his new-found career and achieve satisfaction, recognition, and pleasure. He also wished to avoid doing harm, but effortlessly. The soulful confession of his friend Charles touched him. His old friend was visibly in distress. But the ethical considerations raised by Charles and his baffling talk about nature were distant background noise for Collie. Collie was an empathetic, postmodern man. Reports of refugee tragedies and other calamities on NPR sometimes caught his attention as he sipped morning coffee, munched cereal, and scrolled the computer screen for personal messages, favorite blogs, and the comics. But it was all distant chatter, and shortly afterwards, he was scarcely aware of what he had heard and read as he hurried to work.

Collie and Lou both suddenly looked up to a figure who had come up to their lunch table. Collie recognized the person who had nodded at him earlier, the VP for public information at Kershaw University.

"Thought I recognized you, " he said to Collie. "Great to see you. You'll be getting an e-mail to save the date, but we don't know yet just when. We're having trouble getting everyone together. Maybe next month, at the faculty club, we're having a reception for one of our superstars, Max Brusolowitz—Brucie. You know him."

"What for?" Collie asked, intending to sound casual, only politely interested,

"I know he's just got his 100th patent, so maybe that's it. But I really don't know. But you know Brucie. He's always got something going. The science faculty is putting on the reception. See you there," and he moved on.

"Jesus," Lou said, "what's that about? If that Army stuff is secret like you said, it can't be about that."

"I don't know," Collie said. "Could be something else. I'm going to a dinner tomorrow night and there will be some big people there from Kershaw. Maybe I can find out."

"Where's that?"

"Someone named Martin Dollard and his wife. I remember you said he's an old business buddy of yours."

"Martin Dollard," Lou said with a big smile. "I remember now, when I ran into him a while ago, I told him we've got a real scientist working with us. He sounded very interested. You'll have a good time, but watch out for his wife, Helen," Lou cautioned. "She's a piece of work. Believe me."

"What do you mean?"

"You'll see. She dropped out of college after two years because she thought Hollywood was pining for her. But it wasn't. Then she did some modeling and bit acting—starred in a laxative ad that won some kind of big advertising award. She was about 30 when she met Martin. He has a lot of dough. And I think she figured it was him or doing underwear ads for Macy's. So now she tries to play Grande Dame in a pad that takes up half a floor on Park Avenue. I'm not sure what he does now, but he's got some connection with the university. And she's doing something there, too. Funny couple."

CHAPTER 11

Though Lou took pride in Collie's scientific credentials and expertise, his young colleague was a bona fide failure in science—with no position in the profession, no research publications to his credit, and no prospects in science. True, he possessed a doctoral degree in molecular biology, acquired at a mecca of that speciality, the University of California at Berkeley. But in contemporary science, the degree merely entitled him to pursue further training as a post-doctoral fellow in the lab of a master scientist. Thus he came to Kershaw University to work under a scientific legend, Dr. Elias Fenster.

From Collie's early days in graduate school, the laboratory repeatedly lost out to the bedroom. It wasn't that he prowled for women. Rather, situations arose naturally, frequently, spontaneously, serially, in which he was complaisant prey rather than pursuer. Like a friendly Labrador, he was a big assemblage of affability, and, without effort, popular with girls on campus as well as women faculty, librarians, and once there was even a visiting socialite trustee he was assigned to guide around the Kershaw science complex. She asked him to detour with her back to the university guest house to pick up her sunglasses. As a result, he missed his turn to report to his department's science journal club, a failing, among several, noted by Professor Fenster.

The postdoc appointment was considered a good move toward the ultimate career goal in academic science, a tenure-track appointment, which would bring career-long job security. But pondering the lengthy, and uncertain, road to tenure, Collie felt his passion for research slipping away. Where was the enthusiasm for science that began two decades ago with a middle-school science fair? True enough, as the teen-age Collie realized and accepted at the time, his science teacher, good old lovable "Doc" Middleton, was the concealed performer behind his prize-winning project, titled "Light and Temperature As Interacting Co-Factors in Plant Growth." Collie thus received an early taste of scientific sleight of hand. For the project, "Doc" selected the seeds, set up the plant containers, lights, water-flow devices, thermometers, and other measurement instruments, and record keeping. He served as a "guide" as the youthful Collie wrote up his lab notes. Though the experimental plants grew erratically, conforming to no visible pattern, "Doc" produced smoothness in the tables and charts in Collie's project report. "A little adjustment is okay," "Doc" explained. "Real scientists do it all the time. It's necessary to make things clear." Collie's entry took first place. Winning was exhilarating, bringing with it praise and assurances that Collie's career destiny had been revealed. "Doc" received plaudits for inspiring yet another American youngster to pursue a career in science and thereby keep the nation competitive and strong. The Chamber of Commerce awarded him another plaque, and he received another certificate from a national science teachers organization. In recognition of their science-fair achievement, young Collie and his proud mentor were flown to Cape Kennedy, where they were photographed with a Space Shuttle crew and witnessed a Shuttle launch—all reported, with photos, in the middle-school student newspaper. The thrill of it was overwhelming for young Collie. He became emotionally bonded to a career in science, as intended by the managers of science, education, industry, and government. After all, as they repeatedly warned, the U.S. was short of scientists. Collie, aspiring to help fill the gap, was puzzled later in high school by a "study module" titled "Integrity in Science." Recalling his science-fair triumph, he recognized that Doc's tutelage did not conform to the strict rule of unalloyed accuracy, truth, and completeness in reporting experimental results. Collie wished he could discuss the matter with his old middle-school mentor, who had since been elevated to Director for Science Instruction in the statewide system. But Doc was now beyond the reach of a mere high school student. Collie put aside his doubts and trudged on toward a career in science.

Now years later, abruptly though not unexpectedly, Postdoc Collie was brought to understand that his future in science was dark. On that turning-point occasion, the head of his research group, "The Prof," Elias Fenster, a regal power relative to Collie's plebian presence in science, stopped him in the hall and mumbled that a recommendation for a tenure-track job looked doubtful. "You never know," Fenster speculated, while plainly looking at his wristwatch and frowning, "but you might start thinking about something else." The encounter for delivering the grim message was not by chance. Fenster could have summoned Collie to his office, motioned him to sit down, and humanely delivered the disappointing news. The Prof, however, preferred a quick, surprise thrust that would preclude a mawkish plea for mercy, an emotional outburst, or a prolonged discussion, all of which he had painfully experienced in prior episodes of delivering the *coup de grâce* to troublesome subordinates. Knowing when Collie and his lab partners would be emerging from a conference-room meeting with their section chief, Fenster had carefully positioned himself at an intersection of corridors where he could pull Collie aside for a quick, one-sided encounter. He delivered his message, and then hurried along, leaving Collie with a spreading ache in his gut. Collie was pained but not surprised by this thunderclap of fate.

Collie had previously realized that unlike Professor Fenster's devoted acolytes laboring cruel hours at nearby lab benches, he no longer felt an urgency to deconstruct the fragment of a problem assigned to him by the Prof. He was slowly coming to understand that research wasn't his game, that he didn't care about discovering a surprise anomaly in a phenomenon and building a career on it, laboring on it night and day, weekends included. That's what Fenster had done years ago as a young researcher after he published a paper reporting a hitherto undetected slight decline in the sperm counts of rats in the presence of a potassium compound. Eureka! As the first occupant of this patch of scientific landscape, Fenster took a dominant lead in a career-long series of investigations that assured his primacy in the field. He and his continually growing research group studied the viability of stored sperm from rodent donors exposed to high and low levels of the intriguing potassium compound. They studied variations in inheritability of characteristics, physical and behavioral, from *in vitro* fertilization at various exposures. From these observations, numerous publications were composed, some barely distinguishable from previous publications. Others were not at all distinguishable, save for altered titles to elude computer detection and create the appearance of a fresh report, thereby lengthening the publication list in Fenster's *curriculum vitae*. Recognizing Fenster's dominance in the field, peer reviewers, carefully selected for their scientific knowledge and freedom from conflicts of interest, confidently checked the "publish" box on the forms sent to them by journal editors who sought their advice on manuscripts he submitted for publication.

Replication is the vaunted safeguard against innocent error and fraud in science, but, in fact, it rarely occurs. Money for research eternally falls short of requests for money for research. In the federal government's granting agencies, the guardians of the funds saw no need to replicate Fenster's research, and no request to do so was made. Then came tenure and, eventually, a professorship, all emanating from that long-ago observation and Fenster's indefatigable reassemblage of stale data into new publications.

Danger threatened when Collie and another postdoc, working independently in adjacent wings of Fenster's expanding lab empire, followed their curiosity about Fenster's original research. Comparing the findings from their moonlighting efforts, they agreed that the rodent sperm counts rose and fell within normal range, and were unaffected by the presence of potassium. The colleague, wiser than Collie about the workings of science, cautioned, "We'd better forget about it." Collie, however, was thrilled by the finding, regarding it as his first big discovery in science. Like a child playing with a loaded gun, he did not recognize the risks that this finding posed to the reputation and professional survival of Professor Fenster, and therefore to himself. Excitedly, innocently, Collie brought the discovery to Fenster, who served as his mentor and clutched his professional fate in his hands. Gravely, unmistakably, Professor Fenster counseled Collie that the finding was not correct, could not possibly be correct. He advised him to expunge the data from his lab notebook, drop the matter, and return to his assigned duties. And he did. The episode further eroded Fenster's regard for Collie. On Fenster's list, he became a marked man.

The Prof subsequently was elected to the National Academy of Sciences, a self-perpetuating body comprising the nation's leading scientists. In the prestige rankings of science, only the Nobel prize topped membership in the Academy.

In furtherance of his scientific education, the professionally foundering young Collie Marson observed that Professor Fenster reaped rewards from beyond academe, notably consultancies and contracts with Big Pharma firms and others, too, some interested in sperm counts, others in potassium, and a few concerned with rodents. Some of Fenster's corporate patrons were dedicated to preventing pregnancies in humans, others to promoting them. A vitamin manufacturer concerned about potassium in its capsules contracted for an annual "heads-up" briefing on Fenster's research. Competitively eyeing each other, two firms dedicated to eradicating rats came aboard with annual retainers. The Pentagon awarded a contract, citing its need to keep abreast of scientific advances that might have significance for national security. The U.S. Department of Housing and Urban Development bought in because of its interest in rodent control in public housing. Without explanation, the U.S. Department of Homeland Security annually sent $1 million to Fenster's laboratory, later raised to $2 million, but gave no indication of what it expected in return. Though the checks were honored at the bank, the only response from repeated inquiries to the Department was that it had no record of the payments, which nonetheless continued to arrive.

The Prof's colonies of experimental rats proliferated. Even his abundant funding was insufficient to keep up with the need for expanding animal-care facilities. As a result, the livestock population evolved into a sprawling, reeking, makeshift rodent slum. Among the ranks of graduate students and postdocs intently counting sperm on around-the-clock shifts, the Prof was privately known as the "cum lord." The commonly accepted measure of the significance of a scientific paper is the frequency of its citation by other scientists, who presumably use it as a building block for further scientific advancement. Being scientifically arid, Fenster's papers were rarely cited, though without damage to his reputation. The money pouring into his laboratory more than compensated for the dearth of citations. Prizes and honors stacked up, head hunters came wooing with lustrous job offers. In defensive response, Kershaw anointed Fenster as a Distinguished University Professor, which translated into a munificent salary, a grander office, his first unshared secretary, and priority dibs on graduate students and postdocs. After many years, the odyssey that began with the report of a decline in rats' sperm count had not yielded a practical result or significant scientific value. But in science, an ancient dictum reigns: Never say never.

Despite his renown and overflowing grant portfolio, Professor Fenster was haunted by a recurring, terrifying dream: An official investigative team arrived unannounced and seized his laboratory files. He was summoned to a hearing where all his lab notes, records, and publications were placed in evidence. Trembling, Fenster would awaken just as a verdict was to be announced. On these occasions, he would hurry to the lab even earlier than usual. Among his colleagues and students, Fenster was renowned for long hours and personal attention to laboratory records and documentation. Papers routinely flowed from work-a-day use at the lab benches to a secure archive in his inner office, to which he alone held access. Varying widely in personality and working style, scientists tend to be tolerant of their colleagues' eccentricities. Nevertheless, Fenster's colleagues would occasionally ask about his unusual methods of laboratory management. He was prepared with plausible explanations: Industrial research contracts required strict security for the protection of proprietary information. He also explained that he had a long-standing interest in the history of science and hoped someday to write a fully documented account of his research. And, he pointed out, in our increasingly litigious society, careful record keeping was essential for self-protection.

"In all respects" he explained. "Good science requires thorough retention of all relevant papers." If challenged about the scientific validity of his work, Fenster was uncertain about his ability to mount an effective defense. But he figured that control of paper—the main product of research—was an essential first step for assuring survival. The retained papers supported the publications from his lab. Carefully weeded out were contrary or ambiguous research results. Mainly, however, Fenster counted on avoiding a challenge, rather than surmounting one. Early warning of danger was essential.

Toward this end, good fortune unexpectedly arrived in the person of Fenster's cousin Myra. They had grown up together in the same neighborhood and parted in young adulthood; occasionally, they encountered each other at family weddings and funerals. Myra, children grown, newly widowed, needed a job. She possessed basic office skills, but nothing beyond that. Fenster, learning of an opening for an assistant receptionist in the office of the university president, reasoned that a beholden relative inside the presidential suite would be invaluable. He was especially jumpy after Collie Marson unwittingly came close to exposing his work as sham science. Seasoned in academic rules and practices, Fenster knew that suspicion of scientific misdeeds rattled the bureaucratic apparatus because it soiled an institution's reputation, undercut public trust and fund raising, and brought troublesome inquiries from Washington. Though the university's geriatric president was famously detached from university affairs, the presidential office was in the information loop. With Myra on the job, Fenster would tap into the loop, unofficially.

Myra became the understudy receptionist following an endorsement from the distinguished Professor Fenster to the chief presidential receptionist, along with an assurance of a laboratory internship for the receptionist's nephew. To Fenster's satisfaction, she succeeded to the full-fledged role when the long-serving occupant retired. Myra's debt to Fenster was repeatedly repaid with a reliable stream of information and copies of documents from the presidential suite. Peace of mind eluded Fenster, but he found comfort in Collie's departure from his research group and Myra's presence at Kershaw's center of information and power.

❧

Cast out from the scientific guild, Collie morosely contemplated his vocational options, and found them all grim. The best among his several poor choices was the adjunct route. At Kershaw or any of the nearby universities he could probably sign on to teach a beginning biology course or two, at $3,000 to $4,000 each per semester, and thereby grasp a tenuous on-campus presence that might, possibly, lead to something more substantial. Adjuncts were the migratory expendables of the academic labor market. Sympathetic sentiments regarding their dwarfed status and slight prospects were standard fare at conferences on academic governance. But these needy, vulnerable workers were simply too useful and too easily manipulated for academic managers to dispense with or treat decently. An oversupply of job-seeking, well-trained academic professionals guaranteed a buyer's market and inexpensive staffing, not only for financially pressed universities, but for wealthy ones, as well.

In this dismal setting, dropout scientist Collie Marson, like a lost waif, joyfully spied an opportunity: making money from science done by others, rather than himself trying to make science. He read an advertisement for "well rounded scientist interested in financial career." Following a cordial interview, Lou Crowley offered him the job, and Collie gratefully, promptly accepted. Collie thus made the transition from unappreciated, under-paid, dispensable, unemployed dropout-scientist to beginner venture capitalist, in alliance with Lou Crowley, a scientific illiterate who was the money man in their fruitful partnership. With the job came a starting salary of $200,000, nearly ten times his postdoc stipend, plus a year-end bonus. Not a munificent sum for a professional-class lifestyle in pricey New York. But raised in a family of modest means, and subsisting on spartan income through college, three years of grad school and three years as a post doc, Collie felt wealthy. Even as he achieved new heights in spending, a cash surplus piled up. Collie immediately gave up his shared, furnished student digs near campus. In a fashionable new building, he rented a bright, spacious apartment, with river view, and engaged a recommended decorator, who filled it all at once with contemporary furniture, rugs, prints and other art objects, linens, dishes, and table wear. Collie worried that the overall effect was a bit too hotel-modern, but, plunging into his new work, he didn't fret about his household aesthetics. Lou, delighted with his new staff acquisition, cheerfully explained, "I don't know anything about science, but I know what I like, and Collie knows what I like." Which was early knowledge of research that might flower into a big-selling drug, or that looked so promising that one of the scientifically drowsy corporate giants of pharmaceuticals would buy an exclusive license for a mighty sum just to be safe. Big Pharma's executives were pleased to do business with Lou and others who kept tabs on university research. Research in their own corporate labs was expensive, and, in the nature of research, of uncertain outcome. Selective purchase of promising research from university labs was relatively cheap.

In this business, early knowledge, ahead of the pack, was critical. Collie was eager to provide it and succeed with Lou's company. He realized that he wasn't bringing in enough business to cover his salary, that Lou was patiently investing in him in the expectation of a scientific bonanza down the road. His chances of a return to science were bleak to non-existent. And the contract for his new job contained a standard non-compete provision, which prohibited him from doing similar work for any other employer for three years. He knew he had to deliver for Lou.

C H A P T E R   I I I

Collie gained stature from his connection to Lou's well-regarded firm. As an attractive unattached straight male of marriageable age and financial substance, he became popular on a wide-ranging dinner-party network. The cast was drawn from universities, philanthropic foundations, museums and the arts, journalism, and finance. The participants generally wanted something from each other—philanthropic donations for favored organizations, stock market tips, boosts up one or another social ladder, assistance in getting a kid into an Ivy-track nursery school or a wanting offspring into a selective college, perhaps a job for a witless son-in-law. For parents of college students, summer internships at brand-name organizations were prominent on the favors list. Real-estate gossip was always in fashion. From a few forays into this milieu, Collie found that information useful for his work sometimes circulated around these dinner tables and serious business could be conducted over pre-dinner and post-dinner drinks. People heard things, first, second, or third hand, and passed them along as evidence of their important connections or in *quid pro quo* exchanges. Somebody would relay something from a brother-in-law who was a lawyer for a pharmaceutical firm, or a visiting professor from Italy would boast about a forthcoming publication. Information flowed.

While spending a tipsy, sensuous Saturday afternoon with a recently acquired acquaintance, Loretta, a third-year psychiatry resident, Collie considered begging off the Dollards' dinner invitation that he had mentioned to Lou. He was pleasantly weary. They had skipped lunch and awakened after a subterranean slumber. As they incrementally returned to wakefulness, mutually unspoken thoughts and murmurs and slight motions converged. "But first I think you ought to open another bottle of wine," Loretta softly suggested. "That's what I was thinking," Collie said. Later, another slumber followed. Afterwards, he wasn't hungry, though his most recent solid nourishment was a refrigerated slice of leftover pizza for breakfast. He might be getting a cold. He was undecided about the evening. An awkwardly worded handwritten note on the Dollards' party invitation stated, "Please join us, along with several Kershaw trustees who are here for the special board meeting and other university leaders. Martin." The Dollards were not linked to his usual dinner-party set. But the special meeting, as everyone interested in Kershaw knew, was to select a new president, following the long-awaited death of the geriatric incumbent who had inertly retained the position in the final years of a long tenure. Collie hoped to do more business with Kershaw's science professors, and wondered how the new president might affect the commercial atmosphere. Some academic relics still gagged on professors going into business, and frowned on commercial relationships. Universities varied widely in their attitudes toward faculty business dealings. Some aggressively encouraged commerce, others were cautiously permissive, while a self-righteous few frowned on making money from science. Kershaw's policies and practices were a muddle, reflecting, as in so many other matters at the elite university, the long absence of clear, firm leadership at the top. In the national rankings for academic quality and prestige, Kershaw once led but now was behind its nearby rival, Columbia University, while New York University, a downtown upstart, was coming up from behind.

The Brusolowitz matter rattled in Collie's semi-awakened mind as Loretta hurriedly dressed for night duty at the hospital. Arising shortly after he heard her leave the apartment, he found a handwritten note scrawled on a sheet from a prescription pad bearing her name: "Diagnosis, sex addiction. At this stage, it's only a borderline case. Nothing critical, but condition should be regularly monitored, as this disorder is progressive. Fortunately, there's no cure, and there's nothing to prescribe. Try to get some rest. Further consultation advised. Don't call me. I'll call you. Maybe. Hugs." Collie had heard that Loretta was engaged, or about to be, but, with his customary politeness, had not inquired. Weary, not feeling up to a dinner party, Collie again considered calling in sick, but curious about this particular invitation, he showered, dressed and left for the party.

C H A P T E R   I V

A black woman wearing a lace-trimmed white apron responded to the cathedral-like chiming of the doorbell, admitting Collie to the richly decorated, visibly expensive, grand apartment of Martin T. and Helen Dollard. From the entrance to far off in the distance, many mirrors and paintings covered the walls. Tall vases filled with lush flowers were sprinkled about. In an adjacent room, slumped at a grand piano, a Julliard student, hired for the evening, sullenly tinkled away at the prescribed scores for the evening: Cole Porter, songs from *South Pacific*, and periodic repetitions of "The Girl From Ipanema." An attentive listener might detect insurrectionary, cacophonous outbursts, but the music was masked by the clinking and chirping sounds of partying.

In addition to Lou's explanatory words about the Dollards, Collie knew something about his hosts from *Ultra Ultra,* a slick, give-away magazine. Hand delivered to the city's richest zip codes, it was laden with advertisements for "prestige" international real estate, perfumes, furs, expensive handbags, jewelry, and other upscale trifles. An article titled "Power Couple Plus" gushed that the Dollards were notable for "memorable, imaginative entertaining," and credited Helen with "presiding over a much-envied salon where the city's smart set intersects with the arts and business elite, with A-list Brits adding sparkle to the conversation. The cerebral wattage is dazzling and the gourmet spreads are strictly three-star plus. Crossing the pond has become such a time-consuming bore since the divine

Concorde went to the boneyard, elegantish Euro guests tell us, but they still flock to the Dollards' soirees. You would, too, if you could snare an invite!" The article explained that Martin had recently stepped down from a fabled long run as head of a private investment group, and now was "a rising figure in academic and political circles concerned with societal issues." Helen was described as "a well-known beauty, initially a trophy wife but now with impressive creds of her own in the art world, philanthropy, and university affairs."

The couple's actual c.v. differed substantially from the *Ultra Ultra* version, which was written by a public-relations firm specializing in "image counseling" and "customized editorial services." The article cost Martin $7,500, and he paid another $25,000 for placement in the magazine, where it was presented as staff-written editorial content. Martin told his image counselor that he would prefer publication in the *New York Times,* with *Time* or *Newsweek* as a second choice. In response, he was advised, "There's a tempo to these things, Mr. Dollard. Don't let impatience spoil a very sound, proven strategy." Given the difficulties he faced, and his uncertainties about how to proceed, he agreed. Martin unreservedly regarded the expenditures as worthwhile. But, even with the article, and despite substantial contributions to the Metropolitan Museum of Art, the Museum of Modern Art, and Kershaw University, per his counselor's advice, the Dollards themselves were neither A list nor capable, so far, of attracting A list guests. On the rare occasions when it noticed them at all, the social grapevine graded them arriviste, parvenu. Blogs and the *New York Times* reported many top-rank grand parties, but invitations eluded Martin and Helen Dollard. Helen reviled Martin for multiple types of idiocy—complete, total, pathetic, unbelievable, unconscionable—for *Ultra's* "trophy wife" reference, repeatedly demanding to know why he allowed the demeaning term to appear. His answer, that he relied on the image counselor, ignited secondary explosions and did not forestall further denunciations.

Many of the guests that Helen and Martin drew to their salon were indeed from the city's leading cultural and educational institutions. But they were mainly bland, mono-dimensional financial executives and managers whom Martin had encountered in his long business career. The "brainy people," as Helen called them—renowned professors, glib talk-show gladiators, scholars who opined on

NPR and in *New York Times* op-eds, politicians, prominent entertainers, artists, and writers—frustratingly evaded their net, usually not even bothering to RSVP to the Dollards' stylishly engraved invitations. Their spirits soared when the anchor of a national TV news show accepted an invitation to dinner. His presence—sure to be noted on celeb-tracking blogs—would certify their social importance and set off a chain reaction of other lofty acceptances and socially commensurate invitations. But the TV eminence neither showed up nor sent regrets. Rendered livid by these slights, Helen assailed Martin. "I've had enough of your goddamn accountants and bookkeepers and their dumb, lumpy, size 14 housefrau wives coming here to chew with their mouths open and slop food on the upholstery and stink up the bathrooms with their dollar-store perfume. Next you'll be getting us deliverymen and secretaries. Why the hell can't you get some important people, real people instead of these losers?" she demanded.

"It takes time," Martin explained. "We're making progress. I'm developing contacts at the university and at other places." Martin spoke the truth. He had met with the president of Kershaw University. Martin had proposed, and offered to underwrite, a high-level policy roundtable that would regularly meet at Kershaw to discuss major issues of our time. The participants would be topnotch people from the professional and social ranks that Helen had so far futilely schemed to draw to her salon. As spouse of the roundtable's host, Helen would cordially extend the hospitality of their home to the distinguished guests of the roundtable, using them as bait for bringing in an A-list crowd. Martin had emerged feeling confident about his meeting with Kershaw's president. The old boy, he was convinced, definitely looked interested. Very much so, Martin assured himself. Martin's mood rarely fell below hopefulness and easily soared to ebullience.

∽

From a computer search, Collie located Martin and Helen on Kershaw University's long-term cultivation list for potential big-time donors. As part of a dual-pronged flattery treatment, Martin was appointed to the university's Endowment Advisory Board and Helen was on the Arts Advisory Committee for the university's own collection, as well as for architecture, landscaping, campus sculpture, and the arts curriculum. The arts committee was created at the strong insistence of the university's fund-raising operation, the Development Office, to provide it with yet another opportunity to stalk potential donors. But when the arts professors railed against the prospect of meddlesome amateurs intruding on their territory, a deft compromise was crafted. At the unanimous insistence of the arts faculty, the Development Office promised that the committee would be merely a sandbox operation. And so it was. For the third consecutive year, the Arts Advisory Committee inconclusively labored on a "mission statement," sporadically meeting at the call of its chairman, a former senior curator at the Louvre, who also chaired the arts faculty. He was determined that the committee would never evolve beyond, as he put it, "nascency." His determination drew strength from Helen's aesthetic vocabulary, which mainly consisted of "Fantastic," "I'll have to think about that one," and "No way." Though it was a harmless position, Helen relished her committee membership, believing it provided prestige and made up for a personal deficiency that secretly gnawed at her. Having dropped out of Bryn Mawr after two lackluster academic years for a futile pursuit of ambitions in Hollywood and later in modeling, she was embarrassed by her truncated college experience—so much so that when the "where did you go?" question arose, she replied, "Bryn Mawr," without further explanation.

As he made his entry to the party, Collie recognized an acquaintance, Bill Rhodes, Kershaw University's director of technology transfer, responsible for selling the science produced in its labs. No business triumphs had occurred on his watch. Collie knew that Rhodes was in a shaky relationship with the university. Reports of blockbuster deals at other schools were considered a reproach to Rhodes' performance. Collie and Rhodes had worked out a couple of smallish deals, and got on well. Bill would surely be up on whatever Brucie was into, Collie thought, though maybe not. "What's going on?" Collie asked in greeting Rhodes.

"They don't tell me," Rhodes glumly replied.

"How about the reception for Brucie? We just heard about it."

"They're having some trouble finding a date. Nothing for now," Rhodes said.

Collie was confident that the mighty blockbuster gestating in Brucie's lab—if that's what it was—was bound to become known, though he felt sure that at this point, it was contained. When it got out, he knew, the press and politics and the blogosphere would instantly erupt in wonder, condemnation, and angst. But terrific business deals surely loomed for anyone who got in early and acquired a piece of it. Since Brucie worked on the Kershaw campus, Kershaw would own the patent, but the necessary advanced work on product development and clinical trials would take place off campus, in the private sector. That's the way it usually worked. And that's where Lou Crowley's company could step in with abundant financing—in return for ownership shares. Ideally, the company would acquire an exclusive license for the patent. When Collie had first joined the firm, Lou explained to him that "an exclusive is like owning the toll booths on the Jersey Turnpike."

As Collie advanced into the apartment, a burble of conversation came from a spacious salon amply furnished with upholstered chairs and sofas and nearby tables conveniently clustered for conversation and drinks. The host couple's university connections, and, especially, Martin's previous presence in investing, made Collie wonder whether Brucie might come up in conversation, or might even be there. If Martin Dollard wants a "societal issue," Collie thought to his own amusement, how about no sleep and the other two? But a careful look around the room failed to reveal Brusolowitz or anyone from Kershaw besides Bill Rhodes. But then it was early. Coming up to him unseen from the side, a woman grasped his arm and said, "You must be Collie. I'm Helen Dollard, and we're so glad you're able to join us. Martin has told me so much about you personally and the science you do. There's so much to talk about that we're all mutually interested in."

Wondering what Helen meant about what she had heard, Collie offered appreciation for the invitation. "It's our pleasure," Helen assured him. Collie sized her up as about 40, lightly botoxed after at least one facial overhaul, fresh from a heavy-duty work-over at the hairdresser, and in a stylish, floor-scraping gown probably specially acquired for the evening. From blemish-free teeth to roseate pedicured toenails peeking through sequined pumps, Helen Dollard was the beneficiary of a mobilization of money, medical science, fashion authorities and skilled cosmetologists, perfumers, groomers, dieticians, trainers, and polishers, plus a long-term therapist, currently working on the rising revulsion she felt toward her husband, Martin Dollard.

Helen Dollard's cheerful demeanor and seemingly effortless attractiveness concealed a stressful day that compelled a double dose of calming medication as she presided over preparations for the evening. That same afternoon, while savoring a post-coital cigarette as her therapist lay by her side, she exclaimed, "It's his hands. Little fat stubby fingers. Like a fat baby's. Ugh."

"But he had those very same hands when you married him ten years ago," Dr. Laurence Berlin-Gotshalk softly reminded her.

" I know," she said gloomily.

"And I wish you wouldn't smoke in here,"Berlin-Gotshalk said reprovingly. "Other patients don't like it."

"Oh, screw your other patients," she snapped back.

"If I did," he said, as he rose from the couch, drew on his underwear and trousers and tucked in his shirt, "I would be in violation of the code of ethics of the American Psychiatric Association, not to mention the Hippocratic Oath."

"Oh, Christ," she said, "I'm think I'm going crazy."

"Maybe you should see a psychiatrist." She was not a favorite patient.

"You're so goddamned clever. Your patients must be the cream of New York's wackos."

"*Crème de la crème.*"

"I'm sick of you treating me like an idiot."

"That's something we should talk about next time."

Through the padded, sound-absorbent double-doors between the waiting room and the consultation room, they faintly heard the arrival of the next patient, as usual, anxiously early by at least 15 minutes.

"Who is that, that's always so early?"

"Privacy. Privacy regulations," Dr. Berlin-Gottshalk said, pressing a finger to his lips.

Scowling, Helen dressed and hurried out a separate entrance, arriving just on time for her hair-dressing appointment. "Something troubling you?" Marcel asked. "No," she sharply replied, concerned that the storm in her mind was showing through.

"Where's Vera?" she asked, pointing to a vacant station in the skin- and nail-care area.

"She should be back soon," Marcel said. "There was some trouble at her kid's school."

"I was supposed to have a facial and nails. I can't wait. Doesn't an appointment mean anything here any more?" she snapped.

The overbooked Marcel, recently celebrated in the *New York Times* as the "Da Vinci of coiffeurs," muttered an imprecation that went unheard as she hurried out.

Rushing home, Helen efficiently applied and in sequence removed a chemical cornucopia of facial oil, cream, salve, paste, and emollient, followed by the application of dabs from a jar of yet a different substance, atop which she gently added a fine neutral-colored powder and a bit of rouge. Eye liner, eye shadow, lipstick, a touch or two of perfume, and a strategic application of cologne. Earrings, necklace, bracelets. By party time, the dermatological clarity, glow, and confidence she sought were present. Yesterday's nail care, with a self-administered touch-up, would suffice. The blessed meds had kicked in. As she greeted Collie and other guests, Helen Dollard was a cynosure of style, grace, equanimity, self-assurance, and insouciance. No sign of artifice was present. Collie hadn't met her before, but she was familiar.

Interrupting the conversation of a seated cluster of guests, Helen said, "I want you to meet our dear friend Collie Marson, who Martin says is one of the brightest stars in science today, or science and business." Collie was accustomed to such botched introductions and, in this case, saw no point in offering a clarification. Names Collie didn't catch were recited and he was invited to a vacant place. Nodding and smiling, he chose to remain standing, to avoid being marooned with what he recognized as an uninteresting bunch. "You're in science, Dr. Collie?" inquired a stout man seated opposite him. "Well, in some ways," he said. "So what do you *do*?" the man asked in a demanding tone. "Venture capital. I'm with a company that tries to bring pharmaceutical research to market. Investing in early developments to see if they have therapeutic potential. New treatments. That sort of thing."

The stout man persisted, "So what do you *do*? Explain what you do when you get to the office in the morning." Collie was summoning a minimally courteous reply when a woman seated alongside his questioner broke in. "Speaking of science. My husband and I travel a lot. He's retired from business. We're just care-free. Pack up and go. When we were just in Peru, we met this marvelous couple, absolutely marvelous. He was retired from the University of Illinois, I think it was, and she was a librarian or something. Anyway, he was making a catalog of kinds of plants—bushes, trees, leaves, even grass, things like that. It was absolutely fascinating. It could be something you would find interesting," she assured Collie, who responded with a gracious nod. Suddenly, in a voice reminiscent of escaping high-pressure steam, she hissed across the room: "Jason, that couple in Peru. Was he an archivist?" The addressee of the inquiry, a defeated looking, rumpled man, responded. "Arborist." "Well," she said, "arborist, archivist. What do I know? But if you go to Peru, you really must look them up. Just marvelous people. I'll send them an e-mail telling them you're coming. No problem."

"That's very kind," Collie said. "I will keep it in mind if I go to Peru."

"You should," she insisted.

"How did you know them?" the stout man asked the Peruvian traveler.

"We were getting a health insurance policy for the trip. There's a lot of sickness there. Our insurance man knew them and told us to look them up. So we did. Simple as that. How would we know anybody in Peru? Never been there before."

As Collie contemplated a polite means to evade the empty chair in this cluster, his host, Martin Dollard, reached out to him and introduced himself. "So glad you're here," he said. "Let me get you a drink. Wine, red, white, whiskey, or anything you'd like. And since we're sure to be interrupted at least a dozen times if we try to talk now, let's be sure to try for a chat later in the evening. Maybe when people settle down for dinner. I think we've got some things to talk about."

"Sure," Collie said. Now with a glass of wine in hand, he looked about but still found no one of interest. The door chimes boomed again, signaling an arrival who earned his attention: a young woman, who, having made a quick survey of the room, apparently failed to find a familiar face and stood planted in the doorway, evidently displeased. Helen Dollard hurried to her rescue and, seeing Collie similarly unmoored, guided the new arrival to his side. "Collie, this is Ginny Rosen. Ever since she was a freshman here, it takes 10 invitations and an e-mail from me to her father to get her here for an evening. Her father is Mike Rosen, in Hollywood. I'm sure you know him." Collie did not confess that he didn't, and Helen continued, "I'm so pleased Ginny's able to join us tonight. You two talk. I've got to make sure we feed all these hungry hordes or we'll have a mutiny."

In the distance, the mercenary young pianist savaged the evening's third performance of "The Girl From Ipanema."

Scowling, the girl surveyed the room while indifferently giving Collie a minimal hello. Close up, he figured she was about 22, probably a senior or a graduate student at the university, and clearly possessed of upscale social poise and a good opinion of herself. In dress-up mode, college style: shiny, knee-high boots, a shortish well-fitted skirt, wide belt with a big brass buckle, patterned tights, and a smart, white open-neck blouse. No novice at confidently mixing with new people. No makeup or jewelry. Pretty good looking, he concluded, noting an alert, freckled face and glaring dark eyes from which she regularly brushed back a shower of shoulder-length straw-colored hair.

Collie started to ask her what she was studying.

Before he had completely got the words out, seemingly oblivious of him, she slowly, emphatically declared, "You know, I hate all these fucking people."

She looked hard and directly at him, as if waiting for a response, and, seeing surprise on his face, challengingly carried on: "Maybe you don't, but I do."

"I don't know very many of them," Collie stammered.

"I don't either, but I can tell," she said.

"Tell what?"

"They're, like, mostly a bunch of prehistoric ass holes. What am I doing here?"

Collie did not offer an answer. Then the beginning of a recognition came upon him. "Where did I see your picture?" he asked.

"You probably mean the horrible mug shot with the column I write for *Haywire*. That's the school paper at Kershaw, if you *ever* see it," she said, as though if he didn't, he was inexcusably negligent.

"Oh, yeah," he said, "I get up on the campus now and then"—though he rarely looked at the paper. "And you write about?"

"I write the 'Bodily Functions' column."

"'Bodily Functions?'"

"Yeah. I used to do the sex column, 'Whole in One,' with a W. I started it."

"I think I've seen it—with your picture, but maybe not recently."

" Now I've moved on. But I started with the 'Whole in One' column."

"Yeah. I see," Collie said. Then sensing a conversational insufficiency on his part, he added, "That was something new in school newspapers, I suppose."

"You know," she said thoughtfully, now evidently engaged by the conversation, "actually, it wasn't the first. But *one* of the first. Now there are, like, sex columns in practically every college paper. Readers send in questions. They're looking for advice and information. How to do things. Kids come to school—they're, like, ignorant. So, nothing's off limits for discussion in the column. There's news, advice, analysis. Very reliable. We talk to doctors and experts to answer the readers' questions about any topic: gay, straight, bi-, trans, birth control, blow jobs, orgasm, anal, masturbation, AIDS, herpes, groups, lubrication, sex toys and implements—."

Ginny Rosen obviously was prepared to continue the topical inventory, when Collie interrupted. "I've seen some of those columns," he said cautiously.

"*Everyone* has seen them," she said in a corrective manner. "It's, like, the best read stuff in every college paper. But no one admits it."

Searching to maintain the conversation, Collie asked, "Are there favorite topics that readers ask about?"

With a wrinkled nose and squinting eyes, she contemplated the inquiry for a moment before earnestly replying. "That's a good question. It's hard to say, because a lot of questions from the readers are combos. Like organism and groups, or anal and something else, maybe toys or bi-. But when we did a count of readers' questions last year, masturbation as a *single* topic came out ahead, but not by much. That's understandable, since interests vary."

"That figures," Collie agreed. "But now you do, what did you call it, the 'Bodily Functions' column?"

"Yes. 'Bodily Functions' is a follow-up, building on the popularity of 'Whole in One.' I did the sex column for two years, and it became time for someone else to do it. A fresh look. But same principle. Readers send in questions and I talk to real experts to get the answers, except when I feel that I know the necessary information, which sometimes happens."

Collie searched for a response, settling on a neutral comment. "That's interesting," he said, evoking a staring, blank response that suggested that his remark was banal, inadequate. He hastily added, "But it sounds like there would be some overlap with the other column, the sex column. What are the topics in 'Bodily Functions?'"

"You know," she said, without concealing her irritation, "the fact that you have to ask tells me a lot. A *lot*. Like, what the hell do you think a column called 'Bodily Functions' is about? It's not about how to make strawberries and cream or how to tie your shoes. God!" she exclaimed.

"Dinner. Dinner." Helen Dollard called out. "Help yourselves. It's just a little buffet," she said, pointing to the dining room.

Saved from responding, Collie shrugged, and said, "Let's get some dinner," and gratefully slipped away to join the buffet line. This is a wasted evening, he concluded, deciding to leave as soon as it was politely possible.

CHAPTER   V

Returning to the salon with his plate filled, Collie was relieved at not re-encountering the fulminating young woman. Instead, while pondering where to seat himself, he was overtaken by host Martin Dollard, also plate in hand, who led him to a sofa and said, "Maybe we can have a word here." Martin moved energetically, restlessly. He appeared to be about 60, of medium height with a belly bulge and a bald dome bordered by a gray fringe. His transition from Manhattan real estate and investment executive to public-policy intellectual was reflected in his attire. The double-breasted, dark grey, wide-striped suit that was standard battle dress in his former career was now replaced by a brown tweedy jacket with elbow patches and dark grey trousers. The boldly colored striped ties of yore were succeeded by small, muted patterns; dark brown penny loafers, without tassels, in place of black wingtips. There were, however, several remnants of the old days that Martin had not yet replaced in his new, academic persona. An oversize gold watch on a heavy gold band glowed on his wrist, emitting reflected gleams from lights in the room. Each shirt cuff bore a purple curliqued monogram: MTD, and each was fastened by mother-of-pearl cuff links bearing the initials embossed in gold. Martin strived to appear brainier, better informed, and more worldly than warranted by his internal content. To Collie's surprise, Martin was a supplicant for approval, recognition.

"I keep hearing good things about your work with Lou Crowley," Martin began, accompanying his words with vivid facial expressions and hand gestures. "You know, Lou and I know each other from way back. I'm particularly impressed that you know science from the inside, but you're not part of it. That's a very unusual position these days. It's a good one," Martin assured him. Collie nodded, as Martin continued, "Our own investment group, that is my former group, is quite strong, but not in the area you specialize in. We have—I should say they have—a big gap there. It's not my headache anymore. Done my time, thank you. Now on to bigger and better things."

Collie couldn't sense where the conversation was going. Besides, his head pounded with a rhythmic, deep internal ache. He was fatigued and hungry, his powers of attention eroded after a long day, a skipped lunch, and the residual effects of a considerable intake of wine that afternoon. His condition intensified the effect of the renewed intake of wine provided by Martin. He urgently required solid nourishment. But with the conversation still at an introductory stage, he felt it would be inappropriate to commence eating. He offered a neutral comment. "It's an interesting area."

"At the very least," Martin promptly agreed, warmed by rapport with a fellow thinker. He was accustomed to deference for his money-making prowess, but now that he strived for cerebral recognition, he was wary of being patronized, sometimes suspecting that he indeed was. "I was a business major in my long-ago days at Kershaw. That was a bread-and-butter choice, but poli-sci was my real interest. And that's what I've been getting back to, in a general way. I do a lot of reading," Martin said, with a wide sweep of his hand, "usually eclectically, but with a current emphasis on studies of the future, anticipation of change as it affects society and politics. Some of these studies are extremely interesting—and I get to talk with some leading people in multiple fields. A lot of us share an interest in the changing nature of policy formulation and, in particular, policy architecture. Policy for policy, you might call it. One thing for sure: the low-hanging fruit has been picked, picked clean. Now comes the hard part. I bring this up because the university has been talking to me about founding a roundtable for policy discussions. Bringing in the right people and providing for interactions. We can talk about that later," Martin assured him. "But for now, I'd just like to lay out some thoughts and get your reaction. Okay?

Collie saw no opportunity for dissent. "Yeah, sure."

Martin proceeded. " I don't think there's any doubt that the basis of our society has migrated from the smokestack industries to the knowledge industries to the information era, so that everyone now is on the front lines when it comes to societal impact. I mean this in an epistemic sense. From post-industrial to post-modern, and beyond. One seismic change after another."

Martin expressed himself earnestly, in a slightly hoarse timbre that radiated authority, thoughtfulness and emotional commitment. "From foreign policy to—." He hesitated while groping to finish that sequence, finally settling on "it can be anything. The neurosciences. A lot of activity there, and tie-ins with the genome are bound to be inevitable. About nanotechnology and its societal impact—well, that's in the hazy future, too, but I'm told it's yielding to some very interesting policy investigations. In that case, we have only ourselves to blame if we're surprised at being surprised. Just a few days ago, I was at a seminar on the neurosciences and religion—fascinating. Then there's science and the law, a whole new area that begs for—." For what, he did not say, but proceeded to ask, "Who knows what's next?" Lips pursed, Martin sagely rotated his head from side to side.

Collie didn't know what was next, and furthermore, had no concern nor was able to simulate any. "It is a time of change," he said lamely. Martin responded with a chuckle, "Tell me about it. Ninety percent of all scientists who ever lived are alive today. That gives you something to think about, doesn't it?" As far as Collie was concerned, it did not. Nonetheless, he nodded in agreement, as Martin continued. "The defensive walls around the academic disciplines are a problem, a big problem. Maybe 'one size fits all' used to work, but not today. Call them silos or stove pipes, the isolation of the academic disciplines constitutes a big problem in an existential sense. And I don't mean just in the sciences. Transition is coming, but the big question is will it be seamless or not. We're back to the old chicken-and-egg problem. We need a new paradigm, but just wishing for it won't get it for you. Sorry about that, but let's face reality and finally exit this dilemma." Collie failed to perceive a problem, a dilemma, or an exit, but refrained from inquiring. He realized Martin required no encouragement. The dialog, however, was briefly interrupted as Martin set his dinner plate aside and rose to exchange greetings with a guest.

Collie looked around. At the far end of the long room, he recognized the trustee for whom he had served as a campus guide several years ago. She gave him a flapping wave of fingers, and hurried to him. "I saw you talking to Martin but I didn't want to interrupt," she said excitedly. "Just to say hello."

"You're here for the big meeting tomorrow," he said.

"Yes, at long last. A new president. We hope."

"Who will it be?"

"That's what we have to decide," she said. "Tell you what, if we're done in time, maybe you and I can have a drink and I can tell you whatever I can tell you. I'll be at the same guest house. Just ask for me." She waved to someone across the room and hurried away.

Weariness clogged Collie's mind. He balked at further demands on his atrophying wits, nor could he contemplate a tryst. Having just completed a marathon, he was not up to a jog around the block.

For the dinner, Helen Dollard had engaged an excellent caterer. She had initially contemplated a served sit-down dinner. But with a touch of derision that made Helen cower, her imperious party consultant responded with contrary advice: "Sit-downs are so yesterday for large groups. Guests will simply hate you forever and ever if it turns out that they're forced to sit with people that they'd rather not. The issue is static versus fluid in mixing people, and fluid is in. Go buffet and let them wander and drift and make their own choices of dining companions. It is so much smarter. Trust me."

From the bountiful buffet, a piled-high plateful selected by Collie still rested temptingly untouched on his napkin-covered knees. Martin and the guest finished their greetings. Returning to his place next to Collie, relocating his dinner platter from a side table to his lap, his hands thus freed for delivering emphasis, Martin resumed his elocution. "Consider the impact of emerging technologies on third-world economies. Now that's a can of worms. Try that one on for size and call me in the morning."

Collie mustered, "That's for sure."

A server with a tray of wine glasses loomed over the seated pair, and, removing Collie's empty glass, set down a generously filled replacement. The stem of the glass was long and slender, the bowl resembled a large globe with the top removed. Inside, dark red fluid glistened. Fearing that the tempo of conversation might catch him with a mouthful of food, or that his dinner plate might disastrously tumble down, Collie, though hungrily eying his plate, still made no motion toward it. The wine however, was conveniently situated for safe grasping from the adjacent table and was promptly refilled upon being consumed in a few urgent gulps.

Martin's own serving of food remained similarly untouched as he embraced a new topic. "Someone pointed out to me the other day something quite fascinating that helps calibrate the pace of technological change. See if you can answer this: How many electric motors do you find in the average household today? Try a rough guess." Like an expectant quizmaster, Martin awaited a reply.

Collie stared into the ruby fluid gently sloshing inside the spacious goblet. He raised the glass to his lips, swallowed deeply, and reflected. With some effort, he summoned an estimate. "There are electric clocks and fans and lot of other things. I don't know. A dozen maybe?"

"No," Martin said instantly, with authority, "The average actual number is around 35—it varies, of course, from house to house. But 35 is in the ball park, more or less. That's from an actual survey. There are electric motors in practically everything—your refrigerator, printer, computer, electric shaver, dishwasher, air conditioner, vacuum cleaner, DVD player, blender, and on and on. There's the rotisserie and clothes dryer, too. That gives you some idea, doesn't it?"

"It does, yes," Collie agreed, though idea of what he didn't know.

"You wear a wristwatch," Martin said. "I'll bet it's an electric watch. There's another electric motor."

"Yeah, that's right," Collie agreed, though his watch was of the wind-up variety, a matter he kept to himself for fear that it would set Martin off on a new topic.

His supposition corroborated, Martin smiled cordially and continued. "In the same way that the electric motor has become universal, the semi-conductor chip is the new wave. Digital. That's the point," Martin said triumphantly. "Change, pace of change, in combination with human factors. There's a synergism. In terms of societal impact, some of these things are hardwired and others are not. I mean that in a normative sense. See what I'm driving at?"

Collie offered a "Yes."

"Information," Martin said, falling silent for a moment, to signify the introduction of a new theme. He paused, held up his right arm, and pulled back his jacket sleeve and shirt cuff, holding before Collie his oversized gold wristwatch, which housed several small dials on its large face, along with several protruding knobs on the side of its case. "Look at this," Martin said. "It's an altimeter, a compass, a barometer, a stop watch, an alarm clock, it gives time, date, day of the week, month and year, phase of the moon, a bunch of time zones all at once, and temperature, and it's good to 300 meters—that's over a thousand feet. And there are other things I haven't figured out yet. It's new. But what does it all come down to? Again, it's information."

"Really terrific," Collie said, pondering whether Martin ever descended to 300 meters, and quickly concluding that his pear-shaped interlocutor surely did not. Martin adjusted his shirt sleeve and jacket. "Needless to say, this contraption is primitive compared to today's digital products." Lifting his coat jacket, he pointed to a pouch on his belt. "Blackberry with GPS and who the hell knows what else? But to get back to what we were discussing. The cockpit, the battleground, the epicenter of all this is the university," Martin said. "That's where the true science is being done today. Do you agree?"

"There's no question. That's where a lot of it is."

Further buoyed by agreement, Martin pushed on. "I'm on this committee that advises the university on investments. No real authority. Well, no formal authority, though our recommendations appear to carry some weight. But officially, we just make suggestions. And I like it, because the information flows both ways. I give them the benefit of what I know, and I pick up stuff that otherwise I wouldn't know about. That's fair enough, isn't it? No conflict of interest whatsoever."

Again signaling assent, Collie risked dipping his fork into the rice pilaf, careful not to upset the equilibrium of his plate or overload the utensil, lest the rice grains embarrassingly spill onto his tasteful necktie, pristine white shirt or fine, discreetly patterned wool suit or, even worse, the sculpted upholstery or the undoubtedly precious rug at his feet. He successfully delivered a fork full of the rice, but with his plate precariously perched, and Martin in conversational overdrive, he dared not attempt to cut into a slice of lamb, carved to order at the buffet by a poker-faced attendant in a toque. Lying on his plate, the meat was pink on the side facing him, expertly herbed and crusted on the other. At the buffet, he now realized with some concern, the attendant had spooned an excess of gravy onto his plate, and the fragrant fluid, glistening with globules of fat, was at full tide, perilously close to the rim.

"So you make the rounds of the universities, I understand," Martin said. "You're a scientist and you can go one on one with the scientists. That's a big advantage."

Seeking to avoid a response that might prolong the conversation, Collie cautiously offered a neutral reply. "Some advantage, I suppose, but everything is so specialized these days that even if you're up on one field, you might not be really in touch with others."

Looking puzzled, his food still untouched, Martin fingered his chin. "I suppose, but even so, there's still an advantage. But let me get to the point. I hear about things at the university. That people are working on amazing things. They're developing new materials, synthetics and the like. The psychologists are even working on new ways of thinking. They're doing cognitive research. Brain scans with special equipment. There's a laboratory there doing stuff for the government— psychological or physiological research or something along those lines—that's truly amazing, incredible. I think they call it improving human performance." Collie switched on at hearing these words, but concealed his sudden interest. Martin continued. "But, like I said, I'm not equipped to evaluate these things for their societal impact, which is my area of interest, my real concern. And, besides, the university people play their cards close to the vest. So that's the whole ball of wax. Like I said, the low-hanging fruit is gone. In the end, it comes down to people, but most of all the stakeholders. And synergism. Let's not forget synergism. When I can find time, I'm going to pull this all together in an essay, maybe for *Foreign Affairs* or an op-ed for the *Wall Street Journal* or maybe the *Times*. I'm thinking of calling it 'The Three-Legged Stool of Policy, Technology, and Leadership.' Just a place marker. I don't have the time for anything definitive."

Martin concluded with, "You've let me do all the talking. I'd like to hear your views."

Summoning the remnants of his dwindled capacity, Collie silently, hurriedly reviewed Martin's remarks about research at Kershaw. A great deal of research across a wide spectrum of the sciences went on at the university. And Martin's dazzled reference to "human performance" might or might not reflect some knowledge of Brusolowitz's work. By his own admission, Martin was on unfamiliar ground and could have misunderstood whatever he had heard. Collie made a minimal response. "I'm not specifically aware of anything along those lines, but Kershaw pretty well spans the waterfront when it comes to research. It's got a reputation as one of the top places in the country." Martin was thoughtfully nodding assent to these words when Helen Dollard intervened. "Collie, dear," she said, "when you're ready to leave—I'm not hurrying you off, please understand—let me know. Please stay for dessert. But Ginny Rosen, who you just met, is feeling unwell and is resting in another room. I don't think she should go home by herself. If you're taking a taxi uptown, maybe you could drop her off at her apartment building near the campus? I've offered to have her stay here overnight, but she has to do something at school very early in the morning."

Their conversation now interrupted, Martin and Collie set aside their still-brimming platters and stood up. A sense of deliverance flowered in Collie's mind. To copious expressions of appreciation from his host and hostess, Collie accepted the mercy assignment, grateful that the request terminated his conversation with Martin, though not relishing further contact with the "Bodily Functions" journalist. On the other hand, the unsought escort task was a welcome gift, allowing for an early departure. The evening was a bust for the information he wanted. Liberated from Martin's soliloquy, Collie assured Helen. "If she's not feeling well, I'd better get her home sooner than later." He longingly looked for his dinner platter, hoping for a forkful or two before leaving, only to have a member of the caterer's staff grant him a "thank you, sir," as she cleared away the main course dishes in preparation for dessert. Helen gave him the address—an apartment building across the street from the university's main gate—and said she would call the doorman for a taxi. Collie and his hosts exchanged expressions of disappointment about the premature termination of a lovely evening, along with mutual assurances of pleasure and hopes for reassembling at an early date. Then Collie, with the girl accompanying him, left the Dollards' apartment.

CHAPTER VI

"I could get myself home," she said repetitively and unappreciatively, as the taxi alternately roared and braked uptown, weaving its way through dark, crowded streets.

"Too late to worry about that," Collie said. "They insisted and it's not out of my way."

"Yeah, they're like that, especially Helen. Always barging into what's none of her fucking business. I wonder what's the matter with those people."

Searching for non-provocative words, Collie said, "She meant well."

"You know," Ginny said, "people like that——." She halted in mid-sentence, and released a scream: "Oh, shit!"

Collie braced himself against the back of the front seat as the taxi lurched around a corner. "What is it?" he nervously asked as he devoutly wished an end to this benighted encounter.

"I left my keys back there."

"Where?"

"Back at their fucking apartment. Where do you think? Are you some kind of cretin? When I was feeling barffy and laid down, I must have like put my bag someplace."

Looking at his watch he saw it was almost 10 pm; they had traveled far uptown, and were nearing their destination. Collie quickly, resolutely determined not to return to the Dollards' apartment, fearing the unknowable complications that might ensue from a re-encounter of the couple and the frothing young woman. "We can't go back to get your keys," he said. "Somebody will let you in at your place, won't they?"

"No, goddamn it. They lock the outside door at 9:30, and even if someone lets me in, my roommate is away and there's no way to get into the apartment."

Collie did not care for this dilemma, and did not wish to be conscripted for a solution. "Well, you must have a girlfriend or neighbor who can help you out," he suggested.

"Don't worry about it," she advised him. "You're a real scout. I'll find a park bench, or something. People sleep in dumpsters."

The taxi sped on. Collie silently speculated and calculated: If she disappeared or was found strangled under a bush in the morning, he might find himself in great difficulty. Flashing through his mind: "Last seen with...." And the cops would arrive at his door. Ginny interrupted his doleful thoughts, "Let me ask you something, and say no if you don't want to."

"What?" he asked, incompletely concealing dread for what might come next. After this long day, the extended liaison with Loretta, the wine, Martin's interminable, opaque oration, and now this tirelessly obnoxious young woman, weariness had depleted his resources.

"I don't know what your situation is at your place. No business of mine," she generously conceded. "But if you've got like a spare couch, can I flop on it? And I'll be out very early in the morning. I'll tiptoe out and it will be like I never was there. Okay? I really don't have any other place to go."

Collie rummaged his mind for a safe means to rid himself of this burden. Perhaps a homeless shelter? He didn't know the location of one. But even if the taxi driver knew the way to a shelter, Ginny was no bag lady. Collie didn't know how the shelters worked or whether they would admit a well-dressed and groomed college-age female late at night, delivered by a respectable-looking man who simply wanted to drop her off and leave. They'd probably call the cops, he figured, and then god knows what would happen. She might go ballistic with a mad tirade about bodily functions, implicating him in who knows what. The cops would think there's something funny going on and play it safe by holding him overnight to check him out in the morning. Without an acceptable alternative, Collie reluctantly agreed to her proposal. He told the driver to bypass the original destination and take them to his address.

Inside the apartment, Collie sternly said, "There's the couch and there's a bathroom down the hall, just for you. I'm going to sleep in there," he said, pointing to a door. "And you'll be out of here bright and early. Right?"

"Don't you worry about it," she said. "I'll be out of here very early. Like before seven. Is there an alarm clock? And could you spare a blanket or some kind of cover? Sorry to be so much trouble," she said resentfully.

"I'll get you an alarm clock and a blanket. Why do you have to be out so early?" he asked, making certain not to sound accommodating, hospitable, or even interested. Few classes started early, he knew, since the university schedule generally followed the students' preferred waking hours, roughly noon to around 3 a.m.

"I'm helping this professor, Dr. Brusolowitz, and there's like a lot of stuff he wants me to do."

Collie froze and stared, striving to conceal surprise and instantaneous interest. Could she possibly know anything about Brucie's sleep research? Doubting his capacity at the moment for a nonchalant interrogation, he shrugged and simply asked, "Like what?"

"He's cleaning up his office. Shredding stuff. The place is like a mess, and he's sorting it out. I'm helping him."

Collie decided to ask no further. "I'll get the things for you. Just a minute."

Returning with a spare blanket and the clock from his own bedside he found the room he had left her in brightly illuminated. She had found the light-switch panel and turned on the ceiling spotlights. The unwanted guest stood erect, a blaze of white skin, stripped down to her underpants, otherwise clothesless, staring at him. "What the hell are you doing?" he demanded.

"If you touch me, I'll scream," she assured him in a quivering but threatening voice.

"Oh, shit, go to sleep," Collie groaned, turning away and slumping to his bedroom.

"Just don't try anything. Okay?" she said.

"Oh, go to sleep, you goddamned idiot."

"I'll scream."

Collie started to say, "Go fuck yourself," but clamped his jaw. He tightly closed his bedroom door and plummeted into bed. A few seconds later, he got up and lodged a chair against the door knob. As he fell into deep sleep, two thoughts whirled in his dissolving consciousness: Nut case and Max Brusolowitz.

In the morning, as promised, she was gone when he woke up.

Sipping coffee in his kitchen, scrolling his computer, and plotting his day, Collie was jarred by an unusually early call from Lou.

"Did you find out anything?" Lou asked.

"No, but I'm working on it."

"Well, I heard something you'll be interested in."

"What?" Collie asked.

"Brucie might be leaving Kershaw. Maybe you can check it out. This could be a big deal and I want us to get it."

CHAPTER VII

The special trustees meeting that Martin Dollard referred to on Collie's party invitation was called on short notice to make a critical decision in the affairs of Kershaw University: the long-overdue selection of a new president. The need to get on with it expeditiously was indisputable. Starting a decade ago, the university entered a gradual but continuing decline while its revered, long-serving president, T. Carl Giles, remained in office, increasingly disengaged from university affairs. His intensely loyal staff maintained a reverential silence, leaving the university community intensely curious but unknowing about what he did and when he would depart. University business piled up in his inbox. Fund-raising dropped to a trickle. Plans for new buildings and programs, faculty appointments and poaching of stars from other schools, departmental reorganizations, and other actions essential for maintaining academic vitality—papers concerning all of these critical matters flowed into the presidential suite, never to be heard of again. Long under discussion but still unsettled were several huge gifts contingent on renaming major campus buildings in honor of prospective donors. Such alterations were always delicate and legally intricate, sure to evoke enraged objections from previous living donors or descendants of expired donors whose names currently graced the buildings. Rumors circulated that a Russian oil oligarch had offered a gigantic contribution to the Kershaw endowment contingent on the entire university taking his patronym. But no one knew for sure. Invocation of the trustees' undoubted authority to remove President Giles was unthinkable. In his better days, Giles had handpicked all the current trustees, expertly selecting people who had no experience or interest in higher education, but who were deeply flattered by membership on the Kershaw University Board of Trustees. In choosing trustees, he was guided by two strong preferences: That they would be docile and that Kershaw had a reasonable chance of turning them into major donors. He strongly favored wealthy widows, undistinguished heirs to large fortunes, and bored youngish wives of extremely rich men. He also favored parvenu millionaires hungry for status but uninterested in meddling in university affairs. From these categories, he easily filled the board. Initial appointments were for a probationary three years; those found acceptable by Giles received follow-up appointments of six years and were eligible for renewal. Every year or two, upon his sole recommendation, a trustee would be awarded an honorary degree, while the others politely applauded and wondered which of them was next. Giles was cherished by the alumni, and his fruitful relationships with affluent donors were clearly registered in the robust growth of Kershaw's endowment, construction of buildings financed with gifts, and endowed chairs. But that was long ago. Forced removal, no matter how gently accomplished, would be disruptive and feed factionalism between his sentimental admirers and those alarmed by the university's drift.

The long-serving Giles was an icon of higher education, laden with innumerable honors for scholarship, educational statesmanship, academic administration, and public service. Throughout his career he was a deft academic politician, shrewd at locating the powers to be cultivated, appeased, or avoided, while presenting no threat to established interests. He looked presidential, statesmanlike: tall, lean, in well-tailored, dark, three piece suits, with quiet neckties, a confident but friendly executive manner, sparkling blue eyes, and a durable shock of hair that gracefully grayed in step with his age. His academic speciality, child development, was boundlessly egalitarian, unimpaired by standards of evidence and rigor in data collection and evaluation common to other fields of research. He made his mark by photographing toddlers in the nursery and comparing them to young primates. Giles' doctoral thesis, "Variability in Infant Responses to Selective Stimuli," was repackaged by a textbook publisher into "Origins of Intellectual Variability," which became prescribed reading for many psych courses; a popular edition was titled "The Genius in Your Crib." Both enhanced his reputation and bank account, and imparted thrust to his career. Starting as a bottom-rank instructor, Giles rose in the academic hierarchy, eventually to the university presidency. At each stage, his competitors suffered from some failing. If, in the selection process, the failing went unrecognized, he would discreetly make it known, thus leaving him as the least undesirable choice. Though his presidential performance had been slipping for several years, the downward glide slope was gentle and not readily noticeable in its early stages. Besides, he was away from Kershaw for much of the time to perform the duties of high-level office in prestigious national organizations, mainly headquartered in Washington. These were all part-time positions, in scientific and scholarly societies and associations run by full-time professional staffs that tended to all the managerial and bureaucratic details, including ghost-written speeches, for their drop-in leaders. Fly in, deliver a pre-packaged keynote address to the annual membership meeting, confer with the council of the organization on matters pre-digested and settled by the staff, and return to the home campus. In the aggregate, these offices consumed a considerable amount of President Giles' time. But at this point, whether or not he was on campus, major decisions were deferred and the university lumbered along on auto-pilot. Nonetheless, Giles retained a reputation for deep involvement in important affairs. While serving as the president of the Association of Universities, he was chairman of the board of the Association for American Science and co-chairman of the National Commission on Educational Revitalization. In addition, he served on the council of the Academy of the Sciences. Despite clear signs of slowing, he maintained an excellent attendance record at their many meetings, participated in discussions, and cast his vote on the issues confronting these organizations.

True, his comments often puzzled other committee members, but they received them as oracular and worth pondering—such was his stature. On one of these baffling occasions, during a meeting on space cooperation with China, he remarked, "The Robbins report may have done more damage than good. Time will tell"—possibly a reference to a long-forgotten 1963 report by a Lord Robbins on the expansion of higher education in Great Britain. Unacquainted with that Robbins report, or any other, the participants around the table, all far younger than Giles, exchanged puzzled glances, and returned to their agenda. "That guy's soft as a grape," a lowly staff member at the meeting whispered to a senior staff colleague. In return, he received an upward roll of the eyes and a hush-up finger to the lips.

Of utmost concern to the university's board of trustees and senior management, President Giles's once-formidable fund-raising prowess had slipped away. But to growing despair in widening circles at the university, he indicated no interest in leaving, even as his 65th birthday receded further and further into the past. When he was not away at meetings, he conferred in his office with a steady stream of acquaintances from his long career in higher education, national and international affairs. The purpose of these meetings was the object of campus-wide conjecture, as they had no consequences or apparent relation to university business or the president's many external involvements.

The president's administrative assistant shared in the puzzlement about these meetings, as well as about other matters concerning the president. Stationed in the presidential suite, he actually had little day-to-day contact with President Giles. When he did, he often came away looking down, shaking his head, and talking to himself. On one occasion, Giles rang him on the intercom, and, in his customarily courteous manner, said, "Bob, when you have a moment, could you kindly step in here?

He arrived immediately. Giles, at his desk, looked up, and said, "I was just noticing that 'dwell' spelled backwards is 'lewd,' but with one 'l'."

"Sir?" the assistant asked quizzically, thinking, perhaps, the president had taken up a word puzzle.

"That's just an observation," Giles said.

"I'll make a note of it," the assistant assured him.

"That would be helpful," Giles said. "Something for the files."

"Of course. Anything else?"

"No, thank you, I think that's it." the president said

"One more thing," the assistant said. "The science association sent the text of the keynote speech you're giving next week at the annual meeting. It looks fine. A really strong statement on global warming."

"Their people always do a fine job," Giles said.

When President Giles was not on out-of-town business, his on-campus routine was as follows: A university limousine daily delivered him to his office at
8 a.m. At about 9 a.m., visitors began to arrive. The common explanation was
that he liked to schmooze, and there was no reason to believe that the meetings
entailed anything beyond that. Among those meeting with Giles was Martin Dollard. Expecting that the president would be pressed for time, Martin had carefully
rehearsed a succinct description of his proposal for a university roundtable on
societal impacts. President Giles, however, adopted a leisurely pace, asking questions that opened new avenues for exposition and explanation. Abandoning his
plan for brevity, Martin, in full measure, explained the need for the roundtable,
how it would operate, and the benefits it would bring to Kershaw University.
The meeting ended with a characteristically enigmatic utterance from Giles. "We
might look to innovations that have proven beneficial." Nevertheless, the meeting
with President Giles inspired Martin to believe that the president was favorably
impressed and that the university would welcome the roundtable.

Immediately after meeting with Dollard, President Giles summoned his assistant. "What is our situation with respect to low-hanging fruit?" he asked.

"Low-hanging fruit?"

"Yes," said Giles, with his customary geniality. "That Dollard chap happened
to mention it, and aroused my curiosity about our situation."

"I have no idea, sir, but I suppose Buildings and Grounds might know something about that."

"Yes, of course, they would, wouldn't they? See what you can find out. But
nothing urgent. Low-hanging fruit on campus. Has it all been picked? And if so,
by whom? We can decide later whether we have to look further."

"For sure," the assistant said, backing out of the President's office.

A few minutes later, Giles buzzed his assistant. "It occurs to me that the
Botany Department might be helpful."

Immobilized by Giles's prestige and staying power, but aware of the inevitable, several Kershaw trustees quietly persuaded the board chairman to commission a presidential search—"just to be prepared." The chairman, Saul Goodson,
a former dentist turned millionaire automobile dealer, normally didn't act on

university affairs without the guidance of President Giles, but now he saw the need to move. And fortunately so, because not long afterwards, President Giles failed to appear for his morning limousine ride, and was found expired in the presidential residence. Thanks to the trustees' foresight, an academic headhunter was prepared to present a short list of carefully vetted possible successors. But to conform with federal affirmative-action and non-discrimination laws, the search was presented as a wide-open quest in advertisements in the *Chronicle of Higher Education* and the recruitment section of the *New York Times Week in Review:*

"Kershaw University, an acknowledged international leader in higher education, advanced studies and scientific research, seeks a visionary, transformational new president to take the institution to even higher levels of academic excellence. The successful candidate will have a world-class scholarly reputation, the highest executive ability, sensitivity to the pressing social issues of our time, a firm commitment to environmental progress, the ability to develop consensus among a large and diverse faculty, and a demonstrated capacity for fund raising on a major scale. Kershaw University is an equal-opportunity employer."

The many responses that arrived were filed away unopened. Eager to get on with it, the trustees confined their attention to the headhunter's short list.

CHAPTER VIII

With all 14 trustees in attendance, John Stanley, president of the blue-chip recruitment firm John Stanley & Associates LLC, stood at the head of the long table in the trustees' wood-paneled conference room adjacent to the presidential suite. A former professor of human resources, and author of a standard manual, "Human Resources Administration: Avoiding the Misfit," Stanley had left academe to establish his own recruitment company. He unabashedly charged top dollar for his services, which were rated prime quality in elite educational circles. As the trustees settled down for what they had been told would be a lengthy session, he briefly introduced himself. The discussion, he emphasized, must be regarded as highly confidential, since it would necessarily entail sensitive personal information about the individuals under consideration for the presidency.

"A breach of confidence," Stanley warned, "could result in serious legal and financial liability for the university, the board as a whole, individual members, and myself and my company."

Stanley switched on a PowerPoint presentation, which he accompanied with running comments. He spoke in a low, conversational manner, without gestures or rhetorical flourishes. "More than many of you probably realize, society is rife with a large variety of misfits, many of whom pass for normal and honorable. Many are productive and successful at work, though many are not."

A long list appeared on the PowerPoint screen. Reading aloud, one by one, Stanley highlighted each entry with the jumpy green dot of a laser pointer: "Child molesters, embezzlers, extortionists, tax evaders, money launderers, deadbeats, pornographers, perjurers, shoplifters, spouse abusers, forgers, bigamists, military deserters, fetishists, scientific frauds, plagiarists, and arsonists."

Setting down the laser pointer, he continued, "There are more, many more, as well as others who remain within the bounds of legal behavior but who are problematic for one reason or another, such as nudists, chronic liars, and psychiatric cripples. When mistakenly appointed to high academic office, as unfortunately happens, any one of these, upon misbehaving or being exposed, can inflict serious institutional damage by undermining confidence and offending donors, alumni, faculty, parents of students, foundation staff, government officials, religious leaders, and some elements of the press. The potential for damage is considerable. Maybe enormous is a better word." Pausing for a moment, he said in slow-paced speech: "Higher education is not immune to grossly inappropriate appointments. Not by a long shot."

Hesitatingly, a trustee raised his hand and interrupted. "With all due respect, it seems far-fetched," he began. "I mean, like nudist and some of the others. The people we're considering are all highly accomplished and have passed muster many times to get where they are. Without evidence to the contrary, don't they deserve the benefit of the doubt? And wouldn't we save a lot of time if we gave them the benefit of the doubt?"

"Thank you. This inevitably comes up," Stanley said. "Maybe in the old days. But 'evidence to the contrary' is a new game today. Consider that with computer hacking and the cell-phone camera and other intrusive devices now universal facts of life, derogatory information can be just a few clicks away. And once it's found, *anything* about anyone can be displayed on the Internet, including presidents of universities. There was a very admirable young man—Harvard, Rhodes Scholar—running in a Congressional primary last year. Just the kind of person we'd all like to see in politics. I won't say where this happened, but somehow a video of him picking his nose and then a minute later shaking hands with voters showed up on the Internet. And it was all over for him. That's the new digital world for you."

The scraping of a chair interrupted Stanley. A woman trustee arose. "Excuse me. I think I'm going to be sick," she croaked. She left the room. Stanley gravely waited a moment and resumed.

"From the living room to the men's room and the ladies' room, the locker room and the medical-examining room, and including the bedroom, there's no privacy. For twenty-five dollars, Radio Shack can turn anyone into a first-rate eavesdropper. My message is, 'Don't be naive, be careful.' But at the same time, we want to strike a balance between prudence and informed tolerance for human frailty. None of us is perfect. But I'll remind you: Each of you is legally and morally responsible for this great institution."

Sitting motionless, the trustees absorbed this admonition in stark silence. The gravity of their duty now bound them together as never before.

"Weeding out misfits is just one step in a successful search process," Stanley cautioned. "A clean record is not enough, as it has no bearing on the separate and important issue of competence. Sterling resumes, impressive publication lists, and strong endorsements for moving up the academic ladder are standard. Often they are legitimate. But we must recognize that today anyone with a laptop and a printer can make them up to order. Which is why they are never to be accepted without careful, thorough investigation. How many times do you read in the paper about some dean or president or even a surgeon who, it turns out, never went to college or has something very embarrassing, or worse, in his or her background? Or the President of the United States nominates someone for the cabinet or some other top job, the FBI says he's okay, and then it turns out they haven't paid their taxes or child support for years? Or maybe something worse. The better the resume, the more reasons for careful, thorough investigation."

With evident pride, Stanley noted that "no misfit has ever got past us. But they've come close." Delicately avoiding mention of his fees, which were known to the trustees, he assured them that the price for finding a dean ($50,000) was well worth the cost in catastrophe avoidance; for a president ($150,000), it was an even greater bargain.

Short, squat, square-jawed, with a ruddy face and a tawny crewcut, Stanley proceeded without irony or humor, a consequence of his many years of methodically peering into the lives of presumably upright, honorable people—the celebrated and the obscure—and often finding something unseemly, seriously amiss, occasionally even horrendous. His capacity for trust and faith in good reputation was long gone. He presented a simple message: "Remember the list I just presented. Better to find out before the inaugural ceremony that your presidential choice is a—" and he paused, "—whatever, than to have the hometown paper, the campus newspaper, or national TV reveal it to you and the world, after inauguration day. I think we all want to avoid a train wreck."

With his stock introduction completed, Stanley turned anecdotal and chatty. "Just recently," he related, "we were called in to confirm the short list for chancellor of a major university—I won't say which one. It took some investigating, but we found that one of the candidates on the list—a distinguished statistician who holds a high academic position—is a compulsive flasher, a habitual exhibitionist. He was discreet on his own campus, as far as is known, but on university business out of town, he had a penchant for—well, hanging around women's dorms. Despite dark glasses and a turned down hat brim, a student from his own campus who happened to be visiting there recognized him, and snapped him on his cellphone camera. Checking this out, we discovered the facts."

A trustee started to speak. "Could that possibly be—?" But Stanley cut her short. "Privacy considerations enter into this. I think we'd better move on."

Pausing for a moment while a trustee scribbled a note and passed it to another, Stanley went on to stress that technology and changes in campus culture have made recruitment more dangerous, and screening even more indispensable. "Today's kids grew up on computers from age two, and they can crack most any computer security system and get into personnel files and police and court records and medical records. They can read the mail on your personal computer, coming and going. In addition, there's a big menace that's insufficiently recognized: Work-study programs put students into all levels of university administration, including the offices of the president, admissions, general counsel, personnel, and the campus mental health service. These kids consider it their right, their absolute right, to see everything and make any copies they choose and share them with the whole world via the Internet. It's best to assume that no record is safe. Transcripts, grade point averages? They hack into them and change them as they please. Don't expect today's students to respect other people's privacy when they're routinely posting nude pictures of themselves on the Internet. Also, don't ever assume any e-mail is deleted. It's always out there someplace, and can be found by somebody who isn't supposed to see it. You should keep that in mind for your personal affairs and especially when you're e-mailing about university business.

"As I'm sure you know," he told the trustees, who were now enthralled, "university administrators receive anonymous letters by the truck load from people who nurse grievances and grudges about this or that, real or imagined, in the school—admissions, rejections, the food, tuition, class size, faculty appointments, tenure denial, sexual preferences of people, who's cohabitating with whom, anything. And the rags that pass for school papers get hold of this stuff and will publish anything that comes in or make up anything. A lot of it is pure fantasy, but sometimes there's real dirt—about divorces, drunk driving arrests, unbelievable sexual practices, embezzlement, whatever. In any case, nothing, and I mean that literally, nothing is out of bounds. If I may say so, the student paper here is no exception when it comes to printing trash, but others are worse, if that's any comfort." Many of the trustees nodded in agreement. Guided by Stanley to peer into the abyss of human frailty, they solemnly felt the weight of the responsibility for which they were summoned.

Having completed his introductory remarks, Stanley proceeded further into the complexities of recruitment. "There are generic and case-specific considerations in filling senior university positions," he explained. "Family situations and geographical preferences may impede a move. Personal and institutional chemistry must be compatible. Kershaw, fortunately, can match any university in the crucial matter of the compensation package, but it has its own challenges. It is a large and diverse university, with many important components competing for resources in a difficult financial environment. Any newcomer will have to contend with nostalgia for your late, very distinguished president, who was favored by better times for much of his tenure. There is no ideal, perfect candidate on the face of this earth. But we have identified and checked out some very, very good possibilities. Not perfect, but very, very good. I will frankly give you the upside and downside of each, but in no particular order relative to their merit." The trustees settled into their chairs. Some sipped water and arranged the note pads and pens at each of their places. Others shuffled the biographical summaries provided by Stanley. All listened intently.

"First, on bio sheet number one, we have from California Dr. Corbin, professor of biochemistry and provost. She received the Lasker Prize in medicine two years ago, which is frequently a precursor for the Nobel Prize. She's widely regarded as a comer in the academic world. Just elected to the National Academy of Sciences, which, as you know, is a very high honor. Gets excellent marks for administration, is extremely popular with faculty and students, and is highly regarded for the calming influence she's had on what was once a fairly unruly campus. Age 45, in excellent health. Limited fund-raising experience, but she's never been responsible for much of that. I think she can grow into that role."

"I've heard of her," one of the trustees said. "What's the downside?"

"I was getting to that," Stanley said. "She's on her fourth divorce. It's in court—a bit nasty. It's the kind of situation that fortunately occurs rarely and that few if any of us know about first hand. But it happens. Her husband is a graduate student a considerable number of years younger than Dr. Corbin. He charges her with spousal abuse, and there are some signs of injury, we understand. She's a large person," Stanley said matter of factly, circling his arms in front of him, "and he's—." Stanley held his hands nearly together, suggesting a slight stature and a mismatch in size. "It's a complex situation. Her son from her first or maybe second marriage is older than her current husband, the estranged husband—the graduate student. And the son and the husband had some kind of personal relationship. That's none of our concern. As I said, it's a complex situation that's still playing out, and some people in the wider university community might find it disturbing. On the other hand, apart from these personal matters, Dr. Corbin is an outstanding educator and administrator."

Several trustees exchanged troubled expressions. "What else do you have?" one of them asked.

"There's Russo, in Texas. He's been president of the university for six years and has done wonders in bringing in top-notch faculty and promoting diversity. Great fund raiser, both from private sources and government research agencies. Really tops. I think he's ready to move on to a bigger challenge, and would be a good fit at this stage of Kershaw's development."

"Downside?" a trustee asked.

"As you've probably heard, he's in this controversy about the football budget," Stanley explained. "He refuses to raise it because he thinks football is overemphasized to the detriment of academics. He's insistent on that, and most of the faculty is with him. He's got a lot of support, but also a lot of opposition, especially from the alumni. There's a student group that burns him in effigy outside the presidential residence every evening. They set fire to a full-size stuffed dummy. It's been going on for months, nightly. The campus police say they can't stop it because burning in effigy qualifies as protected speech under the First Amendment. The ACLU represents the students."

"So what's the downside about him?" a trustee asked.

"He cries a lot," Stanley replied. "Gets very emotional and cries. Stands on his porch when they light this stuffed straw dummy every night and cries. Tears running down his face, they say. Some people think he'll be all right if he gets away from the situation. But others are not so sure. I want to make that clear to you."

"Why doesn't he just ignore it? Be someplace else when they do it?" a trustee asked.

"I don't know," Stanley said. "But he's there every time they do it. Seems to think it's his responsibility in some way, we're told."

"Do you think he'd straighten up if he made a move to a different school?"

"We all hope so, but it's hard to know," Stanley cautioned. "It may be this has gone on too long. It could be, he's over the edge, so to speak. But otherwise he has the right stuff. It's your call. All I can do is present the facts."

"Whew!" one of the trustees exclaimed. "What else you got?"

"MacKinaw, former president of a top-notch liberal arts college in the midwest. He left about five years ago for a big job in the U.S. Department of Education, and now he's ready to move back to university work. Strong resume. He has a law degree and a Ph.D. in education, and was a terrific fund raiser at his former school. He's written a good deal about higher-education issues and is highly regarded by several people whose judgment has been sound in the past. I'd say he's a real statesman type."

"Downside?"

"Plagiarism. He says it isn't, but an investigating committee suggested it might be but withheld official final judgment. It's another complicated case. It turns out that in his Ph.D. dissertation, there are some passages that raised suspicion. Those passages were traced to a dissertation by another doctoral candidate, but the texts are extremely confused. Whether or not these issues had anything to do with it, he left for the job in Washington while the investigation was going on. As far as we could find out, the investigation was never completed. So, officially, nothing has been proven one way or the other. But you have to expect that the issue is still there and could be revived. These things often are," Stanley said. "If he became president, he might get into a row with someone over practically nothing, and next thing you know, it's all over the student paper and on the Internet that he was investigated for plagiarism and the case is unsettled. That's how these things happen. I'd advise you to consider him seriously but proceed with caution. One more thing. In our experience, there's rarely such a thing as a single case of plagiarism. If they do it once, they keep on doing it. It becomes a habit. But as I said, this case is unresolved, sort of stuck in midstream."

"You haven't brought us much good news," one of the trustees said. "How about on this campus? We wanted to get some ratings of our home-grown talent."

"We've looked here too, as you requested," the headhunter replied. "At the suggestion of your chairman, we informed ourselves about Dean Roland at the Law School. He's raised substantial amounts of money, and has recruited outstanding legal scholars for the faculty. The LSAT scores show the school is admitting a better grade of student. He has a growing reputation as a legal scholar. Several important law review articles. We point out in the bios you have that one was cited in a recent Supreme Court decision. There are some problems, however. Seems there always are," Stanley acknowledged with a faint smile. "You might call them personality problems. The dean has a reputation for being difficult, quarrelsome, some might call it. In the extreme. He has many feuds going at once, at the school and outside. We found out that he's the plaintiff in a surprising number of private lawsuits." Stanley pulled a sheet of paper from a folder. "At last count, he's suing two restaurants, a shoe repair shop, his co-op board, the principal of the school his kid goes to, an elevator maintenance service, and the Bolivian delegate to the

United Nations. I don't know all the factual details of these lawsuits, but they seem to be about minor things, like late seating for a restaurant reservation or a poor job of resoling his shoes. Except for the Bolivian, these are small businesses, and the owners have tried to settle. But the dean is adamant, and even insists on jury trials. Says it's his right."

"What's with the Bolivian?" a trustee asked.

"For some reason, the court has sealed those papers."

Several trustees shook their heads in wonderment. One of them muttered, "I've never heard of anything like this." Another, with a hopeful tone in his voice, suggested, "Perhaps these lawsuits are some kind of practical law program that he's running for the students so they can get some courtroom experience."

"No," Stanley said, "Dean Roland is scrupulously ethical about separating his personal issues from his law school responsibilities. He's laid down a bright red line on that issue. I can vouch for that. He prepares and argues the cases himself."

Several trustees emitted sounds of discouragement. Stanley sipped water, and continued.

"Now, we spoke with a psychiatrist at the Medical School who holds a joint appointment at the Law School. He teaches a seminar on Medicine and the Law. In his professional opinion, he said, and I quote, Dean Roland is clinically insane. Those are his words, exact words, clinically insane."

"Clinically insane?" a trustee gasped with incredulity. "C'mon."

"Yes, that's what he said," Stanley confirmed in his monotone manner. "He said I could look it up in DSM. That's a handbook psychiatrists use for diagnosis, but I didn't pursue the matter." Stanley waited for the hubbub in the room to subside. "A word of caution," he explained. "I think we have to recognize that when controversies arise, faculty members sometimes become emotional and resort to hyperbole. I doubt that's a real diagnosis. In this case, the dean and the Medical School person had some run-in about scheduling the class, and some difficulty may possibly have arisen from that. I can't say for certain."

Loudly exhaling, Chairman Goodson said, "You also have a report on Dean Swazy at our School of Education."

"Yes. He's done an excellent job there," Stanley said. "High marks for academic leadership, fund-raising, scholarship, et cetera, et cetera. Extremely popular with faculty and students."

"Looks interesting, worth exploring?" a trustee asked hopefully. "Is he our man?"

"I wish he were," Stanley said. "I prefer not to go into details. It's your decision to make, but in this instance, I especially counsel caution. He's fine where he is. His present position doesn't attract much attention. But if he became president, the added prominence would bring closer scrutiny and some things might come out. I'd rather not say. Trust me."

"Look," a trustee said, obviously annoyed. "We're scraping the barrel. Can't you be more specific? I mean, if it's something like that guy you mentioned who was waving his dick around in public, okay, we'd understand. But with Swazy, is it, like, he's got a pile of overdue books from the library?"

Stanley momentarily hesitated. "I emphasize again that this meeting is strictly confidential. So, with that understood—. When he was an undergrad, the Dean was charged with bestiality and suspended for a semester. It was at an ag school, where he was majoring in ruminants—sheep, goats, cows, with a minor in poultry. He was readmitted later on but was required to change his program. That's how he got into education. This was all long ago. The case should have been expunged from the record, but with computers, these things never completely disappear. It could surface again. Just possibly."

"He was charged with what?" a trustee asked.

Another leaned over and whispered to her. She looked aghast. "Well, I suppose," she said, "where there's smoke, there could be fire. We can't be sure, can we?"

"Impossible to say," Stanley replied.

With late afternoon shadows now gathering outside the trustees' board room, Stanley glanced at his watch and said, "I can be brief with the next one. Professor Max Brusolowitz. First-class scientist, many honors. Runs a big lab with a great deal of external funding. A lot going for him in all important respects. However, he's deeply engaged in a major project. I don't know the details, but that's not relevant for our purpose. When we expressed our interest, he seemed to think about it, but then he made it clear that there's no possible way he could drop the project or keep running it while serving as president. It's a shame that some outstanding people can't or won't move on to broader and higher responsibilities. But on the bright side, it's that kind of dedication that gives Kershaw its worldwide reputation as a great scientific university. Another one of your top flight scientists, Dr. Fenster, said he would not even consider the presidency because of his research responsibilities."

"So, where does that leave us?" a trustee asked.

"Last on the list, Professor Winner, in economics." Stanley said. "He was not on our original list of candidates, but I received an e-mail from someone here— I'm not sure who—asking me to check him out as one of the people already here at Kershaw. It turns out that he has not been, so to speak, on a presidential track in his career, but that's for you to judge. We've heard good things about him. We've found nothing of concern in his background. He's a good fund raiser. His own research has been financed by industry for many years. He hasn't held any administrative positions in higher education, which maybe is a plus," Stanley said with a chuckle and a wink. "But to be serious, he's published what some consider to be *the* book on modern management. I've read parts of it. It's rough going, but I will say it covers a lot of interesting ground. And he's got hands-on corporate experience, which could be a great strength for developing new revenue streams. He was in top management with a Silicon Valley firm for several years. I think this is telling: Not long after he left, the firm went into Chapter 7 and was dissolved. But apparently it was doing just fine when he was there."

"But he's just a plain professor, not a dean or VP or something like that?" a trustee inquired.

"Right," Stanley replied. "Just a plain vanilla professor."

As the group fell into a dismayed silence, a trustee spoke up in a firm, confident voice. "I've known Professor Winner for many years, personally and professionally. I can vouch that he would make an outstanding president."

At the end of a long, frustrating day, the emphatic endorsement had a catalytic effect on the weary group.

"Hey," said a fellow trustee, "We've got nothing else, and it's all pluses about this guy Winner. Frankly, the other ones we've been hearing about scare the hell out of me. We've had a law school dean who's a medically certified nut case, another dean who's a pervert with animals, a flasher, a woman who's setting records for getting divorced, and god knows what else. You say there's nothing disreputable or embarrassing about Winner. That's good enough for me. So what if he's not been on a presidential track. Like Mr. Stanley says, maybe that's for the best. If he doesn't work out, we can always fire him and get someone else. We've got to get this settled."

The trustees voiced and nodded agreement. The deliberations had continued far longer than anyone had expected. Departure time was nearing for flights home. On short notice, all had interrupted their busy, tightly scheduled lives to attend the crucial meeting. Business affairs, a grandson's birthday, a wedding anniversary, vacations and medical appointments, including elective surgery, even the funeral of a dear friend had been cast aside on short notice to fulfill their responsibilities to Kershaw University. None of them wanted to return for another, possibly inconclusive, meeting.

"Do I hear a motion to pick Winner?" the chairman of the trustees asked.

"I move that Winner is the next President."

"Do I hear a second?

"Seconded."

"All in favor say aye."

A chorus of "ayes."

"All opposed."

Silence.

"The motion carries unanimously."

And thus Mark Winner unexpectedly slipped into the presidency of Kershaw University. Ambition and drive, luck and craft are common ingredients for success in our competitive society. Winner was lucky and crafty. On the drive to the airport, Chairman Goodson telephoned Winner. Informed of his selection, with a starting salary of $450,000 a year and a campus residence, he accepted.

CHAPTER IX

An emotionally desiccated, solitary, waif-like little man, Mark Winner confided in no one. He neither offended nor frightened anyone. He was not liked or disliked. Though he satisfactorily performed all his academic duties in a long career at Kershaw, he was as close to invisibility as a palpable presence can be. Short in stature, sharp faced, and customarily squinting in a way that suggested skepticism, if not disbelief, when he engaged in conversation, he steered clear of service on the many committees that endlessly, feebly, and inconclusively, grappled with academic affairs. He was not well-known on campus. On the spectrum of ambition, he was at the far low end, grateful for the security of a university position, and wishing for nothing more. Raised by indifferent parents, and barely noticed by his peers, he carried a burden of feeling unlikable. Nonetheless, in the trying circumstances of the Giles succession, the reigning powers deemed him handily available.

On a check list of presidential essentials, there were some unknowns about Winner, but no negatives. The trustees acted with minimal knowledge about their choice, but he filled the bill for a modern university presidency, if only barely.

As always, collegial respect, or an absence of disdain, within the community of scholars was essential for the presidency of a major institution of higher learning. In today's globalized and competitive environment, abilities and accomplishments in the world beyond academe were critically important, too. Managerial skill was essential. Kershaw, like other elite research universities, was a large, complex enterprise, with over 7,000 employees, from professors to security guards, an annual budget of $2.5 billion, an endowment nearing $5 billion, a physical plant comprising over 100 buildings, large and small, and some 20,000 "customers," i.e., students. Involved, too, were the alumni and the surrounding neighborhood, ever resistant to Kershaw's unrelenting grasp for nearby real estate. The president must be sensitive toward modern-day students, who are collectively volatile and prone to demonstrate about a lengthy list of social and political issues and grievances. The president must also cope with a faculty with frail loyalty to Kershaw, as manifested in departures to other schools for even small improvements in salary or status. Fund-raising ability mattered greatly. Universities were no longer coy or dainty about engaging with and accommodating government, industry, and wealthy individuals to satisfy their ravenous need for money. In all things presidential, a sixth sense for sound judgments was indispensable. So was an absence of embarrassing character blemishes, such as publicized sexual misadventures, tax defaults, plagiarism, brazenly conflicted interests and other deviations from scholarly rectitude and good citizenship. To the aforementioned qualities, add public speaking ability and the possession of national stature, and the difficulties of filling academe's major presidential positions are daunting. Rarely did a single individual embody a full complement of these characteristics. Compromises were necessary, though in no respect did Winner fall grievously short of any of the criteria.

Winner's record as a scholar was acceptable. He had published a satisfactory amount of above-mediocre research and commentary in economics, his primary field of scholarship. His doctoral thesis, "Coin Denominations As an Influence on Economic Activity," had attracted little attention in academic circles. When published as a monograph, the few reviews were non-committal or slightly unfavorable. This was to be expected because of the inherent obscurity and insignificance of the subject and the concomitant paucity of scholars qualified to evaluate his work. Even so, given the opportunity to add a few lines to their *curricula vitae* with minimum effort, reviewers were available. For self-protection, the reviewers either safely summarized the book, without rendering judgment, or quibbled about minor points to flaunt their superior knowledge and perceptiveness and the inadequacies of the author. In scholarly circles, "Denominations" did not elevate the author's stature, but it did not diminish it. For Winner, this was a satisfactory outcome, in view of the profession's natural inclination to denigrate competitors for advancement. Elsewhere, however, he fared even better.

To Winner's surprise, the slender volume drew the attention of a vending-industry executive who served on the Kershaw board of trustees. The trustee, who considered himself a keen judge of talent and leadership, felt that in Winner, he had discovered an unrecognized savant. At the trustee's suggestion, Winner was engaged as a consultant for the industry's trade association. Vending machines are useful and profitable but little noticed by consumers as they deposit their money and receive drinks and snacks in return. Upon incorporating clever improvements, such as the capacity to "read" paper currency, deliver change, and heat canned soups, coffee, and hot dogs, the machines long ago reached technological maturity. Nonetheless, they still lack the eclat and dazzle of high-tech consumer goods. The public's enchantment with cutting-edge smart products has never extended to vending machines. The pioneers of vending technology work in obscurity. There is no Bill Gates of the industry. Perhaps because of their low profile, the executives in the vending association felt uplifted by their academic tie in the person of Dr. Mark Winner, Ph.D., professor of economics at the renowned Kershaw University. From the time they connected, early in his career, the vending association annually provided Winner with funds for research, travel, graduate assistants and stipends for a postdoc or two. Though little known to the public, such deals between professors and business are not unusual. Winner prudently declined to be drawn into the nasty contention over whether soft-drinks and sweets should be available in vending machines on school premises. He assisted the industry's Washington lobbyists when they occasionally sought his advice about their Congressional testimony, which strongly disputed a connection between vending machines and childhood obesity. Otherwise, Winner prudently maintained an arms-length distance from his business patron. Though he actually did little for the industry, the relationship endured to the satisfaction of both parties. This profitable arrangement spared him from the arduous grant stalking that occupied many of his academic colleagues, as well as from the faculty's ceaseless internecine intrigue and squabbling over budget shares, travel expenses, office equipment and supplies, and funds for graduate assistants.

Throughout his career, Winner shunned involvement with the various boards, committees, councils, and other bodies involved in governance of the university. And in contrast to ambitious but less-foresightful colleagues, Winner steadfastly avoided opportunities to rise in the administrative hierarchy, knowing that the inevitable lot of department chairmen, graduate deans and provosts is hatred and scorn, which few survive intact.

Winner's unerring aloofness from campus politics and strife was remarkable, given that the university was constantly roiled by controversies that suddenly erupted into bitter accusations, recriminations, and tantrums. If any issue was ever resolved, it was swiftly replaced by another. Conflict would rage over a change in opening hours at the faculty club, a lecture invitation for a foreign thug, a tenure denial or award, the library budget, regulation of debauchery in frat houses, and frequency of trash collections from faculty offices. On one unique occasion, nearly the entire tenured faculty petitioned against a revision in the academic calendar that would change the opening of the fall semester from Tuesday to Monday. Ignored by the administration, which apparently was unaware of the petition, the aggrieved scholars, in a rare display of solidarity, expressed their deeply felt sentiment by simultaneously observing one minute of silence during the new opening day.

Resisting pleas to join in, Winner remained aloof from the conflict and slithering intrigue that was standard fare at Kershaw and other universities. Tenured, well-financed by the vending-machine industry, bearing a modest teaching load, Mark Winner was content with his lot. But, recognizing that the university was not immune to change, and that tenure was not the impregnable fortress that envious outsiders thought it to be, he was amenable to an unexpected opportunity to strengthen his professional standing. A nudge was also provided by the academic timetable, which dictated that it was time for him to produce another book.

In mid-career, sensing the tightening links between academe and industry, Winner took two years' leave from the university to accept an offer to serve as vice president for corporate strategy of a Silicon Valley software firm. No family consideration impeded this decision. At age 50, Winner remained an unentangled bachelor. His improbable detour to the Valley originated with the same university trustee who had recruited him as a consultant for the vending-machine association. The trustee, who also served on the software firm's board of directors, felt confident that the company would benefit from Winner's counsel. Though once highly successful, the firm now competed poorly in a crowded field of battling corporate carnivores. The self-appointed recruiter assured company management that Winner was an uncommonly brilliant, original thinker who could "strategize" the company to success, and pump up the sagging stock options for its management and 1,100 employees. Comfortable in his academic nest, Winner did not relish the temporary uprooting that the company job entailed. Moreover, following a discussion with the software firm's CEO, Winner realized that he was unqualified for the job, knowing nothing about software design, markets, sales, corporate planning, finance, advertising, management, customer and employee relations, or strategy. But the infatuation felt by Winner's board-member champion was contagious. From the CEO's perspective Winner registered as a quirky, intellectually free-wheeling professor, uncontaminated by failed corporate habits—just what the flailing company needed for a jump start to a big-bang rejuvenation and a roaring stock offering. "He comes without any baggage and he thinks outside the box," the CEO optimistically assured his doubting management colleagues, adding, "He'll push the envelope. Get ready for blast off."

Winner was undaunted by his inadequacy and the certainty of failure in the corporate sector. Seasoned in academic values, mores, and *curriculum vitae* padding, he knew that details of his inevitable flop in a faraway corporate setting would not travel back to academe, his preferred realm of vocational comfort. However, time spent with the company, unfruitful as it might be for both parties, would strengthen his marketability should the winds of change affect his comfortable berth. Aspirants for the professional peaks are known for unrestrained, brute striving toward position and power. Winner showed no ambition, even as the fates propelled him to the top. He roused no opposition because he threatened no one's ambitions.

After just a few weeks with the software firm, Winner's executive colleagues were privately referring to him as "Loser." Unlike academe, where the tenured can remain idle and useless for long periods, even indefinitely, without attracting notice or inflicting harm, enterprise aimed at making money is constantly hounded by risks that can lead to catastrophic failure. Mistaken steps or mere indolence can be personally disastrous, which is not the case for those who occupy a bombproof niche in academe. Business and industrial firms annually perish by the thousands. Universities are forever.

In the company's understanding, Winner's role as strategist was to look ahead and counsel management on what to do now so as to profit in the future. Winner was unknowing about this crucial task. But with great skill, acquired over many years of addressing obfuscatory memoranda to his departmental chair, graduate dean, the provost, and vending-industry angels, Winner confounded and bemused his software colleagues with cryptic notes and opaque comments. He made voluminous requests for data about the company and the two merged companies from which it was formed some years ago. Because of frequent personnel changes, institutional memory was nil. The company's current records were in poor order, and the older records had been carelessly dumped into a distant warehouse. As a result, the fulfillment of Winner's requests became a labor-intensive task, consuming the services of an ever-growing contingent reassigned from important duties. His managerial colleagues were initially reluctant to acknowledge their bafflement over what he was doing. Winner's performance was charitably attributed to unfamiliarity that would gradually recede as he learned his way around the struggling company and came to understand its perilous situation. The test of his worth would come at the three-month mark, when he was to deliver the first stage of a strategic plan. Titled by him "Emerging and Transformative Technologies: The Conundrum of Strategic Choice," Winner's plan, some 100 bound pages of colorful, smartly designed text, graphs and charts, was delivered, as scheduled, to the top management team on a Friday for home study by each member over the weekend in preparation for an all-day "brainstorming" meeting on Monday. The Monday gathering, however, was brief and unpleasant.

The CEO, a prematurely aged survivor of two dot.com shipwrecks, was attempting a corporate comeback while experiencing the onset of migraine headaches and a tumultuous marital breakup. Just weeks earlier, his bellicose, operatic spouse, screaming expletives, had carried their domestic conflict into the company corridors, finally leaving only after she was pinned to the floor by security guards and threatened with direct delivery to a psychiatric hospital. Upon entering the conference room, the CEO immediately dropped his copy of the strategic plan on the table, as though ridding himself of a loathsome object. "Dr. Winner," he said, "the burn rate at this company leaves us no time before we go down the tubes. We may already be down the tubes," he gasped with exasperation, "but we don't know, because the accounting department, like everything else around here, is totally fucked up. But that's not your fault. What we need to know from you, now, *now*—not in the next academic year, professor—is what we can produce that customers will desperately love and need and buy when they hear about it, or what they need right now that we can produce, and how to produce it. And we need to know now, *now*," the CEO shouted, "what we should outsource and what we can do ourselves, and what kind of programmers we should hire and maybe fire, and all that goddamned stuff. That's strategy. That's what you're supposed to do for us," the CEO despairingly exclaimed as he experienced a rhythmic bass drum performing immediately behind his glistening forehead. "And instead, you give us all this bullshit about transformation and conundrum and lots of other crap." Now even more haggard than at the outset of his soliloquy, the CEO abruptly sat down and, with his chin slumped on his chest, awaited Winner's response.

Seasoned over many years in academic seminars, where the object is to show a confident acuity under fire, Winner remained visibly, comfortably composed in the face of this frenetic assault. Reassuringly for him, the company's board room possessed an academic ambience, with its book-lined walls, the long table at which they all sat, a secondary row of chairs along a wall for underlings, and the cookies, bottles of water, and napkins thoughtfully set out on a small corner table by a tip-toeing secretary. Silence pervaded the room as members of the management team anxiously glanced between their decomposing CEO and the astonishingly imperturbable Winner. Winner softly cleared his throat, hesitated for a moment, shuffled papers, and then slowly proceeded in a deliberately modulated mumble: "Thanks, Jeff," he said, cordially addressing the distraught CEO, who now rested his face in his hands. "Let me initially make a few preliminary observations and then we can proceed to a discussion. Initially, I'd like to point out that our areas of agreement far exceed the few minor points on which some differences may exist. I think if you reflect upon it, you will recognize that the matters you cite concern *management* rather than *strategy*. I acknowledge that the two merge at some point, but there is a sharp distinction that I have necessarily observed. If you look at the early literature on corporate governance and product development—."

"Jesus," the CEO screamed, jumping to his feet. "Let me out of here. This guy is going to kill us." And, venting a long string of filthy words, he marched out, followed by his management team, leaving Winner alone at the conference table, placid, undisturbed, at ease. As with many personnel deals in the fast-paced Silicon Valley, the firm's contract with Winner was hurriedly written and skimpy in attention to legal detail. As specified, his salary was banked in escrow and automatically paid to him every two weeks. The contract stated no specific duties, merely stipulating that he was to be present during normal working hours, and that he would be provided with an office appropriate to the rank of corporate vice president. Winner was in flawless compliance with the contract.

Now commanded to stay out of the way, shunned by management, and soon forgotten in a ceaseless succession of customer defections, staff layoffs, and financial crises, Winner enjoyed a comfortable refuge in his spacious, fashionably furnished office, with a large picture window looking out on the serene, closely cropped lawn and flower beds surrounding the firm's headquarters. Spared from even the minimal burden of pretending to strategize, he diligently labored on fulfilling the professorial requirement for a new book at least every decade or so. Under his two-year contract with the company, he was untouchable.

∽

The book-length literature promising managerial magic had long ago surpassed saturation stage. To entice a publisher, Winner aimed to be disturbing and interesting, with a puzzling streak of implausibility and ambiguity. Though he never strived to stand out, he realized that his manuscript must compel attention or be consigned to oblivion. The result was an ingeniously perverse work titled "Kill Or Be Killed? A Guide to Modern Management Science and Success." The book posited a new conceptual framework "for confronting the paradoxical requirements of modern corporate management." Rejecting the reigning prescription for executive and labor teamwork, public responsibility, customer-feedback, and operational transparency as the basis for organizational success, Winner's book took a contrarian approach. In bold terms, he argued for the deliberate cultivation of rivalries in senior management and recommended intrigue and deception as effective tools in relations with employees and the public. In a particularly jarring and controversial chapter titled "The Case for Vengeance," Winner asserted, "Profits count and are the ultimate measure of successful management, but not at any price, and that is the metric that modern-day managers must weigh in constructing their strategies. Good works and moral behavior have perhaps been over-valued. Whether workers and executives can flourish in this milieu is a management issue that must be balanced against contemporary cultural values and economic imperatives." On the one hand, the book called for "managerial sensitivity to public concerns about health, safety, community values, spiritual needs, and environmental quality," and advised corporate leaders to "integrate everyday common wisdom with economic necessity and scientific reality" in developing their business strategies. On the other hand, Winner wrote, "In the new era of managerial eclecticism, it may be that conflicts of interest should be cultivated and nurtured, rather than condemned and abolished, in quest of the energies they can release." Bucking the tides, he inveighed against a mainstay of modern managerial style: the adoption of "best practices," warning that the "seeming best can often be a lure into mediocrity. But," he cautioned, "don't throw the baby out with the bath water. Knowing when enough is enough is the mark of the effective manager and the essence of modern, successful management. When it is there, its recognition is unavoidable, and it is incontestable. In the final analysis, identify your goals and do not permit circumstances to distract you from attaining them, but don't drive over a cliff in pursuit of any one goal."

Winner's text was preceded by three pages of acknowledgments, dense with his lavishly expressed gratitude for the invaluable assistance, insights, guidance, and perspective provided by several score well-known scholars, in management as well as in history, economics, sociology, psychology, and law. None of those cited had seen or discussed the manuscript or its subject matter with Winner, and few if any were even aware of him. But for the reader, a contrary impression was unavoidable, though not explicitly stated. The acknowledgment absolved the cited scholars of responsibility for any errors of omission or commission, while dwelling on "the benefits I derived from their pioneering work and generosity." Winner also bestowed warm thanks on several prominent think tanks and university research centers in the U.S. and abroad, as well as philanthropic foundations, government research agencies, the Library of Congress, the secretariat of the United Nations, and the Organization for Economic Cooperation and Development. "Fortunately," he concluded, "scholarship and collegiality transcend enmity and partisanship in this troubled world."

"Kill Or Be Killed? A Guide to Modern Management Science and Success" passed nearly unnoticed in the annual tidal wave of new book titles, but to the minor extent that it was noticed, it evoked sharply conflicting responses. Labeling him "Machiavelli reborn," a well-qualified reviewer concluded that "Winner displays a primitive, jungle mentality that has no place in a civilized corporate world. Adoption of his recommendations for management would mean a return to a fortunately bygone era of rampant irresponsibility in pursuit of profits." One reviewer dismissed the book as "a loony melange of half-baked drivel." But noting the question mark in the title, another reviewer suggested that critics were overreacting to a tongue-in-cheek approach to management, and that Winner was actually in the modern tradition of corporate responsibility. Another concluded that Winner was simply providing a rare, candid description of effective modern corporate management "as it actually exists. This is *real politik* at its best, and let's be thankful for it." And still another pointed out that the book contained contradictory passages and, despite its sanguinary title, was open to differing interpretations, none of which, however, were deemed acceptable by the reviewer. Winner was reticent about his meaning and intent, insisting that the book would have to speak for itself. "Anyone doubting the validity of my assessment," he told a C-Span interviewer, "need only look around today's corporate landscape."

৩৩

Soon after Winner returned to campus, President Giles passed away. With the presidential seat unoccupied, and the position of provost long unfilled, the presidential receptionist, Myra, though officially no part of the university's ruling hierarchy, temporarily became the personification of power. All communications to the presidential suite arrived on her desk. Trustees Chairman Goodson relied on Myra to dispatch urgent messages nationwide to the board members to assemble just two days later. Myra was directly in touch with the presidential headhunter about arrangements for the crucial meeting. Upon receiving his short list of presidential possibilities, she asked him to run a quick check on a last-minute addition, Professor Mark Winner, in the economics department. Winner was strongly endorsed by the entranced university trustee who knew him as an adviser to the vending-machine industry and former strategizer for a Silicon Valley firm, since defunct. Puzzled when the trustee informed him of his nomination, Winner shrugged and accepted. Before adding Winner's name to the headhunter's list, Myra consulted her cousin-patron and confidante, rodent meister Elias Fenster, who was attentively monitoring the presidential search. Declining an opportunity for his own candidacy out of fear of leaving his laboratory, Fenster dimly recalled Winner as a pale presence, uninvolved in the many controversies that engulfed the campus. "Why not?" he replied to Myra, who promptly added Winner's name to the short list of presidential candidates.

CHAPTER X

Upon learning of Winner's succession to the presidency, the Kershaw community was apprehensive. Extremely little was known about him. Under the university's bylaws, the president, directly or indirectly, possessed power over budgets, appointments, tenure, departmental reorganizations, and external relations, as well as many other important facets of university life. Those on the periphery of Kershaw, like Collie Marson, Lou Crowley, and the Dollards, were also concerned. In the sensitive area of links to the non-academic world, including tech transfer, the president sets the tone—radiating, as the case may be, enthusiasm, tolerance, or wariness and opposition. Across the nation, the situation varies from campus to campus. Though cloistered isolation has gone out of fashion, some schools retain a semblance of aloofness from brazen commercialism. Kershaw's president possessed authority over non-traditional enterprises, such as the roundtable espoused by Martin Dollard. True, ultimate power was vested in the board of trustees. But handpicked and adroitly managed by Giles over many years, the board had withered into passivity. Even during Giles' somnolent final years, the board remained docile. Its quarterly meetings adhered to a skeletal agenda and were brief and tame.

During the two-month runup to Winner's inaugural, news about the president-designate was eagerly sought. *Haywire*, the student newspaper, boldly headlined his appointment with "It's a Winner!" But it was plain from the accompanying article that few on campus knew anything substantial about Winner, and elsewhere information about him was sparse. He declined to be interviewed, saying only that it would be inappropriate for him to speak until he was inaugurated. Not even his colleagues in the economics department could say much about him, professionally or personally. The campus bookstore experienced a run on his immediately forgotten monograph, "Kill Or Be Killed? A Guide to Modern Management Science and Success." As was the case when the book was first published, these latter-day readers found it impenetrable. Some ascribed their incomprehension to the novelty of his arguments and their own unfamiliarity with the subject matter. Others dismissed the book as nonsense. A few sycophantically called it profound and important, an unjustly neglected breakthrough, long overdue for wide recognition as a seminal work.

Though Winner had been at Kershaw for his entire academic career, except for time out in a Silicon Valley software firm, he had left no imprint on campus. His departmental base at Kershaw was famously riven by irreconcilable theoretical approaches, compounded by incompatible personalities. The department, like others at Kershaw, had a geriatric tilt because of the federal law against age discrimination, which restricted forced retirement. In the absence of incontestable dementia or other disabling infirmities, professors were assured life-long employment, as long as they could get to the campus. The department housed multiple sects of economics: Keynesianism, mercantilism, monetarism, Henry George single taxing, libertarianism, and neo-Marxism. There were Friedmanites, as well as gold and silver nostalgists, flat taxers, and a non-repentant bi-metalist. Randomly present among these adherents were various personality disorders, including hair-trigger, uncontrollable tempers, chronic sulkiness, and irremediable grudge-bearing. In combination, the beliefs and the personalities had long ago spawned bitter conflicts, both in the columns of learned journals and in face-to-face encounters at scholarly conferences and chance meetings, on and off campus. Many of the economics professors, like their colleagues in other departments, were months, sometimes years, late in delivering articles and reviews promised to professional journals, and many were years overdue in fulfilling book contracts. Nonetheless, conflict took priority.

The department chairman would surely know something about the long-serving Winner. But in despair over the unrelenting din, the chairman had departed, unannounced, to a visiting professorship in Great Britain. No one knew when, or whether, he would return. The departmental secretary retained her post, but with her responsibilities considerably lightened by the chairman's absence, she spent most of her working hours at Kershaw earning extra income as a telephone canvasser for a credit card company. Department members seeking her assistance were accustomed to being put on hold while she completed a call related to her credit-card duties. The belligerent factions missed their chairman, because, while they fought, he attended to essential routine administrative tasks, such as drawing up budgets, scheduling classes and allocating office space. The dean of graduate studies or the provost would normally appoint a full-fledged or acting replacement for the missing chairman. But under President Giles' hands-off management, the dean and the provost had departed some time ago and the positions remained vacant. In an unprecedented cooperative effort, the economics professors directly petitioned President Giles to appoint an acting chairman, though they split many ways on who that should be. Like so many other papers sent to Giles, the petition disappeared into the presidential suite, and months later, at the time of his death, remained unanswered.

The warriors and spectators of campus politics naturally assumed that at some-time during his long presence in the notoriously strife-torn department, Winner had taken stands that would illuminate his attitudes on crucial campus issues. But, alone among the members of the department, Winner was not associated with any of the factions, and his beliefs on the issues that regularly sent his colleagues to the barricades were unknown. Interrogated by campus journalists and others, veteran members of the department confessed to knowing little about the president-designate; several younger members said they had never before heard of him and were surprised to learn that he had been a full-time member of their department for many years.

While waiting for Winner's inaugural, the Kershaw community parsed and analyzed the few bits of information that came out of the presidential suite. There wasn't much, which tended to magnify interest in whatever little became known.

Unbeknownst to any, because Winner confided in no one, the incoming president felt a jolt of destiny from his unsought, unforeseen, improbable ascent to the presidency of one of America's great universities. The chairman of the history department achieved a short-lived celebrity on campus when reports circulated about a conversation that he allegedly had with the president-designate. Various hearsay versions appeared on the Internet, followed by a report in *Haywire* attributed to an interview with the chairman. The chairman, however, remained silent on the authenticity of all accounts of the alleged conversation, thus compounding the aura of mystery around the incoming president.

In the *Haywire* version, he was quoted as stating, "Winner asked me to come to his office, and when I got there he said he wanted to talk to me in confidence. I, of course, assured him that I would honor his preference in all respects. Then he asked me if I knew anything about President Woodrow Wilson. Of course he had to know that I wrote a biography of Wilson. I told him I have studied and written about Wilson. And he said to me, 'Wilson was President of Princeton, wasn't he?' I was somewhat taken aback by this, since it's common knowledge about Wilson. And so I said indeed he was. And Winner then says to me, 'How did he become President?' Not clear about the question, I asked, 'How did he become President of Princeton?' And he said, 'No, of the United States.' And I said, 'That's a long, complicated story.' Then he asked me if I could find an article or a short book on the subject and send it to him. I said I would certainly do that, and he thanked me. He also asked about Eisenhower being president of Columbia before he became U.S. president. I told him I didn't know very much about that. Just as I was leaving, he said, 'Let's keep this just between the two of us.' I assured him that it would be no problem."

Asked by *Haywire* to confirm or deny the reported conversation, the history chairman replied, "I'll say for the record that the whole thing is ridiculous. That's all."

On the hugely popular, anonymously written blog *KershawRealist.edu* both the history chairman and the incoming president were described as "identical twin scum bags who deserve each other." The comment evoked scores of responses along a wide spectrum, some wholeheartedly endorsing the description, others dismissing it as inaccurate, outrageous, or both; some called for additional information. Interest in and commentary about the history chairman and the alleged presidential conversation were superseded by reports of reconstruction of the presidential suite, located in the elongated base of Monument Hall, the landmark, central administration structure dominating the campus. The modest suite occupied by the late President Giles was torn out, and a major enlargement was in the works. Winner declined to answer *Haywire's* inquiries about the project, again explaining that it would be inappropriate for him to speak on presidential matters until after his inauguration.

The building housing the presidential office suite had been constructed in stages over half a century, as budget conditions and suppression of aesthetic contention permitted. Monument Hall was a misshapen architectural mongrel of neo-classical, gothic, and art-deco design, with some elements of mid-20th century academic plate glass, red brick and raw concrete. The building's unique character had been ratified by an official historic preservation designation, which rendered the exterior of the structure immortal and unchangeable. Near the main entrance, a pile of rusting steel girders left over from a late phase of construction had been scheduled for removal, but was deemed artistically meritorious by the art faculty and left in place. At all hours, some two dozen young demonstrators trudged in a circle near the entrance, monotonously chanting,

Ho, ho, ho,

Hee, hee hee,

Time to drop

Rule 23.

The demonstrators had been there for as long as anyone could remember. A passerby's inquiry to one of the chanters about the nature of the objectionable rule brought the response, "I'm not from here. Just helping out. It's like something to do with how they make investments. Murray can tell you when he gets back."

A lone counter-demonstrator was usually present, bearing a placard reading, "Keep Rule 23."

For the loyal sons and daughters of Kershaw University, Monument Hall was the emblem of their alma mater, with colorful renditions baked onto the surface of beer mugs, dinner plates, and other alumni kitsch. Decals of the building deco-rated the rear windows of many automobiles.

Haywire and campus bloggers appealed to Winner for an explanation of the reconstruction of presidential facilities, but, adhering to his previous refusal, he remained silent.

∽

Winner's inaugural address was another virtuoso performance in the long suc-cession of enigmatic compositions that had marked his career. Titled "The Omni-University in An Era of Evolving Values and Constrained Resources," the address evoked conflicting interpretations. Overall, however, the reaction was favorable. In an editorial titled "Winner's Win-Win Agenda," the *New York Times* commented, "Like it or not—as many do and many don't—Kershaw's new president has delin-eated some of most vexing problems now facing our higher-education enterprise and has courageously proposed bold solutions. Not all of these will be to every-one's taste," the *Times* pointed out. "But, in the aggregate, Doctor Winner's clear-eyed catalog of problems and proposed solutions provides an unparalleled starting point for addressing the difficulties that confront the nation's universities. For far too long, statesmanship has been lacking in the upper echelons of academic lead-ership. The gap now appears to have been filled by Dr. Winner's elevation to the presidency of one of the nation's leading universities. We are particularly struck by his internationalist approach to education, coupled with his recognition of the importance of incremental planning, financial integrity, and the evolving role of science and technology in both the educational process and the national economy. The big difference in Dr. Winner's approach—and for this we especially applaud him—is that he grants equal time to the arts and humanities, which too often have had to settle for crumbs in the budget process. Quite properly, in regard to change, he has emphasized the importance of proceeding cautiously but decisively where successful, well-established approaches, programs and projects have proven their worth. Thus, we welcome his trumpet call for university scientists to play a bigger role in discovering new and better products for the American people. In too many universities today, an antiquated sense of Ivory Tower purity needlessly interferes with promising opportunities for science to repay the public for many decades of generous support. On the other hand, as Dr. Winner noted, the single-minded pursuit of profit has been shown to be detrimental to scientific progress. We applaud his call for a balanced approach. But, as he also noted, success in taking research to market brings many benefits, not least among them greater revenues to ease the burden of tuition on middle-class families. The early signs suggest that Kershaw University has picked a Winner."

CHAPTER XI

Though carefully sifted for omens, Winner's inaugural address did not fill the void that had proven so puzzling and frustrating during the interregnum.

The day after the inaugural, Lou Crowley, holding a copy of the speech, stood in the doorway of Collie Marson's office. A copy of the speech lay on Collie's desk. "What the hell is this guy talking about? You know anything about him?" Lou asked.

"Nothing," Collie replied. "I've asked around at Kershaw, but nobody knows a thing about him. The speech is the usual crap you get from these guys."

"Yeah, but all I care about," Lou said, "is if this guy is good or bad for us. He plays it both ways in the speech. Do we do anything about Brucie and his no-sleeping pill, or do we sit and wait? The more I think about what you told me, the more I want some of it. I think you're right. This is a big one."

"Yeah," Collie said, gratified by Lou's endorsement of his find, but also increasingly uncertain about getting inside to make a deal. "Right now we don't know any more than what I've already told you," Collie conceded. "But I've got a couple of old grad school classmates at Kershaw who maybe know something about Brucie and his project. I'll nose around the labs and see if I can find out something."

෴

Martin Dollard felt nearly certain that his roundtable proposal had been favorably received by the late President Giles. A sliver of doubt intruded because, as he worriedly recalled, old Giles seemed at times to veer off the conversational track. Giles was known for that, Martin reminded himself, and apparently it did not affect his understanding or leadership. No one else was present during their meeting, one of the many held by Giles in his waning days. Perhaps Giles later dictated a memo describing Martin's idea; maybe he endorsed it with a lot of enthusiasm, Martin told himself. But Martin had had no further contact with Giles or anyone at Kershaw concerning the roundtable proposal. On the upside, Martin remembered, Winner's inaugural address invited innovation and change. Recollection of this theme elevated Martin's spirits. Feeling pleased, he considered executing the *fait-accompli* gambit that he had devised and profitably used during his successful business career. He would write a memo to the new president that would matter-of-factly, casually but clearly, proceed from the premise that the roundtable had been approved by Giles, that it was a done deal. To reinforce that point, the memo would pointedly note that Martin had gone some distance in organizing and underwriting the project and shedding other responsibilities in preparation for serving as chairman, "per my understanding with President Giles." If Winner took the bait, Martin would suggest a public announcement from the university. Winner would no doubt agree to this reasonable step, Martin assured himself. The resulting press release would publicly ratify the project and provide a boost up the social scale for both Dollards. Martin foresaw inquiries from top-notch people concerning participation in the roundtable. With the right issues and cast for roundtable discussions, he optimistically assumed, public television would be eager to broadcast some sessions, perhaps all of them, maybe even some in their entirety. Maybe the networks would want to get in.

But then a need for caution occurred to Martin: Maybe old Giles had left behind a memo *rejecting* Martin's proposal. Suppose Winner came across a negative memo. It would be disastrous to claim Giles' support if Winner had a piece of paper stating the opposite. Too risky. Better to wait for Winner to settle into office and see whether anything surfaced about the roundtable concept. Even if Giles had rejected the proposal, Winner might love it. Martin hopefully day dreamed that Winner would be in touch with him, saying he wanted to follow up on an interesting proposal that his predecessor had strongly endorsed, according to a memo found in the late president's files. Martin envisioned the new president calling him in and saying, "Mr. Dollard, great idea. Let's get going on this. You have my full support." Martin knew that his proposal was sound, far-seeing, and would be a plus for Kershaw. In his meditations, he now approached the issue from a different direction: Why wouldn't Winner support it? Martin could think of no reason.

⁂

Helen Dollard blankly gazed at a copy of the inaugural speech that Martin had thoughtfully printed out for her, with a reference to the arts circled in red. "Could mean big new role for your arts committee. Let's hope!" Martin wrote in the margin. As Helen's tolerance for Martin's presence continued downward, his efforts to placate her increased, leading to a further descent. But Martin's homing in on the arts was a shrewd move. Helen had no illusions about the origin of Kershaw's interest in her. A realist, particularly on money matters, she recognized that Martin's wealth, rather than her faint aesthetic sensibilities or negligible knowledge of art, accounted for her appointment to the arts committee. Like everyone else, she knew nothing about Winner. At Martin's urging she scanned a copy of his book "Kill or Be Killed?", copiously underlined and annotated in Martin's hand. In the margins he had scrawled "true," "good point," "excellent analysis," "nicely said," "I agree," and other presumptuous idiocies of which she had had more than enough. Helen ignored Martin's notations. Like most others, she found the book indecipherable. The arts committee, she realized, was a tenuous connection to the university, but because of her educational deficit, it was all the more valuable for her. On several occasions, she had pulled a one-up on rivals, friends, or acquaintances by casually mentioning her membership on the Kershaw University Arts Advisory Committee. She never introduced it in a contrived or boastful manner, but when appropriate, she would find a discreet way to get it on the record. "Lunch Tuesday? Let me check my calender. Oops, got a meeting of the Kershaw arts committee Wednesday and must do my homework. How about Thursday? "

Sadly, the arts committee rarely met, and when it did, the devious hand of the chairman of the arts faculty was behind its meaningless agenda, which remained rigidly focused on developing a mission statement. The chairman's antipathy to the committee of amateurs drew inspiration from the Battle of Verdun in his native France: *"Ils ne passeront pas,"* he vowed as he sowed a minefield around the committee. "In composing the mission statement," he explained to the members, "we must, first of all, define the role of the arts in the historical context of the university. And then we must design an agenda that will relate the committee's work to the specifics of this institution and its relationship to the broader sphere of the arts in contemporary American civilization and beyond that, Western civilization, with a particular emphasis on the arts in higher education. We want to shake off the dead hand of expired artistic sensibility, but we cannot ignore tradition. That's for certain," he told the committee members. All drafts so far had been found wanting by the chairman, who earnestly urged the committee members to return to their task and at last get it right. "Absolutely essential. We can't function without it." As usual, the next meeting would be some time later, at his call.

While Helen gloomily pondered this deplorable situation, a light gleamed in the dark distance. Based on experience, Helen held great confidence in her one-on-one skills. But, always realistic, she recognized that she was a naif when it came to bureaucratic intrigue, having never been involved in the internal affairs of a large organization. At a reception, she had once tried to talk to the late Giles about the arts committee, but though he nodded graciously, he didn't seem to grasp what she was saying. Before she could press her case, a concerned-looking assistant deftly intervened and led him away. A new president, she now reasoned, might, for all she knew, be especially interested in the arts. In any case, he might want to shake things up a bit and take credit for bringing the committee to life, despite the intransigence of the chairman of the arts department. She surely didn't want the chairman to become aware of a direct approach to the new president. From TV drama and friends' tales of office life, she had gleaned enough about bureaucratic protocol to realize that jumping the chain of command might stir resentment and produce a setback. But Martin might know some way to get Winner's attention. No, she thought, Martin is such a dim, clumsy fool, forever babbling and boring people to death with his societal impact crap and roundtable plans that he would probably kill any chance of gaining the president's interest and support. Better to try some other way.

As the youngest child in a household of rivalrous siblings, Helen had discovered a means of instantly winning parental approval. It was a method to be used sparingly, she instinctively understood, but when efficiently executed, it worked: Surreptitiously create a problem that rendered the family flustered and frustrated, and then produce a solution. This tactic had originated in a mundane, long-ago family incident: When not in use, the single set of keys for the family car was always supposed to be in a spare coffee cup situated on top of the refrigerator. But one day, when father was in a rush to drive off, the car was in the driveway but the keys were not in the prescribed place. A frantic, all-hands search ensued, including desperate groping through the accumulated dust balls under the refrigerator, and interrogations between father and mother about who had last used the car and "are you are sure you put the keys back?" and "did you check all your pockets?" and "did anybody move anything on top of the refrigerator?" and "why don't we get a spare set of keys?" Merely age 10, Helen vigorously joined in the search. Then, casually venturing out of the apartment while the others methodically pillaged the place like police raiders, she triumphantly returned with the keys, explaining that she had found them on the outside stairs. Her siblings glowered with doubt and resentment. Father was boundlessly grateful.

That mode of winning ingratiation was inscribed in Helen's book of life tactics. It was not to be used often. In fact, few opportunities for using it came along. But when a situation and an opportunity for applying the tactic matched up, it was worth trying. Then she recalled that nice young man, Collie something or other, who took Ginny Rosen home from the party when she became sick. She remembered he had some connection with Kershaw. Martin spoke very well of him, but, from experience with the quality of Martin's judgments, she knew that didn't mean a thing, one way or the other. She'd have to find out how to get in touch with him, and see what he knew about the new President and his plans. Then she might find a way to make progress.

꩜

At the Army Research Office, Project Manager Charles Hollis somberly studied the latest progress report on Project Zap-Hypnos from Professor Max Brusolowitz, at Kershaw University. As usual, Brusolowitz reported good progress. This time he added a note suggesting that thought be given to setting up a clinical trial. Advanced planning was essential to get approval from Kershaw's Institutional Review Board. "We have to think far ahead," Brucie advised, "because of the unusual nature of the project and the way we've carried it out on campus. A trial might be conducted without IRB approval, but that might be risky," he added.

Hollis had lost a good deal of weight since he unburdened himself to Collie Marson several months ago. Mindful of the security oath he had taken, he dwelled on the breach of secrecy he had committed in telling Collie about Brusolowitz's project. Collie could be trusted, he felt certain. Nonetheless, Hollis had violated security, a dereliction that grated on his devotion to responsible behavior and adherence to commitments. Bad enough, but the underlying cause of his turmoil was the project itself, which he increasingly regarded as an affront to nature and a threat to societal stability. Despite his wife's anxious inquiries about whether he was experiencing trouble at work, he hadn't told her, or anyone other than Collie, about his festering worries. As upbeat progress reports from Brusolowitz spilled over into a second file drawer, Hollis recalled his conversation with Collie and found comfort in being on the record with his concerns with at least one human soul.

The Colonel in charge of his section at the office was an infantryman, not a scientist, serving a rotation to link research to the battlefield requirements of the troops. The bemedaled officer felt confident that he knew how to manage his brainy crew of civilian Ph.D. subordinates, most of them tenure rejects who had signed on with the Army after they failed to make it in academe. Jobs in science were scarce and the Army pay for civilian scientists was quite good. Now, as desk-bound administrators, it was their job to dispense the Army's big research budgets to scientists who had made the grade in research. Untutored in the cultural and professional intricacies of science, the Colonel lectured his subordinates, as they furtively rolled their eyes, furrowed their brows, and whispered cynical wisecracks to each other. "You got to show them respect," the Colonel explained to his staff, speaking of the university scientists. "But you got to keep them focused on the mission, because they're professors and they like to wander off and look into any-thing new and interesting that they encounter along the way, even if it's of no importance to our mission. You got to herd them, like sheep. Their sense of time is different from ours. And their reward system is different. They want to publish papers about every new minuscule thing they find, because that's how they collect career points in their universities. We've got different priorities. We want to get stuff out to the troops that will help them kill or avoid being killed."

Known for his egalitarian camaraderie with soldiers in the field, the Colonel carried that style into his office assignment, backslapping his subordinates and labeling them with affectionate nicknames of his own choosing. At times he ad-dressed Charles Hollis as "Chuck" or "Chuckles," sometimes as "Chas" (rhyming with class), and at other times as "Chucky." Charles Hollis usually admonished anyone who took liberties with his given name. But, fearing a clash, he was silent with the Colonel.

On this day, in one of his encounters with Hollis in their suite of cubicles, the Colonel proudly predicted, "Chuck, when the no-sleep pill hits the battlefield, the troops will stand up and cheer the professor who invented it, our Brucie at Kershaw. But they should also cheer *you*, because you're a big part of the whole thing. Our boys, and these days our girls, too, don't forget them, will be able to keep going 24/7, bright-eyed and bushy-tailed over hill and dale while the other guys are dragging their asses, half-asleep. When your stuff works out and if we can get permission to use mini-nukes on the battlefield, we can clean up all the messes around the world real quick. Keep the pressure on that professor Brucie," the Colonel urged.

Charles Hollis usually lunched at his desk, sipping from a thermos jug of soup brought from home. That day, he took only a frugal sip or two, sat motionless in thought for a time, and then carefully closed the container and put it away in his backpack for the bicycle trip home at the end of the work day. By managing the project, he was in violation of his own personal morality, and by revealing it to Collie he had broken his oath of official secrecy. Hollis saw a turncoat in whatever mirror he faced. His racing thoughts turned to the new president at Kershaw. Maybe he could find a way to talk to him about the project. Hollis had no clear idea of how that might be done, or even what he might say to the new president.

But he strongly believed that a means for eliminating sleep should not proceed in deep secrecy, and probably not proceed at all. Nature should rarely be disturbed, and only for extremely good reasons, he felt, though not with unerring consistency.

Hollis tiptoed through nature. He avoided genetically modified vegetables and farmed fish, and was of mixed mind on abortion, accepting it as socially necessary in certain circumstances, but clearly at odds with nature. He had doubts about *in vitro* fertilization, and frequently worried that the search for extra-terrestrial life might discover something terrible. As best he could, he aimed his lifestyle in accordance with these guideposts. He was sparing in the use of pharmaceutical drugs for himself and his family, feeling that their intended interference with illness was somehow unnatural, though, he conceded, sometimes unavoidable. He felt good about substantially reducing his household's carbon footprint, while continuing to search for further reductions. He diligently recycled glass, metal, and paper. In all these endeavors, his wife was a grudging conscript rather than a voluntary collaborator. She complied with his insistence on organic groceries, though doubtful that they were healthier. "When you look around and see what everyone else is doing," she complained, "we're the ones who are unnatural." Nonetheless, for domestic harmony, she generally went along, though rejecting his insistence on an absolute ban on fast food for the children. "A Big Mac is not the end of the world," she said. "I love McDonald's," their five-year-old gushed. "You get a present with the hamburger and fries," he explained, showing his father the figurine of a bayonet-wielding soldier acquired in his last fast-food outing.

Outside his home, Charles was not an activist or proselytizer about his personal values. In his work, however, he realized, he was an essential cog in a secret government project to eliminate a fundamental of life—sleep. "This is too crazy," he told himself. But his grasp of the underlying science told him it was not impossible. The project saturated his thoughts. In a forgotten school book of poetry and prose quotations that he had recently come upon at home, he found numerous references to sleep. These words, inscribed in his memory from repeated readings, would come to him unexpectedly. Now, as he gloomily thought about his complicity in Brucie's work, a line from Keats occurred to him:

"Mortality weighs heavily on me like unwilling sleep."

The line harmonized with his gloom, but he was not certain of its meaning. Going to the Internet to study the full poem, he found the opening word of that line rendered as "Morality." A typographical error? Mortality or morality. Which was correct? He didn't know. He felt confusion and an inescapable weight of doing wrong.

∽

Bill Rhodes, the director of Kershaw's Technology Transfer Office, the TTO, for the past five years, was yet to score a blockbuster. As much as he'd like to deal with Collie and Lou and other venture capitalists focusing on university labs, he was dependent on Kershaw's scientists for marketable science. He could sell only what they produced. But they had to tell him about their research so that he could find a company that would leap for the science and pay plenty for a license to exploit it. Or maybe if further research were needed, he could bring in a venture capital firm like Lou Crowley's, which would put up money in return for an ownership share. Unfortunately, Rhodes and the scientists weren't connecting. Kershaw's chief financial officer needled Rhodes with memos and news clips whenever another university scored big by licensing research to pharmaceutical companies and other industrial firms. "Hi, Bill, FYI," the money chief would e-mail, gleefully, it seemed to Rhodes. "In case you missed it, looks like Emory's landed a huge deal. How we doing?" Plugged into the tech-transfer grapevine, Rhodes required no notice from the CFO. He suffered from these deals. Blockbusters were rare, and other TTOs shared his difficulties. But the occasional big deals scored by other research universities were nonetheless embarrassing for him. A dropout from a doctoral engineering program, Rhodes was doing well as marketing chief for a computer company when Kershaw hired him because of his solid reputation as a dealer and moneymaker. But Rhodes wasn't making it at Kershaw, which had recruited him with a generous pay package and assurances that big deals were waiting to be plucked. Maybe so, but the harvest eluded him.

Upon arriving at Kershaw, Rhodes found himself thwarted by the aloofness of the science professors and the lethargy that infested the university administration as the coasting Giles regime continued its long decline. Rhodes' marching orders came from Kershaw's vice president for administration, since departed and, in the end-stage Giles era, typically not replaced: "We've got all this science here—over 900 professors grinding out papers on everything from monkey sex to ice on the moon ," the VP gravely explained to the newly arrived TTO chief. "At other places, they're making piles of money licensing this stuff to industry and businesses. We're getting close to zilch from the clowns at our place. Your job is to make us some money—lots of money—from all this science. Find out what the professors are already doing that's saleable, and sell it, because we know they're not lifting a finger to do it. Or if they're doing stuff that's not saleable, give 'em a nudge to do something else, something useful, saleable. It's not hard to do, but somebody's got to do it. You're our guy!"

"Easy to say," Rhodes found himself thinking as he learned his way around Kershaw's science departments. TTO was a sales organization. It had no say about the research program. In the university's social and professional order, the TTO director was an oddity, an outsider. The people who mattered most were the long-time principal figures in universities: teachers, researchers, and academic administrators. Virtually all held Ph.D.s and had started out as faculty members. On a separate, lower-status career track were the money managers, PR people, and others who kept Kershaw running smoothly but were walled off from academic functions. Rhodes was yet another variety, a new type in academe: the science-savvy-broker-businessman-salesman, hired to sell what the scientists produced, but with no authority to steer them toward the market. The tenured professors decided what they wanted to research and what they wanted Rhodes to know about their research. "We're the best judge of what works in science," the chairman of the chemistry department told Rhodes, with a touch of belligerence in his voice that signaled "don't mess with us." Depending on their skill and luck in getting money for research, the scientists did as they pleased. Any attempt to interfere with them, or even a gentle push toward marketable research, would ignite resentment and cries of attacks on academic freedom and scientific creativity. Practical research was particularly abhorrent to Kershaw's scientific royalty. At commencements and other public gatherings, as speakers or listeners, they approvingly clucked over an ancient, oft-told tale: "What good is electricity?" Queen Victoria asks Michael Faraday. He replies, "What good is a baby?"

Alternatively, and probably apocryphal, Prime Minister Gladstone asks the electricity question, and is told, "I don't know, but someday you'll tax it." Among the faithful of science, these tales possessed biblical authority. Scientists wished everyone to understand that wisdom, goodness, and social benefit were inherent in their choices of what to research and how to research it. And, on that basis, they should be given money and independence. Outsiders must not interfere.

Rhodes realized after a brief time on the job that some of Kershaw's scientists were dealing with industry, but directly and not through his TTO. Rhodes knew that Professor Fenster, with his prolonged studies of rodent sperm, had evolved close, financially robust relationships with industry. The same, he learned, was true of Professor Mark Winner in economics, who was working with the vending-machine industry. The two professors were guarded in discussing their work with the TTO director, citing the inviolability of proprietary information. But as far as Rhodes could tell, few others on the faculty were connected to the business world. They conveyed an impression of indifference to the commercial opportunities that TTO was supposed to develop from their research.

When he was allowed a few minutes to evangelize for technology transfer at departmental meetings, Rhodes nudged and pleaded with Kershaw scientists to focus on problems of interest to industry and to consult him about commercial opportunities. "You can perform patriotic duty, help Kershaw, and make money for yourself in the process," he explained, emphasizing that scientists credited with research leading to patents were entitled to a one-third share of royalties from licenses sold to industry. The department members who attended his portion of the meeting—most skipped it—expressed little interest. Some openly resented suggestions, no matter how tepid, about what they should do in their laboratories.

Rhodes soon received enlightenment about Kershaw, science, and commerce. It came from a disgraced and disgruntled postdoc who had attended one of Rhodes' pleading lectures. Accused of swiping a fellow student's research, and facing termination from the program, the postdoc arrived unannounced in Rhodes' office one day. "I heard them bum-rapping you after your talk about tech transfer. You didn't hear it from me," he said, "but these guys all have their private deals for selling research to the companies. They're consultants, advisers, chairmen of science advisory committees, or they have their own spinoff companies someplace or other. Why cut Kershaw in on the deal? So they don't."

Rhodes understood the legal underpinnings of direct dealing. To promote innovation and economic activity, federal law prescribes that when the government pays for research, any ensuing patent belongs to the university, which must attempt to license it to industry. However, government research money is often intermingled with other funds. Research that's co-financed by industry, philanthropy, private angels and other sources falls into a gray area. Legally or not, profs with multiple financing were making their own deals, and leaving Kershaw out. Like most great universities, Kershaw refrained from keeping a close watch on its professors' dealings. Anger a star researcher and off he or she goes to a rival university, taking along, en masse, grants, graduate students, postdocs, technicians, and special equipment. Arrivals and departures from faculty lineups affected the coveted academic rankings in *U.S. News & World Report.* A drop in the listings could bring pesky inquiries, even wrath, from alumni, trustees, donors, and parents of students.

Rhodes knew that time was running out on his job. TTO, he recognized, would not do well in the campus-wide evaluation of programs customarily conducted by a new president. Rhodes needed a blockbuster deal to show President Winner that he was delivering for Kershaw. Rhodes hadn't met Professor Max Brusolowitz, but he knew of his reputation as the most prolific scientist on campus. Parts of Brusolowitz's lab were off limits to outsiders because of some sort of sensitive work going on there. Rumors had it that the celebrated Brucie was soon to be honored for receiving his 100th patent. Going over the files, Rhodes found no record of TTO involvement in any commercial deals involving Brucie's discoveries. Alerted to the free-lancing practices of the science profs, Rhodes recognized that Brucie could be happily enmeshed in many profitable industrial deals without Kershaw's knowledge. He thought hard about how to find out and how to close a deal that would gain the admiration of President Winner and save his job and his reputation.

CHAPTER XII

Martin Dollard identified himself to one of the work-study students stationed at the gateway to President Winner's office suite in the great Monument Hall. He was promptly escorted to a receptionist, who guided him to an inner office. There he was received by Winner's secretary, who motioned him to a seat in the waiting area, which was under the gaze of Myra, the chief receptionist. Winner appeared a few minutes later, led Martin into the presidential office, pointed to a seat, and then took his own place behind a desk. Martin was delighted but surprised by the invitation to meet with Winner, which, without any explanation or prompting on his part, arrived a few days after Winner's inauguration. After reviewing his extensive wardrobe, Martin went tweedy-academic for the occasion, with a heavy-knit grey wool necktie, blue button-down shirt, grey flannel trousers, and loafers.

Martin's primping and high spirits about the invitation irritated Helen. "What the hell does he want to see you about?" she groused as he checked himself in a full-length mirror, adjusted his tie, swept a hand over his bald dome, and dusted off his shoe tops with a Kleenex.

"He didn't say," Martin replied in a crisp, self-important tone, "but I did have a very successful talk with President Giles about societal impact and the round-table, and I think it's reasonable to assume that it's in connection with that. The old man must have dictated a memo about our meeting, and I assume that President Winner has read it and wants to move along. The more I think about it, the more strongly I feel that the roundtable is a very, very good idea. I'm convinced of that."

Helen thought, "What kind of idiot would fall for that bullshit," but held back the words—though only barely. "If it's not too much trouble," she said, "put in a word for my arts committee. That goddamned Frenchman isn't letting it go anywhere."

"I'll try my best," Martin promised, "but understand, I'll have to gauge the situation step by step and see if there's an appropriate opening. If there's anything I've learned it's that these professors have their own way of doing things. It's not my way, and not your way. But we have to go along. I'll have to play it by ear and see how it's going. But I think things are looking up. We're making progress, like I told you." Helen didn't reply.

Seated across the desk from Winner, Martin looked at the new president, whom he was meeting for the first time. He found Winner's appearance drab, uninteresting, disappointing. Slight in stature, with a narrow terrier-like visage, Winner wore his characteristic skeptical squint, suggesting doubtfulness about whatever he was looking at or hearing. He employed a surprisingly rapid-fire conversational style in a small, low voice. Winner's unruly strands of gray hair were overdue for barbering. And his rumpled gray suit and polka-dot red necktie struck Martin as inexcusably un-academic. Like a mid-level clerk, Martin thought. Expecting a grander figure, he was displeased. If he was going to do business with the president of Kershaw University, he expected a presidential figure, someone with the physical stature and sartorial judgment to match the importance of the position. Giles had his deficiencies, particularly in the latter years, but he could have modeled senior corporate fashions for Brooks Brothers.

"Dollard, thanks for coming in," Winner said. "Let's get down to business. Busy days here."

"I'm sure," Martin said. "I imagine you must have—."

Winner cut him off. "You're on this endowment advisory committee. I've checked you out. Background in handling big money and so forth. Retired, or at least not listed as doing anything. What are you doing now?"

Martin saw the opening he had hoped for and expected. He was prepared. "Since stepping down from my business responsibilities, I've developed and pursued an interest in societal matters—you know, the impact of technological change on society, and related policy matters. Let's call it policy for policy. As a matter of fact, I had a very encouraging talk with President Giles about establishing a university roundtable—."

"That's old business, water over the dam," Winner said with a terminating sweep of his hand. "What they tell me at the endowment office is that you're on the advisory committee, and that unlike the other members, you know numbers and that you're pretty sharp about money. Is that right?"

Martin experienced a cognitive disruption. "The endowment?" he started to say, when Winner resumed speaking. "Okay, let's agree that you know the numbers. Save time. Okay? Now what I need is somebody who can nose around our finances and find out for me what's really going on here without stirring up the animals. You won't be the only one doing this. I don't like to depend on just one person for anything. You'd be one of them. That's what I need."

Martin tried to mobilize his thinking. "I'd be happy to provide whatever assistance I can, but as I mentioned, my real interests—."

"Happy or unhappy has nothing to do with it," Winner declared. "I need a certain kind of help, like I said, and the society and policy and technology stuff, or whatever you called it, has nothing to do with it. We've got people all over this campus jabbering all the time at round tables and square tables about this stuff. A lot of B.S. We don't need any more. I need help. I inherited plenty of people from Giles, some them dozing in the same job for twenty years. I need some independent people to help me figure out what the hell is going on here."

"President Giles seemed to think—."

"Look, Mr. Dollard, let's stop wasting each other's time. Giles gave up thinking about anything at least 10 years before he checked out. So, we're not pegging anything to what the old gentleman seemed to think. Like I said, I need somebody to help me with the numbers. To be frank, someone who isn't trying to climb the pole here or sleep on the job for another twenty years. You understand me?"

Martin was seasoned in distinguishing between a deal and no deal. "Sounds interesting. Count me in."

"Good," Winner said. "I'll be in touch with you. We got a lot of work to do. From what I can see, this place is a—." Winner checked himself, then simply concluded, "Thanks for coming in."

The work-study student who had led Martin in was suddenly at his side. "I'll show you how to get out of here," she said, leading him to the street entrance.

When he returned to the apartment, Helen was unrestrained in interrogating him about the meeting. "So, what happened? What did he want?" she immediately demanded.

"It was a broad discussion, a good one. We covered a lot of ground on various topics."

"Wait a minute, you weren't gone for very long. So how much could you talk about? What various topics? Did you bring up the arts committee?"

Martin knew that he had to tread carefully to avoid setting off a major storm. "Let's sit down. I'll get a drink and tell you all about it."

Helen read him with ease and accuracy. "You never brought up the arts committee, did you? What bullshit, just as I expected."

"Not specifically," Martin said, seeking, as he spoke, to choose words that would dampen, if not avert, an eruption. "We ranged over a broad group of general topics. I sensed that there was a tacit understanding—unspoken but it was there—that we were not excluding anything, which I take it to mean that there's no reason the arts committee cannot be on the agenda for future meetings. In the academic world, as I'm learning, there's a somewhat different approach than we're accustomed to when it comes to evaluation and decision-making."

"Jesus," she exclaimed. "What are you talking about? Can you tell me in less than ten thousand words what the hell you talked about?"

"Yes," Martin said. "We had good rapport. Excellent, I'd say. President Winner is quite impressive. He wanted to establish contact for meetings later on. He expressed interest in my financial background, and said that might be of some assistance to him. We have to understand that he's just taken the office and is still becoming acquainted with his responsibilities. But he showed considerable interest in the roundtable concept, though we didn't have much time to go into it in detail. That was more or less what we talked about. My talk with Giles came up, and we talked about it a bit and the roundtable idea."

Helen sat in exhausted disbelief, lips pressed tightly, scowling. She doubted that he would yield anything more. She even doubted that he possessed a clear recollection of his discussion with Winner. She had long ago concluded that

Martin was an irremediable buffoon, that, without awareness, he helplessly oscillated between reality and wishfulness. "Sounds like a waste of time," she said, offering the most conciliatory response she could summon. "Gotta go," she added. "Got a shrink appointment."

∽

Bill Rhodes' summons to the presidential office followed soon after Martin's. They were among many summoned to discuss their duties, experiences, and ideas with the new president. Winner went directly for the vulnerabilities that chronically worried the TTO director.

"Sit down, Rhodes," Winner began, glancing at a sheet of paper. "You've been here a little over five years. At the start, TTO was costing Kershaw about $500,000 a year for staff salaries and expenses, including more for you than we pay the professors." Winner paused, set aside the sheet of paper, and muttered half aloud, "Interesting testimonial to relative worth." Then speaking directly to Rhodes, "And TTO's costs go up about 10 percent a year. So, TTO under you has cost us about $3 million. And in the time you've been here, TTO has brought in less than $1 million. You're not a profit center, are you, Rhodes?"

Rhodes was knocked off balance by the absence of customary conversational amenities at the outset of their meeting and the suddenness of Winner's assault.

"It takes a while to build up momentum," Rhodes began, without knowing how he would develop that theme. While Winner stared at him from across the desk that separated them, Rhodes hesitated, and then said, "I hope that if you look back at us about a year from now, you'll see—."

"That won't wash," Winner said. "I don't know and you don't either what we'll see when we look back a year from now. One or both of us might not be here." Holding up a file folder, Winner said, "I've got all these news reports here about TTOs everyplace else bringing in cash that pays their way and then a lot more."

Regaining some mental traction, Rhodes attempted to broaden the picture of the TTO world. "Actually, there's some new data that shows that about half of the TTOs don't cover their expenses until they've been in operation for five to ten years. There's a learning curve. And some people are turning to the idea that income is not the best measure of effectiveness. I can get you a report—."

Winner cut him off. "Don't bother me with reports. I've got them up to here," he said, motioning toward a two-feet high stack of folders and binders on his desk. "I don't care about the TTOs that aren't making it. And you know what you can do with your learning curve. We've got maybe a thousand scientists here. Are they sitting around all day playing with themselves or are they doing research? If other TTOs are making money, how come ours isn't?"

Rhodes was reluctant to introduce the preference of Kershaw's scientists for conducting their own rogue dealings with industry rather than loyally working through his office and thereby profiting the university. But he was low on ammunition, nearly defenseless. "Many of our scientists are sort of loners when they see commercial opportunities," he plaintively started.

"What do you mean?" Winner demanded. "They work for Kershaw. They're not in business for themselves. Or are they? Is that what you're saying?"

"Some of them, maybe a lot of them, like to end run the university and make their own private deals with companies. They find all kinds of opportunities. Maybe it's legal, maybe it isn't. Hard to say. But it's difficult to find out what they're up to when they won't tell you. You know, the scientists make up a pretty tight little club, and outsiders are not welcome. And on top of that there's some stuff going on that no one will talk about at all. Maybe from the Pentagon, I hear, but there are all kinds of problems about finding out what it's about. If it's got commercial potential or not, we don't know. I'm not complaining, but there are a lot of problems. I'm working on them, but it's a steep uphill all the way."

Rhodes' gloomy assessment grabbed Winner's attention. "This is all very interesting. Like what's from the Pentagon? The rules say no classified research on campus. So how come they're doing it here?"

"I'm not sure, but I hear they took it up to Giles and he okayed it. He granted an exception. Simple as that."

"Who's doing it and what's it about?"

"I'm sure you've heard of Brusolowitz, Max Brusolowitz. He's got appointments in a couple of research departments. He pretty much does what he wants to do. The scuttlebutt is that the Army gave him a huge research contract, but I don't know for sure what it's about. Something about improving human performance. I haven't been able to find out anything more. Like I said, it's classified, or whatever they call it, but there's no information. Zero."

"Brusolowitz. Okay," Winner said, as though filing the name for later retrieval. "Okay. Now one more thing. What about Fenster. We're always hearing about him getting this prize or that prize. I understand he's got the biggest operation on campus. You get any business out of him?"

Worn down by Winner's uncompromising assertiveness, Rhodes mumbled, "It's probably my fault, but, no, nothing. He runs a buttoned-up operation, and I haven't been able to make any connection. I've talked to him, but, no. It's pretty well known that he's doing work for some companies and stuff for the government, but he doesn't give out any details."

"Yeah," Winner said, "that's all interesting stuff."

The work-study guide suddenly appeared and guided Rhodes out to the street entrance. Rhodes emerged shaking from his meeting with Winner. After he left, Winner sat thinking. For his first few weeks in the presidency, he had met daily, one at a time, with members of the Kershaw community—professors, administrators, librarians, students, grounds keepers, and others. The meeting with Rhodes, he felt, was one of the more productive in his ongoing explorations. Many more were to be held, as he methodically proceeded with developing his presidential agenda for Kershaw University. As a result of these diverse inquiries, no one knew more about Kershaw than its new president. But what would he do with his growing store of information?

಄

The Kershaw community futilely searched for clues. But none were found. Winner had come to the presidency without a track record in institutional management, a grand plan or even fleeting thoughts about how he would preside over the university. His craft and energy had been wholly invested in a modest quest for personal security. He was unprepared for leadership. Would he be a status-quo manager? A reformer dedicated to cleaning up the faculty's personal financial dealings? Would he go for broke in bringing in money—clean or soiled—for a growth binge that would enhance Kershaw's standing in the academic world and elevate him to greater things? Clues were lacking because Winner didn't know what he would do.

Winner's brusque style in the exploratory interviews quickly became the talk of the campus, with reality, conjecture, and fantasy freely mixing. "We're reliably informed," *Haywire* reported, "that he calls in Kershaw's top people and screams at them without letting them get in a word. One of the victims of this ordeal told us that at one point, he felt that President Winner was losing it. But others say it was a good discussion, though Dr. Winner did most of the talking."

The 'Bodily Functions' columnist, Ginny Rosen, "taking the liberty of DE-PARTING from my usual subject matter," judiciously urged her readers to reserve judgment. "Many professors and others here spent their WHOLE CAREERS un-der Dr. Giles, who as we all know died. Whether our new president is a MENTAL CASE, as suggested in some reports, or is just doing his job, I cannot say. But I do know that CHANGE can be difficult and disruptive, but sometimes is neces-sary! Let's WAIT AND SEE!" she recommended. A "PS" followed the column: "Sorry for the diversion. Back to my report on 'Ten Myths About Diarrhea' next time."Ginny received a hand-written note from Winner thanking her for "percep-tive reporting."

෨

Unease about Giles' inevitable departure had long rattled Elias Fenster, Kershaw's impresario of redundant rodent studies. In his twitching, nightmar-ish introspections, Fenster feared that his laboratory would be caught up in the campus-wide review customarily ordered by a new president. He anxiously con-templated the uncertainties. Though he rigorously maintained personal control over the laboratory's operations and records, a skillfully conducted independent audit could be disastrous for his reputation and career. So far he had been shielded by a gleaming reputation that forestalled a close look by outsiders. Government research agencies occasionally dispatched visiting committees to check on the re-cipients of their grants. During his long career, Fenster had been spared any such intrusion. If one were proposed, he was prepared to stifle it by quietly appealing to friends in the Washington bureaucracies that financed his work. Fenster felt confident he could block that danger by pleading that an inspection would disrupt critically important work. He could enlist the help of his Congressman and several Senators with whom he had cultivated friendly relations. But Collie Marson's foolhardy trespasses into his research nearly five years ago still terrified him, whether awake or asleep. Though he had expeditiously expelled Marson from the lab and from the profession, Fenster knew that he was the subject of invidious whispers, some coming from his grad students and post docs. Others came from the many Kershaw gossips for whom a day without defamation was empty, wasted. He had heard that Marson was working for a venture capital firm and was occasionally on campus for business dealings. Who was whispering about him? To whom? And what were they saying? Fenster didn't know.

All very worrisome, but, even so, Fenster had grounds for confidence. His research enterprise continued to flourish, publishing papers in large quantities and bringing in envied volumes of money from industry and government. With multiple consultancies, Fenster was personally doing very well financially. The university systematically took its cut for overhead costs, which left the university's managers—always a potential for trouble making—satisfied and incurious.

Rhodes and his Technology Transfer Office were another threat to be fended off. Fenster played on Rhodes' timidity, making clear that the tech transfer people were not welcome. The lab was busy with important work, he explained. TTO's aim was to license patents derived from research on campus. Fenster and his lab held no patents. For knowledge to be patentable, it must be new, not obvious, and useful. The work in his lab satisfied none of the criteria. Fenster saw no need to discuss the matter with Rhodes.

The drowsy Giles administration, a model of decentralized management, had posed no threat, and had left nothing behind concerning Fenster's operations that might invite the interest of the Winner regime. Also on the favorable side, Fenster knew that change-of-command reviews were not invariably invasive or thorough. They could range from superficial to exhaustive. A bright thought raised his spirits. Even assuming the worst, there were ways of fending off troublesome inquiries and even turning them to advantage. Potemkin Village showmanship extended to science, too. He could put on a powerful presentation about his lab's accomplishments. The program officers in government and industry who channeled money his way were naturally disposed to speak favorably of his work, and often did in memos and other communications. He could compile a brochure of these laudatory expressions, accompanied by vivid photos and extracts from his innumerable publications in leading journals.

Other thoughts occurred to him. He was distantly acquainted with the big research program that Max Brusolowitz ran on the Kershaw campus. Their labs were distant from each other and their scientific interests did not overlap. But, on alert for campus gossip, Fenster heard that Brusolowitz had somehow drawn an impermeable curtain around part of his laboratory. Secret stuff, which he wasn't allowed to talk about, even if he wanted to, or so it was rumored. No one could say for sure, but Fenster sniffed Pentagon money. If Brusolowitz could hide behind the flag, he could, too. But after a moment's reflection, Fenster sidelined that thought, at least for the time being. The Pentagon annually provided him with hefty grants, but did not impose security restrictions on his lab. All his work was in the clear, open and publishable. An entanglement with government security regulations and the Pentagon's capacity for strong-arm tactics could take unforeseen turns and create unpredictable problems. Leave things as they are, he told himself. No drastic moves were necessary, since he was in good shape for handling a routine review, if it ever came. Nonetheless, he remained concerned.

Fenster knew that surprise storms coming from unexpected quarters could suddenly upend old ways of doing business. A recent painful example stuck in the forefront of his troubled thoughts.

A colleague at a state university had for many years run a personally profitable sideline in his campus laboratory, utilizing student assistants in preparing customized reagents for sale to industrial labs. But then, under pressure from a state legislative committee, a wave of righteousness swept the campus, leading to a witch hunt for conflicts of interest, of which many had flourished without challenge as far back as anyone could remember. These included sitting on advisory boards that doled out state research funds to scientists, including members of the advisory boards. Worse intrusions were to come. In a rampage of piety, spotlighting conflicts of interest and denouncing and humiliating their beneficiaries were not enough. The search was extended to "conflicts of commitment," which focused on how professors spent their working hours. Were they attending to personal business on university time? Were they giving their students, research, and other campus duties a full measure of time and effort in return for their state salaries? Widespread academic custom allowed faculty members a day a week for consulting and other off-campus activities. However, no system existed for keeping track of professorial comings and goings. If written rules existed, their whereabouts were unknown. A vagueness surrounded "conflicts of commitment." Suddenly, with the atmosphere poisoned by legislative politics and grandstanding, the moonlighting professor-entrepreneur, admired and honored in the past, was publicly vilified for illicit financial dealings, abuse of public trust and neglect of duty. Scant attention was given his pleading that the students received real-world, job-related experience from employment in his commercial dealings, along with invaluable hands-on involvement in entrepreneurial activity; or that his profits were negligible, considering his seniority and the time he devoted to his reagents business. Besides, he insisted, he was tenured. Nonetheless, the university administration relentlessly bore down, threatening, for starters, to eliminate his lab space and reassign his grad students and postdocs. Next would be leaks to the press that would forever blight his chances for government grants. A wisp of scandal and federal research agencies, fearful of Congressional ire, would suspend their grants pending "clarification." With the hardnosed encouragement of the administration, and no other choice in sight, Fenster's unfortunate friend soon afterwards departed for a community college, where he was required to teach longer hours for lower pay and had no opportunity for engaging in sideline enterprise. Lacking a prestigious research university as a home base, he was stricken from the rolls of professors favored for reviewing grant applications and papers submitted for publication. This was a loss for Fenster, who had had a mutually beneficial relationship with the stricken professor. They had endorsed each other for grants and awards, and helped each other in the many ways that seniority brings to the normal governing processes of science. But now that was all gone. On Fenster's ledger of anxieties, his colleague's gruesome experience added to his fears of a surprise blow bringing him down.

Fenster's office was located on a balcony overlooking his sprawling laboratory. With open doors and windows admitting the scent of rodents, the murmur of workaday conversations of researchers and technicians, the tinkle of glassware and the whirr and buzz of a centrifuge and other equipment, Fenster gazed on his science empire. He alone had built it, from nothing. Now he must be prepared to defend it. He had already taken an important preparatory step prior to Winner's improbable appointment to the presidency.

Though the timing of Giles' departure was unknowable, the late president's steadily declining condition suggested that it was not far off. A successor might opt for the status quo. But recent trends in higher education seemed to favor the so-called reformers. Fenster moved accordingly to buttress his own position in anticipation of a new president—identity at the time still unknown—barging in with blazing rhetoric extolling probity, integrity, transparency, accountability and other cheer-winning nuisances that would make academic life hellish.

Fenster held the presidency of the Kershaw Faculty Senate, a semi-inanimate body which chronically experienced difficulty in finding candidates for its various offices. The meetings of the Senate were rare and poorly attended. Gatherings of the officers required laborious scheduling to settle on a common date and then repeated reminders to make a quorum, though usually this was beyond reach and official business listlessly proceeded with Fenster clutching a handful of proxies. In the brief period between Giles' death and Winner's appointment, Fenster moved quickly to assemble the Senate officers and adopt a resolution that would strongly endorse the status quo and uncompromisingly, unmistakably signal resistance to cutting faculty prerogatives. With the requisite proxies backing a motion for adoption, the Fenster-written document became official:

"Resolved, that the Kershaw Faculty Senate expresses its deep regret over the untimely death of President Carl Giles, and extends its profound sympathies to his bereaved family. Under President Giles' inspirational and foresightful leadership, the university prospered intellectually, materially, and in the highly regarded *U.S. News & World Report* ratings. Indispensable to this success were President Giles' strong belief in and unwavering support of academic freedom and faculty independence. The hallmark of his highly successful administration was strong trust in the tenured faculty and a strictly maintained non-interference in academic matters. The strength that he bequeathed to the university assures a successful future, assuming that the new leadership recognizes and builds on this legacy. The

Kershaw Faculty Senate unanimously endorses President Giles' time-tested policies and principles and strongly endorses their continuation in the future as indispensable for the university's progress."

❦

The Senate resolution was lying on Winner's desk when Fenster arrived for his tête-à-tête with the president. "Ridiculous," Winner said. "You know and I know and everyone knows that Giles was a cipher, not only in the end, but practically from the start. A textbook case of precocious Alzheimer's. So, what's this all about?"

Fenster, who increasingly bore a resemblance to the rodents he had studied throughout his adult life, froze in his seat across the desk from Winner. He had heard about Winner's bludgeoning tactics, but was unprepared for an instantaneous assault. Mustering his resources, he opted for a conciliatory response. "We all know that some doubts existed about President Giles in his later years. But for many, his going was a sad event."

"Yeah," Winner said, "and so?"

Fenster realized he was losing the opening moves. The best he could summon was a neutral retort. "The old gentleman had a lot of charm and quality, as you well know, having been a faculty member here for many years. My colleagues in the Senate and I desired to go on record with our appreciation for his leadership."

Winner remained silent. After a pause, Fenster nervously resumed. "At the time the Senate met, the trustees hadn't yet made their selection, so we weren't able to include the warm greeting that we all desired when your selection was announced. We'll of course get to that at the next Senate meeting."

"We won't waste any time on this stuff," Winner said. "I want to hear about your lab and research. Help my education in what makes your place tick."

Fenster braced himself. With instincts honed by decades in the academic ring, he knew to show no fear to a dangerous adversary. But he didn't know what Winner was after. He comforted himself for a moment with the thought that Winner was merely exercising his notoriously boorish manners and wasn't after anything. After all, Winner had spent decades at Kershaw without leaving an imprint.

"Last year was good for the lab," Fenster began, "and this year is shaping up as even better. We expect—."

"What was good about it?" Winner interrupted. "I want to know what's going on there, what's it good for, who's paying for it, and why?"

"You probably know that we're one of the oldest, if not the oldest, continuously operating research group on campus, and maybe one of the longest running in the country."

"You've been studying rats for thirty years, maybe more. What's there left to find out? Look, I don't know much about science, but I know a little bit," Winner declared. "First of all, who's paying for this stuff, why, and will they keep on paying? I'm told you've got the feds in Homeland Security giving you a couple of million a year. For what? What do they want?"

"That's an odd situation," Fenster explained. "Their payments started to arrive several years ago, but we haven't been able to establish a meaningful dialog with Homeland officials. We continue to try, but we assume that their support is predicated on the need for maintaining an important research resource, in the event of a national emergency. Frankly, we're flattered by their confidence in our work." Winner leaned across the desk, staring at him. "Yeah, keep going. Tell me more."

Not knowing how little or how much Winner knew about research, and, in particular, the peculiar brand of research practiced in his laboratory, Fenster carefully fashioned a reply. "We study rodents because the more we know about them, the more we can apply that knowledge to using them for the study of disease. We're doing basic research, the best kind of research. Really basic, fundamental, of great potential for the advancement of science. It's the most important kind of research, and we are dedicated to it, and intend to keep at it, because it's good for science and for the country. That's widely recognized, as I'm sure you're aware. There's a lot of support for our kind of science."

At that moment, Winner recognized that Fenster was not a passive punching bag. "We're all for basic research," Winner said. "But I'm just kind of puzzled by what's going on in your program." As these words spilled out, Winner was thinking: The Senate resolution, obviously engineered by Fenster, was a call to arms against intrusions on the privileges enjoyed by the tenured of Kershaw. And none was more privileged than Fenster, with his own laboratory, independent finances, and accountability to no one.

Winner knew that Fenster had declined to be considered for the presidency. That was unusual but not unheard of, Winner realized. Fenster was well-known on campus as a peculiar character. His laboratory was an anomaly, officially part of the biochemistry department, but autonomous in its operations, financing, and even in its location, in a separate building on the edge of campus. It was well known that he was a hands-on lab director, closely involved in all activities, from formulation of the research program to routine record keeping. Winner could point to nothing specific, but too much about Fenster existed beyond scrutiny. The lab was a great success, by the accepted measures of science: money, publications, top-flight grad students and postdocs. But then there were the rumors and vague reports that suggested something amiss, something serious. Fenster's involvement in the moribund Faculty Senate invited interest. In Winner's many years on the Kershaw faculty, he was barely aware of the Senate's existence. Winner's nose for academic squalor picked up signals that might elude others. Sure, Winner realized that he himself was an odd duck, too. The loner fashion he had followed throughout his academic career was unusual. But his activities on and off campus were an open book, whereas Fenster's were veiled and difficult to assess.

Winner knew that he would be allowed a presidential honeymoon for making changes, but not any drastic changes in policies and practices dear to the tenured faculty. The faculty might settle for maintaining the status quo. But its strong preference would be for expanding Kershaw's traditional non-accountability for faculty performance and behavior. The new president could win over the faculty by backing that preference. But there was no guarantee, since there was always a risk of inadvertently running afoul of the tenured faculty on one or another of the many issues that it held sacrosanct, non-negotiable. These included annual pay increases, lax to near-non-existent conflict-of-interest and conflict-of-commitment regulations, and ample pools of powerless grad students, postdocs, and adjuncts to minimize professorial workloads. As a safety net, the faculty favored disciplinary procedures that virtually assured acquittal for members accused of abusing subordinates, seducing students, committing plagiarism, fabricating data, or violating the one-day-a-week limit on money-making outside dealings. But formal disciplinary proceedings against faculty members were extremely rare. The most recent case—the first in many years— involved a foreign visiting professor whose sexual marauding among undergraduates, male and female, became too brazen to ignore. He jauntily shrugged off a summons to a board of inquiry. But upon receiving a macabre vengeance threat from an outraged parent who sounded all too credible, he hastily decamped for his home university, where he indulged his extracurricular proclivities without hindrance.

Studying Fenster across the desk, Winner concluded that he was alert to danger and possessed sharp senses and a quick readiness to do what was necessary for survival. Winner clearly understood that the Senate resolution was a warning shot, which, if necessary, could be followed by a full Faculty Senate vote of no confidence in the new president. The Senate was a sham, but that made it all the more accessible as a weapon for Fenster. Few faculty members bothered to participate in or even follow its proceedings; almost all who did compliantly followed Fenster.

Open conflict between the fledgling president and the eminent scientist would play out on and beyond the campus. Long gone was the era when academe was walled off from the surrounding society. In their pursuit of money, academic managers had broken down the walls to reach out to wealth, public and private. Public relations and offices dedicated to chasing money were as integral to the modern university as the English and athletics departments. Academic gladiators formerly found their hostilities confined to campus or meetings of their speciality societies. But now the press was attentive to even pitiful rows involving distinguished professors, or, better yet, the presidents of top universities. And the wise combatants of the modern era knew the importance of feeding information and clever quotes to the hungry press. Bloggers had neither the skill nor the inclination to unearth information, but taking their feedstock from conventional news organizations, were capable of infinite discourse and commentary, much of it abusive and flavored with paranoia.

Winner understood that a Faculty Senate vote of no confidence in his presidency would be a fabrication, but Fenster would make sure that the *Times* and the education press received the text and a full load of vituperation about his regime.

Fights between profs and plunges from academic heights make good news stories. An avid student of the press, Fenster knew that the education reporters on the adult papers and on TV mined *Haywire* for news about Kershaw, and plucked negative items for passing along to their own audiences.

In the event of a showdown with President Winner, Fenster knew he would have to play the trustees with caution, since it would reflect poorly on them if the Winner regime were repudiated by the faculty shortly after the inauguration of its unanimous choice for president. But having declined consideration for the presidency, Fenster could credibly cast himself as selflessly working for the university's best interests. Adorned with that halo, the president of the Faculty Senate could turn the trustees around with the argument that mistakes happen. The important thing is to correct them.

Both men realized that their strengths and vulnerabilities differed. Winner benefited from the attention, respect, and resources commanded by the office of the president. If Winner lost the struggle and was toppled as president, his former place on the economics faculty and his livelihood would still be sheltered by tenure, which he retained. The plummet from the presidency would be a humiliation and a painful defeat. Nonetheless, he would survive. Fenster had long ago become an icon of science, though few if any of his admirers could explain why. But Fenster understood, with dread, that if his rodent-based sham were exposed, he would be disgraced, defrocked and ousted from Kershaw and the community of science, including his memberships in the prestigious National Academy of Sciences and other professional organizations. Criminal prosecution for fraudulent use of government funds was not out of the question. Congressional science bashers might compel him to the witness chair for a televised battering about crooked scientists.

Gone would be his chance for receiving the presidentially awarded National Medal of Science in a White House Rose Garden ceremony—an honor he considered deserved and overdue. In the hierarchy of scientific honors, the Medal was of dubious importance, given that it was unaccompanied by a cash award and was subject to the political whims of the White House, rather than strictly scientific criteria. Nonetheless, for national TV, the awards ceremony provided a low-cost opportunity for demonstrating respect for science and scholarship. Fenster envisioned himself shown on national TV news, humbly shaking hands with the president, gracefully expressing gratitude for the award and praising the chief executive for supporting science. Often rehearsing his acceptance remarks, he would avoid any hint of hubris by attributing whatever success he had achieved to "standing on the shoulders of giants." A popular line among medal recipients and commencement speakers, it was always well received.

A few years earlier, Fenster had received a $500,000 MacArthur "genius award." The lucrative, highly publicized prize brought him no joy or peace. Awarded in a secretive selection process by the eccentric MacArthur Foundation, the prize—except for the money— was not esteemed by the scientific establishment, which deemed peer review, by recognized scientific experts, as the *sine quo non* for certifying scientific excellence. Well financed by his government and industrial clients, Fenster deposited the MacArthur money in a special rainy day account for use if the feared catastrophe occurred. The Nobel Prize did not enter into his fantasy life. The Nobel is for scientific accomplishment of the highest order, as documented by teams of knowledgeable scientists, who carefully study laboratory records and the scientific literature to identify the greatest science of our time and the individual or individuals who first accomplished it. Fenster could claim no great scientific accomplishment. He was notable for acquiring research grants, because he was notable for acquiring research grants. But unlike genuine breakthrough research, his research did not reverberate across the world of science. Intelligent and realistic, he knew his place in science and how he got there.

The conversation between Fenster and Winner took place in measured tones, despite its high emotional content. They finished with congenial lines masking the underlying tension, simulating civility as their conversation dwindled down. "I gather then that things are going well in the lab," Winner said.

"In my line of work," Fenster replied in a grinning, self-deprecating manner, "you're as good as your grad students and post-docs. And, as usual, I've got a great bunch this year, like every year. We old professors are just coaches on the sideline. The kids make the difference, and Kershaw gets the best. At least I can take pride in their willingness to sign on with me and work the long hours that I demand. Come over and visit the lab sometime. We can show you some interesting stuff."

"I'd like to do that when I get out from under the paper load here, if ever," Winner said, pointing to his piled-high desk. "Not that I'd understand anything going on in the lab—not my line of work. I imagine you do a lot of traveling. So let's talk later about working out a good time when you're here."

"Actually, I stick close to home base. We have an old joke in science: A great scientist can never be found in his own lab, and a really great scientist can't even be found in a lab he's visiting. Well, that probably says something about me. I can always be found in my own lab. Let's see what we can work out when you find the time."

Then, just as the work-study guide arrived to escort him away, Winner said, "Hey, one more thing. I'm hoping to meet with one of your science colleagues, Brusolowitz. Hard guy to get a hold of, but I hear he's doing some interesting work."

"Brusolowitz? You know, Kershaw is a pretty big place, and our labs are at opposite ends of the campus. I know him," Fenster said, "but really don't know much about what he's doing. Our fields of interest are quite different. But the real problem is you get so immersed in research that you never look up to see what else is going on in the world. I'll see what I can find out, if you'd like me to."

"Nah," Winner said. "Just asking."

As the two men parted, similar thoughts flitted through their minds. *Gotterdammerung* would occur only if Winner broke the peace with invasive changes that threatened the faculty, and Fenster in particular. The faculty expected a docile presidency and would accept nothing else. That was the unspoken message from Professor Fenster to President Winner. Each perfectly understood the tactical situation.

The next move was Winner's. He remained uncertain about which course to follow.

CHAPTER XIII

Collie Marson figured it would be risky to pump his old grad school buddy for more information about Brusolowitz and the Army's anti-sleep project. Charles Hollis had visibly teetered near an emotional crackup three months earlier when he spilled his concerns to Collie. A renewed conversation might push him over. Also, the secrecy stamp on the project signaled caution. Prosecution of a leak was unlikely, because of the publicity that would be stirred up. If they ever found out about it, cartoonists and late-night comics would feast on the Army's goal of inoculating soldiers against sleep, with the elimination of nature's dual imperatives as a tag-along bonus. But if the Army suspected that information about the project was seeping out, it would reinforce security, maybe even relocate the project from the Kershaw campus to a fenced-off Army base. The rumor that Lou Crowley had picked up about Brusolowitz leaving Kershaw had not checked out, as far as he and Collie were able to find. But then Collie factored in what the "Bodily Functions" columnist told him about helping Brucie sort out his lab records. What was that about? A routine cleanup or part of packing up and moving away? Collie briefly considered getting in touch with Ginny Rosen to see if she might spill anything useful about her job with Brucie. But recalling her demented behavior, he feared she might run to Brucie and tell him—who knows what? Or say something bizarre to the Dollards that would get back to Lou. She could say anything.

Or maybe do something nutty, with unforeseeable consequences. He dropped the idea of contacting Ginny.

Instead, as he had originally told Lou, he would see what he could learn from a previously unexploited source, a grad school colleague, Hal Ebbett, who was in a prolonged postdoc holding pattern at Kershaw while hoping and angling for a tenure-track appointment. Hal didn't work for Brucie, but he was active in the union-style association that sought to minimize professorial abuse and exploitation of post-doctoral fellows and graduate students. Having been both, Collie knew a couple of things about these underlings of science: They regularly swapped stories about their bosses, and they were receptive to invitations for upscale meals they couldn't afford on their crummy stipends.

When he met with Hal, Collie adopted an ingratiating tone and a flattering line, aimed at boosting Hal's ego as a hands-on researcher on the front lines of science. Collie spoke wistfully. "I miss the lab," he said after they placed their lunch orders and he picked a bottle from the wine list. "Looking for tech-transfer opportunities is pretty interesting work. Sometimes really lots of fun," Collie added, "But I envy you guys still working at real science."

Hal was a characteristically cheerless member of the post-doc proletariat, recognizable by their pallor and depressed demeanor from long hours in the lab, minimum-wage life style, imperious bosses, and uncertain vocational prospects. Postdoc appointments originated as a final polishing of scientific skills upon completion of long, formal studies. But even after investing over a decade of undergrad and graduate training in their career aspirations, postdocs were still vulnerable to derailment, as Collie knew from his terminated career. The postdocs were prey to many terrors: A peevish superior, a misstep in carrying out directions, pilferage of their good ideas by bosses and co-workers, and budget gyrations that sporadically paralyzed the job market. The path from scientific subservience to independence was lengthy and perilous. Tenure track was the next step up from postdoc. With good fortune, and six to seven years of hard work, the track would culminate in a tenured appointment, which improved the prospects for obtaining a research grant and the coveted title of Principal Investigator. PI signified independence and the right to pursue one's own research interest, and reap the glory, if successful. But in a difficult job market, postdoc appointments also provided a holding pattern. As an alternative to unemployment, successive post-doc appointments were not unusual. Gallows humorists spoke of elderly scientists retiring with the rank of "post-doc emeritus."

"Yeah," Hal sluggishly responded to Collie's remarks, "your work sounds pretty interesting. Maybe I'll try it someday, or something. But I've come this far and maybe there will be an opening. People get hired on tenure track every year, so why not me?" he said, as if appealing to the gods of scientific employment.

"That's a good attitude," Collie said, as he tested the wine and signaled the waiter to pour.

They exchanged "Cheers," both sipped and then Collie casually turned to business: "So what's going on in the lab these days?"

It was Hal's signal to perform for his lunch. "Nothing very interesting," he began. "My prof is waiting to hear about a grant that was rejected and that he resubmitted with the recommended changes. They're mostly for the worse. The original application was better. But what are you going to do? You can't argue with the reviewers or the program directors. So, there's a lot of spinning of wheels, but he's got some good ideas, and lots of bad ones, too, but if we can get going, we might have something. If we get the grant we can do what we proposed in the first place, and nobody will know or care. The system, you know."

"Sweating out grants is always tough," Collie said sympathetically. Hal was ingenuous, straightforward, occasionally inclined to optimism even in his gloomy circumstances. He worked in a Kershaw lab that existed solely on "soft money," the fearful term for government grants of limited duration, usually three to five years. The university provided no support. Without a new government grant, a renewal, or an unlikely helping hand from the university, the prof would lose the lab. The lab's graduate students and postdocs would then be without the research positions essential for their advancement. Kershaw would be obliged to keep a tenured prof in such circumstances, perhaps in an administrative job or for teaching freshman sections, maybe in another lab that possessed funding of one kind or another. But the grad students and postdocs would have to scamper for other berths—always a dicey prospect in the overcrowded, underfinanced realm of advanced science training.

Collie and Hal were silent for a moment as they weighed similar thoughts. Then Collie said, "I hear Brusolowitz has some interesting stuff going on. You ever hear anything about what's going on there?"

"Yeah, a little. You know, he runs a bunch of labs. I had a good friend who was doing a postdoc with him in one of them, but switched to another department after a year or two. It's a funny operation that Brusolowitz—they call him Brucie—has there. Nobody knows for sure, but you hear around that he's got some Pentagon money, from the Army, I think, and it's classified. How they get away with that on campus we'll never know. Something about physiological enhancement or performance improvement, but I never found out just what it is. But he says Brucie was doing a lot of really fantastic stuff. My friend was doing brain imaging on a colony of rats that Brucie was working with, and he says he's never seen anything like it. Brucie's got them all rewired so that their behavioral characteristics are radically altered. Really strange stuff. I don't think anyone else is doing anything like this."

"Like what?" Collie asked as he motioned the waiter to refill their wine glasses.

"Like I said, it's all classified, so my friend was pretty careful about talking about what was going on. But I got the sense that it's really far out. The Army, or whoever, won't allow any publications about the project. My friend figured he'd better get the hell out of there and do something that he can put on a resume."

"Is this friend of yours a pretty reliable guy?"

"Oh, yeah," Hal said. "He worked with me at the post-doc association on the usual issues—you know, working hours and health insurance, grievance procedures, stuff where we never get anyplace. I got to know him pretty well."

"How about dessert?" Collie said, quickly adding, "You think I might get together with your friend?"

"Oh, Christ, no," Hal said with alarm. "He'd be real pissed off if he knew I was telling you anything about this stuff. He had to sign some sort of security form when he went to work with Brucie. And when he left, they lectured him that the project was classified and made him sign something again. He used to blow off steam with me, but he really can't talk about it. Yeah, I'll have some dessert."

The lunch meeting provided some useful information, particularly the reference to brain imaging. But quickly adding things up, Collie had to admit to himself that he hadn't made any real progress since first telling Lou about the anti-sleep project.

❧

Parting from his lunch companion, Collie walked along the street, juggling fragmentary thoughts. A bold, direct-action idea occurred: Go to Brusolowitz and tell him you know about the project, that it's too important to keep wrapped up, and make a pitch for going commercial. That was a bum idea, he quickly realized. First of all, the Army probably owned the whole thing. Brusolowitz would tell the Army that word of the project had leaked out, and the Army would clamp down with even stricter secrecy. Obviously, Collie told himself, Brucie must believe the project was worth doing, or he wouldn't be doing it. And if Brucie wanted the world to know about his work, he didn't need a scientific nobody, Collie Marson, to get out the news. Collie felt hemmed in. There was no place else to get the information he needed. Maybe, after all, he should try to get in touch again with his old friend Charles Hollis, the hand-wringing manager for the Army project. But then he reminded himself of Hollis's sad emotional state and vulnerable status as an Army employee. Their conversation had arisen from a bump-into encounter at a crowded scientific conference, and they went to have a drink. It happens all the time at these meetings. But a direct, deliberate approach to Charles Hollis would be something else. Charles would be suspicious. And there was another possible danger: Charles' negative attitude toward the project could easily have been noticed by the Army people in his office, putting him under some kind of surveillance. If it looked like he was squealing, he'd be pushed out from his job as project manager, or worse. That would close Collie's only window on the project. No, Collie decided, at least for the moment, he would stay away from Charles. An occasion might arise again for them to get together in a casual fashion, perhaps at another of the many big scientific conferences that filled the calendar. Then Collie could tiptoe his way around to the topic and gently encourage Charles to open up.

Not the best choice, he admitted to himself, but what else was available? Nothing. Then he switched to worrying about his relationship with Lou Crowley.

Collie realized that his excited, enthusiastic report about the anti-sleep project had left Lou with high expectations. Collie now feared that he would appear ineffectual if he failed to make real progress toward learning about the project and getting all or a piece of it for Lou's company. Lunch with Hal Ebbett hadn't added anything important to his knowledge. And still to come—but only if he made progress—was the really hard part: getting connected to the project in some fashion and making money from it. That's what Lou had hired him to do, and why Lou was paying him far more than Collie brought into the firm. Sure, the Army and the secrecy around the research created unusual difficulties for going commercial. But that was no consolation or alibi. Someday, somehow the world would ultimately find out about Brucie's research, and some people would make fantastic amounts of money from it. Collie was determined that Lou's company would be there in a big way. There was big money in sleep. It seemed that half the world bought pills to get to sleep, while the other half bought pills to stay awake. But these products were pharmacologically crude, reflecting a poor understanding of the underlying biology, and there was a lot of dissatisfaction with them. Brucie's revolutionary discovery would eliminate the need for sleep and could open the way to many variations for controlling the sleep cycle. The market potential and the consequences for society were unknowable, but they would both be colossal, Collie felt certain. He was grateful to Lou for taking him into the company. Lou trusted him as the scientific scout for his venture-capital firm. Collie's comfortable and rewarding employment sharply contrasted with his past shabby post-doc existence. Lou treated him very decently, and Collie was fond of him. One goof wouldn't end the congenial relationship with Lou, but it would be a setback. From the demise of his scientific career, Collie knew that misfortunes could start small, accumulate and eventually mushroom into serious trouble or even disaster. If gold was to be had from the Army's strange project, Collie didn't want to miss out on it—for Lou and for himself.

"Collie!" a voice called out as he walked along the crowded sidewalk with these thoughts tumbling in his mind.

He looked about and saw Helen Dollard briskly emerging from the university bookstore, flashing a gleaming great smile at him. For a quick outdoor errand she wasn't aesthetically groomed to top level. But still, as always in public, she looked smart—hair nicely done, makeup okay, tailored jeans tucked into high-heel suede boots, a stylish beige tweed jacket and bright red turtle-neck sweater, and a large leather bag with gleaming brass fittings slung over a shoulder. She had studied the look in *Vogue*, and matched it perfectly. Helen had ventured out in connection with her own research project. The package under her arm contained the Kershaw University directory. She had first sought it on-line but her keyboard skills were not up to the task. Helen hoped the directory would provide a clue about gaining access to Kershaw's new president—perhaps through a strategically placed acquaintance whom she had overlooked in her scheming or at a social event on the university calendar. "Honest, I'm terrible at names," she said as she and Collie greeted each other. "But I do hope that I remembered right that you're Collie, and I want to say that you were an absolute angel to take that poor girl home."

Soon they were seated at a small table in the bookstore coffee shop, smoothly, easily conversing as they reconnoitered each other. "Martin is very encouraged about President Winner," Helen said, as though confiding a sensitive confidence. "And I'm so happy for Martin. Perhaps he told you, he's been working on this fascinating idea, all his own. He had conferred with the old President Giles about setting up a regular discussion group, a roundtable, as he calls it, with some of the biggest people from all sorts of places—TV, publishing, Congress, the UN, all sorts of places. It's a long story," Helen said, "but when we all get together again, Martin can tell you about it. It's such a good idea. He's met with Dr. Winner and came away very, very impressed. Martin is a very good judge of people," she confidently declared. "A very good judge." Recalling the drench of banalities that Martin had inflicted on him during his misbegotten evening at the Dollards, Collie merely nodded and said, "That's really good to know. Kershaw needed some new blood at the top. Everyone says so."

"That's what I hear, too," Helen immediately agreed. "But what's up with you? Martin told me that you're involved with scientific research at Kershaw, but that it's not so much working in a laboratory as it's developing ideas for industry.

So fascinating," she said, as she recalled her previous thoughts about whether Collie might somehow provide her with access to the new president. He confirmed that she had it right, that he was involved in connecting the university's researchers to the commercial world. "Trying to," he modestly amended the explanation. "It's not always easy." But nothing he said suggested that he had access to Winner or anyone near him. Helen referred to her membership on the arts committee, and her hopes that the new president would taken an interest in its work. Collie said he hoped so, too, but the subject plainly did not resonate with him.

They had long since finished their coffee, but conversation, back and forth, though of little substance, held them there. And as they chatted, easily and pleasantly, each looked more closely at the other, and each felt good, and then better and better, about their fortuitous encounter. As Collie was telling a funny story about his ruinous post-doc experiences with Professor Fenster, he unthinkingly reached across the table and put his hand on top of Helen's. They looked at each other for a quick moment as he took it away and managed to finish the story. Helen giggled appreciatively, shaking her head up and down approvingly and saying, "Oh, that's so funny, that's so funny." Collie realized that he felt comfortable with her. The waiter suddenly reappeared, tapped on the check, which had been sitting on the table untouched for some time, and pointedly asked if they wanted anything else. Collie paid and they walked out together.

"Which way are you going?" he asked.

"I'm going to get a taxi and do some errands," Helen said. "And then I have to meet Martin. But this has been such a delight. Let's get together again. I love that story you told me about that funny professor. What a riot."

Greatly pleased, Collie repeated the rodent-lab story to himself, this time recalling several funny touches that he now wished he had included in regaling Helen about his post-doc days.

∽

Collie was prudent and principled. Though opportunities occurred, he refrained from intimacy with married women. He took pride in a strictly observed resolve not to be a home breaker. Equally, or perhaps of greater importance, he did not want to be within blast range when collapsing marriages went berserk. He had had no experiences of that nature, but he had heard enough to opt for caution. No circumstance had yet arisen that caused him to deviate from, or even reconsider, his prudence and principles in this regard. But he was not robotically inflexible. The brief meeting with Helen was unusually pleasurable. She lodged in his thoughts, even at times displacing the gnawing problem of Brusolowitz and the anti-sleep project. From his ample experience with women, Collie knew that when attraction was present, and opportunity available, a predictable succession of steps easily followed. But not necessarily in every instance, he assured himself. Besides, he felt confident that his acquaintanceship with Helen came with built-in safeguards that would strongly, naturally compel him to be reserved and restrained. Lou and Martin were friends of longstanding. Not very close, Collie sensed, but there was a connection that went far back. That gave Collie a strong incentive to avoid any difficulties involving the Dollards, he reasoned. Helen was inviting, but her repeated expressions of admiration for Martin suggested domestic harmony and an absence of adventurousness. Collie decided that if now and then he had a drink with Helen or they met to discuss something or other, these built-in safety factors would guide their behavior. He didn't welcome the thought that Martin would probably be on the scene. But accept it, he told himself. Martin probably would be there. Why not? Helen was his wife. So, Collie concluded, there was no real problem in entering into a casual, friendly relationship with Helen Dollard. Just friends. He had never done so before with an attractive woman, but in this instance, special circumstances made the difference.

Helen did not indulge in such puerile ditherings. As Collie told the hilarious story about Professor Fenster, she was on a cognitive dual track, rapidly proceeding to a basic decision, and then swiftly, directly to considering the means of implementation. All the while she smiled at Collie, nodded, laughed and uttered approving words, her mind was racing along. Yes, he was a very interesting, attractive young man, and surely they would have a relationship. The logistics, however, would require extreme care. Her parting words about nearby errands and meeting Martin were simply the first deception in the undertaking. She had no errands to perform or plans to meet Martin. But as accidental as her sidewalk encounter with Collie had been, and though they were barely acquainted, there was a danger: They were visibly enjoying each other's company, not in the casual fashion of two unconnected people, but as a man and a woman drawn to each other. Any sentient passerby would recognize that. Seated at a window table in the crowded coffee shop, who knows who might have observed them animatedly talking and laughing? Suspicions easily flourished. Quality gossip was incessantly in demand, always in short supply. But then, for a moment, Helen realized she was yielding to paranoia. An innocent street encounter was easily explained, if it ever came up, which was not likely. But why compound the risk, Helen calculated, by proceeding down the street together? Her hurried thinking left her undecided, confused, as she switched to pondering the future in their relationship.

Since retiring, Martin had whole heartedly thrown himself into his societal-impact interests. Occasionally, a seminar or a professional society meeting took him out of town—to many exclamations from him about the awesome workload he had taken upon himself because of insufficiently recognized impending societal upheavals, calamities, and misfortunes, compounded by poor policies. Martin hoped to alleviate them through the discussions he would organize. Helen normally paid no attention to his policy rantings or his travel plans, except to experience relief from these absences, which unfortunately, she felt, were too rare and never for more than a few days. Now she searched her memory but didn't recall Martin saying anything about going out of town.

Because of this surprise development with Collie, there was so much to be attended to. She would terminate the extra-curricular relationship with Berlin-Gottchalk. The shrink's supercilious manner was having an unwholesome effect on her self-esteem. Whether she would continue as a patient—well, that was to be seen, though she was now inclined to drop out. Suddenly she told herself, "You're acting crazy. You barely know this guy." But that realization faded away, almost instantly.

Where would they meet? she wondered. Their respective apartments were absolutely out of the question. Doormen, cleaning people, neighbors, chance encounters in the lobby made it too risky. Hotels? Also risky. Seared in her mind was the catastrophic experience of a girlfriend whose carefully planned liaison, and marriage, crashed horribly when the hotel registration clerk looked up to greet her. The smiling young woman behind the hotel desk, she belatedly realized, was the daughter of one of her husband's business partners. "Just a summer job," the college kid said, as she lasciviously processed and comprehended the significance of this woman she knew nervously claiming a reservation under an unfamiliar name. Helen shuddered at the thought of a blow up with Martin or even rousing any suspicions. For her material needs, life with his wealth was too good to throw away. She had signed a pre-nuptial agreement without more than glancing over its closely printed legalese. Experienced in calculating life's choices, she saw no alternative. The physical side of her relationship with Martin had been nightmarish for her from the start. But, increasingly, she was able to fend him off by claiming a need to work out problems with her therapist. Martin was incredibly understanding. No hotels, no risks, she repeated to herself, as she searched for a solution. Helen rarely ever traveled out of town without Martin, but she might do it on some pretext, maybe once or twice, but no more than that. A promising solution quickly came to mind: a small, furnished apartment in a building with underground parking and an elevator directly to their secure love nest. Not absolutely safe but, by far, the best of all choices.

Collie was unaware that this problem-solving exercise was rapidly progressing in her thoughts as they chatted, exchanged smiles, and sipped coffee. After they parted, she felt the strain of her intense deliberations—something akin to the exhaustion that followed long end-of-term examinations during her abbreviated college days. Waiting for a taxi, she remembered the package in her hands—the university directory that she had purchased for ferreting out some means of getting to Kershaw's president. So much to do, she anxiously reminded herself.

CHAPTER XIV

"The trouble with this university, Dr. Winner, is that it's coasting on old glories. It's full of big-name professors who gave up working, even gave up thinking, long ago. Some of them get money for research because the feds are in the habit of giving it to them. That's how the system works: the rich get richer, at least for a while. But the people who hand out money are going to catch on and it's going to hit us hard in the pocketbook, and then things will really fall apart. There's no reason to feel pride in this place."

Bentley Grimes, president of the Kershaw University Alumni Association, required no preparation for his meeting with the new president. His grievances had accumulated and festered without relief throughout the lengthy downward drift of the Giles presidency. Grimes had several times delivered his complaints directly to the progressively vacant Giles. But in each instance he shared the dismaying experiences of many others who tried to communicate with the president: Giles smiled graciously, nodded, gestured, and uttered encouraging conversational cues— "Yes," "Go on," "I see"— but said nothing of substance, nothing that signified comprehension. After a time, an assistant would move in and signal an end to the conversation. No results ensued from these encounters. Talking to Giles' handpicked trustees was similarly futile, Grimes found. None of them seemed to know much about the university or show interest in learning about it. It was as though Kershaw were a finished product, immutable, done, like an old museum or a well-filled cemetery. Nonetheless, Grimes, the founding head of a thriving advertising and public-relations agency, figured that the trustees' choice for a new president had to be an improvement over Giles. That's why he asked for the meeting.

Winner, well along in educating himself about Kershaw from the perspective of the presidency, figured that a meeting with Grimes might be beneficially differ-ent from most of his exploratory discussions. Unlike the many Kershaw professors and administrators with whom Winner had conferred, Grimes wasn't on the Ker-shaw payroll or career track. He was a successful businessman, a big-doer with no personal stake in maintaining the Kershaw status quo. He wasn't in the tenured ranks that scrutinized Winner's words and moves for early warning of ill intent toward their privileges. Blustery, confident, bullying, he displayed impatience with whatever had his attention and an eagerness to move on to something else. He was notorious for an absence of tact. Tiring of selfish pleas by Kershaw's elite, Winner looked to Grimes for a different message.

" You don't feel pride in this place? My apologies. But tell me more."

Grimes, seated across the desk from the president, opened up. "I've been in advertising and PR for a long time, which means I know a lot about bullshit—how to produce it and how to recognize it. My two specialities. And there's a lot of bullshit going on here, a lot of stuff about excellence that everyone knows doesn't really exist. Makes it hard for our grads to find good jobs. Top companies have wised up and are cutting back on recruiting here. Same for the big law firms. They go to NYU and Columbia and other places. They don't come here. The medical school is a menace to public health and safety. Whole departments are on proba-tion by the accrediting agencies, and the profs are all on the take from pharmaceu-tical companies. You want a drug to look good for FDA approval? Put Kershaw profs in charge of the clinical trial. Hell, with our gang, rat poison could pass muster for baby powder. If you don't already know about all this, you should. This place is no source of pride for us grads. The Kershaw brand doesn't get respect."

"That's an unusual introduction," Winner cautiously responded. "How do you know all this?"

"I'll tell you. I find out a lot of things by talking to students. Sometimes I buy them a beer in the campus joints, and we hire a few as summer interns. They're

the ones who know what's really going on. You've got all these tenured professors here, not doing much, yammering about academic freedom whenever anyone
asks any questions about what they're doing. Teaching loads are the lightest in
the league. They don't publish much. It's a mystery what the hell they're doing,
besides traveling to conferences. We're not getting all the good students we need.
The student newspaper is a cesspool, with sick articles about perversion, puke and
toilet habits. Unbelievable stuff. Parents are wise to what's up. They know what's
going on here and they're choosing other places for their kids. Okay, we're still
doing pretty good in the *U.S. News* ratings—but speaking of bullshit, that's nothing to rely on. At other universities, they're building up and cashing in on their
research, getting lots of venture-capital money. Not here. Dr. Winner, I'll tell you
what you have to do."

Winner was entranced, but neutral in his response: "What do I have to do?"
he asked flatly.

"Shake up this place. Pulp the deadwood. Raise some big money—I mean
big. And put Kershaw back on the map. Believe me, it's not hard to do. When you
look at the boneheads running some of the top-rated schools, you have to conclude
that it can't be hard to do."

Winner's skepticism clicked on: "Hey, wait a minute. What's all this
to you? Let me ask you straight: Are you looking for a PR or advertising
contract?"

"No. That's ridiculous. You're too small. We don't do this kind of business.
I'm strictly *pro bono* when it comes to Kershaw. But you ask a fair question about
why I'm here. I went to Kershaw. It was a long time ago, when it was a hometown
school where we all went. I kind of got to like this place, though I wouldn't send
my kids here the way it is now. It hurts me to see people laughing at Kershaw,
like it's a has-been or a diploma mill trying to pass itself off as a real university. I'd
like to be proud of it. I got elected president of the alumni association. Easy to do,
since no one else wanted the job, and most grads forget about this place as soon
as they get out. I tried to talk to Giles, but it was hopeless. But I hope something
can be done now that Giles is out of the way. Maybe not."

"Like what should be done?" Winner asked, less uncertain but still wary about
the trustworthiness and intentions of his glib, confident visitor.

"Let me paint the big picture as seen by Bentley Grimes. It's like this," Grimes said, as Winner listened with rising interest. "Harvard is better than this place, true. But mainly because they've held steady while we've sunk down. Sure, Harvard's older by a couple of hundred years, which really means nothing when you think about it. It's got the biggest endowment, but they're stingy about spending it; so money really isn't a huge difference. What Harvard's got is this big glow around it that makes people think it's the ultimate, the only one of its kind. The press is brain dead, and kneels down when it hears 'Harvard.' But mixed in with a few superstars, Harvard's got its deadwood, too, plenty of it. The difference is they beat the drums when they buy up a big professor or they add a shelf in the library. And they always talk down to the rest of higher education. These things add up. Big-name profs attract the top students, top students make the profs feel good, the image helps draw in grants, and the publicity shop gets more stuff to shout about. Kershaw should do a lot of this, but under old man Giles, it wilted away."

Observing a look of entrancement coming over Winner's face, Grimes proceeded with rising confidence. "Think about what you see in the papers when Harvard is involved in some way. Someone gets appointed as an ambassador or is elected mayor of somewhere. He's a lawyer. If he went to Harvard, the papers always point out that he's a 'Harvard-trained lawyer,' or a 'Harvard law graduate.' Or if he was just a Harvard undergrad, they say he's 'Harvard-educated.' Same if he becomes a big-time CEO or he's arrested for extortion, porno, or murder. Or even if he gets murdered. He's Harvard. It really doesn't tell you anything important, because lots of nitwits get in and out of Harvard, same as other places. When Obama was running, the papers always pointed out that he went to Harvard Law. But where did Joe Biden go to law school? It wasn't Harvard, so no one cares. Harvard is a brand and people salute it. It's like Tiffany's or like Cadillac used to be. The jewels and the car aren't any better than some other brands, but they got the glitz. If some guy in the news went to law school in Minnesota, they don't routinely say he's a Minnesota-educated lawyer. When Larry Summers was forced to resign at Harvard, it was in the national news for weeks. When presidents of other universities get booted out, it's a local story, and no more. At Harvard they've got half-baked teaching assistants running lots of classes. But on the outside, all you hear about are the Nobel prize winners, ex-Senators, and assorted geniuses that the kids never see. Harvard's got this mystique. Others don't, and Kershaw doesn't either. You have to change that."

Grimes' emphatically delivered words hooked deeper into Winner's attention. Most of the prior messages delivered across the presidential desk focused on preserving or expanding the tenured faculty's special benefits, exemptions from rigorous standards, and other advantages. The pitch from Fenster, the rodent meister, was the ultimate, with his barely veiled warnings of retribution if the Giles' system of tenure privilege were cut back.

"Yeah, I see what you're driving at." Winner was beginning to feel a warming sense of comradeship with Grimes. "But everything here is fortified to keep it the way it is. On paper, I've got power over appointments, budgets, tenure, and all sorts of stuff. But in the last ten years under Giles the powers were never used, and sort of melted away. The board shows up for meetings, but doesn't know or care about what's going on and does nothing. The senior faculty runs this place for its own comfort. If I hinted that a professor should get off his butt and teach a class or two, or at least do some research, the Faculty Senate would rally around him and put out a statement about an invasion of academic freedom. And then the AAUP gets on the case. They can put Kershaw on probation, or give us some other kind of black mark. And they feed stuff to the *Times,* and the *Times* makes it look like there's a real controversy going and President Winner is the anti-intellectual heavy; that I'm the enemy of the honest, decent, hard-working professors who are dedicated to teaching and research. They do it in a nice balanced way. The *Times* will tell you that some people think the president is right, some think he's wrong, and others hold mixed opinions, and the reader is supposed to figure it out for himself. But you know the effect. You got to figure on that happening, Mr. Grimes. Things were peaceful under Giles because he got the message: 'Do Not Disturb.' I'm new in this job and I've got to be careful about getting off to a bad start that these bandits can exploit for their advantage. They're watching, and they're ready to jump."

"Okay. You've got problems, but let me tell you—."

Worried that Grimes didn't fully grasp the difficulties he faced, Winner kept talking: "Yeah, and about all that filth in the student paper. It's a third rail. Touch that and you're dead, you're against freedom of the press. Enemy of the First

Amendment. That brings in the ACLU and editorials in the big papers and by the blowhards on TV, and the bloggers. They won't say that students should be free to write about shit and sex with dogs in the campus paper. What they'll say is that President Winner wants to deny the students the opportunity to mature into responsible journalists. And about marketing our research. Sure, we've got research going on here that could be licensed by Kershaw, but these guys in our labs are making their own deals, and if I try to get a cut for the university, they holler about scientific freedom. They're doing drug testing for pharmaceutical companies that should land them in jail for fraud and conflicts of interest—maybe even murder. But don't mess with academic freedom and freedom of scientific inquiry. That's their pitch. We've got a VP on our staff who's supposed to be working on tech transfer deals for the university—selling stuff that's discovered in our own labs, not that there's much of it, as far as we know. But he tells me that the people in the labs are cutting all kinds of deals for themselves with companies behind our back, and they won't even talk to him. I just found out that there's a research project right here on campus, and we don't even know what it's about, and nobody will tell us. Somebody said it belongs to the Pentagon, but I don't know and can't find out. And I've been trying to get the professor who's running it to come in and talk to me, and so far, no response. I'm beginning to feel like I'm just a mannequin here sitting in the president's chair." Sweat was gathered on Winner's brow. He had never before expressed his rising accumulation of grievances.

"Look,"Grimes said, "you've got big problems. I can see that. But there are things you can do. For sure, you can't take these old profs head on when they're dug in so deep. If you try, they'll wipe you out. You're right. But there are ways. First you've got to prepare the ground with a lot of little moves that give you two priceless things—prestige and visibility. Then you can make the big moves. I'll tell you what to do, if you want to listen."

Winner hadn't sought strategic counseling when he agreed to meet with Grimes, but now that he had a taste of it from his blunt-talking visitor, he wanted more.

"You got to make this place stand out. Kershaw has no big sports tradition. That's good, so let's not try going for football or basketball. It takes too long and costs too much and gives the wrong message. But with other things, you can count on the newspapers and TV to play on your side and build up your prestige and image—if you do it right. Let me give you a first, easy step. Okay?"

"Yeah, okay. Go ahead."

"Raise the tuition. Real high. Make this the most expensive school in the whole country."

"Are you joking? What's that going to do, except piss off the parents and scare off applicants and get the press on our tail for being greedy?"

"No. I can see that you don't know anything about the marketing of what's called luxury goods. Designer rags, jewelry, high-end luggage, perfume, watches, ladies handbags. Take watches. The brands with foreign-sounding names that are advertised in the *Times*, the *New Yorker*, and the fashion mags. Except for a little gold or diamond chips, they really aren't different from your twenty-buck Timex, but they go for five grand, twenty-five grand, and they sell. It's not the watch that sells. It's the price, the price. Makes an insecure jerk feel good, important and sure of himself if he's wearing a watch that everyone sees is expensive. Same with ladies handbags that sell for two or three grand, and even more. No different from the $39.95 version. Hell, go to Chinatown and they're peddling beautiful knock-offs for practically nothing. Same with luggage. Lots of wimps worry that the bellhops or desk clerks won't show them respect unless they have a brand-name bag. But the only real difference with the K-Mart version is the price. You've got to price college here like a luxury product. What does it cost now, undergrad with room and board, and all the other stuff?"

"We figure it at $50,000 per year, give or take a few bucks. About the same as Harvard and the other big private schools."

In a cool whisper, Grimes instructed, "Go to $75,000!"

"What?" Winner exclaimed, slapping his forehead in disbelief, but Grimes kept on talking.

"The newspapers and TV will grab it right away. They love stories about big spending, like $2,500 bottles of wine and $5,000-a-night hotel rooms. Tuition at seventy-five grand will be a big story with lots of echoes. The bloggers and columnists and editorial writers will be shouting and fighting back and forth, non-stop, for and against, and why it's happening and what's the meaning—they love what's the meaning—and the politics, the cultural significance. They'll call it a 'pivotal moment in higher education,' 'a watershed event,' 'a critical turning point.' Comments on comments, rebuttals, and all that stuff that keeps these pin heads feeling important. With all that screaming going on, people will figure there must be something special about Kershaw since it charges those prices and gets all that attention. From that, it's a short step to the idea that this school is an elite center—no, the peak— of excellence for teaching, research, and public service. Let's not forget public service—because, whatever it is, it adds to the image. Why will they get the idea that Kershaw is all these things? Because that's what you're going to tell them—in a dignified way, of course. You calmly point out that there's no substitute for excellence; that excellence and Kershaw are synonymous. Kershaw will settle for nothing but excellence. And you tell them the tuition accurately reflects the value of the product. Otherwise, how could this school charge those prices and why would parents pay them? Also toss in something about transparency. That's hot these days, even when it doesn't make a damn bit of difference. And then you'll be anointed with the highest honor. The higher-education crowd and the newspapers will call you a 'transformational president.' Transformation is very popular."

Winner contemplated Grimes' strategy for a moment before protesting, "Everyone complains that tuition is too high, that it keeps going up above inflation, and you want to make it go up even higher. They'll attack us, especially me. They'll say we're out of touch with what's happening to families in this economy, and—."

"Right," Grimes interrupted. "They will attack you, but only if you do it the wrong way. Do it the right way and they'll praise you as a statesman of higher education. Not just a plain statesman—but a *leading* statesman. Most of the time when tuition is increased it's done without any public announcement, sort of in a sneaky way, like it's something dirty or crooked that you don't want anyone to know about. There's a lot of explaining about the consumer price index and inflation, and how the school is really holding down prices. But you're different. You're transparent. You don't quietly raise tuition. No. You call a press conference to announce it with a big splash. But with it, you also announce a big new scholarship program. You say the aim is to increase financial aid and especially to enable kids from the poorest families to get the same excellent Kershaw education as kids from families that can shell out the seventy-five grand. Excellence and opportunity for brilliant poor kids, at no cost to them. Great combination. You'll see. The first thing that will happen is that applications for admission will increase. They'll go way up."

"What makes you so sure?"

"That's what happens with luxury products when they're managed right," Grimes explained. "Raise the price and the customers come rushing in. A lot of them will be rich rejects from better schools—let's face it. But they've got to go someplace. And it might as well be Kershaw. Others who can pay up will make it their first choice because they think it's something special and they don't want to miss out. The poor ones will come because it's free. And if you raise the tuition, you get a bonus."

"What's that?" Winner asked as he tried to absorb Grimes' exotic strategies.

"If the number of applications increases while the number of student slots remains the same, Kershaw automatically becomes an *exclusive* school. Do it right and it can be one of the most difficult to get into in the whole country. Maybe the most difficult. It becomes a hot school. The top Ivies say they accept only one out of nine or ten applicants. Kershaw can beat that. Even if it can't, with this numbers game you can say anything you want. There's no way for anyone to check up. And that will give us that special glow that comes with exclusivity. It's like a restaurant you can't get into. People start scheming to get reservations, not because the food is great, but because they want to be able to say they got in there. And the newspapers play along, with insider advice about how to get reservations when nobody else can. You'll see articles on how to get into Kershaw, interviews with the lucky ones who made it."

"Maybe," Winner said, "but we've got a problem. Our SATs will drag us down in the *U.S. News* ratings. A lot of marginal students—to be polite—get in here because they're cash customers. Some are legacies with rich fathers who we want to soften up for donations. We're in the cellar for SATs."

"Oh, boy," Grimes said, "I wish all my problems were as easy as this. If you've got lousy SATs, just drop the SAT as an admission requirement. A lot of other schools have done it, for one reason or another. Why not Kershaw? But you take the high road. You say that the SAT is culturally biased, class-oriented, that it fails to recognize late bloomers, original thinkers, and ethnic minorities. I read someplace that Einstein would have done poorly on the SAT. We'll write up a good press release for you. Gratis. Something along the lines of 'Kershaw Drops SATs as Discriminatory.'"

"Okay, so we drop the SAT. But I see a problem. Scholarships cost money. Where do we get the money for the poor kids? We're in pretty bad shape here."

"You don't need much money. In fact, you'll come out ahead if you do it right. With enough tuitions coming in at $75,000 a pop, you can hand out a few scholarships to the deserving poor. It doesn't have to be too many. Nobody on the outside really knows what the hell goes on inside a university. You just say that all admissions are on a need-blind basis. Money is no barrier. But you don't stop there. You've got to have a multi-pronged program—lots of things at the same time. So, when you announce the scholarship program, you also announce a big fund-raising campaign. You know, at any one time, there are about 50 universities with fund-raising campaigns for a billion or maybe two or three billion each spread over two, three, four years. The goal becomes inspirational. At times they announce they're behind schedule, at other times they're ahead. No one on the outside really knows where they're at, but the announcements stir up the rich alumni and philanthropic fat cats and foundation staff looking for something special to do. Most foundation managers and execs couldn't hack it in the real world, so if they're lucky, they end up in the wonderful position of giving money away, which means their betters regularly line up to kiss their butts. Empowered mediocrities—that's what they are. You notice, whenever a new foundation president comes in, he conducts a study and then junks everything started by the last guy. One day something is core mission. The next day the new boss arrives, and it doesn't deserve support. The foundation staffs know they're wasting most of their money on useless, deadend projects. But they've got to spend it someplace or some Congressman wonders why they're hoarding it, and their board starts wondering why they're not shoveling it out the door. So, why not let them spend it at a university that's newly dedicated to excellence and elite education for poor but brilliant kids? That's Kershaw. So, you announce, let's say, a two-billion fund-raising drive for these lovable goals, and you invite in foundation directors and board members to explain your admirable plans. Give them the whole schmear.

PowerPoints, glossy brochures with pie charts and tables. Make sure you serve them a skimpy lunch. Shows you're careful with money. Foundation staffs will perk up, take notice. But we have to expect returns will come in slowly. Foundations are cautious, always waiting for the other guys to go first. You won't get much in the beginning, but you keep announcing big returns, even if you're not getting in much. Call it anonymous gifts. No one ever tries to check up. If they try, tell them you're bound by privacy requirements. Phony statistics make the world go round. Newspapers pad their circulation figures, TV claims viewers it doesn't have, candidates rig the polls, bond-rating companies invent ratings, stock salesmen will tell you anything. Remember, some numbers always beat no numbers. And that can get things going, and then later you can move on to the next stage, maybe announcing plans for a new building or two and renaming old buildings in honor of big donors."

Winner protested: "The old buildings are named in honor of past donors from when we were getting money. How can we take off the name of some long-gone donor and put on the name of a new one? Sure grounds for a law suit from heirs or relatives."

"Dr. Winner, that's what lawyers and stone carvers are for. Don't worry about it. If enough money is on the table, the names can be changed. It happens all the time. You'll be in good company with the best schools. There's no flip-flop wizard like a university president on the money trail. You've got to get in step."

"What about the faculty here?" Winner asked. "I can make all these changes and raise the money, but they're still here. What do I do about them?"

"Okay. Money intake is all anybody cares about in a university president. No higher praise than 'he's a great fundraiser.' Once you're raising big new money, or at least you look like you are, you'll have the magic that's known as prestige. Then the alumni will start paying attention, because their old school is now looking good, and they'll be on your side. I'll see to it that you get an award from the alumni association for outstanding leadership. And we can drum up some other awards. No problem. The younger faculty will be on your side because they don't like getting kicked around by the older ones who are clogging up all the tenure slots. And the newspapers will say you're doing good things, because next to trashing you when you're down, they like to discover heroes winning against the odds. Then you can start dealing with the old guard.

"First thing is you deny them annual raises. That will put the old profs on a fast track to a collective mental breakdown. Then you propel them along by setting minimum teaching hours. Then you take some of the new cash that's coming in and set up a few special chairs for distinguished scholars at high salaries—picked by you from *outside* of Kershaw. And with research in the labs, you crack down and make it clear that the university owns that stuff. It doesn't belong to the professors. And they've got to tell you what they're doing. They can't keep it to themselves, like they do now. Also, that the highest ethical standards will apply to testing drugs and doing other dirty work for the drug companies, like lying to the FDA about the safety of a new drug. The old farts will see what's going on and they'll try to fight you, but if you publicly bash them for selfishly resisting needed changes, the newspapers will hail you as a courageous reformer taking on the bad guys. After all, you're the guy who challenged the selfish interests and turned things upside down to provide scholarships for the blessed, neglected poor. The old profs will fall in line or leave. It might get rough at times, but if you go about this right, you'll come out on top. I can see the headline: ' Kershaw Profs Attack Reformer President.' David and Goliath stuff."

Hesitating for a long moment, loudly exhaling, Winner finally said, "It's a lot to think about."

"Yeah, think about it. But there are lots of other easy things you can do to start building up the momentum for the real big changes."

"Tell me more."

"I know this guy, a former client of mine, who tried to get Giles interested in a really good idea, but got no place. Giles seemed to listen, but was out to lunch, as usual. This guy wants Kershaw to set up a kind of public forum or roundtable for discussing big issues of our time—something that could draw national TV interest and put Kershaw on the map as a place where important people get together for big-think stuff. The kind of thing public television might run. Maybe get coverage on the networks and in the papers when someone important says something that makes news. You know what I mean."

"Someone was in to see me with an idea like that—maybe the same guy. Dollard?"

"That's the one. He was a client of mine for a long time. Now retired, with lots of dough, and he wants to get out there and look important. These talkathons are usually a lot of bull, but people go for them. His idea could be very useful for Kershaw, and best of all, he'll put up all the money."

"You think there's something to it?" Winner asked, remembering his brief discussion with Martin Dollard.

"There's a lot to be said for it. You see, here's another place where you get the papers and TV working for you. When they see politicians, best-selling authors, ex-prime ministers from here and there, Nobel Prize winners, and all kinds of ce-lebrities showing up at Kershaw to yak about the great issues, they'll start paying attention. These things feed on themselves. The famous people show up because the famous people show up—the old story. And then the press and the blogs start arguing back and forth about what they said, and it all traces back to the famous Kershaw roundtable."

"Whew!" Winner exclaimed. "You're throwing a lot of stuff at me, and I wasn't expecting anything like this. Interesting stuff, I'll admit, but these things have to be approached carefully. I think you agree with that, don't you?"

"Dr. Winner," Grimes said with a trace of disparagement in his tone, "you can tiptoe around, looking busy but really doing nothing, or you can try to make something of this place. Think about it, but then do something. For starters, talk to this guy Dollard and see what he's aiming at. Setting up this roundtable would be an easy first step. And like I said, he'd pay for it. Meet with him and his wife. She's real charming, and if I remember right, she has some connection with Ker-shaw on some committee or other."

"Okay, I'll think about it."

"Good," Grimes said as the student guide arrived to perform her escort duty. At the door, he paused and turned around. "One more thing. You mentioned that there's a research project here that's secret and they won't tell you anything about it."

"That's what I'm told, but I really don't know."

"That sounds like it could be big trouble. You better find out what it's about. But better yet, get rid of it. It can't do you any good. Students are always looking for something to demonstrate about and close down the university. Secret and research, maybe Pentagon money—that's a bad combination that can really set them off in a big way. Student demonstrations make great visuals for the evening news. Get rid of it before it turns into a PR calamity for you. But be very careful about how you handle it. The military plays rough. If you piss them off, they'll say you're unpatriotic, that you don't care for the young Americans who are in harm's way. And that can bring real trouble. Believe me," Grimes said emphatically as he left.

CHAPTER   XV

The love-nest plan that sprouted in Helen Dollard's fertile mind proved difficult to implement. She faced a timing predicament: Should she first progress in a relationship with Collie, or should she first secure a clandestine meeting place? They had merely chatted; a tangible relationship scarcely existed. For a practical reason, the sequence was important. Money would be required to rent an apartment. Helen did not work and had no income. While doting on his youthful wife, and unstinting in satisfying all her material wants, Martin Dollard controlled the family money—tightly. He amiably supplied her with unlimited pocket money, but this never amounted to much—a few dollars for taxi fares, lunch with a girlfriend, small purchases and so forth. In the desk in his study, Martin kept a pile of cash for her convenience, to be taken as needed. Petty cash, he called it, not worth accounting for. For larger expenditures, he provided her with credit cards and checks. Martin routinely paid the credit-card charges she incurred and replenished the checking account. Regularly scrutinizing the canceled checks and credit-card bills, he occasionally inquired about an item, but only, he insistently explained, to guard against accounting errors, fraudulent alterations of checks and erroneous credit-card billings. "A lot of thieving and simple mistakes can easily happen," Martin said. Resentful of what she regarded as his snooping, Helen repeatedly told him not to bother with these tedious clerical chores, pointing out that he had never yet found a discrepancy. "Let the accountant do it."

"He's for the big stuff. He wouldn't bother with this. Not important enough."

"Then why do you bother with it?" Helen asked, exasperated that she couldn't make a move without providing Martin with a documented financial trail.

Martin explained that he was governed by discipline developed long ago in the financially precarious startup of his successful business career. "Just an old habit that keeps me feeling good," he cheerfully assured Helen. Helen thus found herself in a paradoxical position regarding money: She had all she desired. Martin never objected to her purchases or expenditures. In fact, he was lavish with approval for any addition to her capacious clothes closets, as well as for all other acquisitions. But Martin's generous money-dispensing system, for which she had no alternative, deprived her of financial privacy. Martin knew how much cash she was taking and had an exact record of all her major spending.

Helen had studied the real estate ads in quest of a suitable apartment—nicely furnished, neither minimal nor grand, cozy, romantic— and had made a few telephone inquiries. Fearing detection, she was careful, calling from a pay phone, leaving no electronic billing trail. She clearly remembered the time when Martin, punching keys on a new hand-held computer device, chuckled and gasped about the wonders of the information age, leaving her wondering whether he was sending her a warning: "Look at this," he semi-shouted, reading a web site that specialized in reporting new gadgetry. "Now they got this thing the size of a dime that you hang on your dog's collar or put on a kid's clothes that tells you *exactly* where they are at any time, down to the inch. Amazing," he gleefully exclaimed. "There's no place to hide anymore." Silence for moment, and then, "Hey, maybe we should get some of those things."

Helen looked up from a magazine. "You worried about getting lost?"

"No. Just for laughs. Maybe play tricks on some friends."

The monthly apartment rental would be at least $2,000 plus a security deposit of one month's rent. Far too much to stash away unobtrusively from her pocket money, and obviously she could not cover the costs with a check or credit card. From what Martin had told her about Collie's professional situation, she concluded that Collie could comfortably provide the needed amounts, thus leaving no financial footprints that Martin could trace. But, then, she reminded herself, she knew nothing about Collie's personal circumstances. And she could not be certain that his thoughts were in harmony with hers, though the vibes she felt during their chance encounter gave her confidence that they were. But then she cautioned herself: Maybe he's living with someone, or getting married next week. She didn't know, and saw no way to find out. She dismissed that thought, telling herself, no, he's available. Then she wondered, maybe he's gay or weird in some way. But that notion instantly dissipated. Of course, he's neither, she decided. From his looks and manner, she could tell.

Helen plotted a two-step procedure. First, she would locate an apartment but would refrain from making a move to rent it. Then she would get together with Collie on some pretext or other for coffee or a drink in a café or a bar. Nothing unusual or risky about that. And then when the voltage kicked in between them, she would suggest that it would be great to have a place where they could enjoy privacy. She'd regretfully explain her domestic-financial circumstances. Collie would have to sign up for the apartment and attend to the money part. Surely he'd lovingly agree. And then they'd be all set, she dreamily told herself. Martin was accustomed to her going to museums, discussions and matinees. Good things to do, he heartily agreed. "I wish I could come along." But his concerns about societal impact left him no time for cultural enrichment, or much of anything else. A schedule crowded with attendance at seminars and lectures, plus piles of books and journals in his study, with overflow on his night table, were a testimonial to Martin's daunting workload. As he packed his briefcase for a full day dedicated to societal impacts, Helen looked up from her breakfast newspaper and remarked, as casually as she could: "Martin, I feel so bad about cutting the evening short for that nice person, Collie something, I think it was, the one we dragooned into taking Ginny home that night when she got sick. She can be so difficult. I hope she was nice to him. We really ought to do something to make it up to him. He was so sweet."

"Ah, here's my *Economist*," Martin said, pulling the magazine from his briefcase. "Been looking everywhere for that. Oh, you said something about Collie. Very nice young man. We should have him over or something. Yes. I had an extremely good discussion with him."

CHAPTER XVI

During the first few months of his presidency, Mark Winner refrained from policy changes or attempts to accomplish anything tangible. The Grimes agenda was appealing, but as he reflected on it, as he often did, he chose to remain poised and watchful rather than risk a stumble. The dramatic initiatives suggested by Grimes could be taken later. Looking back with satisfaction on a career safely guided by cautionary principles, Winner felt confident that he had so far proceeded wisely. But always the realist, he recognized that his grace period was ending. The time to move was at hand—but carefully, slowly, he frequently reminded himself. The campus community, Winner learned during his long career at Kershaw, was inherently querulous, sanctimonious, uncompromising, combative, on alert for slights, and untiringly wary of change. During the interregnum between his appointment and inauguration, and now in the president's chair, he developed a deeper, finer understanding of its pathological bent. Many, maybe most, inhabitants of the Kershaw community started from a position of distrust and dissatisfaction with the administration, irrespective of its actions or inactions or the matters at hand. Efforts to mollify the community inevitably spawned suspicion and accusations of concealed, malign motives. At its most quiescent, the Kershaw community was inclined to carp and quibble. Professors and their families, students, and administrative staff easily embraced defamatory allegations, no matter how improbable, credulously accepting that there must be something there. Tales of brazen plagiarism, scientific fraud, financial malfeasance, and nepotism were the stuff of daily campus conversation. Many favored maintenance of the status quo, not because they were satisfied with it, but because they distrusted change, any change. Others, stockpiling fanciful and authentic grievances, expected the new president to do something, especially after the prolonged inactivity of his predecessor. But no consensus existed on what ought to be done, and whatever might be done was bound to spawn new grievances and resistance in one quarter or another. The community was incapable of emotional equilibrium. Overwork was a common complaint, but professors, administrative staff, and students found ample time for grousing, arguing, scheming, and, occasionally, mobilizing for public demonstrations.

Once, after a sustained bout of discord, a peaceable group of professors and administrators issued a collective, poignant appeal for civility, cooperation, and collegial behavior: "We are members of an institution that has historically valued and benefited from decision-making based on reason, evidence, good will, and trust. Let us, from hereon, go forward in a spirit of cooperation, cordiality and dedication to the common good." On many blogs, the message was attacked as a cunning diversionary tactic, and was quickly forgotten as controversies continued to roar.

Over many years, the grading system for undergraduates had deteriorated to merely a record of class attendance as the criterion for successfully completing a course. The student body generally opposed any change, while many professors and some of the better students demanded higher standards. A major row was set off by the claim that strict grading would elevate Kershaw in the *U.S. News & World Report* rankings, with attendant gains in high-quality students, eminent professors, government grants, and other indicators of elite status. "We'll not be driven by a crummy magazine's sales gimmicks," a popular, inflammatory professor told a gymnasium packed with wildly cheering, foot-stamping students. Virtually all students opposed tuition increases, but were stridently in favor of smaller classes, expanded financial aid, renovating old dormitories, building new ones, and modernizing student sports facilities, along with expansion of the food court and more video games in the student center. How to finance these improvements was not their concern. The vegetarian and vegan offerings in the student cafeterias were denounced as insultingly insufficient in variety, freshness, quantity, and nutritional quality. The food manager, earnestly aiming to please, hired food consultants, and, meticulously following their advice, greatly improved the menu, to no avail. The complaints continued, while vegetarian and vegan sales remained the lowest, and wastage the highest, in the entire food service.

The senior faculty sought, as always, a reduction in teaching requirements accompanied by higher pay. How was this to be financed? Not our problem, the professors said, but if it had to be done by raising tuition or dipping into the endowment, they agreed, so be it. The administrative and clerical staffs sought more respect, higher salaries, and benefits on a par with the academic staff, including the university's traditionally long Christmas and Easter holidays, and summers off. As a conciliatory gesture, they refrained from demanding sabbaticals with pay, though they asserted that they deserved them, too. Portions of Kershaw's various sectors were united in favor of or in opposition to fighting climate change, boycotting third-world sweatshops, and opening the university swimming pool to impoverished children in the neighborhood. Strong support was vigorously expressed for more parking space and a reduction in parking fees. Bicyclists and skate boarders, however, opposed both proposals, as did many environmentalists.

On all these issues, the new president remained watchful, and silent.

Reports supposedly emanating from Winner's numerous exploratory discussions with campus figures filled the blogosphere and e-mail traffic with rumors, speculations, and calls to arms for or against whatever the blogger deemed worthy or deplorable in what the president was said to be thinking, doing, or not doing. An editorial in *Haywire*, the campus newspaper, asked whether Winner was a "reincarnation of the dead President Giles, who was famous for being here, but nothing else?" The editorial warned that "the honeymoon is over, Dr. Winner. It's time to get up and out and do something for this school." The things to be done were not specified. Belatedly curious about the basis for Winner's appointment to the presidency, the paper sought to interview members of the board of trustees. Repeated requests were not even acknowledged. Frustrated, *Haywire* demanded in print: "Did the board or any of its members meet with him before he was selected? What was the reason for choosing him?" *Haywire* reported rumors that in a "remarkably undistinguished field," Winner was the last surviving candidate at the trustees' hurriedly called presidential-selection meeting. Silence from the trustees filled the blogs with suspicions and sordid speculations.

Fearful that the sniping and expressions of disappointment might prod Winner into unpredictable, possibly dangerous activity, rodent meister Elias Fenster, president of the Faculty Senate, sought to exploit what he perceived to be the president's wobbly position. By publicly praising Winner, offering him a hand of friendship in difficult times, the president would be grateful and indebted for his support, Fenster reasoned, and not likely to poke into his precariously based scientific reputation. In a sparsely attended meeting of the Senate, where Fenster was re-elected without opposition, he congratulated Winner for "maintaining uninterrupted continuity with the successful policies established and nurtured by the late President Giles, the recognized builder of the modern Kershaw. We should all be grateful for President Winner's leadership." Fenster then pushed through a resolution listing faculty demands, including "additional teaching assistants so as to enable senior faculty to devote more time to research," "an expansion of travel funds for senior faculty," "modernization of office facilities for senior faculty," and "a suitable (i.e. increased) budget for refreshments at scholarly gatherings on campus." Explaining this last item, Fenster observed, "When visiting academicians of international renown attend functions at Kershaw, it is regrettable that our entertainment is financially constrained and limited to crackers and cheese and soft drinks." Fenster asserted that "These improvements are necessary for maintaining Kershaw's position in the increasingly competitive global market for outstanding scholars in all fields. Absent these changes," he predicted, "the high standing that Kershaw enjoyed in the academic world at the time of President Giles' tragic death will be seriously and irreparably compromised. Fortunately," Fenster concluded, "President Winner, by following in the footsteps of his predecessor, is showing early signs of the statesmanship we all hoped for and expected." *Haywire* published Fenster's declaration, describing it as "deserving serious consideration, though it is not necessarily the right prescription in all respects for improving conditions at Kershaw and maintaining this institution's high reputation."

In accordance with university custom, Winner did not attend Faculty Senate meetings, but he cordially responded to the resolution with a public statement thanking the Senate for its expression of confidence and assuring the faculty that he would sympathetically review its recommendations.

❧

Guided by his instincts for self-preservation, Winner decided it was time to make presidential moves, locking his attention on two of the safer initiatives proposed by Bentley Grimes. First, he would look into proceeding with Martin Dollard's proposed roundtable; second, he would seek information about the secret project in Brusolowitz's laboratory, with the aim of expelling it from the campus or, if it was acceptable by Kershaw standards, bringing it into the open. The large tuition increase advocated by Grimes struck him as too radical and chancy. From among Grimes' many recommendations Winner's two favored choices were dictated by practicality and experience, his trusted lode star for career navigation. The roundtable was attractive because it was cost-free, appeared easy to implement, and could bring visibility and prestige to Kershaw. As Grimes had explained, it would strengthen Winner for undertaking further initiatives. Winner knew that faculty members would angrily demand the redirection of Dollard's philanthropic money to the direct benefit of the faculty, such as the increase in entertainment funds sought by Fenster. Winner resolved that he would point out that Dollard's offer of funding was exclusively for the roundtable. We take it on Dollard's terms or lose it, he would explain, terms understandable to even the most obtuse faculty member. For a sweetener, he decided, he would tell faculty members that they would be eligible to take part in the roundtable, depending on the relevance of their scholarly field to the subjects under discussion. But, he would make clear, participation would ultimately be at the discretion of the roundtable director, whom he would appoint. Without that provision, Winner knew, faculty members would claim roundtable participation as a right. For enforcing claimed rights, their armory was stocked with a variety of weapons, and there was no limit to the strife that could ensue. As for Brusolowitz and the secret project, Winner worriedly remembered Grimes' warning that if it became known, it could ignite a student shutdown of the university. It could be a ticking bomb, Winner feared, a menace to be eliminated before it blew up, taking his fledgling presidency with it.

As usual, Winner did not confide his thoughts or intentions to the senior administrative staff that surrounded him in Monument Hall. All of these officials—including the general counsel and the chief financial officer—were holdovers from the Giles regime. Winner trusted none of them, correctly sensing that because of his unconventional route to the top, they regarded him as a usurper, an illegitimate occupant of the throne. The Giles presidency, with its predictable inactivity, suited them, whereas they didn't know what the future held under the Winner regime. For the present, a polite, but cold peace prevailed between the president and the next level down in the university hierarchy.

Winner's first step for carrying out his plans was a call to a delighted Martin Dollard. "Mark Winner here, Mr. Dollard. Last time we got together, we talked briefly about a couple of things that I'd like to discuss further with you. Maybe we can have a dinner meeting, and you bring your wife along. I understand she has some connection with the university."

❧

"What's it about?" Helen cautiously inquired as Martin euphorically regaled her with news of the invitation. Overjoyed, he rhythmically hopped about the room.

"I'll tell you his exact words, but the bottom line is it's good news. Good news," Martin repeated with emphasis and a broad smile. "He said he wants to discuss some of the things I brought up with him at our first meeting. Now, let's recall my initial conversation with President Winner," Martin said, unassailable as the impresario of the moment. "As I told you at the time, I brought up the roundtable, and we talked about it, but not exclusively, though it was obviously a matter of interest to him. He had some other matters, of a financial nature, on his mind, and we delved into those, to some extent. Now, without any doubt, it seems—."

"Oh, for god's sake," Helen burst out, "I can tell he didn't say what the hell he wants to talk about. And why does he want me to tag along? You didn't say anything about the arts committee, you told me. So, what's this all about?"

"I told you we're making progress. Now we're really moving along. It's entirely possible that he wants you in on the conversation so that he can discuss the arts committee. Your membership on the committee has probably come to his attention. We can't ignore that possibility, though, to be perfectly frank, the matter did not come up directly in our initial discussion. But that does not preclude the possibility, the likelihood of discussion at a future date."

"I got that the first time," Helen sullenly reminded him. But she was also thinking of the social doors that would swing open to them if the roundtable came to reality, with Martin as its maestro and Helen as the stylish hostess for its A-list discussants, aspiring participants, and celebrity chasers.

☙

Good luck and a combination of academic and street-level savoir-faire had enabled Winner to survive on the sinuous route to the top at Kershaw. But, as many could not fail to observe, he lacked social polish, a deficiency rendered even more conspicuous by his indifference to the expected graces of his elite occupational position. He was conversationally withdrawn, except when discussing topics of interest to him. Courteous patter—e.g., "so good to see you"— never delayed his direct approach to his main point. He was intolerant of slow wits and disagreement, impatiently expecting his words to be understood and accepted at first hearing. He was not averse to interrupting and shutting down irrelevant discourse. And, as Martin had unhappily observed at their prior meeting, Winner dressed poorly for a person of lofty status. A very odd choice for the presidency, many concluded upon meeting him.

A mystified Helen silently shared that assessment as she and Martin sat across from Winner at the long and broad table in the baronial dining room of the presidential residence, a spacious structure on a quiet patch of the otherwise bustling campus. The dining room and several adjacent great rooms in the building were intended for official entertaining, but up to this time, none of them had been utilized by President Winner. His invitation to the Dollards was, in fact, the first for anyone to dine with him since his inauguration. Nor had he yet accepted any of numerous invitations to dine out. "Tell them I'm too busy," he instructed his secretary. In his first few months in the presidency, he oscillated between his office and his official residence. The chef available to the university president was on call from his regular position in the faculty-club kitchen. At the outset of the Winner administration, the chef had attempted to meet with the new president, but receiving no response, sent a note to the presidential office saying he was available for preparation of meals, day and night for large and small groups. Winner told his secretary, "Tell him thanks and he'll be called when needed." But so far, Winner had not called.

As during his professorial days at Kershaw, when he lived alone in a small apartment near the campus, Winner remained a frequent patron of home-delivered Chinese restaurant meals, occasionally alternating with carry-out Mexican fare and pizza. Sometimes he microwaved a package of lasagna from a stash in the freezer. For his dinner with the Dollards, several white cardboard, wire-handled containers, each imprinted with a red pagoda, were arrayed on the dining table, along with porcelain dinnerware bearing the university seal. "Chinese. Help yourself and we can get down to business while we eat. Chopsticks, if you want them, and there's plenty of rice," Winner said, as Helen, incredulous, tried not to gape in astonishment. Her preparations for this occasion included, after deliberation at several speciality shops, the purchase of a conservatively tailored, grey pin-striped pants suit—"very university looking," the saleslady assured her when she mentioned dinner with the president of Kershaw University. Helen had put in the requisite time for hairdressing, facial treatment, makeup, and nails. Though anxiously hoping for the arts committee to come up during the meeting, Collie and the apartment dilemma were preeminent in her thoughts, no matter how much she tried to concentrate on other matters. Nonetheless, for the evening at the presidential residence, she felt at ease, composed, and therefore took only half the prescribed daily dose of her mood-settling meds. Having cut off her visits to Dr. Berlin-Gottchalk, she wondered about the medical advisability of this pharmaceutical reduction. But no time to worry. She felt fine. Now, while making sure to maintain a smile, Helen inwardly winced at Winner's attire: an ill-fitting gray suit, a matching gray necktie, and a pale green shirt, apparently with short sleeves, as cuffs were not visible. Later in the evening, she glimpsed that he wore athletic shoes. Her irritations and annoyances with Martin were countless, but along with his bountiful open purse, she credited him for excellence in dress.

Addressing Martin, Winner said, "Last time we spoke, you brought up your idea for a discussion group that we could run here. Roundtable, you called it. Now, I need more information. And once we've done that, there's something else I want to discuss. I'm sure we can keep it short."

"Easily done. I realize that you've got tremendous responsibilities," Martin briskly responded. "I can clearly extrapolate from my own former business experience that running an enterprise of this scale and complexity requires a grasp of detail and degree of concentration that—." Recognizing that Martin was gunning his conversational engine in preparation for releasing the brake, Helen cut him off with a request "to pass that one over there, Martin, I think it's orange chicken. And then President Winner can continue."

"Yeah, help yourself, whatever it is," Winner said, quickly adding, with a nod toward Martin, "Let's get directly to the topic I want to discuss first. You have a plan for setting up a discussion group here—the roundtable. Tell me, *briefly*, how it would work, what it would cost, where's the money coming from and how soon can it get going. Understand, at this point I'm not saying we want to do it. In that order. Keep it short."

"Martin can boil it down, Dr. Winner," Helen interjected. "I've heard him tell the whole story practically in seconds. Right, Martin?"

"No problem. Absolutely no problem," Martin said. "You see, I've observed, and I'm sure you and many others have too, that much of the discussion of public affairs tends to be circumferential, by which I mean that it repeatedly comes back to certain basics, fundamentals, you might call them." As Martin spoke, Winner sat tapping the fingers of one hand on the table, with an accelerating tempo. "The roundtable stems directly from my concern about societal impacts, which I hope we can discuss at a later time. But, sticking to the topic at hand, the roundtable concept is aimed at getting to the basics through a process of open and direct discussion by principal figures. What the public will recognize as important people. And we can expect, with some considerable confidence, that the news media will recognize the significance of these discussions and amplify them. Now what are benefits that we can anticipate?" Martin asked. But before he could begin to answer his own question, Winner held up a hand in a stop-sign motion.

"Okay," Winner said, "Just tell me yes or no if I've got it right. Kershaw invites in different, supposedly important people to discuss a subject at the round-table. And we make this open to the public and the press. And maybe it gets on TV, live or taped, or the newspapers report something that was said, maybe by a Senator or someone from a foreign government. And this spotlights the subject and by the way brings the university some good measure of public attention, recognition. Now, basically, just tell me, yes or no, is that about right?"

"Yes, that's fundamentally the essence of it, I will say that, though we'd have to be selective in picking the topics and the people—."

"Okay, I got it. Something like Meet the Press, but with its own special twists. Right?"

"To some extent," Martin began, "but in our case—."

Again, Winner cut him off. "Yeah, I understand. Now, how much is this going to cost and where's it coming from? As you know, we're a little short these days, and with the professors always squealing for raises, I don't have any loose change for extras like this. Do I understand correctly that you're going to pay for the whole thing?"

"I've made some detailed cost studies in consultation with various people concerned with similar activities," Martin began, "and I think the return on expenditure will be extremely beneficial—."

"Look," Winner interrupted, "how much and who pays? That's all I need to know for now. Got it?"

The rising irritation in Winner's voice propelled Helen into the conversation. "I've heard Martin say a million and a half for the first year, give or take 10 percent. Martin will provide the full amount as a donation to Kershaw."

"Good on all counts," Winner said. "We've got a sound stage here that we can use, and the TV and audio can be handled by the journalism department. I assume you'll need to hire a moderator or host, like they have on these shows, and some staff people to line up participants, and maybe some people for research. And odds and ends for various other things. And that's all in the million-five. Right?"

"Approximately," Martin said. "I've costed this out with several people who are familiar with such activities and we're in the ballpark, more or less. I might add that I contemplated a role for myself as moderator, but—."

"We can get to that when the time comes. Good. You've done a good job," Winner said, hoping a dab of praise might quell Martin's feverish loquacity. "So, we've had enough on that. To help me think it over, maybe you can draw up a short memo giving the numbers and the operational details. Okay? If it comes out yes, I maybe want to move fast on this. But understand, there's no commitment at this point."

"I can get the memo to you in very short order," Martin replied. "But what I'd like to point out—."

"There's nothing that needs pointing out," Winner declared with finality. "What I want to do now is get to a second topic. This is kind of sensitive, so we'll just keep it among ourselves. Okay?"

"No difficulty whatsoever," Martin said as Helen nodded her agreement.

"Okay," Winner said, pointing at Martin. "Your volunteer work with the endowment advisory committee gives you a pretty thorough view of all the money coming in and going out of Kershaw. Right?"

"In conjunction with looking into the management of the endowment, I've had an opportunity to look into the university's various revenue streams and expenditures. There's a great diversity, ranging from—."

"Yeah," Winner said, again cutting him off. "Do you get into our research accounts? How much we're getting in research funding?"

"Ah, yes," Martin replied. "That's very important in the overall picture, so I've—."

"Good," Winner said. "There's a research project here that may or may not be off the books, may or may not be kosher. My worry is that it could turn into a big problem for us. You know how people here feel about secret stuff going on. Maybe the Pentagon's involved. I don't know. The project, whatever it is, got some special approval while Giles was here, and now it's hard to find out what they're doing. They're not talking. I've got no one I feel comfortable with to check this out. I suppose I could take a look myself, but that might create a big fuss. Besides, one laboratory looks like any other to me. But if they're doing work here on campus something should show up in the financial accounts for research. I'm thinking, too, that if they're doing anything that has commercial value, there might be some patent rights that we should know about. That's what——."

"No problem," Martin broke in. "I'm sure, with a proper——."

"Let me finish. Wherever the money comes from, maybe they wrote down something about the goal of the project. So, I need someone to check the books. Second, I really want to be careful and make sure we know what we're dealing with. So, it would be a good idea to get someone to visit the lab for a look-see. It's run by a hotshot professor, Brusolowitz—they call him Brucie. Maybe he'll explain what it's all about and save us a lot of time and worry. Famous guy, and pretty sure of himself. Too busy to see me, if you can believe that. You're not a science man, Mr. Dollard, not that I know of, right?"

"I can't claim any competence in science, in a conventional professional sense, but I have had many opportunities to discuss some of the problematics arising from the impact of science on society. And I'm certain that either directly or indirectly, I can provide you with assistance——."

"Okay, okay. You can check the books. But I figure we've got to get somebody into the lab who understands this stuff. It's got to be low key and look normal, routine. Call it a survey for the new president. I don't care what. Anything, just to make it seem normal, ordinary, to get in there and take a look around without alarming anyone there, maybe talk to this Brusolowitz. We need somebody who's got some smarts about science and who we can trust. Most important of all, someone from outside the university, because you never know what connections someone inside might have. As I said," Winner emphasized, "this is very sensitive stuff, and we don't want to stir things up. Got it?"

"I completely understand. And I feel certain that through my extensive networks, a suitable person can be found for this task. You can be confident——." As Winner motioned Martin to be quiet, Helen experienced a rising interest in the confidential mission to the mysterious lab. "Can you maybe tell us a little bit more about the project," she said with a winsome touch of timidity. "Martin knows so many, many people that I'm sure he can find the right person. But it might be helpful to have some additional details."

"I've told you pretty much all I know. It's a dicey thing. The feds aren't supposed to run secret projects in university labs, unless the university signs on that it's okay. Even then, it's considered a no-no because it's hard to get security clearances for foreign students and if it's classified, you can't publish, and you've got to keep things locked up. Lot of problems, but somehow this one got in and going while Giles was here. I haven't been able to find out what it's about, and, like I said, they're not rushing to tell me. So I'd like a little scouting to be performed before I decide on the next step. If you can find me someone who can do a bit of snooping for me, that would be helpful. But it's got to be all very quiet."

"I understand completely," Martin said. "I have a circle of colleagues in the sciences outside of Kershaw from my activities related to societal impact—."

"Yeah, I got it." Winner assured him. "Like I said, you check the books to see what's there. And try to find someone who can drop into that lab. Tell him to call my office for an appointment so I can tell him what we need to find out. Just tell him to say that he's calling at Mr. Dollard's suggestion. I'll see to it that my secretary knows what it's about. Well, good to see you and to talk over some of these things. Don't forget your fortune cookies."

∽

Martin and Helen were just out the door, heading for the main avenue bordering the university to hail a taxi, when Helen suddenly stopped. "Goddammit," she exclaimed, slapping her forehead and stamping her foot, "nothing about the arts committee. Why the hell didn't you say something?" she screeched at Martin.

"We'll have other opportunities," he quickly responded, positioning himself to stifle a storm. "The agenda didn't allow for us bringing up items that were not directly germane to his—."

"Oh, crap," she said, "what am I going to do now? Here was the chance and we blew it. You blew it," she corrected herself. "You're the one he wanted to see and the two of you did all the talking."

"What we have to do without delay," Martin said, "is prepare a very convincing memo for Dr. Winner concerning the roundtable. The case for going ahead is so good that I can't imagine—."

"Yeah, you do that, but keep it under 500 pages. He's a busy man."

"And I'll have to work through the endowment office to see what I can find out about that research business he's interested in."

The two resumed their way down the street, Martin bouncing along, animated by the meeting, Helen slumping, falling behind, disconsolate. "No need for concern," Martin assured her. "I'll concentrate the information about the roundtable in a very readable form. Concise. I can see that's the way he wants it, and it's my style, too. I may even have to leave out some points, but if that's necessary, it will have to be done. Nothing will be accomplished by going overboard with fine details that can be filled in later. Like they say, less is more."

While inwardly seething, Helen saw an opportunity for bringing up the idea that germinated in her mind as Winner spoke of his need for a scientific scout.

"What about that laboratory stuff he wants someone to look into?" she casually inquired. "I mean it would be a good thing to help him out, but I just wonder if we know anyone who can do that."

"Please," Martin exclaimed. "As usual, it's always too many things coming at the worst possible time. On top of the roundtable memo and checking out the financial records, there's finding someone who can go to that laboratory. That item will have to be priority number three. He brought it up last. The roundtable comes first."

"You know," Helen said nonchalantly, though her heart was thumping wildly, "what occurs to me is that that nice Collie that we were talking about the other day—he might fit the situation. I remember you telling me that he's a scientist of some kind. I didn't get to talk to him very much. Didn't Dr. Winner say he wants a scientist to do it?"

"Yes, yes, he did." Martin exclaimed, genuinely taken with the suggestion, relieved to get away from the topic of the arts committee, and delighted by the opportunity for a response that might soothe Helen. Coming to a halt on the street and facing her, he effusively said, "That's very good thinking. As you know, I had a long talk with Collie the evening we had him over and he showed an impressive grasp of the sciences. I was quite taken with his broad knowledge across many fields. That's an excellent idea. But as this is a confidential matter, I wouldn't do this by phone. Better to meet with him and explain the situation as Dr. Winner explained it to us."

" You call him and see if he can do it," Helen cagily suggested.

"Hey, there's a taxi," Martin said, bolting into the street, and wildly waving his arms, setting off a screeching of tires and frantic horn blowing as he gyrated between cars. Martin prided himself on his taxi-snaring skills. Helen caught up as the taxi braked alongside him. Martin declared their destination. "About getting someone to look into that lab for President Winner," Helen said, knowing that if she didn't reintroduce the subject Martin would automatically revert to the topic of the roundtable. "Do you think Collie would be the right person?"

"Difficult to say with any certainty, but very much worth trying," Martin said. "He might be just the right person to do it. I'm going to be tied up with this memo for Dr. Winner. Got to get everything essential into it, and keep it to a reasonable length. Could you call Collie? Let's give it a try. If he can't do it, I'll find someone else. But not just now."

"I barely know him," Helen said. She had not mentioned their chance encounter near the Kershaw bookstore. Since there had been no reverberations from that meeting, she felt certain that it had gone unobserved by anyone who might tell Martin about it. Rehearsing all contingencies, however, she decided that if Martin somehow heard of their meeting and brought it up, she would simply say they had bumped into each other and had a quick cup of coffee and it had slipped her mind. In a low-key manner, appropriate for something inconsequential or slightly burdensome, she agreed to call Collie. "Sure, if you want me to. I can call him, maybe for a lunch." For additional insurance, she added, "But only if you promise to join us."

CHAPTER XVII

Lunch in a busy, brightly lit restaurant, unabashedly in the open. That would be the best cover, Helen decided. Any acquaintance who chanced upon them could only conclude that the comely Mrs. Dollard and her attractive male companion had nothing to hide, which would not be the conclusion if they were spotted in a dark corner of an out-of-the-way restaurant. As an alternative, she had considered meeting in Collie's office, but never having been there, she didn't know whether the layout would be suitable for a sensitive conversation. A restaurant was clearly the best choice. For an extra measure of safety, Helen would again urge Martin to join them, fulsomely offering to arrange the date to accommodate his overburdened schedule. Martin knew so much about science, and she knew so little, she would plead, that his presence was absolutely indispensable. There was some risk in this tactic. Receptive to flattery about his extensive intellectual interests, and never averse to regarding himself as indispensable, Martin might accept—though with loud dismay about his burdens. But Helen figured that in this instance he would decline. Martin was busy preparing the crucial memo for Winner. If he could avoid any task not directly linked to the roundtable he would grasp the opportunity. He would do so regretfully and wordily. Nonetheless, he would decline any diversion from his pressing task. But, if by remote chance, Martin agreed to come along, then Helen would have to contrive another meeting with Collie so she could delicately initiate the next phase of their relationship.

❧

Helen's carefully composed, rehearsed telephone call to Collie's office proceeded smoothly and successfully. Would he join her and Martin for lunch? Yes, he'd very much like to. A few days later, Helen and Collie rendezvoused in the same crowded, popular restaurant where Collie had first told Lou about the Brusolowitz project. "Sorry, at the last moment, Martin couldn't make it, and sends his apologies," Helen explained. Collie politely expressed hope that he might get together with Martin at another time. Helen seconded that hope, while searching Collie's face and parsing his words for clues about his thoughts. He naturally radiated an uncomplicated ease, an absence of guile. He felt comfortable and pleased, happy to meet again with Helen. Faded away, or at least not pressing on his mind, were concerns that difficulties might ensue. Collie retained his reservations about married women, especially one married to an old friend of his boss and mentor. But, from his earlier calculations of the pluses, minuses, and risks, he remained confident that an expanded relationship with Helen would be possible, pleasurable, and harmless. They would just be friends, no more than that, he told himself.

They inaugurated their lunch meeting with amiable chatter. "Yes, I like this place very much. Good choice," Collie said as they were led to a table in the main dining area, as she had requested in making the reservation. Good, Helen thought to herself, noting that some tables were tucked away in distant, dim corners. "My boss and sort of mentor, Lou Crowley, and I lunch here now and then," Collie told her.

"It is very nice, and so convenient," Helen said, as they scanned the menu and placed their orders.

"I better not forget," Collie said. "Lou sends regards to your husband. They know each other from way back, he says."

"I think Martin's mentioned that," Helen said. First some conversational trifles, as she expected, and then she could proceed to crucial matters.

Collie felt a warming glow as she smiled and chatted so near to him. "I like your earrings. Very unusual and attractive."

"Oh,"she said, touching one of the objects of admiration. "Jade. I got them long ago at a flea market in Paris."

"I've never been to Paris," he confessed.

"We—. I mean you should go," she replied.

Silence for a moment as the waiter set their orders before them.

Helen decided to take charge. "Couple of things that I hope we can talk about—that Martin and I wanted to talk about with you, but unfortunately he's tied up."

"Sure," Collie said, sensing they were now moving past superficial matters.

"Martin does some financial advising for Kershaw. And the new President, Dr. Winner, asked us over a little while ago to discuss several things. What came up was that he's concerned, maybe really worried, about some research program at the university, maybe involving the Pentagon—." Helen abruptly stopped talking as Collie winced and appeared to have difficulty swallowing.

"What's the matter? Are you all right?"

"Yeah, yeah, I'm okay. I was afraid something was going down the wrong pipe. Sorry. Just go ahead with what you were saying."

"Thank heaven," she said with relief. "I never got it straight about how you do a Heimlich."

"No, I'm okay. Sorry. You were saying something about a research project at Kershaw."

"I don't know if I really have this right," Helen said apologetically. "But Martin and I both thought it's something you might be able to help out with."

Collie did his best to feign polite attention in place of the searing interest and urgent questions welling up inside him. Now picking at his lunch, he listened intently as Helen provided a sketchy recollection of the conversation with Winner. "The project he's worried about was okayed by the old president, but Dr. Winner is worried—well, I don't understand all this, but it's what the project is really all about. The director of the laboratory—some funny Russian-sounding name—is keeping it secret and Winner says he hasn't been able to find out anything."

"That's okay, okay," Collie said, still trying to quell his astonishment at the unexpected reappearance of the Brucie conundrum. "So, how can I help?"

"Well, let me explain. It's sort of complicated. Martin has been talking to President Winner about a special project of his own. We talked about it a bit last time, when we ran into each other. A kind of discussion group Martin wants to sponsor. He calls it the roundtable. Maybe he told you about it."

Collie dryly acknowledged, "He said something about it."

Painfully familiar with Martin's marathon conversational style, Helen figured Collie's bare response signaled disdain. "Well," Helen continued, "Martin is encouraged, because the president does seem to be interested. But Winner is also interested in finding out about this research project that I mentioned. He told us it's very sensitive. I got the impression that he's really seriously concerned about it, like there's some awful problem there. Martin wants to be as cooperative and helpful to the president as he can be, because of the circumstances. Of course, doing a good turn for the president won't hurt Martin's plans for the roundtable and all that. I'm sure you understand how something like that might work. It's very important for him."

"Sure, if there's anything I can do." Collie said.

Encouraged, Helen continued. "Dr. Winner said he wants someone from outside to take a look at the research project. It's funny, but he's new there, and it's like he doesn't trust the people around him. That's the impression I got. He asked Martin to help him, but Martin honestly told him that he doesn't have a scientific background, though I think he's pretty well informed about science. But Martin is so tied up with his regular work. We thought about who might help out and we thought of you. Martin asked me to see if maybe you could. He says from his talk with you when you were at our place he feels that you have the scientific background. I surely don't," Helen said. "I'm sorry I'm not more clear about this, but science was not exactly my favorite subject back in college."

Collie remained silent for a moment, trying to recover from the sudden, unexpected opportunity. "Well," he said, with as much reserve as he could summon, "I could give it a try. No guarantee that I can—."

Helen sought to reinforce her case. "Maybe you could even find some investment opportunity in what's going on in that lab, whatever it is. I don't know how those things work, but who knows?" she said.

Collie felt a surge of excitement. After experiencing despair, he was overwhelmed by the unexpected opening of the door to Brucie's lab.

"There could be something there," he said as casually as possible.

"Probably wouldn't take up very much of your time. It's just that Winner needs some help. He said to call his office and tell them you're calling at the suggestion of Martin Dollard. They'll know what that's about and put you right through."

"Sure. I'd be happy to do what I can. Sounds interesting."

Helen was silent, uncertain whether the moment was right for switching to the more important topic on her agenda.

Collie resumed the conversation. "You mentioned college. Where did you go?"

"I was at Bryn Mawr." Hesitating for a moment, she confessed, "But actually I didn't finish." The unusual admission emerged spontaneously, surprising Helen. While plotting the deceptions she would have to employ in pursuit of a relationship with Collie, she instinctively felt she should be honest with him.

Collie was sympathetic. "I'm kind of a dropout, too. I told you about that lab I was in." She smiled and nodded, indicating recall of his hilarious story about the rat scientist's laboratory.

"It's so hard to talk in these places. So noisy," she said.

"I read someplace they do that deliberately, to make a buzz. People seem to like that in restaurants."

"Not me."

"Me neither," Collie agreed. Harmony was forming.

Suddenly, as they silently gazed at each other, Helen began speaking, without premeditation. "Have you ever done anything real crazy?"

Collie sensed a new chapter opening from their brief relationship. He looked down, but she continued to stare at him. "Real crazy?" he cautiously asked. "A couple of crazy things. But I don't think I should talk about some of them. You might get the wrong idea——."

"That's okay. I won't pry into your crazy secrets," Helen told him. "But let me tell you a crazy idea that I have."

And, as they finished their lunch, Helen concisely described her plan for acquiring their own secret, private meeting place. Their conversation stopped while the waiter cleared the table, and they remained silent, in thought about this momentous conversation, until after he returned with coffee. Amid their busy public surroundings, Collie strained to maintain an impassive expression while folding his hands together under the table to preclude reaching to touch Helen.

"Sure," he said, "that's a great idea."

"The money is no problem?"

"Absolutely not," Collie said. He was making it faster than he could spend it. His bank account was flush with money, even before Lou told him the New Year would bring a raise. "You just tell me what you need and we'll be just fine. And I can do the signing up for the place when we're ready. What a great idea."

"Not just great. It's a *fabulous* idea," Helen said, pressing a finger against her lips to signal conspiratorial silence. "But just one more thing. Something important. Where should I call you?"

Communication would be a problem, Collie realized. No calls to the office, where Lou might somehow learn of their connection. "Call me at home," he said, jotting down his number for her, "and if I'm not there, just leave a message."

"You can't call me back at home," she said, knowing that Martin irregularly rushed in and out of their apartment, leaving no predictably safe time for telephone contact. "Try my cell," she said, though she fretfully wondered whether Martin might have a means of checking on her calls in the same systematic way that he checked on her spending.

"Okay, cell phone," Collie agreed, as he glimpsed the logistical complexities that lay ahead in his relationship with Helen Dollard.

༠༽

Collie detested withholding anything from Lou. Nevertheless, he told Lou only half the story of his meeting with Helen. Following Helen's suggestion, he explained to Lou, he had telephoned Winner's office and would soon meet with the Kershaw president. The hideaway plan with Helen was not mentioned.

"Meeting with the president—that's a great break," Lou said. "He ought to be able to get you in to see this Brucie guy. Or maybe tell you something we need to know. Hell, I'm really impressed."

Collie glowed under Lou's approval. "It's been frustrating," he told Lou, but now he was hopeful that, at last, they could get reliable information about the anti-sleep research. If it looks good, Lou declared, they should move quickly and boldly to try to acquire a financial stake. "We're in a position to dump in a lot of cash," Lou assured him. In an added boost for Collie's confidence, Lou said, " I'm relying on you. You're custom-made for this one, professor." Then, in a tone laden with innuendo, accompanied by rolling eyes and a furrowed brow, Lou added, "That Helen Dollard, like I said, she's really something. Isn't she? You never know what she's up to."

Collie felt offended by Lou's vague but slighting words about Helen, but he kept his pleasant demeanor. "Nothing to worry about, Lou. She was just trying to help out her husband and figured I could do something. Lucky for us, huh?"

&

Winner lived constantly with Bentley Grimes' ominous warning about the menace he faced from the secret project on the Kershaw campus. His deepening knowledge of the collective Kershaw psyche told him that the project could ignite passions and paranoia that could abruptly topple his presidency. Pro and con factions would mobilize. Defenders would rush to his side in support of whatever was going on in the closed-off lab. But they would be as difficult, dangerous, and unpredictable as those who took an opposite stance. For carrying out a scouting mission, Collie came recommended by the Dollards. But what did they know about him? Maybe nothing, the caution-bound president told himself. Winner felt isolated at the apex of the Kershaw hierarchy. Suspicious of the senior staff he inherited, he wanted his own appointees, but the recruits he sought for the presidential staff were interminably undergoing pre-hiring background checks by Human Resources. HR's director regularly emitted cautions about the unacceptable risks of haste. Grisly cases of poorly screened appointees bringing disrepute to their employers were graphically brought to Winner's attention. The HR director advised him to read the standard work in the recruiting field, "Human Resources Administration: Avoiding the Misfit," by John Stanley, often referred to as the dean of headhunters. "It will give you nightmares," he warned the impatient president.

Winner needed help, and there was Martin, assuring him that he could provide it. But Martin Dollard, he had quickly realized, was a fatuous windbag. Nonetheless, it seemed that Martin did get around and knew a lot of people in the scientific community. In his dependence on Winner's cooperation and good will for going ahead with the roundtable, Martin was obviously eager to please and wouldn't be pushing a dimwit. This Collie Marson might be just the guy for taking a look around the lab and reporting back to him.

"So, you did your postdoc here," Winner said as he and Collie settled down to talk. "Who'd you work with?"

"Professor Fenster. Elias Fenster, on his rodent research."

Winner immediately perked up. "Fenster. I met with him. President of the Faculty Senate. Interesting man. Good to work with?"

"Not bad. He's pretty demanding, and I think some of the postdocs in his lab have problems there."

"Like what?"

"It's been some time since I was there, so my experience is probably out of date." Collie realized that they were straying from his urgent goal in meeting with Winner—access to the elusive Brucie. But in his mixed sentiments about leaving a scientific career, resentment toward Fenster remained intact. Maybe he could get in a well-deserved, long overdue jab at the rodent meister.

"Some of us wondered about Fenster's research, his methods and the way some of the research was written up. But in any lab, there's usually a lot of griping, especially among the postdocs." Collie paused for moment, then added, "Still there were questions."

Collie wondered when Winner would ask him why he had dropped out of a research career, but Winner, though curious, sensed that might be a touchy matter and held back. Registering Collie as a fount of valuable information about the thorny president of the Faculty Senate, Winner figured he had gone far enough on that topic. He could get back to Fenster at another time. "Did you ever get to know this guy Brusolowitz—Brucie?"

"I've heard of him, of course. He's well known, but I never had any direct contact with him when I was here."

"I don't know how much the Dollards told you about my problem with this Brucie. It's a little sensitive for me, just starting here. So I need a little bit of—let's call it scouting. You know your way around the labs. The government is in the picture in some way with his research. But as I understand it, there are unusual restrictions on Brusolowitz's lab. You can't just barge in. My tech transfer VP— okay, he's not the brightest kid in the class—says he got no place with them."

"Give me some idea of what you want."

"Okay, but just between us and what I told the Dollards. I really don't give a damn what they're doing there in the lab. But you know how the kids on campus are these days. They don't like anything to do with the military, and they'd shut down the whole damn university in a minute if they found out that we've got secret military research here. I don't know what's there, but you've got to figure that there's something fishy or they wouldn't be so uptight about it. I'm amazed nothing has leaked out so far. But before I try to boot the project off the campus, I've got to know what the hell they're doing. I don't want to be crucified for inter- fering with national security or endangering the troops. You know, that 'harm's- way' crap. Once I know what's going on there, I can move or maybe not move. So I need someone to sniff it out for me—nice and quiet."

Pondering this unexpected convergence of interest in Brucie's lab, Collie re- alized that he knew more about the project than Winner did. Collie chose to be non-committal. "Yeah, I see. We'd have to figure out some way to get in there." He didn't tell Winner of his prior interest in Brucie's project.

"I want to know what the hell they're working on," Winner said emphatically.

Though surprised by the president's lack of information, Collie didn't say anything about the anti-sleep goal, but he leveled with Winner about his interest in the tech-transfer potential. "We've been able to make some good commercial connections for lab results here. Nothing great so far. But my firm is looking for tech transfer opportunities, and I'm hoping something might come out of Brucie's project. No way of knowing right now what's there and what might pan out. But never say never."

"Never say never," Winner agreed. "Like I said, I don't know what they're doing there, but if it has any commercial value, you'll get first crack at it. Patents belong to the university, I understand. I'm not against us all making money, preferably lots of it."

"It can be good for all of us," Collie said.

"Maybe there's nothing going on that we'll care about, for all we know," Winner added. "But you figure out an approach and if you need anything from me, let me know. But we're agreed, right, that this is all confidential, and that it's important that we don't rile up the Army, Brucie, or the students. We want everyone to stay calm. Right?"

"Right," Collie agreed.

On his way into Monument Hall, Collie, like all visitors to the president's office, was spotted by several students who zealously monitored the administration for missteps that could provide calls to action. By standing arrangement, they immediately obtained Collie's name from the work-study students who checked in visitors at the entrance to the presidential suite. Thus "Collie Marson" was promptly entered on WinnerWatch.edu, the campus blog for keeping tabs on Winner, his comings and goings, his utterances (public, private, actual and spurious), and his visitors. One of the few who recognized the Collie Marson listing was a devoted monitor of the blog, Elias Fenster.

Seeing the name, the rodent meister experienced an uncomfortable chill. Instantly recalling the threatening circumstances that compelled him to deny Collie a tenure-track recommendation, Fenster speculated on the reasons for his visit to the president. Ordinarily, he could count on a surreptitious supply of information from his devoted cousin Myra, the presidential receptionist. Unfortunately, she was on vacation that week. Fenster knew that Marson was in venture capital and tech transfer, but contracts and other matters in that area were routinely dealt with far below the presidential level. Unable to conceive of a legitimate purpose for Collie meeting with Winner, Fenster's agile mind leaped to the likelihood of vengeance as the motive. No doubt Marson was telling Winner about his disastrous postdoc sojourn in Fenster's lab. With equal agility, Fenster contemplated countermeasures for safeguarding his career and the continuing prosperity of his rodent-research enterprise. Fenster was now convinced that, if unchecked, Winner's presidency would subject him to boundless peril and, ultimately, destruction. He reminded himself to instruct Myra to be especially watchful for anything at all involving Collie Marson and the president.

CHAPTER XVIII

Something funny must be going on, Collie thought, because he didn't meet any difficulty in setting up a visit to Brucie's lab. He gave his name to the youngish-sounding woman who answered the lab's telephone, explaining that he was a consultant to President Winner and a member of a venture-capital firm; he would like to visit the lab and talk to the director. His name evoked no special response at the other end of the line. The young woman said she'd check with Dr. Brusolowitz and would call back. In a return call that same day, she told Collie, "He's here in the afternoons. So just come in and ask for me, Ginny Rosen, and I'll take you to Dr. Brusolowitz."

Throttling a gasp at again encountering the "Bodily Functions" columnist, and without acknowledging their brief, bizarre acquaintanceship, Collie politely thanked her and said he would be there the next day. Neither his voice nor his name provided a reminder for Ginny Rosen, who hadn't registered his name during their tumultuous evening together. He realized she would recognize him when he arrived at the lab, but that should be no problem, he told himself. He'd check in with her, as directed, she'd escort him to Brucie's office, and no further contact with her would be necessary.

The next afternoon, Collie entered the main science building on campus, passing through a metal detector installed in the panicky days of terrorism fears. Perhaps set off by Collie's keys or cell phone, the apparatus sounded a loud bong-bong-bong. The work-study student attendant, slumped nearby in a canvas folding chair, was engrossed in a pornographic video rated "excellent" by the student newspaper. He waved Collie through without looking up from his laptop. Originally called Lavoisier Hall, in honor of the famed chemist martyred in the French Revolution, the building had been renamed again and again over the years in response to fund-raising successes—a tribute to the deal-breaking prowess of Kershaw's Office of General Counsel. At this time, however, the building was officially unnamed, and simply known as the science building. The most recent name on the portico, memorializing a philanthropic sandwich-chain mogul, had been removed to make way for a hedge-fund operator who delivered the first installment on a record-breaking endowment pledge. When the second payment came due, he was bankrupt and on the run. Accordingly, his name was removed, leaving the building nameless, pending the acquisition of a new donor.

Collie's scientific career had terminated in Fenster's own building on the other side of the campus. But labs are pretty much alike, and the sights and sounds he encountered in the science building were poignantly familiar. Piles of discarded research equipment lined the corridors—common lab detritus as government grant money brought in new equipment, routinely purchased, whether needed or not, because of the peculiarities of the research-grant economy. Government grants remained viable during the federal fiscal year for which they were awarded, which ran from October 1 to September 30. After that, unspent money reverted to the U.S. Treasury, leading to the rule "use it or lose it." The approach of the cutoff date brought urgent ordering from the equipment catalogs. Walking along, Collie absorbed the familiar aromas, sounds and sights of research in progress. Through open doors to the labs, he saw the present-day versions of the young Collie, in white lab coats, eyes behind protective glasses, hands in safety gloves. A young woman, hunched over a cluttered lab bench, concentrated on pipetting reagents into a tray of glassware. At a blackboard, several researchers conferred with an older scientist, apparently their mentor, while one, looking mesmerized, sat before a computer screen, munching a candy bar. The career compulsions and vulnerabilities that drove them were invisible in this commonplace panorama of young scientists at work. Collie knew for sure that each felt career angst, and that many, maybe most of them, would not complete the route to tenure track, tenure, and the cherished rank of grant-funded Principal Investigator. Nonetheless, they appeared composed, purposeful, satisfactorily engaged with their duties. Feeling a mixture of regret that he had left research and relief that he had found a refuge with Lou's firm, Collie arrived at the entrance to the wing of the building reserved for Brucie's special laboratory. A sign stated: "Secure Area. Do Not Enter." Sprawled over a desk partially blocking the way to a long corridor, a student in a sweatshirt, baseball cap with visor to the rear, shorts and sandals continued at text messaging on a cell phone while indifferently asking, "Whadya want?"

Recognizing an easily intimidated laboratory underling, Collie adopted an authoritative tone. "I'm here to see Dr. Brusolowitz. I have an appointment," he said, suggesting more certainty in his visiting arrangement than was actually warranted.

Since express-mail messengers and deliverymen pushing hand trucks were usually the only visitors to the lab, the young guardian was doubtful, but also concerned about offending a well-dressed visitor, who might be legitimate and important. "You got a pass or something?"

"No, I was told to ask for Ginny Rosen."

"Ah, Ginny, okay. I'll see if she's here." He punched numbers on the phone on the desk. "Ginny, some guy is here to see Dr. B. Says he has an appointment." Listening for a moment, he said "Uh-huh. Okay," and hung up the phone. "Ginny says there's some problem, but you can talk to her. Down the hall, turn right and the second door on the right. Can't miss it."

As Collie made the turn, he saw her standing in an office doorway, in standard, undergraduate, on-campus attire: sweatshirt, jeans, torn at the knees, and flip-flops. Gone was the fraught expression that he vividly remembered from the abnormal conclusion to their last encounter. Upon recognizing him, astonishment and delight lit her face. "Jesus, this is like the most amazing thing," she exclaimed, eyes and mouth wide open. "I didn't remember your name. I didn't know it was you. I've been trying to find who you are so I could tell you thanks for that ride and apologize——."

Recalling the lamentable evening, Collie sought to maintain minimal contact. "Hello. Forget about it, it was nothing. I'm here to see Dr. Brusolowitz."

"Yeah, I know, but let me explain. I never got your name, or maybe like I didn't remember it from that night, and the only way I could get it was to ask the Dollards, and I wasn't going to do *that*. So, I didn't know—."

"That's okay. Is Dr. Brusolowitz available?"

"Problem," she proclaimed, holding up a hand, as if signaling traffic to stop. "He said it was okay when I asked him yesterday, but it turns out this may not be like the best day to see him. He's really having a fit about something. But if he can't see you now, I can try to set up something for later on. No problem, really no problem, because I'm here a lot of the time."

"How come?" Collie asked, though reluctant to expand his acquaintanceship with the young woman.

"Making money, so I can get by with as little as possible from my father. You know, that's how I know the Dollards. Before she got married, she was nosing around Hollywood and got to know my father." Collie saw no way to interrupt her talking streak, which continued as they stood in the doorway while people in lab coats passed nearby in both directions. Ginny was unperturbed. "Jesus," she continued, "when I was a kid I used to like sneak looks at his diary when he was out of town. It was so totally gross. There was stuff about her. Anyway, she makes a pain of herself with me because she knows my dad, and I'm sure she still thinks she's got a chance in the movies someday. Ha, ha, that's a big-time humongous joke. So she like keeps inviting me over. I hate 'em all. Equal opportunity."

Determined to minimize contact with her, Collie repeated, "Maybe we can check on Dr. Brusolowitz?"

" I don't know, but let's go see." Flip-flops slapping on the polished floor, she led him further down the corridor to a set of double swinging doors embossed with "Director's Office" and in letters just below, "Dr. Max Brusolowitz, Ph.D," followed by "Authorized Personnel Only."

Pushing open one of the doors, and extending her arm as a signal for Collie to halt just inside, she whispered, "Let me check."

Then, from inside a nearby office, Collie heard a voice, loud, emphatic, and angry, booming through a speaker phone. "Listen, Colonel, you're a military man, so you're familiar with projectiles. You can take the official papers, roll them up real tight, and lubricated or unlubricated—you make the command

CHAPTER XVIII • 183

decision—shove them up you know where. The biggest, most gigantic, fuck-ingest mistake I ever made was having anything to do with the U.S. Army. God help us in the next war!"

From the unseen speaker phone came an amplified response, pleading and conciliatory, "Brucie, it's not my idea. Believe me. We've got these people in the Pentagon who are maybe a little out of touch, but they've got to deal with Congress, and the Army has to deal with them. We're bound by the Code of Federal Regulations and the requirement for a Funding Opportunity Announce-ment and a Request for Applications if we want to apply for an exemption from competitive-bidding requirements. You don't know the stuff we've had to deal with to keep you going. We still haven't heard back from our application for a Small Business Innovation Research grant. That's why—. Despite what you think, the Army doesn't have any money of our own. We got to get it from some place, and that means paperwork and following the rules, even when we work over the books to make it look like—you know what I mean. One slip and we'll have the Government Accountability Office and the Inspector General climbing all over us, and then it's in the newspapers and some damn Congressional investigation."

"All that crap is your problem, not mine, Colonel. I just want to make it plain to you that it's no go. I'm running this project and I've got my own ideas about how to go. I'm not doing anything, repeat, anything to satisfy some bean-counting asshole policy geek or whoever is bugging you. If you don't like it—."

"Brucie," the plaintive voice broke in, "you're the only one who knows what the hell is going on in the project. You've never told us a thing—."

The speaker phone emitted a loud bang, then silence. "Let me check," Ginny whispered. She knocked lightly on the office door and then entered. The unintel-ligible murmur of a conversation reached Collie. Ginny emerged, looking grim. "It's just a very bad day. You heard. He's upset. That happens here sometimes. Maybe I can set you up with Brucie for some other time, but not just now."

"What's going on?"

"It's a real mess. If you've got time, I'll be through here at four and maybe we can meet a little bit after that and have a cup of coffee downstairs, and I'll tell you about it. Whatever I can. But I've got to stay till four. Okay?"

Collie saw no choice. She was the key to meeting with Brucie. "Yeah, okay. See you in the cafeteria."

扳

"That night is still on my mind," she said the moment she joined him, earnestly insisting, "I got to explain," despite Collie's polite efforts to stifle the topic. He was not curious to learn more about that evening. Ginny, however, was determined to talk about it. The episode intensely interested her, and, therefore, she believed, Collie, as well. "You see, I take anti-depressants, like really mild stuff, but I sort of need it to get going. Just sometimes, not all the time. The student health passes them out for free by the bushel, like they do with condoms and birth control pills and attention deficit pills. They've got morning-after and uppers if you have to pull an all-nighter. You're supposed to see the doctor to get the pills, but that just takes two seconds and they never say no. So, it's practically just help yourself to all you want. The kids call it 'all you can eat.' That night, I was like so depressed about going to the Dollards—practically suicidal. But my dad was on my case to go and Helen was bugging me. So, I took a double dose of the anti-depressant, which really sent me zooming. Boing!" she said, rolling her eyes. "I also took some anti-histamine cold pills, and I had a beer. Real smart, huh? All that really made me like kind of zooming. The combination. Lucky I didn't have a joint."

"That can be bad," he said, reaching his limit for commiseration.

"But I'll tell you something hilarious. You ready? Guess what."

Shrugging, Collie did not offer a guess.

Ginny appeared triumphant. "I had my keys all the time. I thought I'd left them back at their apartment in my bag, but I found them in my coat pocket when I got home in the morning from your place. Isn't that like hilarious? I really must have been spaced out."

"That's really funny," he said, without actually thinking so. Her surliness and outbursts during the taxi-ride from the Dollards' party and the outlandish behavior in his apartment remained a noisome memory. Nonetheless, she was the gatekeeper for Brucie, and he had to deal with her. He adopted a congenial tone in pursuit of needed information. "Let me ask you something. How come you're still working for Brucie? I thought you said you were just helping him sort out some lab records. Isn't that all finished by now?"

"Yeah, we did that with the records. All done. But he's really great to work for and he's got like some general office stuff he needs done, and lucky for me, he said he could keep me on. He doesn't need any money from the university, because he's like got all this money from the Army for whatever he wants. Only—." She put her hand over her mouth. "Oops! We're not supposed to talk about the Army. If anyone asks, it's from the U.S National Institutes of Health. Okay? Just NIH for the special project. Brucie says that's really important."

"Sure, but how come you can't mention the Army?"

"I don't know, but it's really important. We can't mention the Army. Just don't ever say anything, okay? So anyway, he pays students $15.50 an hour, sometimes $20 for special stuff, like on holidays or very early in the morning. And $15.50's like twice the going rate on this lousy campus for work-study and things like that. But if you work for him, you got to be on time and stay to the last minute and do everything just exactly, exactly his way. But Brucie is really a sweetie."

Fearing she might clam up, Collie decided to ease off briefly on the topic of Brucie and the project. "With this job and writing your column for the school paper, how do you keep up with course work? I'm impressed with how much research you put into 'Bodily Functions.'"

"No problem," Ginny replied, savoring the flattery. "Glad you read it. I like get waivers and course credit for work-study and for working on *Haywire*. Kershaw is real cool about that. I'll have plenty of credits for graduation. My major is modern design, with a minor in exercise science. But I've like hardly taken any courses. It's really terrific," she said, effusing satisfaction. "I mean it's not like you can go through here without *ever* going to a class. But it's close to that if you've got other activities and get permission."

"Sounds great. So what's Brucie all in a stew about?"

"I really shouldn't talk about this stuff."

"That's okay. Just give me some idea of what's going on."

"I'm not supposed to talk about anything in the lab. But I owe you one for that stupid night, so I'll tell you a little if you promise, promise to keep it to yourself. I really mean it."

"It's okay to talk about it to me. I don't know if you know this, but I did my postdoc here, and all of us in the different labs used to swap information. So, it's nothing unusual."

"Yeah, I know, but like this is different," Ginny said, suddenly looking concerned.

"Well, then just give me some idea of what's up. That's all. Just curious."

Ginny looked around the cafeteria. Then, lowering her voice: "Brucie usually talks to the postdocs in his office one at a time to tell them what to do and to find out how things are going in their assignments. And he like always tells them to keep quiet about what they're working on or he'll cancel their fellowships and throw them out of the program. He sounds like he means it, and he's got them real scared. But I'm in there lots of the time sorting stuff, taking care of papers, and I hear what they're talking about. And I see the notes that Brucie keeps." Ginny paused and again looked around the cafeteria.

"Yeah," Collie said, trying to control his impatience.

"He's working on this drug for the Army that's supposed to keep soldiers from falling asleep. They call it the Human Performance Enhancement Program. It's got like some other name, Zap or something, but they usually call it who-pep—sort of an abbreviation from the Human Performance thing."

"Oh, yeah, I've heard of that," Collie casually remarked, intimating that the program was common knowledge and could be discussed without restraint.

"Really?" Ginny said with surprise, but she went on, staring closely at Collie, encouraged to talk by his unwavering attention. "It's a funny thing. There's this guy in the Army Research Office down south someplace who's like the program manager for the program. Brucie's office has a special direct phone line to him. And I talk to him on the special line like all the time about reports and payments. You've got to match purchases to the procurement codes for supplies and all sorts of stuff. Vouchers and invoices and like all that business crap—everything has an ID number, even for ordering a pencil there's a number; it's amazing. But this guy in the ARO like goes off on tangents, and I get the very clear impression that he's like some kind of fanatic, some kind of religious weirdo. Talks about morals and research and what's natural and unnatural and all that kind of stuff even when I just want to check out a voucher for some supplies and get off the phone. I've got to keep telling him, 'Hey, dude, let's get back to the topic.' And he like talks a lot to Brucie, too. Sometimes calls up just to talk to him. It's not about the research."

Collie at once recognized she was talking about his old buddy Charles Hollis, the conscience-stricken research dropout who loathed his job managing Brucie's project. Now sensing that Ginny was loosening up, he felt less inhibited about pushing her to talk. "What do they talk about?"

"Brucie is like this multi-tasker and uses the speaker phone so he can do six other things while he's talking, so I hear both ends of the conversation. This guy is giving Brucie the same religious line that he gives me. Scientific ethics, morals, human rights. Oh, yeah, and conscience. A lot about conscience. On and on. Something else: He e-mails like all kinds of articles to Brucie that I download and print out for him, and I know Brucie reads them, because I find them marked up on his desk later on. Little notes in the margins."

"Articles about what?"

"It's like a lot of heavy stuff. Philosophy readings. Stuff about social responsibility. Science, ethics. I took philosophy once, so I've seen stuff like this before. It's all very theoretical, not like everyday stuff in real life. But Brucie seems to eat it up."

"What do you mean?"

"Maybe that's too strong. But he seems to take it seriously. And I think he's like changed a lot since this program guy has been bugging him. I really do."

"In what way?"

Ginny now swung back to restraint. "I really can't say. It's not any of my business. I've told you lots and lots. Let's get off it," she said. Then raising her voice to normal conversational level, "How have you been? It's sort of nice to talk to you. I didn't get much of a chance that night."

Collie didn't want to chill her interest. "It was good to meet you, too," he answered in hope of retaining the connection, but without risking any complicating involvement with her. The reference to anti-depressants and a joint added to his wariness, making him wonder what else she was popping and smoking. Contrived as it was, his pretense at friendliness gladdened Ginny. When he said that he'd call to try for another appointment, Ginny warmly replied she'd do what she could, but cautioned him that it was rare for Brucie to meet with outsiders. "He's like very busy and actually pretty shy," she explained. "And whatever's going on with this guy he talks to, it seems to have him kind of shook up. You know, I was surprised when he said it was okay for you to come in and see him. Even if he didn't see you."

✐

Back at his apartment, Collie clicked through his voice mail, deleting a string of junk calls that had accumulated during his absence, until he heard Helen's voice. "Hey, it's me. The goddamnest complication about this place I had checked out and I thought we could get. Turns out it was the last one vacant. Now they tell me someone beat me to it before I could get in a deposit, and they're all full up, and not sure when they'll have a vacancy. I'm going to check on some others. I'm sure it's going to be all right, but what a pain. I'll call again soon as I can." There was a pause. "Wait to hear from me. Okay?"

He deleted several sales messages before coming upon another that he listened to. "Hi, Collie. Loretta. Got any time for me? Like this weekend, maybe, maybe, maybe, I hope? All or some of it? I'm on duty now. Will try to call you later. Kisses." He opened a bottle of wine, half filled a large tumbler, and emptied it slowly, appreciatively. The telephone rang. He reached for it, but held back, and let it ring again, and then again. A recorded voice came through a speaker, inviting a message at the tone. "Hey, this is Ginny. Now that I can connect your name and address, I got your number. Listen, maybe we can get together. I might be able to tell you some more stuff." She left a phone number.

✐

Rumors of revolutionary science in Max Brusolowitz's laboratory were bound to seep through the Army's security system. Brucie's reputation for scientific dexterity and inventiveness fostered widespread interest in his research agenda. Silence intensified that interest. Only Brucie, alone at the center of the research project, knew all the fine details and intricate components of his research. For security, the work was compartmentalized within his laboratory. There was one section to which only Brucie and a rotating group of carefully selected assistants had access. Reliable information was hemmed in by the military's need-to-know requirement. The system, however, could not be made airtight. In addition to a select inhouse staff of young faculty members, grad students, postdocs, and technicians, the project required the support services of specialized contractors and consultants. Brucie, for example, found it necessary to order custom-formulated reagents from a commercial laboratory, and he required outside assistance in modifying off-the-shelf neural-imaging equipment for the project's particular requirements. Many of the people closely or even distantly involved naturally suspected that the project was aimed at a highly unusual goal. But the hush-hush security assured that no one got the whole picture or deduced the astonishing anti-sleep objective or the unexpected bonus of eliminating human waste. The secrecy inspired speculation and boastful claims of inside information, even among Brucie's terrified postdocs and other subordinates. But given the clampdown on information, the circumstances were not conducive to accurate gossip mongering. Any whispers about the project, realistic or hallucinatory, sent extraordinary volumes of hand-me-down variations ricocheting around the Internet.

Though the Army's role was rigorously concealed, the seemingly unrestrained budget—attributed to the civilian NIH—drew the attention of Kershaw's less-favored lab chiefs. So did the restrictions on entry to Brucie's lab. Immediately after 9/11, the FBI had ordered door checks and other security measures at university labs because of fears of a bio-terrorist heist of pathogens or other dangerous materials. But after a few months, the urgency wore off without anyone seeming to care—except at Brucie's lab, where the staff underwent background checks and the doors remained guarded, if only perfunctorily.

His unusually lengthy absence from publication in the leading scientific journals caused curiosity. These strange circumstances received top-rank attention in the hypersonic blogosphere. According to one blogged report, the famous Professor Brusolowitz was running a project aimed at putting people to sleep in bomb-proof bunkers and reviving them unchanged years later, thus assuring American survival of a nuclear disaster and hegemony in a devastated world. Taking off from this report, another said the survival program sought to miniaturize a carefully selected cadre of technical specialists and political leaders for safe, long-term, anesthetized storage and eventual revival. "After a programmed number of years," a blogger confidently explained, "the automatic injection of a hormone-rich fluid will revive and restore the miniatures to full-size, normal life." The technology of mammalian miniaturization and preservation had progressed to the point where eight adult humans could be safely stored long-term in a 10-liter container for eventual revival, according to a blogged bulletin. The "use-by" dates of the bunkered containers would be "laddered" year by year into a far-distant future to assure survival after the big disaster, whenever it occurred. These blogs evoked skeptical, often abusive blogged rejoinders, providing additional grist for on-line controversy.

In conjunction with the human-storage and nuclear-Armageddon scenarios, the program was said to be developing technology for rapidly converting human waste into palatable, nutritious foodstuffs. "They've been making piss drinkable on the Space Station for years, so it's no big deal to ramp up production," a blogger asserted. Another blogger claimed, "They've been secretly slipping the stuff into the regular food supply to test for long-term effects." A furor of blogging was set off by the claim that an increase in the incidence of autism was attributable to human consumption of converted waste. The Centers for Disease Control and Prevention declared that it would be ridiculous to divert scarce resources to an examination of preposterous rumors. In response, the chairman of the House Appropriations Subcommittee responsible for the disease agency's budget demanded the resignation of the agency's director.

The Internet traffic generated by reports of a secret project at Kershaw University was closely monitored by various groups on alert for challenges to their interests. Several organizations dedicated to international peace denounced the research as a provocative precursor to war. "With America's future safely banked in deep underground storage," they asserted in a collective appeal to the President and the public, "the Pentagon will face no restraints in exercising raw American power as it pleases." A watchdog organization dedicated to ethical behavior in medical research demanded assurances that informed consent would be obtained from subjects selected for miniaturization, storage, and eventual revival; also, that only volunteers would be eligible for participation. Numerous food-safety groups sought assurances that food products derived from human waste would be accurately labeled and in compliance with safety requirements of the Food and Drug Administration and the Department of Agriculture.

Brucie refused to take calls from reporters, insisting that he was too busy with research. But pressed by Kershaw's public relations office to calm the speculation, he explained, "I'm doing routine basic biomedical research. Nothing exotic and nothing very interesting to report at this early stage. Good science takes time."

In Washington, the chief lobbyist for an association of pharmaceutical firms pondered an e-mail inquiry from the vice president for government affairs of a member corporation, accompanied by copies of alarmist blogs concerning the rumored research at Kershaw. "One of our people found all this material on the Internet. What the hell is this about?" the corporate VP inquired. The lobbyist, like most of his ilk, thrived on finding, inflating or even inventing risks in Washington that imperiled his distant clients. Danger in the capital was his bread and butter, necessitating his intervention with powerful figures with whom he claimed long-standing, influential relations. Lobbyists thrive on their clients' fears and anxieties about menaces that fester in Washington's unfathomable bureaucracies, mercurial Congress, and secretive White House. The lobbyist carefully read the blogs about bunker storage of miniaturized, anesthetized humans, hormone-induced revival, and conversion of human waste to edibility. Pure crackpot, he realized, far too removed from reality to provide fodder for alarms that would render the client grateful for his knowledgeable, and costly, services in Washington. But since the client had inquired, a seemingly serious response was mandatory. By prompt return e-mail, he adopted an omniscient but cautious stance, assuring his client, "We've been monitoring this from the start, and continue to check out all possibilities. I'm having lunch tomorrow with a well-placed Senator for health and food-safety issues"—a reference to a trade-association luncheon, in a hotel ballroom, attendance 500-plus, at which the Senator would briefly appear before hurrying to a similar luncheon at another hotel. The lobbyist concluded, "Will be in touch as soon as possible, and, if needed, will outline a plan of response." Several days later, he again addressed the issue. "I've carefully checked and double checked with close contacts at the Pentagon, on the Hill, at the FDA, NIH, NSF, CIA and at the White House. Whatever if anything is going on, it's at a very low level of intensity at this point. To be on the safe side, we'll continue to monitor the situation."

The pharmaceutical VP who made the inquiry felt reassured and relieved and congratulated himself for alerting the lobbyist to keep a watch on his firm's interests in Washington. But others took his place in response to the proliferation of blogging posts growing ever bolder in their speculations and descriptions of the project at Kershaw. Alarmed by national surveys reaffirming a continuous decline of public trust in science, the board of the National Association of Scientists discussed a motion to request an explanation from the government. But upon being confidentially advised that "a serious matter of national security is involved," the board unanimously agreed to put the motion on hold. "We're scientists, but first of all, we're citizens," the board chairman stated, and the members unanimously agreed. Queried at a press conference about reports of an undercover Army research project at Kershaw University, the Pentagon's chief of public information cooly replied, "All military personnel and programs are required to comply with relevant regulations." Asked whether that amounted to "no," the chief replied, "The statement speaks for itself." Going off the record with the cooperative corps of regulars assigned to cover the Pentagon, the info chief quipped, "Hey, guys, the cafeteria here isn't gourmet grade, but take my word, we're not recycling, so to speak." With humor, charm, evasions, and authoritative assurances, the Army dispelled the Kershaw reports as Internet fantasy.

But the persistence of the reports aroused curiosity on Capitol Hill. Asked about the feasibility of shrinking and storing humans for later restoration, the director of the National Institutes of Health earnestly dismissed the notion as further evidence of the dire need for improving science education. "We know about human growth hormone," he told a Senate committee, "but I've never heard of human shrinkage hormone." Then, with an impish grin, he declared, "Downsizing people is not in our research portfolio. If it ever is, I'll be looking for a new job, and I hope you gentlemen will give me good references." The Senators chuckled. Tensions and sniping between federal agency executives and their Congressional overseers were inevitable consequences of the Constitutional system of checks and balances. But when it came to facing a public rife with misinformation, hostility to authority, and immunity to reason, NIH officials and the legislators were battlefield brothers. As frequent targets of demented accusations and deliberate misinformation, the Senators accepted the NIH assurances in a knowing spirit of camaraderie and moved on to other matters.

୧୨

Monitoring the uproar on his laptop, the president of Kershaw University knew that it was a matter of time, probably very little time, before his campus erupted over whatever was going on in the laboratory of Professor Max Brusolowitz. It must be something extremely dangerous or grossly offensive to humane sensibilities, Winner reasoned. Otherwise, why the secrecy? He felt confident that the body-shrinking science-fiction speculations were nonsensical. Nonetheless, risky, objectionable, or outright illegal research of some kind was not impossible. Winner estimated he had a short grace period. The end of the spring semester was approaching, presenting students with a succession of diversions. As the weather warmed, they would be preoccupied with a series of festivals, in which feats of heavy drinking, surpassing the copious norm, would diminish their enthusiasm for manifesting social and political indignation. After a few bacchanalian weeks, they would be diverted by the search for term papers on the Internet and efforts to evade increasingly sensitive computerized plagiarism detectors. Next would come "all nighters" ingesting CliffsNotes and other distillations of the higher learning in frenzied preparation for final examinations. Then, summer job hunting and graduation, with its own attendant festivities. The calendar gave Winner a short stretch of safety. But in late August, he knew, the students would return, rested, not yet burdened by academic concerns, and in peak condition for collectively demonstrating outrage about something, anything.

୧୨

Kershaw University initially took an interest in Martin Dollard because he possessed a lot of money. His appointment to the advisory committee for Kershaw's Office of Endowment Management was a routine ploy to connect to the wealthy with a flattering invitation, and then to nudge, cajole, or entice them into donating to the university. The basic strategy was to make them aware of the eponymous glory available to those who helped rescue the university from its permanently perilous financial condition. Buildings, wings of buildings, and rooms in buildings, walkways to buildings, even benches and trees lining the walkways—all awaited the names of donors, depending on the scale of the donation. Traditional academic departments covered the gamut of scholarly endeavor. But additional immortalization was available through the creation of named institutes and centers that reflected the interests of donors, e.g., the Jones Institute for Middle East Studies or the Smith Center for Public Understanding of Science. Endowed chairs in the name of the donor were available for a price, as were scholarships, fellowships, and special stipends for research and travel.

Appointments as unpaid, part-time advisors to the university's full-time administrative staff were among the artifices for bringing in the wealthy without risking their interference or anything more burdensome for them than an occasional luncheon meeting. "Prestige without power," was the term employed by the architect of the method, the late president Giles. By that route, Martin became an advisor to the managers of Kershaw's endowment. An afterthought about doubling up on the wealthy Dollards led to Helen's appointment to the long-languishing Arts Advisory Committee. The wealth-transfer strategy proceeded at an unhurried pace. Experience had shown that a ripening process was required for impressing the wealthy with the needs of academe and the rewards to be had from satisfying them, now or in the hereafter, via legacies. The most productive fund-raising thrived on a light, ungrasping touch to spare the prey from feeling pursued. Thus the appointments to toothless, harmless roles that conveyed some semblance of importance. Martin's appointment originated in that manner, but eventually took on substantial aspects. His penchant for turgid loquacity was triggered by his mid-life obsession with societal impacts and his determination to address them in an academic setting. But he still possessed the focused, realistic business sense that had made and kept him rich. This bifurcation soon enough became apparent to Kershaw's endowment managers.

Staffed by dross from Wall Street and lesser venues of the financial world, the endowment office prudently recognized its own limitations, and strongly favored safety and avoidance of losses, even at the risk of missing the great gains achieved by financially bolder universities. The timidity in investment tactics dovetailed with the deadened atmosphere of the slowly expiring Giles administration. Martin, coming on board as a financial advisor in Giles' final years, clearly possessed a high level of money skills lacking in the university office. After a few months, the endowment director and staff gratefully recognized his abilities and increasingly turned to him for advice for carrying out their responsibilities. Though wary of making a misstep with Kershaw's money, Martin easily bettered their results by recommending risk-free shifts from low- to higher-interest financial instruments, plus investments in several sure-shot deals that he heard about from old business cronies. Martin thus received grateful recognition and acclaim as a financial wizard. The endowment managers realized that they needed Martin for his skill. Soon they also valued him for his connections to the new president of Kershaw.

With Winner named to the presidency, administrators throughout the university sought to demonstrate that their continued employment was essential to the well-being and future of the institution. The nature of Martin's links to the new president was not known. But it became evident that a relationship existed when word got about that Martin and his wife were the first outsiders invited to dine alone with President Winner. The hurried Chinese carryout dinner that Winner put on for the Dollards was transmogrified by Kershaw bloggers and e-mail addicts into an intimate, elegant dinner party in honor of the fashionable, influential couple—misrepresented as the first "sit-down" held in his campus residence by the new president.

Though Martin was otherwise little known, if at all, in the Kershaw community, the e-mail and blogging buzz received attentive notice among Kershaw's administrators. Playing it safe, they reasoned that his goodwill could be crucial for their survival on the Kershaw payroll. Martin thus received full cooperation from Kershaw's money managers and record keepers when, citing a mission for

President Winner, he requested access to the university's books and data banks for information about the financials of Professor Max Brusolowitz's laboratory.

Martin searched methodically, unhurriedly, and expertly. He understood money—how to make it and properly record it, how to conceal it, legally and illegally, and how to find it. Martin was a hard worker. His tweed sports coat draped over the back of his chair, eye glasses perched on his nose, sharpened pencil in hand, he sat day after day in a cubicle in the endowment office, tirelessly poring over volumes of financial records. Army money was plentifully scattered around the Kershaw campus, for undergraduate ROTC scholarships, graduate fellowships for strategic and language studies, engineering research, and several other topics—a normal military presence in contemporary higher education, repeated at universities throughout the country. But the Army, experienced in financial camouflage, was nowhere visible in the accounts for Brucie's lab. The data showed that his work was primarily financed, in above-board fashion, by grants from the purely civilian National Institutes of Health, plus a smattering of money from other civilian government research agencies, private philanthropies, earmarked endowment income, and general university funds. Scores of labs, at schools throughout the country, were financed in similar fashion. With only acceptable minor discrepancies, Kershaw's own records of government money received matched the official Internet reports of government money awarded to Kershaw. Wise about the ease of deception in money matters, Martin went back, double checked and confirmed his negative finding. No trace existed of Army money in Brucie's lab. None. He felt certain.

ᕕᕗ

The definitive outcome of his search infused Martin with a throbbing sense of accomplishment and importance. He saw it as enhancing his value to President Winner, who was plainly misinformed and needlessly alarmed about a secret Army presence on campus. Martin correctly sensed that Winner was actually frightened. Now Martin could put him at ease. Martin felt certain that Winner's gratitude for his good work would greatly improve—no, surely guarantee, he told himself—the prospects for the roundtable. But first he hurried home to share his findings with Helen. Ordinarily, he might have refrained from a full rendition of his experience in searching the records. Helen never offered more than an uninterested "uh, huh" about his business affairs, and usually not even that. But he felt that Helen was part of the mission he had undertaken for Winner. She was present at the dinner meeting where Winner asked Martin to check out the money behind Brusolowitz's lab. She had suggested asking Collie to conduct the onsite inspection that Winner desired as part of the inquiry.

Because of the Collie connection, Helen was intensely interested in Martin's findings. But she cagily appeared unconcerned, fearing that a departure from her customary indifference might arouse Martin's curiosity. At the lunch with Collie, which she repeatedly recalled to herself in nostalgic slow motion, he had said something about his interest in whatever was going on in that laboratory, something about a business opportunity. Now that she was on the brink of a relationship with Collie, she relished the joy of bestowing upon him something he would value. Martin's systematic tracking of her expenditures precluded the kind of expensive gift that she preferred—a fine wristwatch or engraved gold cufflinks. In this instance, she didn't shrink from prodding Martin to talk. She knew that almost any question she asked would trigger a torrent of words that might include information useful for Collie. Information would be her gift, she decided, precious information that her delightful young friend could use to his business advantage.

"So there's no Army there?" she asked after Martin, at considerable length, described his examination of the books. "You're sure? Because Winner seemed pretty worried that the Army might be there."

"Nothing there. Trust me. I went over every last item. Checked and double checked. Nothing there. This will be good for us, because Winner will appreciate it. He needed help. He seemed to be saying he had no one else to help him. He'll appreciate this."

Uncertain of the implications of Martin's finding, Helen sought to keep him talking, which was not difficult. "Then how come Winner was so worried about what turned out to be nothing? He's no dope. You're saying you know more about what's going on there then he does."

"Anyone can make a mistake. I remember once our company was trying to close a deal and we were worried——." Helen cut him off. "Yeah, yeah, but that's got nothing to do with this."

She wondered whether the blank drawn by Martin's research might be important for Collie, maybe so important that she should tell him about it immediately. But with Martin hanging around the apartment at the moment, she dared not do that. Even if he went out, he might unpredictably come galloping back while she was on the telephone. She might briefly get away from Martin by saying she was going out for a walk, for some fresh air, or to buy something around the corner. But Martin might cheerfully announce he would join her, and tag along, babbling about one thing or another.

Helen silently gauged her poor choices, but seeing no sure escape from Martin for a hurried phone call to Collie, simply said, "Well, yeah, Winner maybe was mistaken. Probably doesn't matter, after all."

"Hard to say," Martin replied, pleased by Helen's interest and an opportunity to dissect his research aloud and minutely explore its significance, both possible and fanciful. "Even if the Army isn't involved, it could be that something else is going on in that research program that still might be of interest to President Winner. I couldn't tell from the financials, like I said. There may be—who knows what?" he said, quickly adding, "But maybe Collie can find some essential item when he visits the laboratory, or maybe he's already been there." Martin was unusually silent for a moment or two, before asking, "When you talked to him, he didn't say when he was going, did he?"

"No, he said he'd try to do it soon. But I don't think we should bother him. He's very busy with his own work."

"I appreciate that," Martin said. "But this is so important that just to be on the safe side, maybe I'll check with him. Just to coordinate this and do as thorough a job as possible, I'll touch base with him before I report back to President Winner. Don't you think that's a good idea?"

Helen was unsure of how to respond. "Wish I knew," she said, seeking to appear indifferent. The need to talk to Collie surged within her. "I'm going out just for a minute," she said. "I need some cigarettes."

"I think I saw a pack in the living room," Martin said, with his customary energetic helpfulness. He hurried off and was back in moment, handing her a pack of her favored brand. "Saved you a trip," he brightly exclaimed before launching a rearranged, finely detailed narrative of his unsuccessful search for the source of spending for Brucie's lab.

CHAPTER XIX

Back in his apartment, Collie sat slumped, motionless, brooding and meditating over his near miss at meeting with Brucie and his failure to add to his skimpy information about the anti-sleep project. The wine bottle was nearly empty. Frustration disrupted his concentration. He preferred easy problems, with attainable, preferably effortless solutions. He looked around his decorator-furnished apartment. He liked the living-room rug, with its bright splashes of burnt orange on a deep blue background. But then he remembered that some visitor—he didn't remember who—had called it gaudy. A few other furnishings were okay, just right, Collie thought, but overall he still felt that the place was too hotel-like. That can be fixed, he told himself, maybe on his own, or with another decorator, when he had time. Then he returned to the Brucie problem. He wanted to report good news to Lou, his benefactor and mentor, but he had none, and he worried that Lou would lose confidence in him. Then he morosely reflected on his aborted scientific career. Maybe he could somehow, someday, go back to the lab and do something great. But it would be close to impossible to find a respectable scientific slot without a favorable reference from his postdoc chief, Elias Fenster. Science remained a master-and-apprentice enterprise. Department chairmen and lab chiefs seeking to fill vacancies depended on each other for rating the young scientists who had worked under them. A glowing endorsement was minimally necessary, though it guaranteed nothing in the over-populated job market. But a negative report, which he could expect from the rodent meister, would be invariably fatal. And, besides, he told himself, it was too late; research moves too fast for dropouts to catch up. He momentarily thought of the pharmaceutical industry and its off-shoots in bio-technology. But both were cutting back on scientific employment. And besides, they focused on exploiting the fruits of university research. They didn't do real science.

The desk clerk rang. "Lady here to see you, Dr. Marson." Collie unsuccessfully rummaged his memory. Then he heard a voice a bit distant from the phone: "Let me talk to him," followed by, in full volume, "It's me, Ginny. Just passing by as it turns out. Okay for me to come up? For just a minute?" Then the voice of the clerk, whom Collie suspected of sly impertinence, arising from envy of Collie's many attractive companions. "It's okay, isn't it, Dr. Marson?" and before Collie could reply, the clerk said, "Okay, I'll send her up." Soon after, the sound of the elevator stopping down the corridor and a light tap on his door.

Admitted into the apartment, Ginny quickly looked about. "It's just like I remember it," she said. "Wasn't that a crazy night?"

Collie noticed that she had changed from her uniform campus duds of that afternoon to a neat and attractive skirt and sweater. A vinous haze from the downed bottle fogged his sense of time, but he realized that only a few hours had passed since their meeting in the cafeteria following his aborted visit with Brucie.

"The apartment is all the same. Nothing's changed," he said. Now returning to the forefront of his mind was the realization that his best, and perhaps only, hope for connecting with Brucie stood before him. "So what's up?" he asked.

She brought a package out from behind her back. "I know you're like tired of hearing me say this, but I'm still so embarrassed about that time, and I just wanted to do a little something to make up for it. So here." She handed him a paper bag containing a bottle. "Take a look. I asked at the store and got something really special."

Collie looked at the bottle. Wine, with an expensive-looking label. "That's really nice of you," he said. "But really, I mean—."

Ginny stepped a bit further into the apartment, and stood silent. Collie wasn't sure what to do. Then she said, "Can I come in for a minute?"

"Yeah, yeah, come in." They were still standing near the door. "Come in, sit down, I've got plenty of time."

"You sure, 'cause you must really think I'm like kind of a flake?"

"No, no," he assured her. "C'mon in."

She sat on the sofa that had served as her bed on the oft-mentioned evening just a few months ago. "How about something to drink?" Collie offered. "Coke, wine or maybe a beer?"

"If you've got some wine. Maybe it will calm me down. I'm off those anti-depressants, except maybe for very rarely. But don't open the wine I got for you. That's like special for you. Okay? I'm sure you've got someone special you can share it with." She wouldn't breathe a word about Loretta's note, which she had found pasted to the bathroom mirror on her previous visit.

Collie didn't know how to respond to that gambit. "That's okay," he finally said, "I've got some other stuff right here," he said, pointing to a wine rack. Nearby stood the bottle he had almost finished solo. He pulled the cork from a fresh bottle, set two filled glasses on a table next to the sofa and seated himself in a nearby chair. "Cheers," he said. "You too," Ginny replied, taking a modest sip. "It's good," she said, quickly following with a succession of modest sips.

Collie ventured, "Was there something in particular you wanted to talk about?" He wondered whether that was a good move.

"Yeah, sort of," she said at once. "After I talked to you this afternoon, I like got to thinking, and I realized that when we talked in the cafeteria that was the only time I've ever talked to anyone about all that stuff, except for the weirdo program manager I told you about. And like I said, I try to talk to him as little as possible when it's not to do with orders for supplies and vouchers and that sort of stuff. But I don't want to bother you about my job. All the kids complain about their work-study."

"It's no bother. I'm really interested," Collie insisted. "If you don't talk to this guy except about business, what's there to bug you about the job? Isn't it just a work-study to make some money? I had a bunch of those when I went to college. It was part of student aid."

"Yeah, that's what it's supposed to be," Ginny said, setting down a now-empty glass. "But it's really gotten sort of crazy, with all sorts of stuff that's really strange. Makes me feel, like, I don't know how, but——." She looked down. "Kershaw's really not a very friendly place, you know, for having someone to talk to. There are all these cliques. And it's so competitive. All these kids, like desperate to get ahead. You'd think——."

Collie refilled their glasses. "So what's the problem? If that Army guy bugs you or whatever is going on, why not just quit? It can't be worth getting all upset just for the extra money that Brucie pays you."

"That's for sure. But I've been helping with the lab records for a long time now, even if it's like sometimes just a few hours a week. And Brucie sort of depends on me. I don't know what you've heard, but he's really a very nice person. I mean it."

Collie wondered what she actually knew about Brucie's research. He figured that Brucie hadn't told her anything. She was just a student assistant doing office work. She wasn't involved in the lab. But what had she picked up from working in his office and overhearing the lab talk? Maybe without realizing it, she knew something. Recognizing her anxiety, he feared that close questioning might push her back into reticence. "That's good that you like him" he said. "Some bosses can be pretty bad."

"Yeah, I know," she said, rubbing a thumb around the rim of her empty glass.

Collie refilled their glasses. Then he cautiously said, "I hear he's made a lot of progress. You know, on some of the things we talked a bit about this afternoon. The sleep stuff, or really the no-sleep stuff."

Ginny downed the wine in two fast gulps, and spoke rapidly, excitedly. "You wouldn't believe it. It's like the craziest thing. But now he's planning to drop the whole thing. He's shredding and deleting all the lab notes and records, so it will be like nothing was ever done. That's what I've been doing for him. And he's going to tell the Army that the project just didn't work out and that his progress reports were full of mistakes. Honest mistakes, he'll tell them. He just wants to drop the whole thing, like it never happened."

Collie restrained his astonishment. "Well, that's strange," he said as casually as he could, "but you've got to figure he knows best, and maybe he hasn't found what they wanted him to look for, whatever that is, and doesn't want to waste any more time on it. He knows best. He's a pretty famous scientist."

"I know," Ginny agreed, now even more agitated. "But the whole thing's not true. He really has made some kind of weird discovery. And now he wants to make like it never happened. All that stuff about morals and ethics and conscience that that guy has been feeding him has got to him. Now he talks like some kind of religious nut. Brucie, I mean. I'm like watching a Frankenstein movie and finding that I'm in it. Really, the way Brucie talks and with what's going on."

"Like what? What does he say?"

"About breaking the laws of nature, and disrupting the natural order of things, and changing the way people were meant to be. Conscience and more about conscience. And doing all this for the military. And like why don't we take care of poor people? He says that if the scientists who invented the atom bomb had thought about this, then we wouldn't have killed all those people with it during the war, or something. You've heard of Hiroshima, I'm sure."

Collie nodded, "Everyone has. But he's not working on anything for killing."

"Yeah, I suppose. But it's still for the Army, and the program manager keeps saying—. I don't know what to do," she said despairingly, and abruptly stopped talking.

Brucie's troubled conscience did not concern Collie. He needed to know about his research. "So where do things stand with his project?" he asked, trying to sound innocently curious. "What's he all worked up about?"

"It's really like totally weird," Ginny said without hesitation. "He's got these rats that never sleep. He injects them just once with this stuff that he's made and they never ever sleep, for months and months, like till they die of old age, rat old age. They keep on going like normal, except for no sleep. And another thing: they don't mess their cages. Never. He made this stuff for the Army, and now they're telling him that it's time to test it on soldiers, not immediately, but to get going on it, because there's a lot of complicated paperwork they have to do when people are involved. Brucie is not ready for tests, no way. But it's his own fault that they want to do tests. There's this Colonel in the Army office, and a few months ago

Brucie made the mistake of just mentioning that it might be a good idea like to start thinking about testing, to think ahead, because there would be a lot of problems about testing on people. Brucie was just talking. But this Army jerk must have told some head honcho or somebody about it, and now they want to do the tests. Like soon." Ginny pressed a hand to her lips. "I'm not supposed to say that, or anything. Jesus," she exclaimed.

Collie now felt he had to keep her talking. "That's really strange," he mumbled, "about the rats and testing, I mean. So where does that leave things?"

For a moment, the young woman was balanced between restraint and an irresistible urge to tell more, to share her distress. After a pause, she resumed talking, lowering her voice, as though signaling extreme confidentiality. "So we're going through all the records and, like I said, just shredding and deleting everything, everything. And he figures the Army's going to have a shit fit when they find out about this, and I'm sure they will. Guaranteed. They've spent millions of dollars on his research. Millions. And they figured they were like getting something fantastic, because that's what Brucie was telling them, until he changed his mind." Ginny realized that Collie was intently gazing at her, drawing in every word. She went on. "He's never told anyone about how he does his research, how he makes the stuff that he injects in the rats. He's the only one who knows. And he figures they're going to come in like big time and ask a lot of questions, and try to make him tell them how he did it."

"That figures. They'll wonder about how he kept the rats going so long. I mean without sleep. That's what he reported to them, isn't it?"

"I think he's going to say there was some mixup with the cages. I don't know, but he's going to tell them that the research didn't work out and—all sorts of stuff like that. There won't be any records to trip him up. That's for sure. We've seen to it ourselves, personally, that they've all gone bye-bye—" she rolled her eyes—"like through the shredder and straight to the dumpster."

"But still, they'll want to know what's up after all the good reports he made about whatever he was doing. They'll ask the other people in the lab." Anxious to keep her talking, Collie refrained from bearing down too hard.

"That won't do them any good," Ginny said with a dismissive gesture. "Brucie's not worried about the postdocs and the techs and grad students, because he carved everything up in tiny parts so each one of them did like only a little piece of the research. He's the only one who knows the whole story." She paused. Then, with a trembling voice, she added, "But there's a scary part."

"What?"

"Brucie told me that since I took care of all the lab notes and supply orders and records and data-base stuff, and I ran the shredder, they'll want to talk to me when they come around to find out what happened. And he said I should just say I just did little odds and ends in my work-study, filing stuff and things like that, and I'm not a science major and don't know anything about the lab work."

"What about the shredder?"

"He said to tell them that we always shredded duplicates and stuff we didn't need to save space. He's saving some records to account for all the time that we spent doing research on their dime, but it's all useless stuff that won't tell them anything about the real lab stuff. Then there's a whole bunch of formulas that he used to give me for entering into the data base. It was like so important that it was the only thing he'd double check after I was finished. He told me he's taken care of that—cleaned out the computer—and that I should just forget about it if anyone asks. 'Just say it's nothing you know anything about, wasn't part of your job,' he told me. I talked to my dad about that and he said they can put me in prison if I lie. It's like government information, and they can do it. My dad's been involved with a lot of legal stuff."

Collie's natural supply of empathy, never large, had been drained by his painful derailment on the way to a career in research. But he suddenly felt a warm impulse of sympathy for the young woman, who had unwillingly been plunged into a dark and dangerous deception. "I don't think they'd do anything like that," he told her. "But if they ask you anything, just tell them what you know. It's always best to tell the truth," he instructed her, though unsure of that principle, he doubted he sounded convincing.

"Brucie said that if I said the wrong thing that would land him in jail, and I'd be in plenty of trouble, too. There's like all the money the Army spent on his lab. Christ," she said, tears running down her cheeks, "I'm not even 22, and I don't want to be mixed up in this crazy business that I don't even understand or care about. But there I am."

Not knowing what to say left Collie in silence. She dabbed her cheeks with a tissue.

"How about something to eat?" he said. "It's getting late for dinner."

"I don't want to bother you with all this personal stuff," Ginny said. "But if you've got a Tylenol. I've really got a bad headache."

"I'm afraid I don't," he said, "but there's a shop just around the corner, and I can be back in a minute. And I'll pick up something for dinner. Maybe you want to wash up in the bathroom while I run out." He wanted her to talk more about Brucie's work and plans, and, most important, he wanted her to set up a meeting with Brucie.

Too stuffed with emotion to speak, still dabbing tears, Ginny nodded appreciatively. Collie grabbed a jacket and hurried out.

Ginny returned from the bathroom, sat on the couch, painfully going over what she had told him, apprehensive but also relieved at having unburdened herself, but no less fearful of the unknowns confronting her. The telephone, at her elbow, next to the sofa, rang—once, twice. She instinctively reached for the phone, but then withdrew her hand as the recorded invitation sounded to leave a message at the tone. "Hi, it's me. Great news," said a cheerful feminine voice. "Lucky, lucky us. I got a place. Not the one I told you about, but even better. Really divine. Starting on the first of the month." The speaker recited an address. "Make a check for $4,200. Mark it rent and security deposit for apartment 704. Fill it out to the building manager, same address. I'll be in touch. Funny, you're never in. Hugs." Ginny instantly recognized the voice: Helen Dollard's. Overcoming her initial puzzlement and then stark astonishment, she struggled to decipher the phoned message, and instantly came to an understanding. Listening for a key in the door, she heard nothing. Without hesitation, she firmly pushed the delete button on the telephone console. A disembodied electronic voice, speaking in syllables, emphatically declared: "Mes-sage-de-leet-ed." Ginny stood up and looked around the apartment. She was shaking. Emptying the remnants of the wine bottle, she tried to steady herself. Just a few minutes later, Collie returned, swinging a plastic grocery bag, muttering about the slow checkout line at the store. She was not in the living room. The bathroom door was partly ajar; no one there. He wondered whether she had left. Then he went to his bedroom. Her clothes were neatly piled on a chair beside the bed. Ginny was wrapped in the covers, deep in sleep.

When they awakened in the morning's early light, they were in each other's arms.

CHAPTER XX

Martin throbbed with the urgency of delivering his findings to President Winner. Conclusion: There's no secret Army research project at Kershaw. Nothing there. He would dispel the disturbing misinformation. He aimed to wrap up his report in one comprehensive package, reap gratitude for a job well done for the new president, and then quickly move on to his real interest—the Kershaw roundtable. But he felt a need for a scientifically worded input from Collie to add heft to his report. Collie could report to Winner on his own, but Martin wanted to be certain that their findings were in perfect agreement. A proper report would explain, first, that Martin had found no unaccounted-for research money on campus; and, second, that Collie had personally confirmed that the ongoing research in Brusolowitz's lab was of an acceptable kind for Kershaw. Double whammy, Martin said to himself. Case closed, Martin would assure the university president. He would complete the task with speed and clarity. Must be well done, he told himself. But to do it right, Martin felt, he must meet with Collie to impress upon him the importance of his share of the inquiry and, if not yet done, the urgency of doing it quickly.

Telephoned at his office, Collie didn't know how to fend off Martin's blustery insistence on a prompt get-together to "wrap up this thing for President Winner."

"I went up to the lab—" he started to tell Martin, who cut him off. "Good, that's what we wanted," Martin shouted into the phone. "I'll just need you to fill me in with the scientific details—the right technical wordage; that's what we're relying on you for. And then I'll write it up and we can unload this thing and get on to important matters."

❧

Collie felt thwarted, useless. Lou was in L.A., working on a complicated shopping mall deal, leaving Collie reluctant to interrupt his mentor with a simpleton call for advice about his prolonged, inconclusive pursuit of the anti-sleep drug he had touted. Recalling Lou's far-back acquaintanceship with Martin, Collie feared an unwitting misstep that might offend Lou or create doubt about Collie's judgment. And then there was the delicate matter of Collie's pending relationship with Helen, which, on his side, had abruptly declined in temperature in the short time that had elapsed since Ginny's unexpected overnight at his apartment.

Collie was thus ill-prepared for Martin, who, self-invited, thundered into his office the next morning, promising, "I won't take up much of your time." He suddenly added, "Before I forget. Helen sends her best." Then speaking hurriedly, impatiently, Martin proceeded. "I just want to get it absolutely correct and be done with this. You visited this Brusolowitz and looked around the lab pretty carefully. That's what I needed, but I have to know exactly how to put it in my report to President Winner." Martin's resonant, jackhammer delivery drew startled looks from co-workers walking past Collie's office.

Collie got up and closed the door. He stared at his over-excited, spouting visitor, waiting for him to subside. Finally a gap occurred in Martin's word barrage. "What I tried to tell you," Collie said slowly, deliberately, "is that I made an appointment and went to the lab, but Brusolowitz got tied up with something at the last minute, and I didn't get to talk to him. I'm going to try for another appointment. I have not seen him yet. I haven't seen him."

"But you were able to look around," Martin said hopefully, "and talk to other people in the lab and see that nothing secret was going on there? Nothing unusual. Right? The same as I found in checking out the financials."

"No, I can't say that. I wouldn't put it that way," Collie responded. The conversation was now approaching sensitive ground, making him uneasy about how to proceed. He didn't want to reveal anything from Ginny's tearful revelations of her job in the lab, or the information he had gleaned earlier from his old buddy Charles, the distressed project manager. He wasn't sure whether he should tell Martin anything he knew about Brucie's lab and intentions, and was less sure that if he did, Martin, erupting and overwrought, could grasp and remember. Charles and Ginny had both made it clear that the Army was there. But, if Ginny had it right, Brucie aimed to cut the connection, soon and completely. Collie ached for Lou's seasoned guidance. While Martin babbled and jittered excitedly, Collie toyed with the notion of reporting directly to Winner, who had personally dispatched him to visit the lab.

"I just don't understand," Martin declared, as though Collie owed him an understanding. "There's nothing in the records about anything wrong in that lab—nothing, zero. So, there's no problem there. The whole thing is just some misunderstanding, or who knows what? But it's nothing for Winner to worry about. That's obvious, isn't it?"

"I suppose so," Collie said, for lack of anything else that came to mind. But then he caught himself. "I just think that maybe you'd better hold off on getting back to President Winner."

"Why?" Martin demanded. "Like I said, I found nothing there. So, that's what I should report to him, but he also wanted someone to visit the lab. And you've been there, and you didn't see anything, even if you didn't get to meet with Brusolowitz." Martin suddenly quieted, and resorted to pleading. "So, where does that leave me? I can't let this drag on forever."

"Yes, like I told you," Collie explained, "I went there, but I didn't get to see what's going on in the lab. Just hold on for a while, and I'll get in there as soon as I can and I'll meet with Brusolowitz and I'll let you know what's up. Immediately, if I can arrange it. Okay?"

"Make it very soon," Martin implored, reaching out and touching Collie's hand. "Time is really important. Okay?"

"I'll make it real soon," Collie said.

As soon as Martin left, Collie phoned Ginny at the lab, and started talking before she completed "Hello." "Collie Marson here," he said, in a strict business-like voice, aiming to head off any personal talk. "I'd like to see if we can try again to arrange an appointment as soon as possible for me to talk with Dr. Brusolowitz. Like I said, it's for President Winner."

"I was wondering if you would call," Ginny said. "Are you mad at me? I hope you're not mad at me."

The call-waiting light flashed on his telephone console. It might be Lou, calling from L.A. "Just hang on a sec," he said, "I'll be right back."

He clicked on the waiting call: "Collie here."

"Collie. Whew! It's you, at last. Did you get off the check?"

The wrong reply, the most impossibly wrong reply, sprang unthinkingly, instantly to his racing mind and passed his lips. "Who's this? Check for what?"

Silence, then he heard exhaled breath, and sensed exasperation just as recognition arrived, and he simultaneously heard, "It's me. Helen. Did you get my message, at home? I left you a message last night. Did you get it?" She helplessly sobbed.

"I must have been out," he lamely said.

"Goddamnit, you're always out. Listen, we've got to have a serious talk. I mean, this is—." She stopped, and then resumed. "Let me see how I can work out things, and we'll get together. Okay?" She stopped, then added. "Please."

"Yeah, sure," he said.

He clicked back to Ginny. "Sorry. Can you get me in to see Brucie? It's really important."

"Yeah, no problem. He said last time that any afternoon is okay. I think he really wants to see you. It's just that he got hung up yesterday. Come in this afternoon. That should be okay."

"Are you sure?"

"I think so. I mean, you know, it's like I told you. Sort of funny things going on. But he's here, so come on over."

"Right away."

❧

Ginny waited on the front steps of the science building. With students and the usual off-campus layabouts tossing frisbees and lounging and chatting nearby, she and Collie instinctively behaved business-like, impersonal when he arrived. "Hello, I'll take you up to see him. Follow me," Ginny said in good guide fashion, leading Collie around the now-untended metal detector and past a recumbent, lightly snoring student posted at the entrance to Brucie's wing of the building. Going down an empty stretch of corridor, she said in a hushed voice, "I'll see you afterwards, okay?" And then in conversational tone, upon entering Brucie's office suite, "He's in. Just wait here, and I'll come back for you." Ginny knocked lightly and pushed open a door. Collie remained in the same ante room where yesterday he had overheard Brucie scorch the Army. Ginny motioned. "Okay, c'mon in."

As Collie entered, she switched to a respectful tone and said, "Dr. Brusolowitz, this is Dr. Marson." Collie tried to speak, but his derailed scientific career humbly silenced him in the presence of Max Brusolowitz. The renowned researcher scanned him with staring blue eyes behind tiny spectacles that appeared precariously perched toward the tip of his nose. Surprisingly lanky, lean, and nimble, with a broad brow and alert face, Brucie projected a lively interest in his surroundings, curiosity, a reaching out to know. At the same time, he appeared confident and at ease. In haute social and business circles, immunity to surprise and an unruffled demeanor are coveted, cultivated personal characteristics, marks of sophistication, knowledgeability, and poise. Affectations of boredom and indifference are utilized as signals of superiority. Scientists vary greatly in personality, but many possessors of the scientific sensibility are very different in this regard, openly relishing and welcoming surprise and the unexpected as clues of something out of the ordinary, worthy of exploration. They ask questions that others avoid for fear of appearing uninformed, inexperienced, or stupid. "I don't know" and admissions of error come easily to their lips. They are not riled by challenges from subordinates. As with children who have not yet been molded into intellectual passivity, their faces are open and readily express wonder and delight. Miraculously, they persist in looking youthful even as they age into the later years. Max Brusolowitz was in this genre. In the many admiring news profiles written about him over the years, he was often referred to as baby-faced, boyish, enthusiastic, tirelessly curious. Reporters who came to interview him found themselves more questioned than questioning.

"Brusolowitz," he said, rising from his desk.

A greeting choked in Collie's throat, leaving him wordless. Brucie was in command of the meeting. He pointed to a chair. "Sit down, Marson," he said, "I've been meaning to talk to you—not you specifically, but someone like you." Brusolowitz spoke confidently—the master addressing a novice.

Collie noted that he wore the same pigtail, and was a bit grayer and somewhat thinner than when he had last seen him, a few years ago in the snows of Aspen. Still, his face glowed with alertness, sensitivity. Attire was carefree laboratory-standard: white coat over an unironed shirt and shapeless trousers. The book shelves and table surfaces were cluttered with journals and scientific tomes. On a nearby table, splotches of color tirelessly rotated on two computer screens. No religious icons, artefacts or paraphernalia were in view, nothing to substantiate Ginny's reports of a spiritual conversion in progress.

"She called you doctor, so maybe you know something about research," Brucie began. "What did you study and how far did you go?" Collie briefly sketched his failed postdoc at Kershaw under Professor Elias Fenster. Mention of the well-known rodent meister induced a skeptical grimace in Brucie. Collie felt inadequate, intimidated. In the presence of the eminent Brucie, he was a callow outsider, a commonplace failure among the many who unrealistically aspire to careers in the elite guild of scientific research.

Brucie announced the start of business. "We can begin. You're here to get information about us for the new president," he said. "And since you're in the investment game, you figure you might pick up something here that you can use for your company. Maybe make a deal. Huh? You've heard a lot of unusual things about what's going on in this lab. Right?"

Collie hesitated to respond, bringing a sternly voiced repeat from Brucie: "Right?"

"There's been a lot of stuff on blogs and so forth, but I don't know—. And President Winner says he wants to review everything going on on campus. That's okay. He's new. So, he asked me—. "

"Yeah, yeah, I know all about that. First of all," Brucie said, "let's forget about President Winner. He'll be out of here practically overnight if he makes a pain in the ass of himself. Happens all the time. University presidents are just hood ornaments. Even at Harvard, the president got bounced out for being obnoxious. So why not here? Right?"

Collie strained to organize his thoughts and steer the conversation toward his mission. "Maybe I should first explain—." Brusolowitz interrupted him. "You don't have to explain anything, Marson. I'll do the explaining. When I checked you out, I was interested to see that you do tech transfer for a venture capital outfit. I think I need a guy like you to help me out, but first you need to understand the peculiar circumstances we're in here. Very peculiar circumstances. Okay? And then I need some information, which is really why I'm seeing you."

Collie managed a soft-spoken "Okay."

"I've got a big research group here. Some really good postdocs and grad students and a bunch of people on tenure track hoping to reach the promised land. All very good people, because I screen out the ciphers. Either you can do research or you can't. Nothing personal, Marson. If we're going to do business, we're going to talk grownup. We're not doing science for dummies." Collie remained silent. "The people I have here are all working their butts off because they know a recommendation from me guarantees a good lab placement or a promotion when they move on. A bad word from me and they'll go no place. So they produce. But there's a penalty for working here, and some people leave because of that. We do no publishing. The reason is the United States Army, which no one is supposed to know about. They give me all the money I want, but they like to keep things quiet. Nothing we do in this part of my lab gets known in the outside world. The Army cooks the books so it looks like we're staked by NIH. We have all the money we need for what we're doing for the Army. I'll come to that. Nice situation. Not many others like it these days. Right?"

Collie indicated agreement.

"Now you know where that money comes from, because I told you, but you don't know what it's for."

Though Collie knew the source and the purpose, he cagily demurred. "There are rumors all over the place," he said, "but—."

"Yeah," Brucie said, "if you want to identify the leading idiots in this country, start with the bloggers. Forget about all that crap that's on the Internet about shrinking and storing people and bringing them back to life—what is it, a hundred years later? Purified bullshit."

His feeling of professional inadequacy intensifying as the monologue proceeded, Collie found himself nodding in agreement.

"Good," Brucie said. "Now you have to tell me something. How much money did you make last year?"

The invasive, unexpected question depressed Collie's sense of worth still further. In making a good income by commercially exploiting the work of productive scientists, he felt excessively rewarded and parasitic. His former postdoc peers and his scientific superiors were deprived and authentic.

Collie felt compelled to reply. "I get pretty well paid. It was about 200K last year, plus a bonus of 20 percent. But I'm just starting out in this work. It usually gets better with experience. I know the firm is still carrying me, but I'm getting better at this stuff."

"Not bad for a dropout," Brucie said, only a trifle contemptuously. "Even with all the Army money I have for research, I'm still limited by the university on what I get paid. There are two accounts: research and salary. The bottom line is I get paid less than you. I get a few additional bucks from royalties on patents. There's always consulting for industry, but a lot of that is pretty damn revolting. I know they want my name and reputation so they can get some crap through the FDA and kill off sick people faster, which is one of the great accomplishments of Big Pharma. Leave me out of that. Okay. You get the picture. Max Brusolowitz, scientific genius, 35 years in the lab, author of too many papers to count, gets paid less than *you*; even less than the MBA swindlers coming fresh out of the business school across the street. Right?"

Collie's sense of personal worth dropped another notch. "Right," he conceded, but then, with a last-hope effort, he again tried to steer the conversation. "Look, Professor Brusolowitz, maybe we can discuss some of the stuff that President Winner is interested in. He wants to know what's going on in your lab. That's what he asked me to find out."

"Okay, I was getting to that. I'll tell you what you need to know. What's going on here is I want to get out from under the Army. I've developed—if you'll pardon me for sounding precious—ethical and moral concerns about what they'll do with my research. Took me a few years to come around to this way of thinking. I apologize for these feelings coming along late in life. Sorry. But I never thought about it before. So now I've got a conscience, you might say—something rare in science, by my observations. Plus, in the spirit of full disclosure, as they say these days, I want to make more money. But I don't trust the Army. Right now my problem is how to deal with the Army. We've made some damn big progress in this lab that can turn out to be important for lots of things. But I don't want to give it to the Army."

"But they'll just take over the research and go ahead without you."

"No way. Because there's nothing for them to take over. I take care of the lab notes and records, and always have in dealing with them. All that will be left is some odds and ends of stuff that won't do them any good. There are no papers, published or unpublished, because, like I told you, the Army said no publications. Right from the beginning they said they wanted to keep it very, very quiet. They told me to keep everything secret. And I've got that in writing someplace from some goddamned general. No sharing of the work. I set up a division of labor here, so no one working in the lab has the big picture. I'm the only one who knows what's been going on and what's been found, and how I found it."

"So what's this research all about?" Collie asked. He knew the answer but he wanted to hear Brucie confirm it.

The answer came in a stately word-by-word whisper: "Big. Biological. Breakthrough." Brucie waited a moment, resumed his natural voice, and continued. "Revolutionary. A lot of people would say what I've done is impossible. But we know the most important rule: Never say never. Right?"

"Never say never," Collie agreed.

"Good. Now I personally want to make a sharp turn. It will be in the direction of good stuff for people, ethical. That's what I want to do. Nothing for the Army!" he said, punching a clenched fist into his cupped hand. "And, I want to make some money, big money. Why not?"

"Why this turnaround?" Collie asked.

"I'm getting old," Brucie said, "and I've done a lot in research—published mountains of papers—but nothing really useful. Maybe a little bit, but nothing much. I developed some special rations for the Army but there are problems with them. Really could be some serious problems. But before I was finished with the research, the Army took the project away from me and went into production, and back then in my naive days, I let them get away with it. They're making tons of the stuff, and the government flies it in big sacks to refugee camps around the world. You know, humanitarian relief. But I don't get any royalties because the Army says it owns everything. I don't understand the legal stuff, but I do know I never should have got mixed up with the Army. And I've been thinking about a lot of things I never stopped to think about before, and reading a lot of stuff. But that's my business." Suddenly silent, Brusolowitz looked down, deep in thought. Then he looked up at Collie and resumed talking.

"You know, most of us scientists are miserably educated. They start us out with science and math when we're kids, and if we show any talent, we get only a smattering of anything else. And we're encouraged to be narrow by all this crap about the country falling behind the rest of the world in math and science and we're short of scientists, and the economy is going to hell. All bullshit, but it keeps the money coming into science, and no matter how much we get, we're organized to scream it's not enough, we're losing the lead, falling behind. We've got all these scientific and university organizations and lobbyists in Washington working on this full time, and the press gobbles it up. They're all for more science, but they never think about science for *what*. Why are we doing some of the things we do? I've only started to do some serious reading and thinking. I know I'm not a deep thinker. But deep enough to know I don't want to be part of this anymore. I still want to do science, but I've got to make some changes. First step is to get away from the Army."

They both remained silent for an uncomfortable interval. Then Collie said, "The Army's not going to sit still for this. You know that."

"Yes, they will," Brucie countered, "because I've got them by the nuts. They know that I can tell the world that they want to turn the brave and trusting sons and daughters of America into military zombies, with their brains marinated in strange goo from a secret laboratory. It will be a scary story. The public is a sucker for success stories about science—miracle cures and stuff like that. But it's also jumpy about risky things that look like science gone amok: pesticides in baby formula, bad pharmaceuticals, radiation leaks, fish kills. The scientist who blows the whistle is a hero. I'll tell the *Times* and NPR and everyone else and they'll run with it. I'm not going to let the Army have my research. They can yell and scream and sue me and arrest me and do whatever the hell they want to do, and I still won't let them have my research. They know that. I control the research. Me and only me."

"You mean for eliminating sleep?" Collie said, instantly fearing he had said too much.

"You know about that," Brucie calmly replied. "I figured something was eventually going to get out. Not too much so far, just a bit about the object, but not the method. Luckily, there's so much crap out there on the Internet that no one knows what to believe. But the longer we go on working here on this project, the less chance there is of keeping it quiet, and the pressures will rise and attempts to steal it will be made. Yeah, I found the secret of sleep. There are hundreds of labs around the world trying to figure out how to get people to sleep or how to keep them awake. I've solved the second problem. I've got rats here that haven't slept for six months and are in perfect condition. No bad effects. And guess what: no defecation and no urination. I didn't figure on that, but it's there. And I'm the only one who knows how to do it. Just me, no one else has a clue. And no one else is ever going to figure it out for a long, long time. Maybe never. You know why?"

Collie felt he was falling under a spell. With difficulty, he mustered a response. "No, I don't, but if you figured it out, someone else will figure it out. Might take a long time, but that's how it goes in research. Someone is first, but there's always someone running second." Asserting a connection to the brotherhood of science, he added, "I know that much."

"Not in this research," Brucie responded with a beatific grin. "What I've done is not a discovery. The nano-biogenetics, endocrinology, and chemo-physiology of sleep elimination weren't just sitting there for someone to come along and find it, like Columbus found America or an astronomer finds a star or an entomologist finds a new insect. No way. This is not a discovery. And it's not like other inventions. If the Wright brothers had never lived, we'd still have airplanes, and if Edison had never lived, we'd still have electric lights. Because the technology was ripe, and these things were going to happen, with or without any particular person. Not so with what I've accomplished. It wasn't going to happen until I did it, and it could never happen without me doing it. It's not a discovery or an invention."

"Then what is it?" Collie shot back, demanding rather than merely asking. He felt misused: badgered by Martin's demands for a quick and decisive visit to Brucie's lab, pressed by Lou for a business deal, and baffled by Brucie's byzantine, boastful account of what he was doing and why. Brucie spoke with passion. Collie could recall conversations with accomplished scientists, both in his university days and as a scout for commercial opportunities in their laboratories, but never had he encountered such fervor. "What is it?" Collie repeated.

"It's a *creation*," Brucie declared. "A creation. Like the Goldberg Variations, or Guernica, or the Divine Comedy, or Michelangelo's David. If their creators hadn't created them, they would never exist. Never."

Collie could not conceal his puzzlement. In college, he had feasted on science and math courses, surviving the arts and humanities requirements as a CliffsNotes scholar. Brucie plunged on. "Same with my compound for eliminating sleep. It's a creation, not a discovery. I made it. It's my work. My own handmade molecules. If I didn't do it, it wouldn't be done, couldn't be done. Simple."

He stopped for a moment to let his visibly baffled visitor absorb the message. Then he continued, "Sure, if it goes into production, someone can get ahold of it and reverse engineer, copy it. Which wouldn't be easy, but it's doable. But if I dump it down the drain before anyone else gets ahold of it, and I don't tell anyone how to make it, no one will ever find out, because there will be nothing to reverse engineer. That's the difference between a creation and a discovery or an invention."

Collie's expression shifted among wonder, disbelief, and confusion. "Look," Brucie said, watching him struggle to comprehend, "Take a poem. All the words in a poem are in a dictionary that anyone can use. Words are the raw material, available to anyone. But only one person writes *that* poem. No two of the six billion people on this earth can ever write the same poem. Same with my creation. It's unique, like a poem. Someone can read a poem and make a copy, but if they never see it, they can never copy it, and they can never make up the same poem, intentionally or accidentally. If I told you there's a Shakespeare sonnet that's never seen the light of day, and I tell you what it's about, do you think you, or anyone, could write it? No. No one could. Not even the thousand monkeys pounding on typewriters."

The monkey reference stumped Collie. "What thousand monkeys?" he wondered, but dared not inquire. A thought raced through his mind: "He's nuts, crazy, or something." Collie then realized that with Brucie's prideful tirade, the conversation had reached a crucial point. He ventured a big question: "Where do you go from here?"

"That's what I want to talk to you about. I want to spin off this whole operation. Take it away from the Army and out of the university and put it into an independent lab. Run by me. And then I can take my invention about sleep, strip out what might be the bad parts, and direct it toward nice things. Useful, helpful things. Nothing for the Army. I don't know that there can be a good use for it. Maybe no good use. It doesn't seem to be reversible in rats. When you think about it, you can see it turning the world upside down, so I'm going to be very, very careful about how this goes. I don't want to be like that song says about that Nazi rocket genius Wernher von Braun—that he sends 'em up but isn't responsible for where they come down. A lot of research needs to be done. And maybe in the end, I'll just toss the whole thing down the drain and walk away. And that will be the end of it—gone from the face of the earth forever. It's possible I'll do that. Maybe not. But one thing I know for sure: nothing for the Army. You understand?"

"I understand. "

Brucie returned to his original business-like demeanor. "You're in venture capital. I'll need $25 million and we can get started and keep going for a while. Small change. They easily spend that much cooking up another shampoo or nail polish remover."

Collie didn't blink. If Lou was game, $25 million would be no problem. "I'll have to talk to my boss. He might be interested. But he'll want to know what's in it for us. You just said that if you don't like how it looks, you'll dump the whole thing—and then we're out $25 million."

"That's right. That's what could happen. But what I've found is so funda-mental, a basic biological intervention unknown to anyone except me, that if I decide to go ahead and bring some of this into the open, it will be worth a lot for anyone who's in on the ground floor. Better than getting in on anti-depressants before anyone ever heard of Valium or Prozac. Billions. But, yeah, you'll be taking a gamble."

"You need twenty-five million," Collie said.

"Soon," Brucie said with impatience.

"I'll see what we can do. Soon as I can."

"Don't take too much time. There's a lot of big money chasing after smart science these days."

As Collie rose to leave, Brucie motioned him to sit down again. "We've got to decide what you're going to tell Winner."

"Yeah, that's a problem. What do I tell him?"

"Tell him I told you that we're just doing some ordinary, pointless basic re-search, and that NIH pays for it. Nothing about the Army, and everybody will be happy. Got it?"

"I'll tell him something."

As he left Brucie's office and headed down the corridor, Ginny appeared and fell in step with him. "Did everything go okay?"

"Fine, fine," Collie said, quickening his pace as he tried to figure out his next move.

In a timid voice, as they strode along, Ginny said, "I hope I can see you."

"Sure, but first I've got to do some important things for work. Okay? Let's talk later," he hurriedly said as they left the building and he waved for a taxi. "We'll be in touch."

"I hope so," Ginny said, adding, with poorly suppressed emotion, "Soon?"

As the cab sped along, Collie recalled a recurrent dream: He was on the high school baseball team. The other players were all bigger, stronger, faster, more ex-perienced. He was playing the infield. At a crucial moment in the game, a sharp line drive rocketed directly toward him. And he awakened in a fright, trembling, on a damp pillow.

C H A P T E R   X X I

After much tactical deliberation, Martin decided to go directly to Winner's office suite without an appointment on the chance that he might luckily get in to see the president and declare his assignments completed. Martin was agitated, exasperated. Over a week ago, he had sent Winner the memo he requested about the costs and operations of the roundtable, but hadn't had a response. Now he was ready to report that Brusolowitz's lab was legitimately funded. He could deliver this important finding by e-mail or in a typed memo, but the message might get lost in the flood of communications to Winner's office. If he called for an appointment, he feared, he might be put off for a week, a month, or indefinitely. And that could lead to back and forth e-mails and telephone calls and further delays. No telling with the busy president. He urgently wished to impress Winner with a job well done. Hadn't Winner told him to move fast to clear up the question of whether a secret research project was running at Kershaw? There was no such project, Martin would tell him. Now, with that issue disposed of, he could request final approval for the roundtable and get on with it. Martin hopefully wondered whether a title of visiting professor might be arranged for him. Or maybe distinguished visiting scholar or something in residence. In pursuit of profitable relationships, universities used several of these impressive titles for outsiders who didn't possess full-fledged academic credentials but still had something to offer. The roundtable would establish him as a policy intellectual, the head of a prestigious public forum for discussion of the urgent issues of the day. It would be quite proper for him to hold a title linking him to the university and the wider academic world. Helen's ambitions for high hostess status would be glamorously, enviously fulfilled in the attendant glow of publicity and celebrity. At long last, important people would flock to their salon. Martin was not vindictive, but he momentarily relished the prospect of *not* inviting certain puffed up, self-important A-list celebrities who had ignored their invitations. He also figured that from the inside, he could put in a word to break the logjam on Helen's arts committee. Of late, he had noticed, she was irritable, impatient, distracted. He felt an urgency to clear the road to the roundtable. Martin still hadn't heard from Collie about his visit to Brucie's lab, but he felt confident that Collie's conclusion would match his own: nothing there. No reason to call Collie or to wait for him to report. No reason to put up with more delays.

Striding along the walk to Monument Hall, Martin navigated around a clutter of placard carriers and several slowly rotating circles of chanting demonstrators. The long-running denunciation of Rule 23, continuing without abatement, was now joined by a new chant:

Livers and toes,

All for sale,

Time for someone

To go to jail.

"No thanks, no thanks," Martin barked as leaflets were thrust at him. "Crazy kids," he muttered to himself. Concentrating on his mission, he only vaguely sensed that the density and agitation at the building entrance were considerably above normal. The clamor was too great to comprehend the chanted words. Besides, he was in a hurry and had no interest in the endless succession of obscure issues that animated the student rabble. How they dressed, he noted with dismay: sweatshirts, ragged jeans hanging off their behinds, and sandals. Some were barefoot. Unkempt hair, and not a necktie or skirt in sight on anyone under 35.

Once inside, his brisk pace and authoritative manner spared him a challenge by the work-study sentries at the perimeter of the presidential suite. Marching on, he received a nod of recognition from the receptionist, Myra, the formidable final barrier to Winner's office. "Martin Dollard," he crisply announced, "Just in the neighborhood and wondering whether I might see President Winner for a few minutes about an extremely important matter. He'll know what it's about."

"Does it have to do with—?" Myra hesitated for a moment, "to do with the medical school and the hospital. Were you supposed to be at the meeting?"

"Meeting? No," Martin said. "Just say it's a private matter."

The receptionist responded with a downcast no-no shaking of her head. "Oh, you're not here for the meeting? Then it's just impossible," she said. "His schedule is absolutely chockablock with wall-to-wall, back-to-back meetings from early to late after what they found."

"What they found?" Martin asked. "Who? What did they find? What's going on?"

"I'm not supposed to say, but since you've been in here before—." Lowering to a loud whisper, she confided, "It's about the body parts." Martin expelled a puzzled "What?" Inspired by his incomprehension and the opportunity to display insider knowledge, Myra continued: "They found that some people at the medical school were collecting body parts—from where, god only knows—and were *selling* them. Maybe to a Japanese drug company. I don't know. There are all kinds of rumors. And somebody told the newspapers. President Winner is very deeply concerned and has been meeting with lawyers and the public-relations people. They're still trying to find out from the medical school just what happened. Someone said the dean there has had a stroke. We're trying to find out."

Martin exclaimed, "Body parts? What kind of parts, for what?"

At that moment, the door behind the receptionist opened and Winner emerged, jacketless, with rolled up shirt sleeves and loosened tie. Appearing sallow and grave, he was followed by several grim-looking, smartly groomed, dark-suited professionals, with well-shined shoes and expensive brief cases. Definitely not professors, Martin said to himself. Then he overheard Winner saying, "I can't put them off much longer," and one of the group replying, "The press statement is practically done. We'll 'lawyer' it as fast as we can and get it over to you. It's better to get it right than to do it fast."

"Do it fast and right," Winner peevishly snapped back.

The group departed, and Winner was turning back to his office when he recognized Martin, at the reception desk, motionless, with a beseeching expression. "Dollard, isn't it?" Winner asked. Then, turning to the receptionist, "Myra, is he on the schedule?"

"No, he's not, but he said it's very important and—."

Now remembering his distaste for Martin's garrulous manner, Winner was about to tell him to come back at another time when he recalled the task he had entrusted to him. "You were going to find something out for me, weren't you?"

Martin nodded affirmatively and was about to launch an extended reply, when Winner said, "Good. We can talk while I have my lunch, but let's make it short. Short. Got it? No calls, unless it's from you know who," Winner told the receptionist. He led Martin into his office, motioned him to sit opposite him at his desk, withdrew a sandwich from a bottom drawer and unwrapped it. Winner did not conceal his impatience or preoccupation with other matters. "Excuse me while I eat," he said, as he bit into his lunch. "Now, what's going on in that lab? You were going to check on who's paying for it and for what."

"I feel confident that we can conclude, on the basis of my personal examination of the financial records for the laboratory—."

"C'mon," Winner said, biting off and rapidly chewing another sandwich segment, "what's going on there? That's what I got to know."

Martin started to reply, when the phone rang and Winner motioned him to stop talking. "Yeah, yeah, okay," Winner said, listening intently. "They're all going to be okay? That's a relief. I'll have to tell the admissions office to cut down on enrolling so many idiots. Thanks."

Turning to Martin, he exclaimed, "Unbelievable. This freshman drinks at least ten cans of beer and falls three floors out of his dorm window and lands in a hedge—right on top of a grad student in the bushes with our Distinguished Professor of Religion, Bio-Ethics, and Social Values. Fortunately, everyone was very loose and relaxed. No one's dead, not even any broken bones. And now, our lawyer tells me to be prepared. He says we're probably going to be sued by the families of all three of them."

Martin was distressed, not by the described event, but by its intrusion on his business. Nonetheless, he expressed commiseration with simulated astonishment: "What can they possibly sue you for?"

Winner, visibly weary, was receptive to sympathy. "They can say the university, and me in particular, failed in our *in loco parentis* obligation for the students and reasonable caution to prevent harm for the professor. What horseshit!" he said with disgust. "I never dreamed—." He cut himself off, and then resumed the conversation with Martin. "We were talking about the lab. Who's paying the tab, and what the hell is going on there?"

"There is no evidence in the financial records—."

"You mean you didn't find anything. Right?"

"That is my conclusion, on the basis of a thorough examination—."

Winner took another bite of his lunch sandwich. "You didn't go there yourself. But you found a guy like I asked you to who was going to visit the lab, just for a look-see. I met him. Seemed like an intelligent person when he checked in here with me. What's he say?"

Uncertain about Collie's share of the inquiry, Martin hesitated while attempting to formulate a safe reply. The telephone provided a respite.

"They've been doing it for how long?" Winner asked his caller. After listening for a moment, he asked, "From patients and from stiffs?" A troubled look settled on his face. "Both, huh? And it's been going on since before I became president? That's some relief. But you still don't know who they sold them to and who got the money? Really? The dean and the chairman of pathology were in on it. Some blogger says the parts were going to China? We gotta find out. Let me know when you have anything else."

Putting down the phone, he turned again to Martin. "And the guy who visited the lab, what's he got to say? I haven't heard from him."

Martin now turned wary. He didn't know whether Collie had visited Brucie's lab. Collie told him he had failed in his first try and would try again, but maybe there was a hitch on the second try. Maybe he did visit the lab. Maybe he had directly reported back to Winner. Maybe Winner was testing Martin for trustworthiness. The president was obviously a crafty operator. The maybes mounted up. Martin cautiously answered. "Because of scheduling difficulties, I haven't checked with him yet, but, as I said, on the basis of my own examination—."

"That's enough," Winner said, picking a fragment of white chicken meat from the sandwich and expertly lofting the remaining bread and lettuce into a wastebasket.

Martin wasn't sure whether "that's enough" applied to their conversation or the sandwich. Winner swallowed the chicken.

Martin hurried to salvage his case. "The visit to the laboratory will certainly corroborate my findings, since the financial records must necessarily——."

"Mr. Dollard," Winner said, "I've got some big problems here that require immediate attention. So, we'll get back to this some other time."

"If I can be of any assistance." Martin hesitated, then added, "Also, we had discussed the roundtable proposal. You received the memo that I prepared at your request, I hope."

"That all sounds like it was a thousand years ago. First things first. Many thanks for your interest, but I don't think anyone can be of any assistance." Gloom in his voice and exhaustion on his face, Winner quietly added, "Trouble is this place is uncivilized, ungovernable. It's always like happy hour in the psychiatric ward. We'll be in touch."

Striding out of the building and into the crowded plaza, Martin grabbed one of the offered leaflets and seated himself on a bench to read it. The nearby tumult continued, now elevated by a new recitative:

Kidneys, eyeballs, bones and skin,

Hurry, get your orders in.

Kershaw's Future Looking Sunny,

Winner's Making Lots of Money.

A choral group on the sidelines responded with:

Hee, hee, hee,

Ho, Ho, Ho, Ho,

President Winner's

Got to Go.

The leaflet in Martin's hand announced that a rally would be held at 1 a.m. that night "at the President's residence to protest the gross mismanagement of this great university." There followed a "Bill of Particulars vs. President Winner":

(1) Failure to provide enlightened leadership of a high order.

(2) Unacceptable neglect of on-campus safety, as revealed in a student accidentally falling from an unsafe dorm window and critically injuring himself and two people passing by.

(3) Illegal activities at the medical school involving human organs and human remains, reported sales of, without permission of source individuals (where applicable), next of kin or significant others.

(4) Lack of ethnic-cultural-health dietary diversity in on-campus dining facilities.

(5) Because of time constraints, this is only a partial list. More items are being collected. Always check WinnerWatch.edu for latest information. Very Important, send in what ever you know about.

Sponsored by the Kershaw Alliance for a New President.

From his presidential suite, Winner could faintly hear the chanters. A copy of the leaflet lay crumpled in his wastebasket. He stared at the front page of the campus newspaper. "What the hell is suddenly going on?" he said to himself. Under the headline "Scandal on Campus: Human Organs for Sale," *Haywire* reported that "campus authorities admitted they were investigating detailed reports of 'biological improprieties' at university medical facilities, but at this point in time were unable to comment because of privacy considerations."

Natural grist for Kershaw's pathologically suspicious inclinations, the human organs scandal was instantly embraced as plausible. The initial report, alleging "wholesale harvesting of body parts from unconscious patients," was spread across the front page of the mass-circulation tabloid *Daily Post*. In slightly rewritten form, it was promptly echoed in the rival *Daily News*. The *Post* reasserted its dominance over the story with a lurid, detailed account of organ collecting, attributed to "sources who spoke anonymously because of fear of losing their jobs and being prosecuted for violating confidentiality pledges." To establish that it was not dozing on duty, the *Times* cautiously noted "unconfirmed reports of illicit transactions in human organs at the Kershaw School of Medicine," thus maintaining its reputation for factual precision, at the cost of elevating the credibility of the reports. The evening TV news plunged in with explanatory comments from expert consultants on the multiple uses of body parts and fluids on the frontiers of modern medicine.

"I am not familiar with the particular situation at Kershaw," a retired veterinarian said on NBC, "but if this is not the tip of the iceberg, I don't know what is." The blogosphere was blanketed with commentaries on the meaning of the scandal and its origins in the deplorable economics of the American health-care system. "Today everything has a price," a leading medical blogger sermonized, "including your genes, skin, and urine." In response to Winner's desperate demands for information, the dean of the medical school adamantly insisted, "I don't know what they're talking about. Nobody here knows anything about this. Absolutely nothing." Winner silently resolved to sack the dean after the crisis blew over. It wouldn't be easy to oust the long-entrenched incumbent, given the lucrative entanglements he enjoyed with the pharmaceutical industry and other sources of financial support for the medical school and himself. Many on the medical faculty had been dealt into these deals, and they would rally to defend their leader. But it must, and will be, done, Winner vowed.

Looking at his desk calendar, Winner saw that the remainder of the afternoon was fully booked with further meetings with legal, public relations, and the dean of the medical school, culminating with a 5 p.m. combined press conference and town-hall meeting for the Kershaw community—in plenty of time for the evening news programs. He buzzed the receptionist. "Myra, anyone calling that I should know about?" he anxiously asked.

"Yes, sir," she replied. "The chairman of the board of trustees said he'd like to talk to you as soon as you have a moment. That Dr. Marson said he's ready to report to you about some research you inquired about and wants to know if he should come here, give it to you on the phone, or send in a memo. Your choice, he said. And Dr. Fenster would like to have a word with you. Something about the next meeting of the Faculty Senate."

"After the press conference," Winner said.

೧౨

The erratic movements of near and distant events, in combination with the news industry's low regard for public tastes and interests, assured wide coverage of Winner's press conference. The media focus on the body-parts revelation was abetted by a brief respite in mayhem, carnage, and bizarre manifestations of human possibility, creating a "slow news day," which left broadcast time and newspaper space to be filled. Assignment editors for print and television organizations, along with many independent bloggers, were therefore responsive to the announcement of a combined press conference and "town hall meeting" at which President Mark Winner of Kershaw University would respond to questions concerning the reported collection and sale of body parts at the School of Medicine. TV news planned to switch between Winner at the podium, an inflamed, shouting audience, and stock footage of surgical procedures and magnified body parts and organs. The excitement on campus was heightened by the presence of TV vans and their high-rising giraffe-like antennas parked near the meeting site. Students, faculty, and campus hangers-on arrived early to fill the hall to overflowing. Reporting live from the scene, a local TV anchor performed a pre-game buildup, reminding the audience "that only last week, this campus was rocked when a freshman student accidentally fell out of an unsafe dormitory window and injured two passers-by. All three narrowly escaped death. Now there's the deeply troubling issue of body parts and fluids illegally removed from anesthetized patients, including young children, and sold on the open market, raising new questions about academic ethics and public safety. Tonight there is trouble in academia, and no great university is more troubled than our own Kershaw University. Questions are being asked about Kershaw's newly installed president. Did the university make the right choice? Is Mark Winner the right man for this tough job? Can anyone handle this job? We're right on top of every aspect of this rapidly developing story, 24/7, with full team coverage. Stay with us."

Winner feared and shunned the press. When interviewed about economic issues, as occasionally happened early in his teaching career, he found his words grotesquely mangled. Thereafter, he dodged or minimized contact with the press, feeling, with sound instinct, that the outcome of any interview was purely a crap shoot. He had initially resolved against any interviews or public statements concerning the body-parts issue, but was quickly turned around by the advice of Alumni President Bentley Grimes, the public relations and advertising success who, early in Winner's presidency, had intriguingly counseled him on steps to achieve greatness for Kershaw. He felt considerable embarrassment in again meeting with Grimes and hearing his counsel. Winner had barely progressed in carrying out Grimes' initial batch of advice. The roundtable project of the insufferable Martin Dollard had been warmly welcomed by the journalism department. But the department chairman and members were, in a rare instance of unity, quietly allied in opposition and committed to suffocating the proposal under a blizzard of picky memos seeking additional information, questioning various details, and citing difficulties with similar efforts elsewhere. Winner was familiar with these derailment techniques, having employed them himself at crucial points in his career, including his stint as a software executive. He was warily unsatisfied with Dollard's failed search for a rogue military research project on campus. Winner recognized that his isolation had foolishly led him to depend on Dollard. He vowed to get free of the officious, babbling intruder as soon as possible. As for the remaining innovations urged on him by Grimes, many were attractive and feasible, but inexplicable slippages thwarted progress toward accomplishing them. The university's finances were inscrutable, and his efforts to achieve clarity produced sheafs of obfuscatory reports, replete with pie charts, tables, and dense, heavily footnoted explanatory text. Briefings by the chief financial officer only deepened the mysteries of Kershaw's finances. His choices for senior staff positions remained entangled in Human Resources' background checks.

Winner realized he had accomplished next to nothing. And now, without a preliminary clue, came the revolting body-parts scandal, which brought Grimes sweeping past Myra's reception desk and barging into his office with an ominous forecast: "If you don't do something about this fast, Winner, they'll be selling *your* body parts. Lance the boil and let the puss pour out," Grimes lectured him. "I warned you about the medical school people. Some are bandits, some are incompetent, and some are both, rolled into one. Few of them are worth a damn. But they'll tell you they're all selfless Samaritans, dedicated to helping humanity, without regard to personal gain. You've got to publicly fire at least one of their big shots and call in the district attorney and open up everything to him. Stolen body parts rings a bell with all people. Call in the press and market yourself as the most outraged person in the whole damn business—even more outraged than the relatives of some guy who was sold off in pieces. A final word," Grimes said.

"What is it?" Winner sheepishly asked, repelled by Grimes' self-assurance and intrusiveness, but unhappily realizing that Grimes was capable of valuable insights that eluded him.

"You'll need some help for getting out of this mess. I'll send over some of my crisis managers. I regularly hire them out for big-big bucks to very rich organizations that are deservedly in deep shit. Like oil companies, banks, and pharmaceutical firms. We're even working on a new image for a Congo general who's on the lam for atrocities. He'll never qualify for sainthood, but we think we can clean him up. No matter how much we pad the billable hours, they're all happy to pay up. But it's free for you and my old school. Count this as another *pro bono* for my alma mater, Winner. These crisis guys are fabulous. Magicians of the mind, I call them. They can make anything smell good—usually."

∽

Seated on the stage of the campus recital hall requisitioned for the press conference, Winner faced an overflow attendance of press and public irresistibly drawn by the exotic topic of body parts for sale. Few among them knew much about Winner, but as president of a university routinely referred to as "elite" and "highly selective," he rated a comedown. The crowd was in a bear-baiting mood. In a prior century, the same mob would have festively attended public hangings. As the bigTV lights were set in place and adjusted, the click-clack of camera shutters and bright bursts of flash equipment continued without interruption, all aimed at Winner. A flunky from the Kershaw Office of Communications and Public Relations proceeded to the lectern and repeatedly pleaded for quiet before finally achieving it. "Thank you, thank you. President Winner will make an opening statement, and then will take your questions."

The alluded-to statement, covering a single page, was meticulously composed by the team of public-relations specialists, medical ethicists, and legal experts donated by Bentley Grimes. It was formulated to soothe public concerns with assurances of Kershaw's integrity, empathy, and the world-renowned professionalism of its medical and administrative staffs.

The leitmotif of the prepared statement was time-tested, plain, simple: The investigation was just beginning. A prestigious panel of impeccably upright, disinterested public figures would review all allegations concerning the sale of body parts. At this point, no wrongdoing had been confirmed. But it was already clear that, at worst, the incident came down to a few rotten apples in a big barrel; a rare, single blemish on an otherwise flawless record of public service. In the prepared statement, Kershaw's budget for charity medical care was repeatedly emphasized, though, in fact, the university fought bitterly with Medicaid for reimbursement of every expenditure for the skimpy service it provided for the poor. Numerous awards for good works were cited, among them several sponsored by pharmaceutical and health-insurance firms that enjoyed profitable relations with the university. Going over the statement, line by line, with the head of the crisis team prior to the press conference, Winner took comfort from the shrewdly composed text and the assistance of skilled hands to assist him through this wretched, unfamiliar ordeal. The crisis team drilled into him the importance of emphasizing certain evocative terms of comfort in the question period that would follow his recital of the prepared statement. "You can't say them too often or too loud," he was advised as his mentors ran down the list: Transparency, ethics, trust, integrity, responsibility, commitment, caring, community, decency, honor, dedication, service. When confronted by a difficult question, he was advised, spew out these words, relevant or not, and take refuge in the obligation to observe privacy laws and regulations and prohibitions against discussing personnel issues and matters under investigation. "Make yourself the angel," he was advised. "You're just following rules laid down by God and the government for the benefit of the young, the sick, the weak, and the poor."

Hoots, whistles, and foot stamping broke out as Winner rose, took his place at the lectern, and stared at the expectant assemblage while adjusting to the blaze of lights. Placing a folder on the lectern, he tested his voice with a few introductory words: "Thank you for coming today. I have some prepared remarks and then will be happy to answer your questions about these unverified and disturbing reports."

Lifting the cover of the folder, he looked down, expecting to see the prepared statement. In its place was a message scrawled in heavy black letters: "You're on your own, you prick." Winner struggled to conceal his shock. Earlier that day, he had reviewed the statement and had returned it to the folder, which he secured under the weight of a marble pen holder on his desk in the presidential suite. Now, the expertly composed, crucial opening remarks were gone. Secured inside the folder with a stout paper clip, the single sheet of paper could not have accidentally slipped out. Within his own office, perfidy had been committed. How and by whom, he did not know, but, clearly, malign intent was on the loose, and it had penetrated his private space at a grievously difficult time. For a moment, Winner thought of turning for help to the communications assistant who had introduced him, but realized that he was on display and must rescue himself.

Though stunned by the deft treachery that left him without prepared words before the baying audience, Winner gripped the lectern with both hands, steadied himself, and said, "Better yet, to save time, I'll dispense with my prepared statement and we can go right to your questions." Scores of wildly waving hands went up throughout the hall. Winner pointed at no one in particular, and the contest began, as one questioner gained the floor by outshouting the others. The questioner was a stooped, elderly man, familiar on campus for distributing unintelligible leaflets on whatever was the news of the day. His younger confreres had migrated to the Internet, but he still confined himself to paper. In a prosecutorial tone, without looking up, he read from a notebook that he held before him.

"Dr. Winner, as you know, or should know, the public is very upset by these events. Will you confirm or deny a report that this was a deliberate, carefully planned scheme by the hospital to close its deficit and that the medical school dean gave prior notice in his annual report to your predecessor and to you. On top of that, what started out with just the sale of some skin and knee cartilage from dead patients later on was expanded to patients under anesthesia for surgery, both elective and emergency, and that body parts and various body fluids were taken from them without their knowledge or consent, and they were billed for the surgical services incurred in taking the parts and fluids. All this has been in the newspapers. Please confirm or deny."

Winner's mind churned to reinforce his answer with the strategic words recommended by the crisis-management team. "Because of federal privacy regulations, I can't discuss personnel matters or individual cases, or matters currently under investigation," he said, as he attempted to project a commanding, confident presence. "But I want to assure the public that the university adheres to the highest standards of transparency, responsibility and ethical codes of professional conduct. Integrity is seamlessly incorporated into all our activities. All patients, regardless of their financial status, age, gender, race, ethnicity, nationality, and immigration status, receive care of the highest quality. All patients are precious to us, rich as well as poor. We are empathetic. It would be irresponsible for me to discuss the hospital budget, as that is under review at this time, but I am certain that everything was in accord with standard accounting practices and appropriate medical requirements, all to the highest standards."

As Winner's response wound down, hands again shot up and shouts for recognition were everywhere in the tightly packed hall. He pointed to a questioner. But the first questioner remained on his feet, shouting, "You didn't answer my question." Collective murmurs of agreement welled up from the crowd. "Answer the question," voices demanded.

"I was trying to make clear that the matter is still under investigation—."

"That's no excuse," someone shouted. "Answer the question."

"Which question?" Winner shouted back.

"The one about body parts."

"I answered the question. Next question," Winner said, pointing to a matronly woman looking directly at him through huge, square eyeglass frames. "Dr. Winner," she began in a lachrymose sing-song, "I'm not a member of the regular press. So forgive me if I'm—. Anyway, I'm in a group called the bloggingmothers. com, and we work together to overcome many of the barriers that today confront young parents, as well as seniors and others, including single, gay, lesbian, transgender, and traditional. What I want to ask you is this: How would you feel if *your* child went to the hospital and they removed some of his or her body parts without your permission, consent, or knowledge? *Your* child. How would you feel?"

The questioner ignited explosive applause, accompanied by piercing whistles and deafening foot stamping.

Winner waited for the tumult to subside. "We've asked for a complete, impartial, thorough investigation," he said. "Everyone can be confident—."

"But, sir," the questioner persisted, "how would *you* feel? Please try to answer that simple question. Please. It is not a difficult question. Please."

The crowd now broke into two choral segments, one rhythmically shouting, "Please. Please," while the other repeatedly roared in unison, "Answer the question. Answer the question."

Winner held up his hands, palms toward the crowd. The roar gradually subsided. "Let's have another question," he said.

He noticed a young man standing in the rear of the hall, vigorously waving a hand, and shouting above the tumult, "Hey, President Winner, hey, President Winner." Staring at the upstart, he suddenly recognized Fenster, the rodent meister, standing behind the clearly determined questioner and insistently whispering to him, while the youth nodded affirmatively. Fenster slipped out of sight as the questioner yelled out, "What about the secret Army project? Why are you selling out to the Pentagon? Is that what we can expect from President Winner? What about it?"

Recalling Dollard's report, Winner suddenly felt confident that he could turn the tide with an emphatic, informed, authoritative reply. He slowed his pace of delivery. "I have had rumors of a secret project thoroughly investigated, and I can assure you that they are nothing but rumors, baseless rumors, unjustified rumors. There is no secret project on the Kershaw campus. No secret Army project or any other kind of secret project, none whatsoever, in any shape, manner or form. I can assure you," he declared.

Winner felt satisfied, but many in the audience did not. "Don't change the subject," someone yelled, to general approval. "We're supposed to be talking about body parts. That's got nothing to do with the Army." Above all, came a stentorian bellow: "That question is a plant to get us off the subject." Shouts of agreement filled the hall.

Feeling the onset of exhaustion, Winner declared, "Next question." A loud voice from a gangly young man in the front row won the decibel rivalry. "I have here a preliminary inventory from a source at the hospital showing the body parts that were collected and sold over the past six months, approximately. I won't go into everything, but it shows hair follicles, liver, kidney, and testicle tissues, ovaries, bone fragments, intestinal sections, sperm, blood, lymph nodes, cuticles—and much, much more. I won't list it all. My question is, when will you apologize to the victims and their families? And if you won't apologize, why not? What's the reason for not apologizing?" Winner gathered his energy for a response. "When the investigation has been completed, I will make the results public and take all necessary action. Thank you. We'll have one more question."

The audience went silent in deference to the host of a popular afternoon TV talk show. "Dr. Winner," he asserted in a resonant baritone, "in all fairness to you and everyone else involved in this tragic affair, we must have the facts before any conclusion is possible." The statement evoked a few approving sounds from the audience. "But," the questioner proceeded, "we'd all feel more confidence if you were willing to make these same statements under oath. Are you willing, sir, to make these same statements under oath? That is my question, pure and simple." Whereupon the audience erupted into clapping, foot stamping, and ragged cheers, taunts, and boos that quickly resolved into a rhythmic chant, "Under oath, under oath."

The crisis coaching hadn't prepared Winner for the intensity of the encounter. Fatigued, puzzled, he stared at the audience for a long count before mustering a reply. "We'll do what's necessary. I can't say for sure until—. But thank you."

Shouts and jeers filled the hall as he hurried off the stage and into the crowd, brushing off questioners who accosted him, pushing his way around knots of excitedly talking people, emerging from the hall, and finally reaching his office. Myra, the receptionist, speaking on the telephone, looked up as he entered, and said, "Please hold a moment." Cupping her hand over the phone, she whispered to him, "It's the chairman of the trustees. He now says it's urgent."

"Okay," Winner said, "I'll take it at my desk."

"Dr. Winner, this is Saul Goodson. I've just been watching the television. What in the world is going on there? First we had students falling out of windows and practically killing some professor. Recently, I heard some totally crazy stuff about people being shrunken at Kershaw and put into long-term storage, or who knows what? For God's sake, have we descended into voodoo? And now there's this scandal about body parts. In 25 years with Giles we never had anything like this. I'm hearing from the other trustees. I've been trying to get them together for a special meeting, but at this time of year, it's impossible so I've been in talks with as many as possible by tele-conferencing. They all want to know one thing: *'What is going on there?'*"

"That's what I'm trying to find out," Winner said. "I've got some people working on it, and I'll let you know as soon as I get something. We're working on it. I assure you."

"I'm sure you are," Goodson replied in a flat tone that did not convey confidence. "But as members of the board we have fiduciary responsibility for the entire institution. The board counsel says there's no wiggle room on this. To cover our asses, we have to demonstrate responsibility on the record. So, in consultation with a unanimous quorum, I've taken the step of initiating a board-sponsored inquiry. I'm sure you'll understand the need for this. It protects all of us, you included."

Winner started to answer, but the board chairman went on without a halt. "I've asked Dr. Elias Fenster to organize and lead an investigation. He was in touch with me earlier to express concerns about the situation there, and I thought it appropriate to ask him to take on this task. He's up to speed on the problems and can hit the ground running. It took some persuasion, but he finally agreed to take time off from his research responsibilities and help us out. I don't know whether you've had an opportunity to become acquainted with Dr. Fenster, but he's a world-recognized scientist of the highest caliber and integrity, and I know we can count on him to conduct a thorough and impartial inquiry. I've known him for years, and have always known him to be a gentleman, a real square shooter. Please don't misunderstand me, but to be perfectly candid, we considered him as a candidate for the presidency after Giles passed away, but he declined because of the demands of his research program. He'll be in touch with you very soon."

"Good," Winner replied, choking on the word.

CHAPTER XXII

Drawing on his intimacy with duplicity, institutional intrigue, and maneuvering on treacherous ground, Winner focused deep diagnostic thought on the damaging, unexpected shocks that had struck his presidency. He ordered Myra, the sentry of the reception desk, to fend off calls and visitors. Cocooned within his office, he felt confident that he could think his way to a successful outcome. His brow nestled in his fingertips, Winner sat and thought, carefully recalling and surgically dissecting the evidence.

Clearly, Fenster was the main causative factor and beneficiary in the cascade of doleful events that afflicted his presidency. Fenster had the motive, the opportunity, and the means to undermine Winner. Winner could be a threat to Fenster's spurious scientific reputation and professional survival. The Senate resolutions engineered by Fenster revealed his fears and anxieties. Winner recalled that Collie Marson, Fenster's former postdoc, had hinted at unsavory doings in Fenster's lab. Marson had been cautiously vague, but Winner sniffed malfeasance in his measured remarks. In his own meeting with Fenster, maybe his body language or facial expressions had hinted at his suspicions about the rodent meister's scientific reputation. From his familiarity with Kershaw's high-velocity, digitized chatter networks, Winner knew that by one route or another, Fenster had learned about his meeting with Marson and naturally regarded it as threatening. Seasoned in internecine academic strife, Fenster knew how to strike at Winner from several vantage points. The Kershaw community feasted on disparaging allegations about ranking figures on campus. With the bar for credibility set low, no great skill would be needed to sully Winner's character and presidential performance and gouge away at his stature. The Web guaranteed an uncritical uptake, lavish embellishment, and energetic recirculation on campus, and beyond.

A meticulous analyst, Winner took Fenster's hostility as a given, but recognized the risk of exaggerating Fenster's ability to produce havoc. Fenster, he told himself, couldn't have had anything to do with the beer-sotted student taking a three-story plunge from a dormitory window, or the amorous couple beneath who by chance served as a life-saving crash pad. But, Winner reasoned, from Fenster's perspective, the bizarre event was a godsend, symbolizing the tawdry condition and misgovernance of the Kershaw campus, for which President Mark Winner was ultimately responsible. Fenster, with his many personal connections in and around Kershaw, could easily have exploited the mishap with targeted whispers suggesting presidential mismanagement and neglect.

Winner continued his analysis, maintaining the same high evidentiary standards. He acknowledged to himself that he lacked evidence of a broadly based denigration campaign, though he did not rule it out. But he felt certain that Fenster was fiendishly involved in spreading damaging reports and alarms about the so-called body-parts scandal. He had spied Fenster coaching one of the questioners at the press conference. And the questioner, visibly at Fenster's instigation, had compounded Winner's vulnerability by introducing the hyper-sensitive, volatile issue of a secret Army project on campus. Luckily, the mob's overriding obsession with the body-parts issue smothered that dangerous spark. For a moment, Winner drew comfort from the possibility that the Army project was a Kershaw figment that, poof, would promptly vanish when yet another crisis or scandal gripped the campus. According to Martin Dollard's report, the Army project didn't exist at all. Talk about it could be baseless, like so much of the fervid conversation on campus, Winner told himself, but his instincts made him queasy about Dollard's reliability. Words, relevant and meaningless, randomly erupted from Dollard like an emergency bowel movement. Nonetheless, now on the public record, the Army project invited exploitation whenever a new issue was needed for rousing campus-wide indignation. Even if ultimately revealed as non-existent, brawling over the alleged project would once more identify Winner with troublesome issues, and thus further discredit his stewardship of the university.

Focusing on the body-parts scandal, Winner contemplated an anomaly: A great disproportion between the howling public uproar and the striking absence of confirmed or even marginally plausible information about the reported collection and sale of body parts. Despite the voluminous coverage in the press and on television, and the ongoing secondary explosions on campus, the reports were flimsy and vague. All were attributed to unidentified sources. No credible person had yet come forward to confirm that body parts were illicitly harvested at the medical school and sold for profit. The medical school dean was a simpleton, destined for ouster, Winner reminded himself, but his professions of ignorance of anything resembling the body-parts allegations seemed authentic. Odd, Winner told himself. Buoyed by a sense of analytical progress, Winner turned to thinking of how Fenster might fit into explanatory possibilities when Myra, in defiance of his orders, buzzed, and then buzzed again. "Dr. Fenster is here. He says it's urgent that he sees you at once."

Despite having ordered solitude, Winner did not hesitate. "Send him in," he said.

❧

Fenster's arrival in Winner's presidential suite did not surprise or disturb Myra. On her scale of loyalties, Fenster's wish to see Winner took precedence over Winner's wish to be undisturbed. Myra was employed by President Winner but was beholden to her blood kin, cousin Elias Fenster, whose intercession had landed her this very good job. Upon becoming president, Winner, with no inkling of how Myra got there, unthinkingly inherited her as part of the presidential landscape. No one knew she was related to Kershaw's rodent scientist, to whom her surreptitious deliveries of high-level information continued without interruption. She was alert and reliable in her official role as the president's receptionist and equally so in her clandestine role as Fenster's informant.

When Bentley Grimes' crisis managers were coaching Winner for his body-parts press conference, Myra promptly informed Fenster. And when the opening statement that the Grimes team had meticulously written and rewritten for the press conference reached final form, the devoted Myra, working from the hand-written, scratched-out original, typed a clean version for President Winner. She immediately checked in with Fenster. who instructed her on how to proceed. While Winner made his unfailing afternoon visit to his private bathroom, Myra stepped into his office, removed the prepared statement that he planned to take to the press conference, and replaced it with a single sheet bearing a brief, black-lettered message dictated to her by Fenster. As Winner stood at the lectern, his copy of the prepared statement was on the way to Fenster by inter-office mail.

☙

"We don't need any preliminaries," Winner said, motioning Fenster toward the pair of facing chairs in his office. "Why the hell are you doing all this, and what do you want?"

"I'll tell you," Fenster replied, "I'd like things here at Kershaw to remain as they are. No big reforms. We can even do without little reforms. We're okay as we are, a nice scholarly community. That's all I want. New presidents come in and they want to shake things up, innovate, make things different. There's no need to review anything. There's no need to change anything." Fenster stopped, fixed his rodent-like visage on Winner, and declared, "And we should be careful about malcontents who try to damage reputations. Don't you think so?"

Not fully recuperated from his press-conference ordeal, Winner snapped back, "Because you're afraid of what would happen if this place adopted decent stan-dards. Right?" Winner instantly regretted that sharp rejoinder, recognizing the need for a cool demeanor in confrontation with this adept antagonist.

Fenster serenely replied, "I'm in favor of live and let live. Ask anyone around here. I'm a peaceful guy. I keep to my own lab. People even complain that I don't get involved with outside activities, committees and things like that. But I prefer to stick to my own business and I don't barge into other people's territory. Once a professor gets settled in here, it can be a nice place. That's the way it's been here at Kershaw for many, many years, and that's how it should continue. We don't need to reorganize anything or make new rules about conflict of interest or teaching hours. That also applies to what's called scientific integrity and all the other stuff that brings out the boy scout in some misguided people. I think we both understand what I mean. We can leave things as they are."

"And if not?"

"You can figure it out for yourself," Fenster said.

"You mean body parts, Army project and more of that kind of stuff."

"You said it, Mr. President. Not me. But let's get down to the business of the moment," Fenster said, adding, "Pressing business, I think you'll agree."

Winner remained silent.

"As you know, I've been appointed by the trustees to look into these shocking reports about body parts being collected and sold at the medical school. Terrible for the public image of this university—and its president, of course. And I'm ready to deliver the findings of my investigation." Fenster removed an envelope from his inside jacket pocket and waved it at Winner.

In silence, Winner gaped at the performance going on before him.

"There's good news," Fenster proclaimed. "Good news. What we've found is that this terrible blowup about body parts is the product of a serious misunderstanding, really a tragic misunderstanding. The medical school and its leadership are blameless, and, by extension, so is the president and the administration. Unbelievably, it all comes down to a silly student prank and a misunderstanding. Details here," he said, again waving the envelope.

Winner could not conceal his astonishment. "You've just been appointed to do an investigation. Goodson called me half an hour ago and said you've just been appointed. You've had no time to investigate anything. How the hell can you produce an investigation report?"

"Actually, he called me last night. But you're right," Fenster agreed. "There's been no time for an investigation. But that's neither here nor there. I'm in charge of the investigation, and I've concluded, as I said, that the whole thing is one big misunderstanding coming from a foolish prank. There's no body parts scandal. Trust me."

"No body parts scandal?" Winner repeated. "Just a big misunderstanding?"

"That's what I found, so to speak," Fenster said.

"So, what's been—?"

Fenster interrupted him. "Let's wind this up. Okay? As my report makes clear, tissue specimens from biopsies and surgery are routinely collected and stored in tissue banks for research and studies. It's all legal and above board, here and at hospitals and research centers all over the country. You know, they collect tissue samples to see whether mercury or other stuff is accumulating in kids' bodies. All kinds of stuff. Same with body fluids. Sperm counts up, sperm counts down—my speciality, though only in rats. Tissue and biological banks trade the stuff back and forth. They use it, they freeze it, whatever. So, we've got specimens coming and going all the time at the medical school labs and at the hospital. FedEx and UPS make daily pickups and deliveries. Nothing illegal or unusual about it. In fact, when patients check in for surgery or whatever, they have to sign away the rights to whatever is cut out of them or drained out of them. That's modern medicine," Fenster chuckled. "You leave part of yourself at the hospital, like it or not."

"Get to the point," Winner demanded. "It's routine, but they're dumping on me on every front page and there's a hanging mob outside my office."

"Yes," Fenster agreed. "Unfortunately, that's true."

"Okay," Winner said, striving to control his anger, "How did this happen?"

Fenster grimaced as though deep in thought. Silence for a moment. Then, "Causation is a complex subject. If A precedes B, we cannot automatically conclude—."

"Cut the crap."

"Okay," Fenster said, "I'll observe that the press is highly competitive, especially the tabloids. Reporters hate getting beaten on a good story. Hate it so much that at the hint of a scandal they're off and running to get into print or on the air as fast as possible, before the other guy. And they like stories about squalor in the halls of medicine and science. You know, saints falling from grace."

"So you told one of those birdbrains at the tabloids that the medical school is stealing and selling body parts from patients at Kershaw."

"*I* did nothing of the sort," Fenster replied with disdain and a prolonged vocalization of "I".

"So you had some stooge do it for you."

"I think we've gone as far as we can go on this topic," Fenster replied. "My report clearly states that a misunderstanding, possibly originating in a misguided prank, was the cause of this very unfortunate event. You know, postdocs, residents and junior faculty gossip. They don't realize the danger of things getting out of hand, especially with the blogs running loose. Reporters pick up things in one way or another, and their competitive situation works against the kind of careful research we'd all like to see from the press. My report will explain all this, with emphasis on press responsibility. Sort of shifts the focus. And for good measure, I emphasize the importance of restraint and protection of individual rights and reputations when wrongdoing is suspected. You know, innocent-until-proven-guilty. Due process, or something like that. Not my field, but I think it's in the Constitution. It adds class to the report. And you should put it in the bylaws if it's not there. I haven't had time to check. The trustees will like that. The *Times* will like that." Fenster paused. "Oh," he added, "and transparency, too. Must never leave that out. The report calls for greater transparency. Can't have too much of that."

"What else?" Winner asked.

"You've seen the resolution adopted by the Faculty Senate. Kershaw is just fine as it is. No need to change a happy situation. The last thing we need are so-called reforms. If it ain't broke, don't fix it."

After a moment's reflection, Winner said, "I saw that kid stooging for you at the press conference. Isn't the body-parts hysteria enough? Why are you bringing up this old stuff about a secret Army project? I've had that checked out. Like I told the crowd, there's nothing there."

"The kid was supposed to hold that item in reserve and just ask about the body parts, but he got flustered and blurted out the Army question. Sorry."

"Still there's nothing there," Winner insisted.

Fenster disdainfully snorted. "Nothing there? I wouldn't be sure. Brusolowitz is a very, very smart investigator. There's never nothing there when he's worked on something for months and months."

"So what's he got?"

"He hasn't published anything or said anything. But word gets around. I hear he gets his money from the Army. Lots of it. But, I can't say for sure."

"So what's he doing?" Winner asked, without success in concealing his exasperation.

"Honestly, I don't know, specifically, let's say. It's not my business, and it's got nothing to do with me. But, as an act of friendship, I'll tell you it's got to be something scientifically big, because that's what he does. Brucie is a *real* scientist," Fenster said with a self-deprecating gesture away from himself. "Whatever he's got, if the drug companies get in the picture, it could be worth a great deal. Maybe many millions even billions over the long haul. That's how those things pay off when they're real big."

"Billions? You sure?"

"No. Control yourself. Nothing's ever sure about these things in the early stages, which is where it's probably at now. But you might consider that if there's anything there, a lot of it would belong to Kershaw, because the work was done here and any patents belong to Kershaw. But I only hear second-hand rumors that my postdocs pass along from his postdocs. I don't know. But you shouldn't think that there's nothing there. Brusolowitz doesn't spend time doing nothing."

"Billions?" Winner repeated. "Really?"

"That's what you get with a blockbuster. Billions—if it's a full-fledged blockbuster. No guarantees, so don't start spending it."

"That's interesting," Winner said, as he momentarily fantasized soaring to presidential greatness on a gusher of boundless pharmaceutical wealth. "Where do we go from here?" The threat he feared from Fenster seemed to have receded.

"Let a few days pass," Fenster said, "and I'll issue my investigative report. Then things will immediately quiet down, and we'll all be back where we started."

Winner could think of no alternative. "Okay," he said. "That's the deal."

"Good," Fenster said, rising to leave. "I'll give you a copy of my report. You might want to refer to it when you call off your own investigation. And there's something else in there you might find interesting," Fenster added, as he handed the envelope to Winner. "Adios, we'll be in touch."

Returning to his desk, Winner opened the envelope and pulled out two separate documents. One was headed "Report to the Trustees Re: Body Parts Investigation, E. Fenster, Chairman." Winner found the other document immediately recognizable. It was headed "Opening Press Conference Statement by President Mark Winner."

As Fenster left the office, Myra bid him a cheerful good afternoon. He responded with a smile and a barely perceptible wink. A moment later, Winner buzzed. "Does anyone ever get into my office when I'm not here?"

"Oh, no, sir," Myra replied. "When you're out, I'm like a watchdog. And when I leave at the end of day, I always lock up. Been doing that since President Giles was here." Before he could respond she added, "When I tidy up, I'm especially careful, because I figure you want things just the way you left them and don't want your papers disturbed." The conversation resumed a minute later when she stepped back into his office and said, "The maintenance people are sometimes in here to check out something in the pipes and things like that. And a couple of work-study kids have been in to help with some copying."

The multiple assurances and explanations registered on Winner's suspicion meter. The truth usually is simple. Excess in alibis, he long ago learned, warrants attention.

Winner stared at the press conference statement, recalling the feeling of devastation and betrayal that nearly paralyzed him when he stood up to speak to the hostile crowd, opened the folder, and found that statement replaced by a mocking message. Then he snapped back to the urgencies of the moment, telling Myra, "That Dr. Marson you said is ready to see me. Get him in here soon as you can."

༄

The half life of bizarre news is brief. In the media, the intensity and volume of body-parts coverage sharply declined over the next few days in deference to other stunning reports and implausibilities. These included an urgent, nationwide search for a bride who fled the altar. Tracked to a hairdressing parlor in an Atlanta mall, her frenzied on-camera thrashings and screams set a one-day record for online video viewing. Several days later, the bride and other newcomers were swept off the front pages and prime time by a resumption of body-parts coverage. The *Post*, which had initiated the original reports, was again in the lead, with a headline proclaiming "Body Parts Hoax." The accompanying article stated that "Kershaw University officials are red faced and fleeing for cover for over-reacting to fake reports of a body-parts racket at the medical school. An independent investigation, led by a nationally recognized scientist, has concluded that the allegations originated as an irresponsible prank and were completely baseless." A *Times* editorial chastised university officials for "reacting hastily to false rumors and thereby raising anxieties and lowering public respect for medical science. Let this be a lesson that can serve as a warning and a guide for the next crisis, which will inevitably occur. There is no room for complacency."

◦◦

Collie was scheduled to meet with Winner on the day the all-clear was sounded for the body-parts scandal. But first there was lunch with Lou. Gripped by what Collie had told him about the anti-sleep drug and its gargantuan financial potential, Lou anxiously waited for Collie's account of his talk with Brucie. Months had passed since Collie had excitedly told Lou about the anti-sleep project, but Lou's company was no closer to getting a piece of it. From long experience, Lou knew that great investment opportunities were rare and quickly scooped up. As Collie described the conversation with Brucie, Lou tried to conceal his disappointment. He was fond of Collie, very much so, but he wanted a deal, or at least real progress toward a deal. He didn't see either. Lou attempted to be gentle, diplomatic. "You science guys are a touch different from us ordinary citizens," he told Collie. "This Brucie oddball's got this fantastic invention, discovery, creation or whatever the hell he calls it, but now he's suddenly got religion and is thinking about dropping the whole thing down the toilet, but might reconsider for twenty-five million bucks. Our twenty-five million bucks."

Collie nodded. "Yeah, that's what he sort of said. It's complicated. He thinks he can get some good out of it without giving the Army anything that might be—." Collie hesitated. He wasn't sure that Brucie could elude the Army and launch a new career in beneficent science.

Lou reluctantly wondered whether Collie was up to handling a blockbuster deal involving a swollen professorial ego plus the legal complexities of tech transfer compounded by the murky rules of military security. Collie was relatively inexperienced in the business side of tech transfer, Lou realized, but lately, too, he seemed preoccupied and inattentive to work. He didn't know the details of

Collie's personal life, but his drowsy visage on some mornings suggested a wearing after-hours social schedule.

Lou and Collie were at lunch at the same spot where Collie had first told him about Brucie's anti-sleep project. It was there, too, that Helen Dollard had popped her scheme for a love nest. Collie had failed to get back to her about the apartment rent and deposit. She had left him several messages. He kept thinking he would call her, but he didn't. That now seemed so long ago. He kept putting off calling her. What would he say? He didn't know.

"Tell me something," Lou said, forcing Collie back to the here and now, "is all this research stuff really in Brucie's head and no place else? Is it him or nothing, and if he dumps the whole thing, no one else can figure it out?"

"That's what he says, and it could be, but I don't really know. The whole thing is very unusual."

"Okay," Lou said, "twenty-five million isn't out of the question, considering the potential if we're in there first and everything goes right. I can see the Big Pharma guys stampeding to get a piece of this from us, and then we'll make out just fine. But what do we do if this flake takes the money and then has another religious vision, or whatever the hell it is that shakes him up, and he decides no dice, he doesn't want to go through with it? Or what if the Army comes after him and says he's got to deliver, that they paid for it and they own it? They can be mean, these Army guys. That's what they train them to be. And if we're mixed up in it, they might have a go at us, too. We might finally win in the Supreme Court, but by then we'd be broke, and maybe dead."

"I'll level with you," Collie said. "I just don't know. You also have to figure in what Winner might do if he finds out that the Army was secretly bankrolling the project. Will he just let Brucie pack up and go? What about patents? They belong to Kershaw, but if Winner tries to claim them, the students might wreck the place. It's a mess. I was going to tell Winner what I found, but then this body-parts thing blew up and there was no way to see him until he called me to come in." Collie paused as the waiter set down their lunch plates. "And the whole thing is even more screwed up because your old friend Dollard told Winner that he checked the books and there's no Army money in the project and nothing secret going on. Dollard swears he's sure there's nothing there. While you were in

L.A., Dollard came charging into my office, yelling his head off that there's nothing there. He was wacko. But I know that he's wrong. Dollard got faked out. So, when Winner finds out, that's the end of Dollard and his big plans for some kind of televised bull sessions, or whatever it is."

"What are you going to tell Winner when you see him?"

"I suppose I'll level with him, tell him what I found out. That's what I agreed to do when I talked to him a couple of weeks ago. Remember, we couldn't get in to see Brucie until Winner cleared the way. I jumped at the chance. That was the deal."

"I don't know," Lou said. "Maybe you should think it over before you see Winner. Maybe just tell him that you didn't find anything."

"I suppose I could do that," Collie said, weary of the entanglements and confusion.

Lou, however, remained focused and eager. "Yeah, think about that," he suggested. "When Winner finds out that Dollard is full of crap, that's the end of him as far as Kershaw is concerned. And then his wife will go off the deep end because she's counting on Dollard getting this TV show with the university."

"You think so?" Collie asked, with faked indifference.

"Who knows?" Lou said, throwing his hands up and cracking a smile to ease the tension between them. "People are funny. But you really got me turned on by this anti-sleep thing, and I'd hate to miss out if it turns out to be a big one. But don't worry about Dollard. He's got plenty of dough to soothe his troubles, even the ones Helen will make for him."

⁓

"You went into the lab, and you talked to this Brusolowitz. Right?"

Collie acknowledged, yes, he had.

"So, what's going on there?" Winner impatiently asked.

Collie had arrived in Winner's office still undecided about what he would say.

"It's a big, busy lab that he's running. Lots of people working there, with very advanced instrumentation. It's got all the indications of a good lab. You can tell," Collie said, stretching out his non-committal remarks.

"Good, glad to hear it," Winner said, "but I need to know what's he doing there and who's paying for it. I hear he's got something going there that might have serious commercial value for the university, and that the Army is secretly sponsoring the lab. What can you tell me about those things?"

"Well." Collie paused and waited for words to come to him. Winner impatiently stared at him, wondering whether Collie had descended into a trance.

"Yeah, what?" Winner said in an urgent tone, as if trying to awaken Collie.

"He's got something big there," Collie said. "Real big. Like a scientific breakthrough that could really—. Yeah, it's real big. Something that could change lots of things."

"Don't play games. What are you talking about?" Winner demanded. "What the hell is going on in that lab? You know, I can send security in there and shut the whole goddamned thing down in two minutes." The threat was empty, Winner knew. Invasion of a lab by campus police would set off a campus-wide student and faculty demo in behalf of scientific freedom. But Collie was visibly jarred by that dramatic thrust.

"If you do that," he began, but nothing further occurred to him. Then talk flowed from him, and, as Winner silently listened with rising amazement on his face, Collie related what Brucie had told him about the anti-sleep project, the Army's concealed sponsorship, and Brucie's moral awakening and decision to cut loose from both the Army and the university. "That's everything I know," he assured Winner.

"Jesus, that's plenty."

"What are you going to do?"

"I don't know," Winner said, "but, I've got to do something, big, drastic." He sat quietly for a moment while Collie stared at him. "And right away, right away. Got to get him the hell out of here before this place blows up."

CHAPTER XXIII

The retrospectives on Mark Winner's short-lived presidency were mainly vi-
tuperative, in the Kershaw style, with a smattering of evenhanded and favorable
assessments. Whatever their opinion of Winner, the commentaries invariably recognized that Kershaw University underwent important changes during his brief
presidential tenure. Tirades and rejoinders on whether for better or worse filled the
blogs for weeks. Of particular importance, it was generally agreed, Winner had
asserted Kershaw's tech-transfer rights, giving the university substantial, greatly
needed income from patents derived from faculty research, especially that of Professor Max Brusolowitz. In the end, Kershaw served as the launching pad for Winner's next career step. The move surprised everyone, including Winner.

∽

The few dispassionate, objective observers agreed that Winner's attainments
and failures were mixed and difficult to disentangle. True, in his first year in
the presidency, he merely survived, narrowly avoiding ruination in the phony
body-parts scandal. By his second year, however, he had mapped the minefields
in campus politics, and was able to navigate safely, basically by appeasing, never
challenging, the existing power centers. Controlled by the ever-alert Fenster, the
Faculty Senate refrained from the nuclear option—the no-confidence vote. There

was no need. Winner accepted the sanctity of tenured privilege and the central, nonnegotiable tenets demanded by the tenured as their inarguable rights: annual pay increases above inflation and limited, preferably non-existent, teaching loads. Adjuncts and other lowly academic workers berated Winner as a tool of the power structure and a do-nothing president. Their barbs pained him, without reducing his commitment to caution.

Feeling the necessity to bring about some change, Winner carried out Grimes' scheme for linking a major tuition increase to scholarships for the poor. As predicted by the ebullient alumni president and public-relations executive, freshman applications and revenues jumped sharply, and Kershaw rose high on academe's charts for admissions exclusivity. The blogosphere was divided on the tuition move, but the mainstream press was enthralled by the unprecedented $75,000 price tag and its charitable coupling to educating poor, smart kids. Laudatory news accounts followed and editorials hailed Winner as an innovative statesman of higher education. "Just like I told you," Grimes gloated in an e-mail to the president. Encouraged by the favorable public attention, Winner acted on another Grimes recommendation, announcing a multi-billion-dollar fund-raising campaign for expanding Kershaw's commitment to "academic excellence and public service." At a press briefing, Winner explained that the two would be coupled "for assistance to the developing world and promotion of educational quality and economic growth and justice in the United States." Expressions of admiration and encouragement came from many sources. Relatively little money actually arrived. But as Grimes had predicted, announcements of anonymous gifts and workshops for program planning created an impression of a whirlwind of activity and important progress. Winner was praised as an educational visionary, in addition to being a statesman and a proficient fund raiser. Though never more than a trickle came in, relative to the lofty goals, the sums were sufficient to finance the highly publicized acquisition of several celebrity professors, sometimes referred to as "public intellectuals," who were well-known on the TV talk circuits, though rarely present in the classroom. They nimbly jumped ship when Kershaw offered a recruiting package that included the usual lures for academic body snatching: higher pay, full or near-exemption from teaching duties, stipends for graduate assistants, ample travel funds, and secretarial assistance. The old-line faculty reacted sourly to the favored newcomers, but as the recruits were few in number—because funds were limited—no eruption ensued. With these and other innovations, Kershaw University, under Mark Winner's leadership, climbed into the charmed top ten of *U.S. News & World Report's* annual rating of American universities. The stature and renown of Professor Max Brusolowitz contributed to the ascent.

ᕳᕲ

Incited by Charles Hollis' morose sermonizing about scientific integrity, ethics, and social responsibility, Brucie felt a swelling, righteous urgency to break free of the Army and keep exclusive control of the anti-sleep project. His resolve deepened when Lou Crowley agreed to invest $25 million for an off-campus laboratory where Brucie and his own specially selected team could explore the potential benefits and evils of his breakthrough research. But now that Brucie actually contemplated the break, his bravado wobbled as he wondered how the Army would respond to abandonment by its long-pampered star scientist. From the Colonel, he had gleaned that Pentagon personnel planners were already thinking ahead to the day when sleepless legions would reduce troop costs and enhance combat effectiveness. Brucie figured that he might scare off a retaliatory move with threats to reveal the goal of creating sleepless soldiers. But what if the Army decided to risk bad PR about zombies in uniform and drag him into court to get its money back? Or maybe prosecute him for fraud or robbery? Brucie knew nothing about the law, which made him fearful about his planned flight from the Army. Charles Hollis, who had evolved from spiritual adviser to breakaway strategist, counseled him, "Better first talk to a lawyer."

Consulting Kershaw's general counsel, Brucie sheepishly confessed he didn't remember whether he had signed any papers in establishing his deal with the Army. "Maybe. I don't know. I sign lots of stuff all the time." The lawyer told him to check his files. Brucie explained that the files were gone; all had been shredded.

The lawyer rose from behind his desk, looked into the anteroom, closed the door, and stood close to Brucie. He did not utter his thought— "So this is a scientific genius?" But he did ask in a near whisper, "Does anybody know about this?"

"Not really," Bruce explained, "just the work-study kid who runs the shredder for me, and does lots of other stuff. But I've talked to her and she won't say anything. She's a good kid."

The general counsel silently considered only the leading possibilities: Misappropriation of government funds, fraud, obstruction of justice, and suborning of perjury. "If anyone asks you about this conversation," he told Brucie, "just forget it ever happened."

In analytic fashion, Brucie concluded that the risk of trouble was not trivial, but he continued with preparations for moving off campus. Lifelong success had shaped his confident view of his abilities. He was sure he would find a way.

ᘛ

Deliverance arrived in an announcement from the White House. Max Brusolowitz was among five scientists selected to receive the National Medal of Science. In Brucie's case, he was to be honored for a long-ago but newly appreciated research accomplishment: invention of highly nutritious, minutely condensed emergency food rations, originally developed for the U.S. Army and later adopted by relief agencies worldwide for humanitarian crises—with the exception of the U.S., where the FDA remained concerned about safety. The prize citation lauded Brucie for "saving countless lives in the war on hunger by revolutionizing emergency food assistance."

Upon learning of the award, Charles Hollis was hopeful, for the first time in the many years since his Army job had plunged him into spiritual gloom. With his political antenna sensitized by his social concerns, Hollis concluded that the science medal immunized Brucie against the U.S. Army. "Now you're untouchable," he told Brucie. "The Army can't prosecute someone who's getting a medal from the President"—no matter how great its wrath and financial losses. Hollis experienced a rare upbeat mood. "Brucie," he meekly suggested, "now that you're going to move on, maybe there's a chance I can join you."

Upon learning of Brucie's unilateral departure plans, the Colonel in command of the research office requested permission from the Pentagon to dispatch a squad of military police to "secure the site and protect government property and national security." As the proposal to send armed troops into a university laboratory was routinely rubber stamped up the chain of command, a junior public relations officer—a politically sentient civilian on reserve duty— urgently brought the matter to the direct attention of the Pentagon's chief public relations officer. "Totally insane," the chief agreed, visualizing the uproar that would ensue from the proposed military raid. "Stop that lunatic before he brings a hurricane of shit down on the U.S. Army."

The severance of Brucie and the U.S. Army was peacefully negotiated by a Pentagon lawyer who arrived in Brucie's laboratory without prior notice. Normally engaged in clawing money back from crooked military contractors, the lawyer was under strict instructions to detach the Army from Brucie's lab silently, without leaving a paper trail, raising a public fuss, or attempting to seize the science or reclaim the money. "As far as we're concerned, the Army never had anything to do with this lab," he told Brucie. "We didn't pay for it, we don't know anything about it, never did and we don't want to know anything about it. Whatever the hell you were doing here was for NIH or whatever, but not for the U.S. Army. We're out of here. We were never here. You got it?"

"Okay with me."

"If you've got any records that say anything different, shred 'em. Okay?"

"Okay, we'll take care of it," Brucie assured him, as his wonder grew about the man's rising agitation.

"Count yourself lucky, professor. We really could have fixed you for good if the Army had any balls. My recommendation was that we prosecute and get back every stolen penny. But the generals are pure chicken when it comes to bad publicity. That's the politics we have to live with."

"I don't see what you're getting so excited about," Brucie responded, genuinely puzzled by his foaming visitor.

"Go to hell," the Pentagon lawyer spat out as he stomped past the packing crates awaiting removal to Brucie's new lab.

∽

Beautiful, appropriate lab space for Brucie's new venture became available when a high-flying bio-tech company was brought down by a bad FDA review of its hoped-for blockbuster drug. The shares crashed, the company went into bankruptcy, and Brucie picked up its lab at auction. With him, on loan from Lou Crowley's firm, came Collie Marson, testing a return to the lab bench, with Brucie's skeptical approval and Lou's instructions to keep an eye on use of the firm's $25 million. Brucie was energized by the move. The early scientific indications were exciting: Brucie said there might be a way to strip out the anti-sleep and natural-function components of his "creation." The result could be revolutionary drugs for controlling diarrhea, a leading killer of children in developing countries, and urinary incontinence, for which immense, world-wide markets existed. And, Brucie speculated, new drugs for both promoting and resisting sleep, without undesirable side effects, might be possible, too. Brucie said he wasn't sure and wasn't promising anything, but Lou felt lucky and certain that a blockbuster was in the works. He was silently ashamed that he had ever doubted Collie's ability to carry out a big deal, and relieved that he had withheld his concerns. The financial prospects for Kershaw, Brucie, and Lou's company were favorable. Because the basic research had been performed at Kershaw, Brucie agreed to assign the patents to the university, thus precluding marathon legal strife if they hit the jackpot. Lou's company held an exclusive license to market products protected by the patents. Aroused by Lou's stealthy placement of exciting hints, big drug firms came calling, offering big bucks for a holding place while the product possibilities were developing in Brucie's lab. In a three-way split sanctioned by federal law, revenues after expenses would be equally shared by Kershaw University, Brucie, and his laboratory. Situated at the center of the deal making, Collie recalled the sorry plight of his friend Bill Rhodes, director of Kershaw's luckless Technology Transfer Office. Now seasoned in the tech-transfer game, Collie saw an opportunity. At Collie's direction, much of the paperwork for Brucie's move was routed through the TTO, where the appreciative director referred to Brucie's lab as a "spinoff" from the university's tech-transfer program. With Lou deftly sowing hints of great things to come, Bill Rhodes was chosen Man of the Year by the national association of tech-transfer specialists. Forever grateful to Collie, he put him at the top of his list for a first look at Kershaw research with commercial potential.

Mark Winner was a beneficiary of Brucie's renown, though he had only recently confirmed the presence of Brucie's Army project on campus. Collie's report to the President ended all doubt: Brucie was running a secret Army research project in his lab. Fearing an eruption of anti-military demonstrations on campus, Winner was determined to get Brucie and his lab off the campus fast and quietly. But even before he could deliver an ultimatum, Brucie had concluded his $25 million deal with Lou's firm and notified Kershaw's Building and Grounds Department that he would vacate his lab, which he did a few days later.

Stunned by the swift-moving events, Winner turned to his most trustworthy adviser, Bentley Grimes, the loyal alum PR executive whose past advice had never failed him. Grimes arrived with a press-release specialist at his side. Having initially warned of the perils of Brucie's Army-backed project on campus, Grimes now reversed course, recognizing advantages in Brucie's connection to Kershaw and his commitment to humanitarian science—with the halo of the National Medal of Science reflecting glory on Kershaw University and President Mark Winner. Rhapsodizing aloud as his PR flunky and Winner scribbled notes, Grimes paced around Winner's office, ad-libbing the basics for a Kershaw press release:

"We've got to point out that this is Kershaw at its best, working for the advancement of science and the health of the American people. Here's how we tell it: This Brucie, or whatever his name is, was nurtured by Kershaw University when he was conducting basic research for which no use was seen by anyone. He defied the skeptics who said it was a waste of time and money, and he kept at it, because that's what great scientists do. They have a vision, they have faith. But to pursue their dreams, they need money and moral support. And that's where a great university comes in," Grimes exclaimed. "Kershaw teamed with this brilliant professor to make it possible. Then, after many heartbreaking disappointments, he pushed back the frontiers of science and got to the stage where he could actually design new, exciting drugs for curing terrible diseases and conditions and new ways for fighting hunger. That's when the White House took notice and awarded him the highest honor that the president can bestow for scientific achievement. It's like the American Nobel Prize. Be sure to put that in."

After a moment's reflection, Grimes resumed with gusto. "Then Kershaw, in tandem with the free-enterprise system, enabled him to take his research to a new level by setting up an off-campus research center to concentrate on product development so that he can deliver the goods bedside to the American people. But even while he's working off campus, he's going to continue here as a professor, training the next generation of young scientists to follow in his footsteps." Grimes directly addressed Winner, "That's right, isn't it? He's still going to be a professor here. And if he isn't, you can see to it that he is. Right?" Winner, looking up from his note pad, nodded. "Yeah, we can work something out."

Continuing his extemporaneous soliloquy, Grimes said, "This is a prime example of synergism between one of America's great research universities and the private sector. Be sure to get that in. But leave out the Army and all that stuff. No one knows anything about the Army being involved, and it's no one's business. Point out that its win-win for everybody, for Americans needing medical help, for starving people around the world, for Kershaw University and its dedication to public service and education, and for the advancement of knowledge. And be sure to get it high up in the release that it all happened under the leadership of Dr. Winner. That what the professor did wasn't possible without the far-seeing leadership and personal, direct support of Dr. Mark Winner every step of the way. Put it all in the press release, nice and polished. And let me see it, and we'll send it out to the whole goddamned world."

ᢙᕉ

Not long afterwards, NBC evening news spotlighted Winner in its "Making a Difference" series, celebrating him as the "epitome of a new breed of innovative academic leaders with the courage to break free of dead tradition by pulling down the walls between the ivory tower and the real world. Mark Winner has emerged as a benefactor of some of the country's brightest kids who otherwise might have been consigned to educational neglect, and he is leading the way in mobilizing science to meet the needs of the American people. Mark Winner, president of Kershaw University. Making a difference, in a big way."

Urging new attention to Winner's long-forgotten book, "Kill Or Be Killed? A Guide to Modern Management Success," *Fortune* cited him as a "leading managerial giant who catapulted a tired university into 21ˢᵗ century leadership. Clearly, Mark Winner is bound for bigger things."

∽

The circumstances of Winner's departure surprised everyone, even Mark Winner. Far away from the Kershaw campus, the state's senior U.S. Senator died in a light plane crash while en route to a golfing weekend as a guest of a defense contractor. Thus ended his indictment, and universally expected convictions, for extortion, obstruction of justice, campaign-finance violations, payroll padding, and income-tax evasion, among other federal crimes. Pending the next election, the appointment of a replacement belonged to the Governor, whose own political fortunes were shaky because of his close alliance with the deceased legislator. Mourning was local, minimal and perfunctory, but the senatorial vacancy itself attracted national interest because of the close division of party lineups in the Senate. Pledging a "clean break with the past" in hope of salvaging his soiled political career, the Governor disavowed party considerations in filling the seat, pledging to appoint "an independent, outstanding leader with an immaculate record of public service who will restore honor and distinction to our great state's representation in the U.S. Senate."

Beset with multiple problems close at hand, Mark Winner, president of Kershaw University, remained unaware of these distant matters.

Though settled into a tolerable *modus vivendi* with Fenster, the rodent meister, Winner realized that a surprise blow-up could instantly be set off by a misstep on his part or a deliberate provocation by any one of countless maliciously inventive malcontents on campus. He felt surrounded by shadowy threats and experienced a ceaseless, oppressive need to be prepared for sudden attacks. Ever since the phony body-parts scandal and the episode of the mysteriously missing press-conference statement, Winner remained troubled by Myra's hovering proximity. Sometimes she remained late in the office, mumbling improbable explanations about catching up on work. As the president's receptionist, she had little work at all, let alone any to catch up on. She matched visitors against a list prepared by Winner's appointments secretary, sorted his letter mail and e-mail, and did some typing, but little else. Surely she would move on without protest if she were offered a better-paying, more prestigious job. Without revealing his specific interest, Winner asked Human Resources for information about available staff positions and their salaries anywhere in the university. Most of these were plum jobs, paying well for little work and minor skill as departmental secretaries or solo assistants for especially privileged professors. HR's director regarded the positions as part of his fiefdom, to be bargained for favors in return. His brief reply stated that all staff positions were filled, and long waiting lists of qualified applicants were on file for openings. Winner knew that he risked a legal eruption if he tried to remove Myra. She clearly preferred to remain just where she was, in the presidential suite at the heart of the Kershaw administration, without onerous duties or supervision. From the frequent reports of personnel litigation that came to his desk, Winner knew that the individual possessed great tactical advantages over the institution. Charges of shoddy work, inappropriate behavior, or absenteeism were promptly countered by charges of sexual harassment, maintenance of a hostile work environment, or racial, gender, or ethnic discrimination. Federal, state and local laws heavily fortified incumbency. Like incurable diseases, cases lingered for years, while evidence was collected and depositions were taken, parsed, and challenged. Lengthy formal hearings rarely settled anything. Appeals were interminable. Myra would stay where she wanted.

⁓

The bereaved Governor sensed an opportunity after an aide directed his attention to Winner's laudatory press notices. The appointment of such a sterling figure to fill the Senate vacancy could be a first step toward rehabilitating the Governor's decrepit political fortunes. While the precariousness of his own situation was constantly on his mind, Winner received a confidential feeler from the Governor discreetly inquiring whether, if asked, he would be available to fill the Senate vacancy. Winner experienced the soaring spirits of a despairing castaway sighting a rescue vessel. His reply was coyly restrained: "I have never considered elective office, but as one who is committed to public service, I would be honored to discuss this with you." A search into his background found him scandal-free, untainted by party affiliation or involvement in public controversies, paid up in his taxes and absent from police and court records. He had been exonerated in the body-parts episode. As with his appointment to the Kershaw presidency, there was no reason for any faction to like or dislike him. While Winner awaited the Governor's decision, his thoughts turned to President Woodrow Wilson. He recalled that Wilson and Dwight Eisenhower were the only former university presidents elected to the White House; that Wilson was the only Ph.D. in the long presidential line; that Wilson and Ike, as in his own case, were latecomers to politics.

Amid speculation and suspense about filling the Senate vacancy, the Governor introduced Mark Winner as the appointee for the crucial post. The setting for the announcement was the nationally broadcast debut of the Kershaw roundtable, with founder and Distinguished Visiting Professor of Public Affairs Martin T. Dollard in the moderator's chair, joined by a panel of celebrity journalists. Helen occasionally glimpsed the broadcast as she moved about the apartment overseeing preparations for a grand party that evening in celebration of the launch of the roundtable. The abundance of A-list acceptances was admiringly noted on several celebrity blogs, and the photography desk at the *Times* had called for the Dollards' address. She was scheduled for an interview with *Vanity Fair*.

Helen had never heard back from Collie about the apartment rental, despite several attempts to reach him. Eventually, she let the matter recede from her immediate concerns, but a residual longing and feelings of hurt and missed opportunity still remained. As always, she was fearful of Martin's electronic omniscience. He frequently guffawed over newly purchased devices that he said could perform prodigious feats of information gathering. Warning, bluff, or just another instance of his purposeless babbling? She didn't know. She had left several innocently worded messages at Collie's office without receiving a reply. Ostensibly concerning some minor matter about medical research or the university, they would be easy to explain away if any question arose. But she was restrained about again calling him at home, where several messages had gone unanswered. As she went over the invitation list, she felt a heart-pounding urge to telephone him with a last-minute invitation to the roundtable party. After restlessly arguing with herself and deciding not to call, she impulsively rang his number. A recorded girlish voice cheerfully declared, "Hi, you've reached the apartment of Collie Marson and Ginny Rosen. We're not in. At the tone, leave a message and we'll get back to you soon as we can. Have a great day." Helen silently set the phone in its cradle. A member of the caterer's staff stood nearby, adjusting flowers in a vase. Her English was poor, but she grasped the barbarous outburst that escaped from the stylish hostess.

Ginny was happy. The closet space in Collie's apartment was cavernous compared to her old, cramped place. And he said that when they had time, they'd pick out an armoire with lots of drawers just for her. "He's like just the greatest guy you can imagine. I hate to think of all the total creeps I used to know," she told a girlfriend.

∽

"Saul Goodson here, Dr. Fenster. I'm sure you've heard the news about our new Senator."

"Yeah, it was an offer too good to refuse, and besides, Winner never really settled in here. Giles was a hard act to follow. Just one of those situations."

"I guess so," the chairman of the trustees agreed. "What I'm calling about is that all this really blew up on us faster than we had any reason to anticipate. With Giles at least we knew that something was coming and we were able to prepare."

"Right," Fenster said, his curiosity rising about the purpose of the call. Of course he knew about Winner's appointment to the U.S. Senate. Thanks to Myra, who screened and routed all presidential communications, he knew about the Governor's initial inquiry even before Winner did. And by the same method, Fenster immediately learned about the decision to appoint Winner to the Senate. "So what's up?" he invitingly asked the chairman.

"No reflection on Winner, you understand, but this time we don't want to rush into it. We're going to take our time. Don't marry in haste, like the saying goes. To get right down to it, Dr. Fenster, you and I have known each other for a long time, and we share a mutual confidence."

"For sure on my part. Always a pleasure to work with you."

"Same here, of course. I know you don't want the job on a permanent basis. Too much going on in your lab for that. But we want you to become interim president while a nationwide search is put together. The whole thing might take six months or as long as a year. You can look in on your lab on a daily basis, but after all the disruptions the university has been through, we need a steady hand at the wheel, someone we know and have full confidence in until we make a permanent choice. I know this will be a big sacrifice for you, but you have to do it for Kershaw and for me and the board. No is not an option."

Fenster calculated quickly, weighing the risks of leaving his lab, even for short periods, against the benefits of sacrificially accepting a call to service, and thereby ingratiating himself with the chairman and trustees. If the crisis he eternally feared actually arrived, he wanted them sympathetic, supportive, deep in his debt, rather than resentfully recalling his refusal to help when they needed him.

Elias Fenster became interim president of Kershaw University on the day Mark Winner took the oath of office for the U.S. Senate.

∽

Brucie's new lab, off campus but nearby and closely associated with the university, did in fact turn out to be the win-win forecast by Bentley Grimes. The good odds of betting on Brucie were long ago recognized as a no-brainer in the pharmaceutical big leagues. Buying from hot academic producers was the new business model, far preferable to the high-cost uncertainties of expensively staffed corporate labs plodding along the frontiers of science in search of potentially profitable leads. Whether or not the company labs produced science with commercial value, their paychecks, operating expenses, and annual budget increases persisted. Science produced in universities, mostly financed with government research money, could be bought up at costs that were piddling for the industry but colossal for the professors and their schools. Better to buy than to try, industry concluded, as it downsized its own labs and shifted budgets to buying and commercializing academic breakthroughs.

Charles Hollis, recently resigned from his job as a civilian science administrator for the Army, joyously signed up to work with Brucie and Collie as the laboratory's bioethics chief. Brucie, a pious convert to the pursuit of science exclusively for humanitarian purposes, bore down hard on Charles: "Don't let us get away with anything," he commanded. "If you think something we're doing isn't ethical or might be harmful, blow the whistle. And even if it just might possibly be bad stuff, blow the whistle."

Lou got the laboratory gossip from Collie. "This ethics crap doesn't bother me," Lou shrugged, "so long as it doesn't get in the way of getting results that make money."

"I don't think it matters a helluva lot," Collie said. "Besides, we owe this guy Hollis. He's the one who put me onto Brucie's research in the first place."

"You're the scientists," Lou said. "I'm just a simple guy trying to make a buck."

"We can't be sure," Collie said, "but I think we can count on Brucie. He'll come up with some goodies. I know some people have their doubts, but remember, never say never."

"Yeah," Lou said. "Never say never."

5597132R0

Made in the USA
Lexington, KY
28 May 2010